ORION Ruined

New York Mafia Vengeance: Book 1

Alexandra Iff

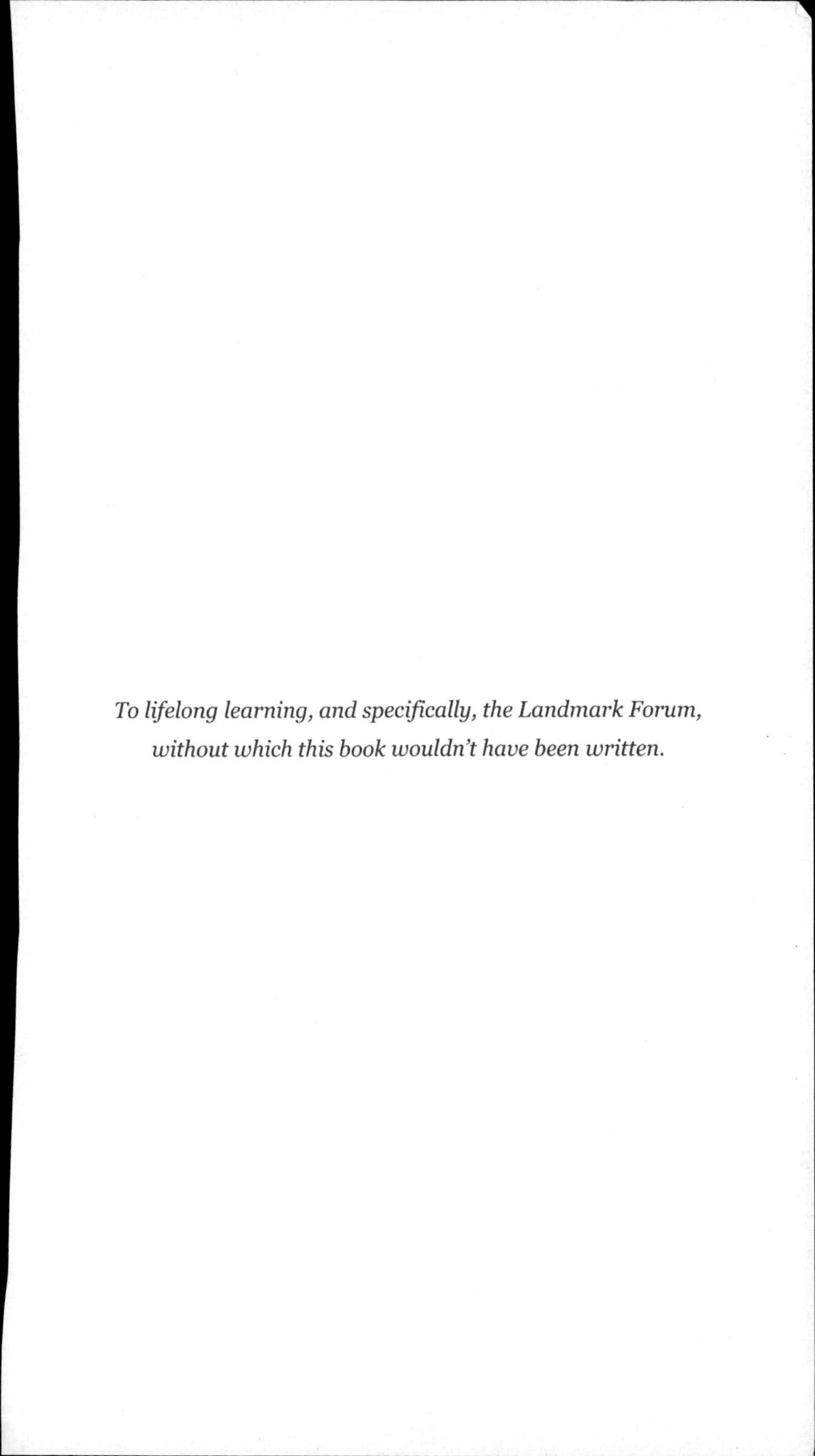

To lifelong learning, and specifically, the Landmark Forum, without which this book wouldn't have been written.

CHAPTER 1

ORION

There is a charged silence in my house as we stare down the wife of Milan the Dog.

This meeting was to be held in the utmost secrecy. The four families controlling New York are finally sitting down to discuss money, murder, and business.

Of course, Milan knew nothing of it because he would instantly reject the invite out of fear that we'd set him up; hence, we needed him to think he'd be meeting me alone. Had he come, the three of us would have proposed life-transforming changes to the syndicate.

But the fucker sends his wife Camila instead. *And to do what? Fuck? Gossip?*

She even has the audacity to come with a bodyguard. Standing in front of us, ten feet from danger, she's waiting on an invitation to sit but I'm dead fucking silent. And irritated beyond belief. I should kill her right on the spot.

I look over to the other side of the room and the two most dangerous men I know, Kai Delgado and Logan Vitali, their eyes burning with the same crazed look. Kai's hands are already closed into fists. He may lose it. He *should* lose it. It's within his right. And Logan–I've seen him kill a man in one move with his blade. It was one of my men. So as much as I fear them, I respect them too.

"What are you doing here? Where's Milan?" I growl.

"Milan had more important things to tend to. He sent me." Camila nods at Kai and Logan. "What are *they* doing here?"

"It's none of your goddamn business!"

"To think that I had to leave the party at LaToya's for this buzzkill," she says nonchalantly, but her eyes betray a special hatred for us, most likely thanks to Milan. "And now when I tell him about you ganging up on him"–she points to my guests–"there'll be hell to pay."

I look at Kai, then Logan. We're in a tight spot, and will seriously have to consider the consequences. She's right, there *will* be hell to pay. And if this gets out, Milan will gain the most. Not one person alive has seen the three of us together, apart from my sister. How on earth, and more importantly *why*, did the heads of the most feared mafia families, Delgado, Vitali, and Carte, get together to talk without blowing each other's brains out? To the world, we are bloodthirsty enemies who despise each other, but between us, we have an airtight connection that nobody knows about, or can break. But if anyone in our families hears of it, they'll get stupid ideas in their little heads.

It's now a standoff. We stare at each other in silence. It seems the voices in Kai and Logan's heads are getting the better of them, as they are in mine. Each of us considering different scenarios to figure out what would be best for our families. To stay alive. To remain kings on the streets of New York.

All of a sudden, a loud noise disturbs the silence. We are jolted by the bell ringing furiously, someone yelling and banging on the door, and that's it.

Kai, Logan, and I scramble for our guns and empty silent rounds on both Camila and her bodyguard. The bodyguard manages to open fire too; one bullet flies right past my face, to no avail. They drop to the floor like flies. There isn't even blood seeping from the wounds yet, it happened so quick; they didn't stand a chance. I instinctively point my gun at the others and they mirror me. After a brief hesitation, we aim them at the door where the banging continues.

"I thought you said we wouldn't be disturbed. Who the fuck's there, Orion?" Kai hisses.

"How the fuck should I know?" I snarl back. "Someone must've sneaked in past my camera sensors."

Logan dives for cover. "Get ready for the door to be blown."

We follow his lead and wait, but nothing happens. Just the yelling becoming subdued, and the pounding slowing down.

Irked by whoever dared approach my house, let alone bang on my door, I decide they don't get any more time. I stand up and motion to Kai and Logan that I'll unlock the door to see who's out there. They nod, get closer, ready to kill whoever shows up. But I know we all have the same suspicion. It must be Milan the Dog. And if that's the case, Camila lying in a puddle of blood just a few feet away would be one of the reasons we have to kill him.

I open the door, ready to rain hell threefold on whoever's there, and find myself blindly pointing my gun at a girl in torn clothes with blood dripping from her. In stunned silence, I glance at Kai, then Logan.

She doesn't say anything. Just stares at me with wide, dark eyes, her chest heaving, like a petrified deer on the road waiting for a car to run it over, until her eyes roll back in her head and she faints, falling at my feet.

I crouch to check her pulse. "Fuck!" This is the last thing I need today.

Kai and Logan stride past me and check the driveway. Only Camila's car can be seen from where I'm standing.

"Clear!" Logan yells.

"Clear," I hear Kai confirm as I lift the girl into my arms and take her inside. I'm not happy about this situation but I have to get her off my porch.

They close the door and join me as I carry her to the living room and lay her down on the sofa.

For a few moments, the three of us stand over her in silence. I'm pumped, ready to kill the next person in line, but looking at her all covered with blood, she's the last person I want to hurt.

"Who the fuck is this?" Kai eventually snaps.

"Let's figure that out later." In situations such as this, we know the drill. "Logan, take Camila's car into the garage. Here." I pull the keys from my pants pocket. "And put the bodies inside. Don't forget to turn off their cells."

"Don't insult me, Orion. I'm not a rookie," he scoffs, taking the keys. "Come on, Kai. I'm gonna need help."

I take a second look at the girl. Who the fuck is she? Who sent her? And why? Why tonight? She has blood all over her. She must be wounded. Her clothes are torn, and her top, well, her top's too small for her breasts, that's for sure. Why am I even looking there? The way she looked at me right before she crumbled at my feet... *fuck*. For that reason only, I'll let her live. For now. Dammit, I hate that she looks so innocent, lying here unconscious. *I bet she's not. She can't be.* Either way, I'll be damned if I don't find out.

I pick her up and take her upstairs, straight into one of the guestrooms at the end of the corridor. The only guestroom on the east side of the house, usually reserved for real guests, or those incapable of going home after a night out.

"I'm up here!" I yell at Kai and Logan when I hear the front door opening.

Since I live alone, my house has always been the safest place for our meetings. Nobody's allowed to walk in unannounced. My privacy is what keeps me safe. I don't allow anyone to come close without me knowing, thanks to the perimeter of sensor-activated cameras around the property. Except my sister Lisa. She often comes with her daughter, but not unannounced, as my cell buzzes each time there's movement in the vicinity. Besides, she's the only one who knows about Kai and Logan. From day one. They met, too. So I don't even consider her a threat. She brings me food and whatever else I ask her for, and I'd give my life for her.

This girl here must've come straight after Camila. I remember my cell buzzing, but I also remember being too angry at Camila's arrival to check.

Kai and Logan join me in the guestroom.

"She's still unconscious," I say to Logan. He's the doctor, after all. He's the one who has taken an oath to save lives. Not me. I'd rather kill them and get it over and done with.

Logan looks at her closely for a moment. "One thing's for sure, her body–"

"Logan," I warn him. I know where his mind goes.

"Whoever sent her must've known about our meeting tonight." Kai glowers at Logan and me. "And us."

I pace around the room. That realization is beginning to weigh heavy on me. "Fuck!"

"Most of the blood is around the stomach," Logan observes.

"How long can she survive a gunshot wound to the stomach?" Evidently, Kai hopes she'll die before she sees any of us again.

"It would depend largely on the gun, and the type of bullet," Logan replies. "A 22-caliber rimfire round would make a hole less than a quarter-inch, and might not 'pass through' but actually remain in the stomach. A 30-caliber hunting round with a soft point or hollow point projectile designed to expand and expend its energy rapidly would probably blow her stomach apart, killing her quickly. There are hundreds of bullet calibers designed for different purposes, so it'd be impossible to go over all the possibilities.

"Another issue would be the angle of the bullet's path. If it only hit the stomach and not the liver, pancreas, a kidney, or a major artery or vein, the chances of survival are much higher. If the bullet were to tear the abdominal aorta, death would happen very quickly from blood loss, not the stomach injury the bullet caused.

"Aside from these observations, a bullet would pass through other materials before reaching the stomach, so a heavily dressed individual might have a different life expectancy. Since this one's practically naked, and she was able to walk here, the chances are that she's not shot," he concludes, scratching his chin.

That's too long a ramble for my liking. I check my watch and frown. "Shit. With Camila dead, we don't have time to waste. As usual, this meeting never took place."

Kai nods.

Logan points to the girl lying on the bed. "What about her?"

"Let me deal with the bodies I already have for now."

"Cleaning crew," Kai states darkly.

I nod. I work with the best cleaning crew on the East Coast, with no connections to anyone in my family. One great piece of advice my father gave me: no matter what you're up to in your life, find yourself an independent cleaning crew.

"Both of you, stay here. I'll be back in ten."

LOGAN

Goddamnit! We didn't have to kill Milan's wife! It took us years to get to where we are, and because all of us are trigger-happy, we now have a dead woman on our hands. She was hardly anyone's role model, but still. She was a good bargaining tool, seeing as she wanted to bang all three of us at some point. And that poor bodyguard didn't stand a chance.

Orion's life-transforming changes he wants to propose to the syndicate, a 'smart' mafia life for all, is great. I'm sold to the life where I step back and practice medicine. But it's hard taking even one step forward with the asswipes that are Milan's men, the Slavs, who never keep their word. I didn't need this today. Had I stayed at home, I'd be tucked up in my bed right now with a girl under each arm. Not getting annoyed that if this gets out, some prick from my own family may want to cut my balls off, our syndicate's calling card. I know, *I* was the one who came up with it–you betray us, you lose your balls. As for death, it will come for sure, but not before a good, lengthy torture. Of course, nobody will get anywhere near my balls as my trusted blade's always in my pocket, and my skills are equivalent to that of a surgeon with twenty years' experience. But still.

If it wasn't for this tempting girl lying on the double bed in front of me, I'd certainly think tonight was wasted.

"I'll be on lookout out front." Kai sounds pissed. He's always pissed. He hasn't stuck his cock in anyone for nearly a year and of course he's miserable. Getting on his motorbike and going at a deadly speed is where he'll lose his head one day, and properly–not like he did last year, over a girl.

"Sure. I'll try to examine her."

I reach out and slowly move her arm, checking for a knife wound, but there's none. I examine her neck and down her body. Her tank top is bursting at the seams, so I undo three buttons and the tops of her breasts spill out. Her chest rises sharply. She takes a deep breath, and moans on the exhale.

Sweet Jesus mama! The sound is heavenly. Her breathing must've been restrained, that's probably why she fainted. I continue my examination. The torn material she wears as a skirt has many slits in it, and I check her legs. She moans again, and her eyelids flutter open.

"Hey, welcome back." I try to sound comforting, like I always do with the girls I check over in my club. But in reality, I want answers. Why is she here? Why was she banging so desperately on Orion's door? *And why is she so unbelievably sexy?*

She sees her top's undone and lifts her hands to cover her breasts which, by my reckoning, are not exposed at all. I'd have to see her nipples for that to be the case.

Panic visibly takes her over and fills her dark eyes, now wide open. She lifts her head and seems to scrutinize every detail of my face, like *I'm* the one being examined, then moves on to surveying the bedroom we're in.

"Do you mind if I check you over?" I ask.

She sits up. "I-I'm fine."

"Whose blood are you wearing, then?"

She stares at me, looking taken aback by my words. Her chin wobbles and tears bubble from beneath her eyelashes. As if she knows that I cannot stand a woman crying, she does exactly that. *My Achilles' heel.*

"Hey, it's okay. You can tell me." I speak softly; it's what always works. I reach out and gently touch her arm, but she jerks out from under my palm. I grit my teeth. Clearly she's been manhandled and can't stand anyone touching her.

"It's from... It's from a rat," she eventually says.

"From what?" Shit. This is bad. Really bad.

"A rat. He was aiming at me and killed a rat instead."

"Who's 'he'?"

Immediate withdrawal. "I... I don't know."

Sometimes I wish I couldn't read people this easy. She doesn't want to tell me who it was. No matter. I won't press. Eventually, she'll spill. "Why did he want to kill you?"

She shrugs, her deep, dark eyes fixed on mine.

"Well, you have nothing to worry about anymore. You're safe here."

I don't even know why I said that when I know how we operate. You see us together, we kill you. End of.

She smiles at me in a sad, broken way. She trusts me, and yet she's known me one full minute. "Is there any place I can clean myself up?"

"Sure. Over there." I point to the door leading to the ensuite bathroom.

She stands up slowly, her body barely covered by the rags she wears, and disappears behind the door.

I'm so immersed in her that I don't sense the person walking into the room is Kai. On impulse, I pull my blade and nearly spin it at him. After the shootout with Camila, my gun's safely tucked in my ankle holster, but my blades will do. They're deadly and silent. What could be better in this world?

"Is she okay?" Kai asks.

"Fuck, man, you should knock, or walk louder. I could've killed you." I tuck my blade back into the special pocket of my pants. All my pants have custom-made leather holsters inside the pockets for my blades. "And yes, she's up." I raise my eyebrows at him and smirk. "Something else is up too."

Kai ignores my joke. "Where is she?"

"Getting cleaned up." He's no fun at all these days. This past year, actually.

"She's hurt?"

"No. That's a rat's blood on her."

His eyes narrow. "A rat's blood?"

"Yeah. Someone tried to kill her and got the rat instead."

"Who?" Kai snarls. He's always taking the side of the weaker person, be they a man or a woman.

"She won't say."

"We'll make her," he snaps.

"Right now, one thing I want to make her is–"

The door of the bathroom opens slightly, and I stop. We don't see her, but we hear her smoky voice.

"Um, are there any clothes I could change into? Mine are not wearable."

"I'm sorry. There are none." My pervy heart rejoices that I may look at this angel's perfect skin longer.

The door opens fully and she comes out, her wet hair draped over one shoulder, her body wrapped in a towel that I'm jealous of, and her arms crossed over her chest. Kai and I both suck in a breath. We're rarely in the company of a normal girl, one who hasn't been passed around and ruined. We don't move, but I bet she sees the fire in my eyes, and probably in Kai's, because she questions my earlier promise.

"I'm safe here, right?" She sucks her bottom lip between her teeth.

"Um, yes. Yes, you are. Kai, stop looking."

She trusts me, I see it in her eyes. But why? I'm a thug. I've killed people. I've tortured more. Not one living soul trusts me these days and yet, somehow, she does–why? *And why am I smitten?*

Kai doesn't miss a beat. "You're in the safest place on earth, baby girl. I assure you."

Huh. Look at him. There's still sap in his balls, I guess. He's been gloomy and indifferent to every one of the girls we sent his way in the past year. And now this. *Good. Fucking great.*

I study the girl in front of us, trying to drink in her normal, sweet, innocent presence as much as I can.

God, are you messing with me?

Long, dark curls fall over her shoulder, and eyes as black as onyx stare at us with pure guilelessness. Her rosy cheeks and full lips are still flushed from the shower, a warning of what's coming next as my eyes travel south to her breasts. Those are the last things you want to lay your head on before you die. Abundant, and virginal.

"What's your name?" Kai asks.

She looks up at him through thick lashes. "Maisy Roy."

"Do you know where you are, Maisy?"

She nods. "Orion Carte's house. Is he here?"

"He will be shortly," I reply. I want to bathe in those dark, bottomless pools of hers, but I also want her to know who's in charge. "And it's 'O-RYON.' I'm sure he'll say something if you mispronounce his name." I chuckle. "I'm Logan, this is Kai. We're his associates. Nice to meet you."

CHAPTER 2

MAISY

With only a towel wrapped around my body, I exhale the breath I was holding. I'm alive, and safe. The gunshot sound was still resonating in my head just before I fainted, having followed me all day since I was shot at. And when I saw Camila the witch getting inside the house, I had to enter too. My ears are still ringing now. I'm a wanted person. The Slavs are looking for me, the assholes from the pits of hell that someone should kill already. The bounty on my head is high and if I show my face anywhere, that's it, game over. And why? Because I don't give up. That demon Milan has taken the most precious thing from me and I'll be damned if I don't get it back.

The answer lies somewhere inside his files. It took me years to sift through most of them, which unfortunately got me plenty of information on his enemies rather than on himself. It seems that his life is devoted to taking down the Cartes, Delgados, and Vitalis of New York, after which he plans on widening his scope, but that's not my concern. At the moment, I'm here, and I'm taking a different approach. I have no other options, even though I know I'm playing with fire. It's either that or becoming one of Milan's whores. I was stupid to think I'd go unnoticed for so long.

At least for the time being, I know I'm safe here. Also, on the plus side, the men in front of me, Kai and Logan, don't seem to want to violate my body.

I haven't seen their faces before, which makes it harder for me to guess who they are. Give me names, addresses, photos, numbers–anything, really, and I'll remember it. My photographic memory has been a curse throughout my life. People have tried to use me, and many succeeded. My ability to merely glance at anything for it to become etched in my head is the reason why Milan kept me alive.

It's also the reason I don't own a cellphone or a laptop. To me, everything I see becomes information my brain chooses to keep, and at times it's overwhelming. It weighs me down like an anchor, each day heavier.

I study Logan as he talks to me in a slow, dreamy manner. His eyes are green, with a mischievous glimmer, and sporadically roam over my body. He doesn't know I've noticed. His teeth flash when he smiles; this person is seductive by nature. Every now and again he sucks in a breath and runs his hand through the dark hair that falls over his face, and he regards me from underneath.

Tall, muscular, perfectly built body, wrapped in a well-fitted suit, white shirt with a tie and a vest. The shiny black shoes finish off the polished look. Not only does he look safe, but there's nothing intimidating about him. He's magnetic.

He's the one who said I was safe.

Kai is different. His piercing blue eyes bore shamelessly into me, appraising me. Messy, shoulder-length blond hair, strong jaw, a scar on his cheek, full lips. If we were in a different place, I'd say he was a model.

Although the black leather motorcycle jacket, tattoos on his hands, jeans, and black leather boots betray him. Tall and buff, he's a menacing sight. I'm not biased but if that doesn't scream *gangster*, certainly in this city, I don't know what does.

They're mobsters, clearly–why else would they be here?–but then again, I don't get that vibe when they talk to me.

I wonder what the vibe is with Orion Carte, apparently the finest criminal lawyer in NY and head of the Carte family.

"We're his associates."

I bite my lip. "Associates, as in, part of the mob?"

"Haha. Cute. No. We *are* the mob." Logan raises his chin arrogantly. Just now, he reminds me of the type of mobsters who dress well, talk well, and kill without mercy. All with smiles on their faces.

Kai's eyes look shocked as they fixate on Logan. "What the fuck, man?"

"Look, she's here already, she doesn't even know who we are, and look at her. She's harmless."

"Do you always think with your cock, Logan?" Kai growls. "Is that how you do business in your club?"

"As a matter of fact, women love to strip these days. It's empowering for them. You should catch up on all the feminism that happened in the last year."

"You work in a strip club?" I purr. I don't want them to argue.

"No, Maisy, I *own* the strip club," Logan explains.

Kai stares at Logan. "Oh, and the girls behind the club? What are they up to?"

Logan narrows his eyes at him. "Shut up, Kai. You're talking too much!"

"Or what?" Kai steps forward and pushes Logan with his chest.

Logan draws a blade in an instant and presses it against Kai's neck, right under his ear. "I love you, man, but you're treading a fine line here."

Kai seizes Logan's lapels, the blade still flush against his neck. "Cut me. I dare you."

I gasp and take a step back, just as a third person walks in. *Thank God!*

"Hey, *hey!*" the new arrival yells.

This must be Orion Carte.

"What the hell are you doing, fuckers? This is *not* what we talked about."

"Fuck, man, this one here's thinking with his cock again," Kai snaps as Logan lowers the blade and slides it back into his pocket.

The three of them exchange glances. It looks like Orion's silently cautioning them. Then, he turns to me and steps closer.

I never would've imagined a lawyer to be this huge. Power spills from every pore on his body, and his demanding dark eyes burrow into mine. Like an animal sizing up its prey. I feel insignificant already.

Clean-shaven, defined jaw and cheekbones, and dark hair in messy waves. On one side of his neck, he has a tattoo of a rope with some sort of knot leading from his ear down to the collar of his buttoned shirt and tie. His sleeves are rolled up to his elbows, revealing tattoos on both arms. There are four silver rings and a silver bracelet on one hand, and three rings on the other together with an expensive-looking watch. Plus, a leather holster under his arm with a gun in it. *Of course*. And he's vexed about something.

He possesses a different kind of darkness, one that I can see lurking as if patiently waiting for something. I recognize it from a photograph of his father and the syndicate's most ruthless gangster, the infamous Willer Carte. But that was on paper. And I thought it was a glitch in the print. Seeing it in person makes me tremble.

Logan aligns himself with Orion. Kai does too.

The three of them are of roughly equal height, too tall, and tower over me in silence, as if I'm a defendant on trial. They are intoxicating, yet strangely comforting. It's been a while since I've been in the company of men who don't want to use me for some selfish cause. Just wait until they know more about me. They always turn into demons.

"She's not hurt?" Orion asks, appraising me.

"No, that was a rat's blood." Logan's staring at my jugular notch for some reason. I cover my neck with my hand.

"She needs clothes." Kai states the obvious, but he's stripping layers of my armor away by acting the uber-protector.

"Rat's blood, hmm?" Orion ignores him and narrows his eyes at me. "Are you a rat?"

"No, I'm not." I speak loud and clear, my chin lifting automatically.

Orion arches an eyebrow. "Then why rat's blood?"

"I was just lucky, I guess."

"Lucky?" Orion scoffs. "Right. You, stay here." He turns to Kai and Logan. "Both of you, come with me."

I'm left in the big room, alone. Not that I mind. I have a huge bed, a TV, and a large window with no blinds.

I look through the window and can just about see the lights of a few houses in the distance. There seems to be a dense thicket of trees around the house I'm in. I peer down at the ground. It's late August and stuffy, but I'm on the second floor, so it's basically safe to open the window.

ORION

"Follow me."

Three different sets of footsteps ring out as Kai and Logan walk wordlessly behind me, down the staircase and into the kitchen. They know I'm fucking mad.

I stop in the middle of the room by the granite island and turn to them. "Why the fuck were you fighting?"

"It's not important," Kai snarls.

Logan tries to deflect. "Let's focus on the problem at hand."

"You think?" I'm exasperated, and losing my patience. It's getting close to midnight. "What are we doing about her?"

"*Maisy*, you mean," Kai corrects me.

Logan and I look at each other. Kai's never corrected me in his life. For once, I'm glad there's still fire in his balls. We were beginning to think he was dead on the inside. In all my annoyance, I can't help but laugh.

"Is that what she said? That's her name?"

"Yes," Kai confirms, while Logan and I smirk.

"What else did she say?"

"She came here to see you."

"To see *me*?" My eyebrows shoot up.

"Yes, you."

"You know we're going to have to kill her, right? She's seen too much," I remind them.

"No," Kai says. His obstinance is beginning to annoy me.

Logan's on his side. "No way."

Look at that. Logan, siding with Kai? I must admit, 'Maisy' woke my dick from its winter sleep when I saw her, and her freshly showered scent wafting under my nostrils made me feel like a horse on drugs, but even so, she's seen us. It's game over for her. In our world of lies, betrayal, semi-automatic guns, and killings, you trust a few people. And these two make my most trusted army, though it's shocking even to me.

"What's this? A mutiny?" I snap.

Kai pleads his case. "Orion, you saw her. She's different. Normal. We don't kill people from outside our world."

Clearly this goes deeper than I thought for him.

"I'm with Kai on this one," Logan adds.

Fools! "She came to my door with rat's blood on her," I point out. "Rat's blood! That's a message for me. Or us. How can you not see it?"

They stare at me, silently resisting.

I exhale a loud sigh. "I can't deal with you two today. Stay the night, but away from her room. We'll talk tomorrow morning."

"Are you gonna kill her?" Logan asks.

"Not until I know who sent her. Come, I'll show you to your rooms, then I'll go and see what she knows."

I take them upstairs again, but to the opposite side of the house, to Lisa and Mya's rooms. My sister and niece are the only family members I allow in my house, so they rightly have a room each.

"Orion, I trust you, brother," Kai insists as he enters his room. "I know you won't kill her."

Logan heads for his room without a word.

"Get some sleep," I tell them.

MAISY

I shift my weight from foot to foot as I wait for Orion. He is the person I ought to get on my side, seeing as I'm in his house and looking for his protection. But somehow, I get the feeling he doesn't want me here. I'm not frightened–even though his eyes are black as a bottomless pit, seeming to magically lure every living creature to him. Mine are, too. Darkness doesn't scare me. What does scare me is that I can't read him. But I'll take that over being on the streets. *I'm finally safe, thank God!* A mantra that's been on repeat in my head. That, and from time to time, the image of the three of them standing over me.

The knock on the door makes me jolt. "C-come in."

Orion strides inside as if he's meeting me in some professional setting, like a boardroom or something. "You haven't dressed yet."

"I have nothing to wear." I chew on my bottom lip. "Maybe I'll wash my old clothes later."

"No. Throw them away. I'll bring something for you."

He disappears somewhere and comes back with a t-shirt, jeans, and underwear. *How often has he been in this situation?*

"I hope these'll fit you." He hands them over and glances at my legs, at the wound on my ankle. The skin is broken and red where I was shackled.

"Thank you."

He sits on the armchair opposite the bed, rests his left ankle over his right knee, and leans back. "Sit," he orders.

I take a few steps backward and sit on the bed.

"What's your name?"

"Maisy Roy."

"I'm Orion Carte. But you knew that already."

I nod.

"Tell me why you showed up on my doorstep in the middle of the night."

"Um, there's a letter for you." True, there *is* a letter for him, except I don't have it. It's one of those 'I glanced at it and now it lives in my head' things. As much as that always gets me in shit, it's saved me quite a few times. And had I not seen it and remembered the address, I probably wouldn't have known where to go. Seeing Camila entering only a moment earlier gave me the strength I needed. Camila the *witch!*

He reaches out with his palm open. "The letter."

"I-I don't have it."

"I will ask you again. And I expect the truth this time. I don't need to tell you who I am or what I could do to you."

There's an infinite void inside his eyes, and I feel it pulling me to him. It must be a cross-examination technique he uses in his work. Or some kind of sorcery.

I nod. "Yes, I know." He's the head of the Carte mafia family, and a criminal lawyer. Which is partly why I knocked on his door.

"So, why did you show up on my doorstep in the middle of the night?" he repeats.

"I told you already." I have a persistent itch under my arm that I try to ignore but it's damn hard, so I scratch as I speak.

"I've seen girls like you on the streets, hungry for a heroin shot or whatever else is available. Whoring themselves out for a moment of peace. Are you one of those girls?"

"No." I scowl. "Of course not."

"Your eyes tell me one thing but your body tells me another."

He keeps looking at my legs, specifically around my ankles.

"Remove your towel and stand still for me."

The fire in my fists ignites by itself. I raise them, using my upper arms to hold the towel tight at my sides. "You will not sell my body like I'm a piece of meat, and I will *not* be your whore! I'm a human being, you asshole!"

Orion doesn't flinch. He seems entertained, even. "I don't want to sell you. I want to see if you have any bruises or whip marks. That usually tells me who you are. Unless you want to start telling the truth."

"Well, I'm not a heroin addict." I raise my chin. I have nothing to be ashamed of. "Here. Read my body, asshole." I remove the towel.

My body's already been seen by at least twenty men today. They all had a nasty comment, a few slapped me, and one wanted more but thankfully was stopped. I was to be 'prepared' and then put into production. *Monsters*.

I watch his pupils dilate as he sucks in a breath. He stands up and moves closer to examine me. His eyes meander all over my upper body, expertly avoiding my nipples, hardened from the sudden rush of cool air. He rubs a hand over his jaw, and his tongue darts out to lick his lower lip.

He reaches for my upper arm and I jolt when his cold hand lands on my skin, expecting him to say something demeaning. He's a man standing with a naked woman in front of him, after all. But his eyes are at peace, black and calm, his head slightly cocked as if I'm overreacting.

He proceeds to turn me around, slowly. "I see."

"What do you see?" I breathe.

"You have a stamp on your lower back from your pimp. A fresh one. Did you run away, Maisy Roy?"

"A stamp?"

He stoops to get a better look at it, checking it out carefully. I'm self-conscious about his face being literally an inch from my bare ass. But clearly that doesn't faze him at all.

"Mm-hmm, done four hours ago. Checked, stamped, dated, contraceptive included, the whole shebang." He stands up and I turn to him fully, as if I'm not naked at all. I look up at him as he towers over me. "This means you're clean and you can start." He twists my itching arm outward. "Here. They inserted you with an implant so you don't get pregnant."

I automatically give my itchy arm a good scratch, almost trying to tear that fucker out from under the skin, and as I do, my eyes stay on him. His are focused lower, on my breasts.

The moment he realizes I've noticed, he steps away and sits back in the armchair. "Please, cover up."

I pick up the towel and wrap it around my body.

"Tell me how long you've been a whore."

A hurtful presumption. *I have feelings, asshole.* The way he looked at me a moment ago is at odds with the impassive expression he wears now. The sight of it doesn't give me any indication of my destiny.

"I'm not a whore, I told you that! Are you deaf or something?" I spit back. I guess this is the only way we'll communicate.

"Then what are you?"

Tears spike my eyes. "I ran away from a man who... who wanted me to... to..."

"And you came running to me? Why on earth did you think *I'd* save you?"

"I don't know. I saw a letter with your name and address on a while back. When that bastard was shooting at me, I ran here. As I got closer I saw Camila coming in. It's then that I realized I had to get in too."

"Camila?" His eyes narrow and turn icy, as if I've stepped on his grave.

"Yes."

"Let's try this one more time. Why did you show up on my doorstep in the middle of the night, with rat's blood on you?"

"Look, I told you. I saw a letter addressed to you–"

"Okay. Who's it from?"

"Your mother. It looked important."

He shifts awkwardly in his seat. I must've hit a nerve. "My mother passed away last year."

"Well, it said it was from 'Mom.' It had your home address."

"When did you see this letter?"

"A few months ago."

"And you remembered my address?"

"Mm-hmm." I yawn suddenly, and lie on the bed. I've been awake for a few days and running on adrenaline for some time. I'm exhausted, and the cool air in the room is making me sleepy.

"You should stop lying."

"I'm not lying. There was other stuff in the box. Baby pictures. Other memorabilia."

"And you're telling me this out of the goodness of your heart?"

"No. Yes. I mean, I needed to go somewhere safe." I'm having difficulty keeping my eyes open. "They want me to work for them... but I won't do it. I'll never do it."

"Who's 'them?'"

"Them." I yawn again.

"How do you know me?"

"I don't. Please, Orion, I'm tired."

"It's O-Ryon. You pronounce it like the constellation Orion."

"The most striking and recognizable constellation in the night sky," I say, pulling redundant information from my head, and close my eyes.

"What do you want from me, Maisy?"

"Right now, can I sleep, please?"

I turn onto my side, place my closed palms under my face, and instantly start to doze off. The bed just called my name.

Orion's still in the room. I hear him sigh, sounding annoyed. "We'll talk tomorrow."

I sense the cover being draped over me, and I feel tucked in, cozy.

CHAPTER 3

KAI

I'm ready for our meeting. I want to get this over and done with. It's morning, and my mind is firmly set on not killing Maisy. The sight of her last night, water droplets from the shower clinging to her thick lashes, her bare shoulders glistening in the light, and two perfect mounds protruding from the towel wrapped tightly around her body, made my heart pound. And she didn't show a flicker of terror that she was being held by the heads of not one, but three crime syndicates.

Orion wants her dead. It'll be tough changing his mind. We've always followed his lead. As someone who's a practicing lawyer, he knows what's best when it comes to liabilities. The funny thing is, I didn't expect Logan to back me. To be on the same footing as him makes me feel good, powerful. Like he's in my corner for once. Since we met thirteen years ago at that deserted factory, despite the pact the three of us made to stick together no matter what, Logan and I have always been in competition. But deep down, we love each other. He's the brother I never had.

I decide I had enough time lying in the bed so I leave Lisa's bedroom and go in search of coffee.

Orion's kitchen is big, with a large island in the middle and an equally imposing wooden table next to the wall, enough to seat fourteen people. Logan and Orion are already there, sitting opposite each other and talking.

Logan's swearing under his breath. "For fuck's sake..."

I pour myself a large cup and sit next to him. They both seem agitated. "What's going on?"

Logan sounds somber. "She knows Camila was here."

My jaw drops. *It can't be. Fuck.* "Then the rat's blood on her face must be for you. Or all of us." My head is spinning as to who knows about us.

"You know what this means." Orion cuts through us like a knife through a birthday cake. "She must die."

I nod decisively. No one's immune from execution when they have that kind of knowledge. Logan looks at me and nods too. *I feel you, man. What protectors we are. We said she'll be safe and now we can't deliver.*

"There's more. Last night she was running away from a pimp. Got stamped, meaning she was medically checked maybe three, four hours before we saw her. They inserted her with an implant, the whole shebang."

"Who's the pimp?" I snarl. At least I can take it out on him when she's gone.

Orion shakes his head. "She won't tell."

Maisy's been cagey about everything. *I wish she'd tell us who the fucker is.*

"Who's gonna do it?" Orion asks bluntly.

I lower my head. This has always been the easiest part. When people have it coming we have no problem killing them. If it's one, or ten, meh, work is work. But now, today, fuck me if I'm pulling the trigger. If I must–if I'm told to–I will, but I don't want to.

Logan looks away, a clear indication he doesn't want to do it either.

"In that case, all of us will pull the trigger," Orion concludes. "Or do you pussies want me to do it?"

In the distance is a faint noise of a door opening, and Orion stops talking. He turns toward the staircase, listening to the barefooted footsteps that grow louder until Maisy appears. She's wearing an oversized t-shirt that comes down to just under her ass.

"Good morning." She smiles, and my cock twitches. I follow her every step as she saunters in front of us and behind Orion, to the coffee pot. Orion doesn't move.

"Good morning." My face lights up. I know it does because Orion scolds me with a glare.

Logan grins. "Good morning, Maisy."

She picks up the coffee pot in one hand and looks around for a cup.

"They're in the cupboard, on the left," Orion says without turning around.

She opens the cupboard. The cups are on the second shelf, too high for her. She pushes herself up on tiptoes and just about grabs one, but it slides from under her fingertips and gets nudged further from her reach. She stretches again, and her t-shirt rides up.

Oh, dear God! She has nothing on! We are spectators in the front row of the show called *Maisy's Perfect Round Ass*. My cock throbs in appreciation, but only for a moment, because I remember I'll be blowing her brains out soon.

"Can someone help me, please?" she purrs.

Logan huffs under his breath, "The way she says *please*, sweet Jesus mama!"

Before we can move, Orion jumps up, pulls out a cup, and sets it on the kitchen counter. "It wasn't that high," he growls at her. "And if I remember correctly, I gave you some underwear."

She frowns at him before pouring herself a coffee. “I can’t wear someone else’s underwear.”

She stands up for herself; good for her.

Orion rolls his eyes and looks at us. “Let’s not make it messy.” His overly composed voice means he’s one step away from a killing frenzy. It’s chilling.

The three of us jump to our feet at the same time. Nobody’s being a pussy now. The screeching noise of our chairs alarms Maisy, who drops her coffee cup to the floor. She obviously senses what’s coming–except the buzzing message on all of our cells stops us in our tracks.

Orion’s clearly annoyed at Maisy for dropping the cup, breaking it into pieces with coffee splattered all over the floor. He reaches for his back pocket and Maisy raises her hands as if to protect herself.

“No!” she yells.

“Orion, stop!” I shout. Maisy’s face is splashed across the screen of my cell, with ‘*Wanted*’ written in the message.

Orion’s staring at me, looking vexed. “Is it okay with you if I check my cell, Kai?” he asks sarcastically.

“Oh, sure, I thought... Never mind.”

“What are you waiting for?!” he yells at Maisy. “Clean this shit up!”

I glance at Logan’s cell. He’s got the same message as I have. I look at Orion and he’s staring at his screen.

He sits down, and we follow suit. Maisy’s on the floor, soaking up the coffee with a tea towel. Her t-shirt gapes at the front and through the opening I have a partial view of her breasts bouncing about.

I’m mesmerized.

She looks up, her eyes shiny with tears.

Orion speaks more softly. “Maisy, come sit here.”

She pushes herself to her feet and hesitantly sits next to Orion. She’s eyeing all of us, looking unsure of what to expect. I make her another cup of coffee and set it on the table in front of her.

“Are you hungry?” I ask.

"No." She takes a long sip of coffee and blinks at me over the cup.

Orion doesn't beat around the bush. "Why are you wanted by Milan the Dog?"

She looks at him, then at us. She takes a few large gulps before placing the cup back on the table. We are silent, waiting on her to start talking.

"I ran away from his pimp last night."

"That's not the reason why he sent every mobster in town searching for you," Orion replies. "There's a bounty on your head. He's not doing that for just any whore."

She stares him dead in the face and talks through gritted teeth. "I'm–not–a–*whore!*"

"You ran away. I get that. But there's something that you're not telling us."

"I wouldn't work for him."

"Have you ever worked for him?"

"No. I don't know." She sighs. "I did some work for Jerry, my landlady's husband. That's how I'd pay my rent. I thought that was working fine. Until the day before yesterday. They came in the morning, killed him, my landlady too, and took me with them. The order was, I'm to work for him from now on."

"Why?"

"While I worked for Jerry I saw loads of documents, both legal and illegal. And when they found out about my... my..." She regards the three of us like she's waiting on something, maybe to see if we know something, but we just stare at her impatiently. "My photographic memory. They know I still have them in my head."

"Photographic memory?" Logan's eyebrows shoot up. "Like some sort of live database?"

"Anything I lay my eyes on, I remember. That's how I knew this house belonged to you, Orion."

"It's O-RYON," he snaps.

I'm confused. "Wait, you saw Orion's address in Milan's documents?"

"Yes."

"What about us?"

"There are many Logans and Kais that I've come across in my twenty years of life. What's your full name?"

"Kai Delgado."

"Logan Vitali."

Her eyebrows lift slowly. She seems to realize who we are, and nods. "Yes, you too."

"Fuck, man. You *are* valuable," I conclude.

"So what, he thought you'd become a whore, and then work for him?" Orion is not letting her forget. "And what would your family say? Surely someone'll be looking for you?"

"I have no one. He thought he'd punish me first, get me to see what that life's like before I submit."

"You ran away, and you came here?" I ask her.

"I saw Camila, and... um, I knew of her. Um..." She takes a deep breath and exhales. She looks at us as though she's letting us in on a big secret. "Over the year I worked for Jerry, apparently I was being filmed in my home and at that time I had a boyfriend. They said they had enough material to produce an adult video. I did things with him that I don't want anyone to see. And I found out Camila produced the film already."

The three of us look at each other. My cock twitches at the thought of Maisy in an adult video. But I shake off the idea just as fast. I wouldn't want to see her with someone else. Knowing me, I'd have to kill them.

"Where is Camila? Did she see me?" she asks.

"No, she didn't see you," I say.

Orion is not easing off with the sarcasm. "And then what? Were you going to ask her nicely for the video recording?"

She nods. "If anything like that gets out, I'll never be able to work as... um, as a schoolteacher."

"Ha, you want to be a schoolteacher?" Logan laughs.

Her eyes instantly fill with tears again. "You think I can't?"

"No, no, I didn't say that. It's just... What will you teach?"

"I don't know. I want to help kids. I can make a career out of it."

"Sure. Sure."

"Maybe you can help me get the video recording back in exchange for the information I know Milan has on you?" she asks in a small voice. *Proposing a deal with the mafia. She's brave.* "If anyone can do that, it's you."

Orion narrows his eyes at her, and we all wait on him to speak. It seems he's not swayed by her full lips and bosoms, not yet. "I'm gonna be straight with you, Maisy. We're the worst people for you to have gotten involved with." He observes her closely, no doubt trying to find any sign of treachery. "Although out of the two evils, we're a touch better than Milan the Dog."

"What does that mean?" she breathes.

"You were as good as dead up until five minutes ago."

"But now you want to keep me for yourself and use me, right? Huh. Figures. Everyone's the same when they know what I can do."

She's being impatient, and that gets Orion every time. He pinches the bridge of his nose. "No. I didn't say that. We'll help you get the tape, and possibly get Milan off your back, in return for the information on what you saw about us. This is not you working for us, or us using you. This is simply us obtaining our data. Milan cannot have information on us if we haven't consented to it."

Maisy runs her tongue over her lower lip. "And then? I get the video recording and I can go?"

"Yes. Meanwhile, you'll have to stay here and out of everyone's sight."

"I get it. Lay low for a few days," she says quietly to herself, staring into her cup.

"Let's start with the name of your pimp," I growl.

She just shakes her head and takes another gulp of coffee.

I raise my voice, frustrated. "Why won't you tell us?"

"*Why?!* I was lucky to get away last night! I read about his operations in Jerry's documents, and it's terrifying what goes on in there. I won't be a number in his books, and get sold off in the Middle East!"

"Kai, we will not be going about killing people. We need to be smart about this," Orion says, trying to mollify me, but it's no use. I could kill every person who ever touched her by the end of the hour.

Maisy's eyes widen. "What are you going to do?"

Orion delivers his response by leaning in, speaking straight to her face, clearly expecting some sort of reaction. "I don't think we'll be telling you all our plans, Maisy. After all, you could be lying about everything."

"I'm not!" she protests.

"Says the whore with a stamp on her back."

Visibly hurt, she scrunches her brows. "I–am–not–a–whore!" Eyes filled with tears, she stands up and runs out of the room.

"Orion, man, come on!" I scold him as I get to my feet. "She's not one of your perpetrators. Cut her some slack."

I run after Maisy and stop in the doorway of her bedroom when I see her sobbing, frantically trying to put on her jeans. She buttons them up, curls her hands into fists and lunges at me.

"I'm not a whore, I never was! You hear me?!"

I pull her perfect body into my arms. "Calm down, Maisy. Ignore him, please."

"No! Let me go! I want to break his face!" She fights me, kicking me hard and punching me wherever she can reach.

"You don't want to do that. He was only joking. Hey. *Hey!*"

I hold her firmly, wrapping her in my arms, her scent overwhelming me. After her earlier teasing, now that she's nestled in my chest she's even harder to ignore it.

Easing off, she cranes her neck to look at me. Her eyes are full of innocence. Her lips are parted and she's breathing heavy. She definitely needs air.

I let her go and cup her face instead. “I will never let anything happen to you. Is that clear?”

Within my hands, she nods. I wipe her tears away and lower my lips to kiss her forehead. All of a sudden, she pushes herself onto her tiptoes and kisses me.

She doesn’t know what that does to me. I’m not hiding it, but I’m sure if I reciprocate, I won’t be able to stop myself. Still, I press my lips to hers and kiss her back. She moans softly.

I have to tear myself from her to speak. “You don’t have to do this.” My cock is getting hard and I’m reminded of all the filthy things I want to be doing to her.

“I’m sorry. I... I just... I’m sorry.” She turns around and stands with her back to me. “Please, go.”

My heart hurts for her, but I will not use this moment of weakness to sleep with her. She deserves better. And more. I may be a sadistic and cold-blooded murderer, but I’ll be dammed if I ruin another woman again.

I turn and walk back to the kitchen.

ORION

While I grow more frustrated by the whole situation, Logan pleads.

“We don’t ever get to hang with girls like her anymore. Or ever,” he’s saying. “She could stay with me. I’ll keep her safe, you know I will.”

“Do you want to go jerk off and come back in ten?” I ask.

His reason to have her in his home holds up 100%, but I need his balls empty when he talks to me. Usually, he doesn’t oppose me because deep down I’m always thinking straight. And that’s saved his life too many times. Why? Because my cock knows when to make an appearance. And now is not the time.

"Just imagine being in the company of someone normal–" Logan starts, but I've had enough of his crap.

Kai walks in, which is good. He's equally irresponsible, so he too can hear what I think of it.

"Imagine what?" I snap. "We'll be holding her prisoner, and when we're done with her... then what? Nobody knows about us. Do you want to put that at risk? We don't even know who she is, for God's sake!"

Logan doesn't respond. He knows I'm right. Kai too.

"Do your research on her. I will too. We have a good reason to ask questions now, seeing as everyone's talking about her." Exasperated, I stand up. It's time they leave. "Go home. They must be looking for you all over town."

I walk out of the kitchen still in disbelief. A schoolteacher! I've seen a fair share of liars in my life and she's by far the worst. And why wouldn't she give us the name of her pimp?

She thinks all men think with their cocks. Well, I'll be glad to change her opinion.

CHAPTER 4

MAISY

I've been in this room for a week now, away from everyone. There's always a lot of noise coming from the kitchen downstairs, yet nobody has ventured to my room.

Except two days ago, when I heard someone walking up the stairs. Orion's thunderous voice boomed through the house in warning: "If you're tired, get the fuck out of my house! This is not a hotel! Get the hell out!" There was the sound of someone grumbling, and then... silence.

Kai and Logan came a few times, together and separately, so I got to spend time with each of them and get to know them better. In fact, I've been doing my own research with them. I already knew Logan was involved in the adult industry and I wanted to find out in what way. He's a doctor but doesn't really practice, although if he could, he would. He told me about his life, and his days spent around naked girls who strip for living. A pang of jealousy hit me when he talked about them giving him lap dances on a daily basis. Apparently, that's how he's been brought up: whiskey, and lap dances. He mentioned his mother, and how he wished he knew her. He even showed me a small heart he had tattooed over his left pectoral muscle, in her honor.

Kai, on the other hand, is a boxer: a mean killing machine. At least he's channeling his negativity in the boxing ring. Labeling oneself as a professional boxer is apparently the best thing one can do in their line of work, especially when they know killing someone in the ring doesn't make them guilty. And he has killed a lot. Legally, as he says.

I told them as much about me as I could, as I didn't want to complicate things. I do like them a lot, and not being honest is, for the first time, tough. I haven't had to be honest with people in a very, very long time. They genuinely look after me, without asking for anything back. And for me, that's new. I have no point of reference as to if or when it will all go south. But I'm sure it will. That's why I protect myself. I cannot tell them the truth yet.

"What shall we do today?" Kai asks as he makes himself comfortable on my bed, lying down with his head where my feet are, propped on his forearm.

"Let Maisy choose. She's the one that's stuck in this room," Logan responds softly. Ever since we met, he's been acting as if I need to be taken care of. He's on the bed too, sitting opposite Kai, with his legs crossed, while I'm propped on my pillows against my headboard.

"Hey, don't treat me differently just because I'm in here. It's my choice that I'm here, no one else's."

"Yes, we know," Logan chuckles and shuffles the cards.

"How about poker?" I grin.

"Poker?" Kai's eyebrows flash. "Do you know how to play poker, baby girl?"

"Ha! Of course I know!"

"Hmm." Logan is gazing at me, his eyes roaming from the nape of my neck down to my leggings, oozing that particular vibration that brings heat between my legs. "Don't forget, we're quite good at playing poker. We were taught how to play poker before we could walk."

I chuckle, that's funny. But Logan keeps his cool. The way he's observing me, he's taking off my clothes, one by one. I think I like his glare, although I could be wrong. He doesn't give anything off.

"You have no money to play," Kai's raspy voice gets my attention.

"Come on guys," my chuckle suddenly drying out. I'm calling their bluff. "I have other things. Like, clothes. I'm sure you two are not afraid to lose a few of your garments in a poker game with a girl."

They glance at each other, contemplating on the consequences should they win and undress me. I continue before they respond. "Suit yourself. None of you stand a chance anyway."

They chuckle, this time out loud.

"Oh, sweetheart, you're so on." Logan gives me the deck of cards to cut. "Kai? Let's teach her a lesson."

"With pleasure." Kai sits up and crosses his legs too.

I lean in, and focus, now I definitely mean business. I'm wearing a t-shirt, leggings and panties underneath but it won't come to that. I know poker.

Logan deals the cards, and we're in a game. Immediately, I start noticing their minute movements. Poker is all about nuances. Kai leans back slightly, I notice that Logan bites his lower lip twice, and he stops. He has something. Kai tries to look cool, clear sign he has nothing at all.

Kai would have to fold, and Logan is now the real threat.

"Hit me." Kai says and my lips crook. Is it going to be this easy?

Logan looks like a proud father holding his cards. Bluff? Does he have the king? Maybe king and queen?

It's as if Kai wants to take off his clothes. After a few rounds we place our cards on the table, and I grin. Damn.

"What's it going to be, Kai?" I grin.

"Let her decide." Logan is quick to interrupt him.

He's wearing a t-shirt, and jeans. If I go for the jeans I'd seem cruel.

"T-shirt."

Kai doesn't say a word, but slowly pulls his top over his head, revealing his bulky pecs, six pack, and inked arms, leaving me speechless. I see his jeans are low cut and, without the t-shirt, I distinctly see the V below his abs.

"Close your mouth, Maisy." Kai glares at me like a brooding animal that's going to attack.

I'm cool, although uninvited heat pools between my legs.

"I was just celebrating my win. It's Logan's turn next." I smirk as Logan chuckles defiantly.

"I'm out. I can't bear the humiliation, seriously, I felt like a piece of meat as I was undressing." Kai laughs and moves next to me.

His aftershave, mixed with the scent of his leather jacket, is pure bottled testosterone. It overwhelms me and, I'm sure it's because of it, I lose the next game.

Which is unheard of because I actually have photographic memory, and therefore, remember everything. I count the cards. Clearly I'm distracted. Clearly.

"What do you want me to take off?" I ask, knowing perfectly well I have no bra under my t-shirt.

"Leggings." Logan says and rolls his eyes. He knows he does not have much of a choice.

"Don't do that. I'm playing fair and square. You want me to take something off, I will." Do I want him to ask me to take off my top? Yes. No. Don't know. He wouldn't dare though.

I stand up and take off my leggings in a clumsy way, nearly falling down on my butt. "I would have taken my top off if I needed to."

"You need lessons in stripping, Maisy." Logan chuckles and Kai joins him. "I could arrange it if you want."

"Just deal the next round, Logan."

Naturally, I won that round. Of course I did. But just as Logan was about to take off his pants they both got a message on their cells, and our party was over. It must have been Orion.

Still, for a few days we hung out, watched TV, talked. It's funny; all either of them wants to know, from under their masks of testosterone and hardness, is what it's like living a normal life.

Normal? Only up until the day I turned twelve was my life normal. I had a mother, a sister, and a stepfather, who later turned out to be the biggest monster out there. And everything was 'normal' up until Mom died. Cancer does that to people. Takes them away when they are most needed. Since then, my life has been anything but normal. But I don't tell them that. I stick to the parts when I was little, that I remember. I don't feel right making things up so when they ask me about my teens, I stop. They'd probably poke and ask more questions, but somehow our time together is always cut short. It's as if Orion has put some kind of embargo on me. *Asshole.*

I've left my room only once. It was past midnight and I was in the kitchen when I heard grunting sounds coming from the basement. Quietly, on tiptoes, I pushed open the door and took a few steps down to what looked like a huge space under the house and probably beyond–part gym, part boxing ring. Step by step I followed the sound, until the room opened up to me and Orion came into view. I was still mad at him for insulting me and I wanted to say something, to tell him off, to stand up for myself.

He was lying on his back on a bench, in his shorts. I saw his black sneakers and muscly legs first, then his naked torso, a sight to behold: glistening with sweat, one side full of tattoos from his neck down to his arm and chest, as well as his thigh down to his knee. What got me flustered was how the weight he pushed away from his chest triggered a grunt, and the bulging of his pectorals and biceps–all that was more than enough for a wet heat to develop uninvited in my core.

I stood there, immersed in him, watching him sweat and grunt until he finished his reps and sat up. His eyes landed directly on me, as if he'd already known I was there. He couldn't have. But somehow, he did.

"Keep showing up like this and you'll get your ass spanked, Maisy."

I was there to put him in his place but for some reason, I became mute, just staring into his eyes. It felt as if he took away all my cognitive power, but when he stood up abruptly, my petrified little heart skipped a beat. I spun on the spot and ran. Up the two flights of stairs and straight to my room. Imagine him saying that. *You'll get your ass spanked.*

And since then, I dare not go out. Thinking about him gets me flustered a lot. He was clear: I'm not allowed to be seen. And I wasn't–it was only that night that he saw me, but he said if someone else sees me, he cannot protect me. Lying low is the best plan for the moment. Until they forget about me.

At least he remembers to feed me. It's always early in the morning and late at night. Judging by the scent in the air, he brings the food himself, leaving the tray outside my room. I don't know if someone prepares it, but the food is superb. And morning and evening, there's always on the tray a small punnet of strawberries, sweet and juicy.

He's also brought me basic toiletries, pads, five packs of boring black panties (clearly he doesn't look at me in *that* way), jeans, leggings, cami tops to sleep in and so on. He even got me a cellphone, but I gave it back immediately. I don't have anyone to talk to in this world, and as for the internet, no thank you. I don't want to inject more information into my head. I have enough. What he failed to bring me was shoes. That's probably to remind me to stay in, I'll bet.

In my boredom I turned to Netflix, Disney, Hulu, Apple TV, Prime... I have a feeling I've seen everything already.

Finally, I found a pen and paper in one of the drawers and started to communicate with him via letters.

I'll sit and write him a message on how I loved or hated the food, how I love the strawberries, but what's the point if there's no cream? And why did he say what he said in the basement? Trying to sound normal. My intention is to become relatable, because when I'm in his presence, when he looks at me in his particular way, I'm overpowered. Another thing I hate myself for.

What's really odd is that he hasn't asked anything of me yet. People don't stop with their requests once they know what I know, and that worries me. Maybe they're planning how to kill me this very moment. In any case, I can't run anymore. In here, I'm free. There's nothing to do but eat and watch TV. And be normal, I guess.

Today is the same as any day. It's past midnight, and I'm watching something on Disney Plus when I hear a knock on my door.

I put the TV on mute and listen.

"Come to the kitchen, I'll cook you something to eat."

I never knew Orion's voice could sound so inviting.

"One moment!" I look down at myself. I haven't showered since yesterday and I've been in bed all day. I may have even gained weight.

I jump up and put on jeans and a t-shirt before leaving the room, practically running to the kitchen. Why, I don't know. Well, I do.

"Hello, Maisy." Orion greets me with a steady gaze. He's dressed impeccably in a suit, minus the jacket. There's a speck of joy in his expression, I'm sure of it.

I lean on the table, a few steps away from him. "I thought you'd forgotten about me."

"How could I? You've been eating all my food, and complaining about it." His impassive expression makes him impossible to read.

"Not always."

"Not always, true." His deft fingers begin to loosen his tie. The rings draw my focus, together with the tattoos on his forearms peeking from under his rolled shirtsleeves. I remember the tattoos on his body and wonder how they would feel beneath my fingertips, tracing them from end to end.

He must've finished work now; his outfit is for anywhere but the kitchen.

"So, what's the occasion? Did you get laid?" Asking it doesn't feel right, but was that where he was all this time?

He cocks his head to one side, regarding me intently. "Would you have wanted me to get laid just to let you out of your room?"

I blush. "If that's what it takes. Whatever."

He comes to me. My neck cranes as he pinches my chin, urging me to look up at him. "I don't trust you. There's still something you're not telling us." His eyes drop to my lips and he sucks in a breath.

"I told you everything," I mutter, and pull my face from his grip.

"Yes, you did say that." He sighs. "Look, I'm sorry. I've had a long day. And you... you're just, you. Let's start again. What did you do this week?"

I don't need dull conversation. "Watched TV. I just finished watching *The Mandalorian*."

"Huh. You like a man in a helmet," he remarks.

"Keep me alone for longer and I'll like–" I stop myself. I shouldn't say such things.

"What?"

"Nothing. Never mind. Sorry. It was gonna be rude."

"You don't think I can take rude? I invented rude."

"It's not that. It wouldn't be conducive to, um, our relationship. Forget about it."

"Our relationship?" He raises his eyebrows. "I didn't know we had one."

I ignore his comment and nod toward the kitchen counter. "Are you going to cook, or what?"

He chuckles at my awkwardness. "I was hoping *you* would."

"Me?" Can I cook? Barely. Only so I don't die from hunger.

"Make something, anything. I'm starving."

"How about pasta?" I ask.

"At this time of night?" He's surprised, maybe even shocked. I'm just used to eating whatever there is. I never choose the food, the food chooses me.

"Why not?" I smirk.

"Great. I love a good pasta. I have a ready-made sauce in the cabinet." He crouches, opens a cabinet door, and pulls out a tomato and mascarpone pesto. "Would this do?"

"Yes, I love pesto. Any kind."

"Good. Now, where's the pasta?"

He starts searching every cabinet, and I remember seeing a packet at the back of the shelf where the coffee cups were. I open the cupboard and spot it. I push myself onto my tiptoes and try to reach it, but no luck. I reach again and as I turn my head to tell him I've found it, he's behind me, reaching for it himself.

My breath hitches when our eyes meet, and he grinds into my behind. Or so I think. The muscles deep in my belly clench. My mind plays tricks on me as his eyes, dark like the night and determined, stir something inside me.

Orion isn't moving. He pins me there, our bodies almost glued together, when he takes a lock of my hair and tucks it behind my shoulder. His touch is all I'm aware of. He does something to me; on purpose or not, I don't know. It's the power he has.

I look away, anywhere but his eyes. "Please, take a seat, I got this." My face is burning.

He smirks. "Sure."

I place the pasta in a pot with water and put it on the stovetop in the middle of the island. It's one helluva high-tech stove. Figuring out how to turn it on would require a master's degree.

Just as I'm thinking that, his masculine scent overpowers me yet again. I sense him behind me, not pressing against my body but standing a few centimeters away. Close enough for his gravity to work. He lowers his head over my left shoulder, past my face, to look at the stove. I turn to him and my lips graze his cheek.

"This, here–you press for two seconds, and the stove comes on. Once you're there, it's easy. And over here..."

He points at something with his finger, but I'm still looking at him. *Why is he doing this to me?*

He turns to me without skipping a beat, as if he enjoys torturing me. "Hey," he mumbles, his breath warming my lips. We're so close he could practically kiss me. He lifts my chin and angles my face toward the hob. "Over here's where you choose which ring you want to turn on."

I breathe silently. "Okay."

"Maisy, are you turned on?" he whispers in my ear.

"Wh-what?"

"Is the stove turned on?" he asks.

I'm hearing things, and that's not good. "Oh. N-no."

I lean forward to turn the stove on, and I'm sure I can feel the steel ridge of his erection at my butt. I swallow hard as I bravely step back into it, and I'm right. He moves back, but not before I feel his cock bulging through his pants. I look back at him and his eyes are closed; he's breathing through his nostrils.

"Darling." As if he knows I'm watching him, his eyes open and look directly at me, now hooded, fire blazing within. "Stay away from me."

"I'm not... I..." I stutter and turn away, my back to him. *I didn't do anything!*

He bends down to my left ear and with his right hand, out of my line of sight, reaches around my body and pinches my nipple hard, rolling it between his thumb and index finger.

"This... is what you get for making me hard."

I moan from the pleasure of his touch, the pain too, and arch my back into him. Our bodies merge but the moment doesn't last long. He releases my nipple and, without a word, leaves the kitchen.

I still feel his presence like an after-effect, marking my body as unused, and yet... ready.

He's gone, and I'm left alone in the kitchen to cook the pasta. He messed with my head yet again, but I'm not petty. I make the food anyway. I even add parmesan and I'm not hungry at all now.

I serve it onto two plates and, stupidly, I wait. Twenty minutes later, I realize he's not coming back. The lump in my throat is getting bigger. I leave everything as it is and run to my room. What was the point of him calling me downstairs, just to make me feel like shit?

Tears prick my eyes at his rejection. *I'm not that ugly, am I?* I bring my hand up and smell my breath–it's not bad. I close the door and I let go. I haven't cried in a long time.

KAI

I try to erase Maisy from my head but her presence is torturing me every day, as if she's imprinted on me. In my mind, she's mostly in the shower with me, her eyes begging me to protect her, to kiss her, to fuck her, which makes it so fucking hot that when I do, I explode like a volcano.

I've seen her more than a few times since she showed up last week. We hung out at Orion's and each time I'm left wanting more with her. She makes me feel like a teenager.

I'm not sure she's serious about being a schoolteacher, though. I'm afraid she may be a little naïve, but I don't know. Who am I to say anything about teaching kids?

In any case, I'm seeing her tonight. I didn't plan to see her for another few days, and I was surprised when Orion texted me saying she needs company. Of course, I wasn't going to argue. I think he gets to spend the most time with her anyway.

I texted him to make sure the way was clear as I was riding in. The Cartes are set up in such a way that gives Orion, the head of the Cartes, the space and freedom to move about. In my eyes he's a legend, years ahead of mine and Logan's families. But ultimately, all he aims to do is live a normal life. Or at least, he lies to himself that he does.

I ease off the gas pedal on my bike as I enter the Cartes' CCTV blanket. This is Orion's baby; he has the controls but on the off-chance that someone else sees me, there'll be a commotion and as we agreed a while back, I'm to shoot.

The way is clear. I turn off the engine and park my bike behind the high shrubs next to Orion's house, where I always do.

His house is grand. With CCTV in place it looks like a fortress, but it does have a few weak spots. For example, if I climb the nearest tree to my bike, which is coincidentally outside Maisy's room, I'll get to her quicker than if I go through the main entrance. I chuckle to myself. Entering through the window reminds me of old times, except back then I'd break and enter for work, meaning whatever nasty deed my father wanted me to do.

I climb the tree quickly and jump onto the window ledge. The latch isn't even secure, that's how cocky Orion is. I pull it and the window opens easy. Orion must've seen me by now. I wonder if he'll come up. He never talks about Maisy so seeing as he asked me to come, I think something must have happened.

Her room's dark, just a sliver of a streetlight beam hitting the corner, but once my eyes adjust it's clear where everything is. She's in her bed, sleeping peacefully. Tissues are spread out around her. Either she has a cold or she's been crying. It's the latter, I'll bet. Orion has his ways with girls, but they love him for that. That's normal in our world. Maybe she needs time to warm up to him.

Wearing a cami top and panties, she's lying on her back, her left knee open and bent, her face pointing to the right.

This is the first time I'm entering Maisy's room through the window. I don't want to scare her when she's lying there fully exposed.

I make enough noise taking off my leather jacket and boots that she stirs, and I leave my gun over my jacket, still within reach.

"Hello gorgeous," I whisper as I lie down next to her, subtly tilting the mattress and her toward me.

She wiggles about and turns to me, burrowing into the crook of my arm. "Mmm... Kai?" She raises her head and sleepily opens her eyes. "I didn't hear you come in."

I stroke her hair. "I came through the window, baby girl. How did you know it was me?"

"Leather, fuel, and... that sexy aftershave," she purrs.

Nestled in my arm, her palm flat over my chest, she hooks her leg over mine as she lies there, eyes closed. I hear a sigh. "Thank you for being here. I feel safe with you around. And seen."

She dozes off as I continue stroking her hair. I've had a hard day–although my enemies should be singing Maisy's praises, since my torture methods were much bloodier before I met her. She has a strange effect on me. She calms me.

My hand moves down to stroke her back, then I run my fingers softly back up to her shoulder. A soft hum escapes her lips and she adjusts the hook she has on my leg. Her cheek presses more firmly against my chest, and her hand moves down to my abdomen. *Fuck*. My cock twitches and I think I stop breathing. I've been hanging out with her, true, and wanting her desperately, but never like this, in her bed.

I tuck her hair out of the way, gradually moving it strand by strand and exposing her throat, and brush my fingers softly over her shoulder and neck. She sighs softly and moves her hand over my jeans, to my swollen cock.

I stop moving. *Is she doing this on purpose?* The last of my blood rushes to my cock and I forget how to operate two body parts at the same time. She reminds me, though. She jerks her shoulder slightly, gives me a short, sweet moan and another shift of her leg, hooked over mine, and now I wonder if she's rubbing herself on my thigh. *Fuck!* I resume brushing my fingers over her shoulder, and now I'm upping the game, I must figure out if this is what she wants. I play with her cami top, pulling the strap aside and down her arm.

And that's it for the next half hour. She's dozed off. But my dirty fucking mind keeps me wide awake as her hand is still on my cock that's now so hard it hurts.

I'm imagining and focusing on all the things I want to do to her when I hear the door opening. I reach for my gun and wait.

It's Logan. I'd recognize that frame anywhere. He walks in and quietly closes the door.

"Logan, dammit! Make yourself known when you come in, I nearly shot you!" I hiss at him, careful not to wake Maisy.

"Is she asleep?"

"Yeah. She's been crying."

He rolls his eyes. "Orion."

I shrug. "She'll warm up to him soon."

Logan takes off his shoes, the gun holster from his ankle, and the three blades from his pocket, then lies down on Maisy's other side. The moment he does, the bed dips and she takes her palm off my cock, reaching out to feel who's behind her.

"It's me, sweetheart," Logan says quickly. I guess he doesn't want to frighten her either.

We haven't been with her in this situation yet where, knowing Logan's thinking, and mine of course, we're hoping things will happen. Things *better* happen, because my cock may explode otherwise.

"Come closer, please," she breathes. "I want to feel safe."

Logan scoots in closer and spoons her, wrapping his arm around her waist. "You're always safe with us, remember that."

I withdraw my arm from under Maisy and she repositions herself as she's spooned. The leg that was over me moves and hooks on top of Logan's behind her. She's open to him, and all I can see is how she could be fucked if only her panties weren't there.

She lays her head on the pillow between us. Her hand that was under her is now on my stomach, fingers spread open, claiming me too as she lies on her back. She's keeping us connected and I can only pray it's for one thing. I'm on her left side, Logan on her right, and she's snug between us, her legs slightly open, and there's no way I'm going to be able to sleep. My cock is talking to me for the first time in twelve months.

We lie like that in silence, and every now and again she hums sweetly, wiggling her butt and her shoulders between us, burrowing further into Logan's groin. It's agonizing. My cock is so hard I'm in pain. I try to shift it and notice it's out, peeking above the waistline of my jeans.

Maisy turns to Logan, whose head is propped on his forearm as he gazes down at her and strokes her face. As he does, he pulls aside her hair.

"Has my Maisy been a good girl today?" His voice is hoarse and slow, deliberate. Her eyes are closed, but her lips crook upward. *She likes that.* "Yes? Would you let the doctor check you over, Maisy? Just to make sure?" His hand goes down to her leg that's draped over him, and he squeezes her inner thigh as he talks.

Maisy's hand at my stomach moves down and over my cock, cupping it gently. I put my hand over hers, squeeze it, then take it away and thread our fingers together. I'm going to fucking come if I let her touch my cock again.

I see Logan's hand gradually moving up, and when he reaches her panties he doesn't stop. He rubs her there, gently, up and down the dip that's formed. She grips my hand and turns to me with lust in her eyes, and total surrender. She is gorgeous.

"You okay?" I ask.

She nods. I lean in and press my lips to hers. I'm starved for her, for her scent; I want to make her mine in every sense of the word.

She responds as I devour her mouth, weaving my tongue with hers. It feels like we feed off each other's need.

I swallow her moans fully before I move my lips down her neck and bury my face into it. When I've had my fill of her scent for now, I start to gently bite and suck her collarbone. I finally lower myself to her nipple–I've been focusing on the hard pebble poking under the cami top and calling my name for some time.

I pull the silky top beneath her breast and bite into the flesh until she moans out loud, and until I feel I've left a mark. I release her and bite on the nipple between my teeth and gently squeeze it, and suck it, never letting go. She moans and slides her hand under her top, touching her other nipple, pinching it herself.

I take her hand and pin it above her head. "Nuh-uh."

All of us have a demon inside, but right now hers is free, unrestrained, and needs us.

I watch Logan hooking his fingers under the band of her panties and sliding them into her arousal.

He then raises his hand, like a trophy. "Soaking wet, Maisy..."

With her nipple still in my mouth, I look at Logan's hand. My cock has a double ration of blood coming to him. *Can't wait for my turn.*

Logan makes a deeper entry into her panties and pulls them harder until I hear a small rip, and see that he's made enough space to brush his middle and index finger over her entrance.

I let go of her nipple and press my lips to hers, devouring her mouth again and swallowing her moans as Logan progressively finger-fucks her.

"This is good, very good, Maisy," he mutters.

I fully pull down her cami top to reveal her red nipples, sore and hard. I lower my head and continue to suck the bud into my mouth, gently tugging it between my teeth.

"Kai!" Maisy gasps.

I take the other one and do the same. Her sweet whimpers of pleasure are all I want to hear for the rest of my life.

But I know Logan, and he's losing patience. If there's an obstacle in the way of him receiving pleasure, he'll throw a tantrum.

He sits up between Maisy's legs. "Maisy, close your legs, sweetheart. Let the doctor take your panties off. You must be taken care of."

Maisy closes her legs and lifts her ass to allow him to slide her panties off. Once he's done, he unbuttons his shirt and throws it to the floor. Free from obstructions, he takes one of her legs and starts kissing her ankle before making his way up.

I'm sucking and nibbling at her skin but my eyes fall to her perfect mound that I want to conquer. As Logan moves along her leg, my hand goes down to her entrance and I play with her silky folds.

I slide my index and middle fingers in; they enter her hot cunt snugly and coat in her juice. She moans as I take them out and swirl the arousal over her nub. On the second go I jerk my fingers deeper, to the knuckle, and do this a few times before she bucks and raises her hips into my fingers. I collect her arousal on my way out and rub it over her swollen clit as I suck on her nipples. She grabs hold of my forearm with both hands and looks at me with a crazed lust while I continue to make circles around the nub.

I chuckle. "You like this, baby girl?"

Logan's kisses have reached her inner thighs and he's holding her legs open by pressing them firmly against the bed.

She moans as I keep sliding my fingers inside her and rubbing her nub, and I repeat the motion, over and over, until she throws her head back. "*Kai!*" she cries.

"You're so pretty when you're moaning my name, Maisy."

Rush of cum dribbles out of her divine pussy, her hips jerk up into my hand as she rides the waves of pleasure with her orgasm exploding under me. She feels so fucking good.

I bring my soaked fingers to my lips and lick them. "What a fucking taste. Logan, you're in for a treat, man. She's like a portal to a different dimension."

Logan leans in and blows on her, up close. Meanwhile, I'm unbuttoning my jeans. My cock needs air. The moment it's out, I fist my hand around it and pump a few times, the precum glistening under the streetlight. Immediately, Maisy's warm, soft fingers wrap around me and she takes over. She fists my cock, twisting at the base in a heavenly stroke and, I groan.

"Is that right, Maisy?" Logan blows on her folds and inhales as he looks at her from between her thighs. "Is Kai telling the truth?"

Maisy's looking at him through hooded eyes, unabashed.

"What do you say? Should the doctor take a look?"

She nods.

LOGAN

I press the flat of my tongue against her pussy, soaked with arousal, and lick up to her sweet nub.

Sweet Jesus mama! This girl has been sent to us by God himself. I've wanted her every moment of every day for the past week and had to sate myself with constant lap dances and endless jerking.

Even Bobby, my number one, noticed I was permanently hard. "Fuck five whores and you'll get it sorted," he said. But if I'm saving myself for someone, not even fifty whores will do the trick.

I made sure I'm clean so I can ride her bareback. I did all the tests I usually do, except this time I did them much earlier.

Was it presumptuous of me to think I'd ride her? Fuck knows, but if the opportunity knocks, which it clearly is, I will. This pussy is going to experience the doctor in his full glory.

I would've thought Orion would've done something with her already. We've shared women before out of necessity, just so we know they aren't fucking anyone else. Between the three of us and seven days of the week, they couldn't walk. They'd think they were fooling us by jumping from the bed of one mobster family to another, but we were in on it for a reason. In our world there's too much sex, and none of us want to get AIDS or gonorrhea. And of course, all of us hate condoms.

But this is different altogether. I'm here for Maisy because she truly needs us. She's different in so many ways. Maybe that's why Orion's wary. Seven days in her company and the blue-ball-itus would drive me mad for sure.

Kai nibbles and sucks on her neck as I push my tongue at her entrance, lapping up everything she has. I hold her thighs firmly open, keeping her in place; she bucks downward against my tongue, jolting and moaning as I continue to devour her swollen nub.

"Doctor!" she breathes.

Did she just call me 'Doctor?' I pull back to cool off, compose myself. *She's gonna make me cum in my pants.* "Yes, Maisy?"

"There, just there." She raises her hips again and I wrap my forearms around the backs of her thighs to keep her in place.

Kai pinches her chin and pulls her to him, kissing her hungrily.

I lap up her juices and devour her pussy, which clearly now belongs to me. My tongue swirls over her nub, sucking on that little fucker until she screams in Kai's mouth.

Kai plays with her nipples, then slaps them, making her tits bounce and jiggle. As he does, I push two fingers inside. Her thighs begin to tremble and she treats us to a whimper that becomes one long moan. She coats the bed and my hand with her juice.

"Logan!" she shrieks.

MAISY

God!

I'm thrusted up into the clouds while a tornado wreaks havoc inside me, merging my body and mind. Is this real? Am I in bed with two of the most feared mafia heads, who are ready to protect me no matter what and give me heaven on earth?

Kai has been respectful with me from the start, despite my kissing him on the first day. And he responded, too. That in itself was too much of a pull for me to forget. And Logan... His eyes scream *Fuck me* every time he talks to me, especially when he licks his lips and smirks at me. I recognize the thoughts in his head. At night, when I lie in my bed, the same thoughts have crossed my mind. This natural flow of having two men touching and kissing me is new on so many levels, and comes with passionate, crazy, extraordinary orgasms. I love when I'm loved. But doesn't everyone? And when I'm loved, I'm giving. Right now, I'm loved, and I'm *safe*. That's the key word.

But I wonder why Orion doesn't want me. He was clearly aroused earlier, yet he ran away like a chicken. What was I going to do, eat his cock?

The thought has crossed my mind.

"Are you okay?" Kai asks, grinning.

"Mm-hmm," I murmur.

"Good, because we're not done with you. Go on, up on all fours, facing the wall," Logan orders.

Kai helps me peel off my cami top and positions me with my ass in the air and my hands on the headboard. He kisses my shoulder. "Hold here."

He looks at my body, my boobs swaying below me, then grabs a handful and massages it before slapping my ass. "You're gorgeous, Maisy Roy."

He's on his knees next to me, his big, girthy cock springing up, while Logan takes off his pants. I'm not sure I've had anyone that big. Without thinking, I turn to him and fully lower my mouth onto his cock, managing not to gag.

"Oh, fuck... *Fuck!*" Kai exclaims.

I bob my head a few times until he tangles his fingers in my hair and pulls me away. Lowering his lips to mine, he begins to devour my needy mouth. "Not yet, baby girl," he mumbles at my lips. "Not yet."

With my ass up in the air, Logan spreads my knees wider on the bed. I'm certain I'm fully exposed now.

"Let's see." He slides three fingers into my cunt. Then he takes my arousal and smears it over my ass and *Oh dear God*, my body is vibrating in a whole new way.

He does the same again, and as he swirls his finger over my entrance the urge to buck against it is too strong; and then he pushes a finger into my ass. I whimper at the intensity. I hear Kai groaning as he pumps his cock and moves behind me on the bed, next to Logan.

I look back and see Logan's fisting his cock. "The doctor will be riding you bareback, Maisy. Is that okay?" he asks.

And suddenly, everything stops, and there's no touching anymore. They don't move, but I want to continue. An answer is expected, and I turn to Kai in panic. I know *I'm* clean, since those fuckers prepped me for whoring, but them?

"Kai?" I'm waiting for some sort of confirmation.

"He's fully checked, baby girl, I promise," Kai assures me. "I am too. But we have condoms if you prefer."

"Whatever the doctor wants." I breathe, and instantly I feel Logan brushing his cock against my arousal, going up and down my folds, and I begin to buck backward into him.

"You'll have to hold still for me, Maisy. Is that okay, sweetheart?" Logan asks.

I bite down on my lip. "Yes."

He rubs my nub. "Once you get adjusted to my size, it'll be heaven."

"I know," I whisper.

"Easy now." He thrusts slowly, attempting to enter me, but it's slow going. Slow, and fucking *heavenly*. On the third try, his cock gains traction and begins to stretch me out. It's fucking too much pleasure as my cunt adjusts to his girth, accommodating him and adapting to heaven as he thrusts into me.

"Sweet Jesus mama!"

He's fully in, following the trail to paradise and back as he starts to pound into me with slow, measured strokes. I sense every vein on that cock as I'm stretched out, but it doesn't last long.

"Fucking *heaven!*" Logan cries.

He pulls out, and I groan in frustration. *Why?*

I look back and see Logan pumping his glistening cock. Kai's moving in, and his cock is just as big, if not bigger, but the path has been made for him already. He rapidly brushes his cock against my arousal, going up and down my folds, and enters me. I whimper. It burns. He stretches me some more.

"Maisy, baby girl, open up for me. You're squeezing me too tight."

I raise my ass higher, opening my legs as wide as possible, and feel my arousal gushing.

"Oh, yes... *Yes!*" Kai growls as he enters me to the hilt. "This is what heaven feels like!"

He digs his fingers into my flesh, holding my hips with both hands, and starts pounding me. He's big, and now that I'm accustomed to him, I never want to let him go. After a few thrusts, he tries to slow down, but I don't let him. I buck backward, milking his cock as if it's the last one on earth. He gets the message, and picks up that driving force again.

Logan cups my breast and squeezes my nipple between his fingers, then repeats the action on the other. My volume's increasing at the pounding Kai's giving me but when Logan reaches under me and rubs my swollen clit I go wild, straight into bucking bronco territory.

Kai slows down. "Oh, fuck! Easy now."

Logan brushes his lips over mine as he rubs my nub. "Maisy, do you want to tell the doctor if you've been with two guys before?" he mutters, moving to tug my nipples again and rendering me unable to think straight.

I was floating on cloud nine, but his question has abruptly brought me back down. I look at Logan, then back at Kai, and hope they won't see the panic in my eyes. *No, I haven't been with two guys before.*

Kai seems to sense my hesitation. "Don't worry, we won't do anything you don't want to do." He slows down, easing me off and lulling me back into that need, that craving for him.

"Aren't I with two guys now?" I ask.

"You are," Kai says, beaming, "and you like this, don't you?"

"Yes," I moan.

"I can't hear you," he pants.

"*Yeeessss!*" I cry as he reaches under me and rubs my swollen clit. This will be the death of me. The sweet, orgasmic, hedonistic death of me. And it will be worth it many times over.

Kai pulls out and moves aside, making space for Logan again. That moment of emptiness, of an empty hole that needs to be filled, is a moment in time that may drive me insane. I cry out in frustration.

As if he's reading my mind, Logan enters me. He reaches down and swirls my juices over my clit, while the fingers of his other hand dig into the flesh of my hip.

I whimper, and moan again. "Logan!"

And just like that, Logan is out and Kai is in, pounding into me again. Well, it could be either one of them at this stage–I'm not even looking back at them and they swap of their own accord. At the moments in between when I'm empty the craving only grows, that desire and hunger for their cocks to fill me.

"Yes, baby girl, that's right, take me all in." The familiar fingers dig into my hips and the pounding to the hilt continues. But this time, my arousal is taken from under me and smeared over my ass. Kai pushes one finger, then two into my ass, preparing me, and I can't stop the vibrations from thrumming through my body. This, I don't think I'll withstand.

Just as I'm about to cum, I'm taken aback by them stopping, feeling like I'm being teased into oblivion.

"Kai, I think she's ready."

They both get off the bed, and I hang my head and become aware of the nerve synapses roaring through my skull in brand new ways.

When I manage to open my eyes, I see they've taken the rest of their clothes off. Kai lies on the bed and lifts me over him. I straddle him immediately and guide his cock to my entrance. The emptiness is killing me and I'm chasing my rainbow, the one that they deprived me of. He sucks one of my nipples into his mouth as I sit up and start riding him but he holds my hips firmly down, not allowing me to weave my magic, to squeeze his cock and to pull it deeper inside me.

"Oh baby girl, no, no, this is not what we had in mind... Fuck, you'll make me cum."

He pinches my nipples with both hands and pulls me down to lie over him. I moan and follow him, lost in the pleasure of his cock and his touch. While he peppers kisses on my neck, I sense Logan's legs moving at the side of the bed. He repositions himself behind me and I feel him rimming my ass and pushing a finger inside. Kai lifts me off himself, and as soon as his cock is out, Logan's fingers are inside, taking my arousal.

"You're so fucking wet, we don't need lube at all," he says, smearing my arousal over my ass. As he does, Kai slams into me again, and I sense more fingers in my ass.

I stop. I haven't been like this with anyone before and though my body's willing, my mind is afraid.

Kai must've sensed my alarm. "Shh, just be still. This"–he holds my hips and moves his cock in and out–"is what I want you to focus on, okay?"

I nod.

"The doctor knows what he's doing."

Logan edges his cock a few inches into my ass and *fuck*, it's good. I buck into it. My mind is hazy from so many sensations at once, but I know I'm close.

"Baby girl, the best is yet to come." Kai holds me as Logan nudges deeper inside. "Pace yourself."

Logan groans. "Your ass is so tight. I'm gonna have to do something about that, Maisy."

His words make me gush arousal over Kai, and his cock in my ass does something else.

"I'm going to move, just a little bit deeper... and deeper... and deeper..." He's taken on a rhythm that's now working alongside Kai's, making my whole body vibrate to a different level of orgasmic pleasure.

"Yes, yes... You're a fucking *star*, Maisy!" Logan rasps.

He kisses my back as he holds me and Kai has his lips pressed to my breasts, sucking them one after the other.

"You're so beautiful, baby girl," Kai pants.

The three of us bounce in a magic rhythm as Kai and Logan use my body in the filthiest ways possible.

I finally lose myself when both of them begin to growl like animals. When I do it's long and hard, yet fast at the same time.

Logan is fucking me into oblivion. "I want you to look at me when you come," he orders.

I turn my head back to him and I'm there; I've been there for a while. I buck, and whimper, and let out loud, staccato moans as Logan grabs my chin and urges me to kiss him. He bites my lip as he pounds me faster and faster.

"Fuck, fuck, *fuck!*" he shouts, emptying his seed inside me, each spurt pulsating in my ass.

"*Fuuuuckkkk!*" Kai follows, emptying his balls inside me. I can feel every inch of his cock as I squeeze every last drop from him.

The vibrations inside me travel to every nerve ending in my body. Lightheaded, I collapse onto Kai's chest, panting for breath.

Logan exhales shakily. "You are *perfect*, Maisy."

Sitting in a big mess of sweat and cum, I have never felt better in my life–or more loved, respected, and protected.

Logan slides out of me and lies down beside Kai, rubbing my back. I rest my head on Kai's chest, facing Logan, while Kai strokes my head.

My heart is still reminding me of what just transpired between us and I feel content. Two men protecting me, fucking me, looking after me. *This is the way.*

Logan is tracing my face with the pads of his fingers.

"Is the doctor happy with me?" I purr.

Both of them laugh quietly.

"Very happy," Logan rasps. "Come on, let's shower and go for seconds." He slaps my ass and gets up, heading for the bathroom.

I lift my head and look at Kai. "Is he serious?"

"About having seconds?"

I nod.

"What did you think? That was it? Oh, baby girl, you're in for a treat," he laughs.

"But I don't want to shower," I murmur. "I love having your cum in me. I love being all sweaty and stuck to you."

"You're already giving me a hard-on. You can have my cum whenever you want it, Maisy."

I giggle and unglue myself from his body. He shudders when he slides out of me. I hear Logan turning the shower on, and I head toward the bathroom. Kai's on his feet too, following me.

"Don't hog the shower, Logan, there's a line!" Kai yells.

"Who's next in line? If it's Maisy, send her in, I got a present for her," Logan calls.

"I'm next in line and thank you, but I got the same present in my hand for her." Kai holds his cock and balls and snickers. "Hurry up!"

The steam's starting to pour into the bedroom through the open door.

"Keep your voice down, Kai," I warn him. "Orion could hear you."

He nods toward the door. "Hear me? I bet that perv was jerking while we were playing."

"What?!"

"Yeah, baby girl. You don't think someone like him would have everything under control? Over there." He points to the corner of the ceiling above the door, where I spot a small dot that looks like a squashed bug.

I start to panic. "Has he... Has he been–?"

"What?"

"If Orion's been videoing me all this time..."

"No, no, it's not like that–"

"Really? Orion's a jerk! He doesn't like me. What's stopping him from selling me out to Milan? Or anyone else?" I demand.

Logan comes out of the bathroom, his towel wrapped around his hips. The V just above his pubic area is clearly visible and his glistening abs and pecs pull me in, even in my distraught state.

"Maisy, you're fully protected in this house," Logan says calmly. "If he didn't want you here, you wouldn't be. His right-hand man, Jonah, wanted to use this room a few days ago and Orion was clear with him about staying away. He doesn't do that for just anyone."

The certainty he speaks with is comforting, but ultimately my life's goal is to right one wrong, not make another one. *This is how it started with my sister. It's all too familiar.*

"Please tell me you're not in on this." I search for reassurance in Kai's face, but all I see is his nostrils flaring as he sucks in a breath.

"I never want to hear you ask us anything remotely like that again," he says in low grumble, then turns and walks into the bathroom.

Logan takes my hand and sits on the edge of the bed, lowering me onto his lap. "Maisy, you don't understand how we operate. On the face of it, Kai, Orion, and I are mortal enemies in this world. Everyone sees us that way. But the truth is that we're brothers in blood. We've killed together, we've tampered with evidence, we've threatened and killed snitches and brutally tortured many souls. And when I say many, trust me, that's a lot. We trust each other with our lives. That's what integrity is. It means when we speak among ourselves, we speak the truth. You're the only person ever to see the three of us together and live to see the next day. Why haven't we killed you? Fuck knows. We enjoy your company. Right now, please forget about Orion. He'll warm up to you. He's saved our asses God knows how many times and even if he films us *killing* someone, it means shit. That will never come back to bite us. If he records us fucking, again, it means nothing." He presses his lips to mine. "Okay, sweetheart?"

I nod. Logan has a way of convincing me to trust him.

"Now, how do you want to tell the doctor you're sorry?" He undoes his towel to free his cock and smirks as he fists his hard-on.

I decide to play along and kneel between his legs. "I can't, Doctor. My tongue hurts."

"Oh, Maisy. Open wide and take your tongue out. Let me see it."

I open my mouth and show him as much of my flattened tongue as I can. He lifts his cock and drives my head down, my tongue landing on his balls.

"Suck for a while, let me see how it works."

I lick and suck his balls until his cock grows to its full length.

"Good, good. That's a good girl. Now open wide again."

With my mouth open wide and my tongue out, he slaps his cock against my face, over my forehead, my cheek, while watching me with hooded eyes. "Yes, *yesss*," he rasps, and my pussy clenches in anticipation.

When he cannot possibly get any harder, he slides his cock into my throat. Deep. Lucky for him I don't gag. I take him in fully.

Upon realizing what I can do, he throws his head back. "Oh, sweetheart! You... you.... *Yes!*"

I swirl my tongue around his head and bob, sucking him. His fingers tangle in my hair, and that's when he takes over, fucking my mouth, faster, his rock-hard cock swelling even more. He rams me a few more times before stilling inside of me, groaning as he empties his seed deep into my throat. I swallow every drop.

"Sweet Jesus mama!" He collapses back onto the bed, panting. "How is this possible?"

I push myself up onto my feet and wink at him. "Let me apologize to Kai, too."

I enter the bathroom and see Kai under the shower, leaning with his forearm on the wall. With the other hand, he's slowly fisting his cock.

I step under the water next to him and lift my head toward the flow, allowing my face and hair to be drenched. A ridge of tattooed abs and pecs fill my vision until he lowers his head and slams his lips against mine. He drinks me up with his might.

What I have with Kai is something special. He feels me, he protects me, and I sense it in every kiss. His need for me.

I peel myself away from him and kneel, the water falling directly onto my face. His cock is sprung up, waiting for me. I open my mouth and take it in, gazing up at him. Our eyes lock as his cock enters my mouth, deep, and the moment his glans touches the back of my throat I close my eyes.

"Eyes on me," he hisses, making me open them again.

I bob my head on him, throat-deep each time. He's staring at me with that wild look in his eyes and grunting with each thrust. The sounds coming from him are heaven sent. I'm there, wanting only to please him, and when his hands grip my hair, he takes the lead, quickening the pace. His grunts change into a growl, getting louder and longer until I feel the hot cum shooting down the back of my throat. I swallow it, gulping down every last bit of him.

He's such a sight to behold, still holding my hair with his hands, his knees slightly bent, his back hunched. I swirl my tongue one last time over his cock, making him shudder, and push myself up to my feet.

Immediately he searches for my lips and kisses me, devouring me as he cups my cunt in his hands, rubbing my swollen clit. I need release badly. He swirls his thumb over my nub and slides two fingers inside my folds, finger-fucking me rapidly while rubbing my clit at the same time, so deftly that my legs start to give out. I have fully surrendered to his mercy.

"You're so beautiful, Maisy." His fingers slow down, but I crave my orgasm badly, and buck against his hand.

"What, this?" He rubs harder, then stops again.

"Yes," I whine. I'm lost. He starts again and jerks his fingers deeper, and rapidly massages my clit until I find my release, gushing like a waterfall. My legs tremble, but he manages to hold me up.

"Kai..." I kiss him deep, greedy for him as I wrap my arms around his strong body.

I'm in Kai's arms, unable to stand on my own, when Logan's somber voice interrupts my daze. It looks like he's already dressed. "Kai, we got to move. Shit's happening."

Kai turns the shower off and helps me out, seeing that I'm still high from the oxytocin. "Are you good?" he asks before letting me regain my balance.

I nod, and pick up a towel to dry off.

Logan passes his cell to Kai. I glance down at the message he reads.

Milan the Dog's looking for guns to buy. His wife was found dead outside LaToya's, with her bodyguards cock in her mouth.

"Camila's dead?" I blurt out.

Both of them turn to me, but neither says anything.

"If she's dead, how am I going to find those video recordings?" The realization suddenly comes to me. "Oh my God! You killed her! She came to you that night when I saw her, and you killed her!"

Kai shrugs. "Hence, the reason why Orion wanted you dead."

"And you?"

"I told you, Maisy, nobody's seen us together and lived. I don't care that she's dead, she was a bad person. I just hate that you know of it," Logan says.

"It may also make you greedy," Kai interjects. "You could take that information to Milan in exchange for your videos."

"How could you say that, Kai? If I show my face anywhere, I'm dead." I pause, and make a decision. "Take me with you. Please, I want to be with you all the time. With either of you."

"We can't. It's not safe." Logan cups my cheek. "But we'll be back soon, I promise you, and we'll have news for you. Okay, sweetheart?"

I place my hand over his and nod. It's *not* okay, but I have no other option. Unless Kai wants to take me to his house.

Logan presses his lips to mine, kissing me deeply. "We haven't finished what we started today," he mumbles against my lips.

Now fully dressed, Kai comes up to me, wraps his arms around my waist and pulls me to him. "Don't worry, baby girl. We got you."

The black t-shirt underneath the leather jacket is stretched over his pecs and abs, which I was lying on only a half hour ago. I miss them already.

They leave me in silence, but I'm sated in a way I have never been in my life.

It's been a wicked night.

CHAPTER 5

MAISY

I pat my body dry, put on another pair of the unglamorous panties and a cami top and jump back into bed to burrow in Kai and Logan's pheromones. Lying here in a bed that smells of us having sex is exactly what I need to doze off peacefully, if that's at all possible.

I only wish Orion would look at me the way they do. He says he'll help me and protect me, but I don't feel it.

The sudden loud rumbling of my tummy makes me realize I'm starving. I'm not sure I'll be able to fall back to sleep at all.

I lie awake for some time when I hear a familiar knock on the door. It's Orion, I know. I sit up. I don't know why he bothers with it. It's as if he's creating the illusion of privacy by knocking, but he's taking it away by filming everything I do.

I decide I'm not going to take any more shit from him.

Orion walks in and looks around. He spots Kai and Logan's towels on the edge of my bed. Ignoring them, he sits in the chair. His chair.

"You're a little too late," I tell him.

He holds my gaze. "Late for what?"

I lift my chin slightly. "I'm not hungry."

"Oh. I see. I don't have food for you, even if you are." He chuckles. "The pasta was great, by the way."

"Why are you laughing at me?" I cross my arms over my chest. "Are you happy with your video recording?"

He looks perplexed. "What are you talking about, Maisy?"

"I know you've been filming me on your security cameras!" *There. I told him.*

"I have, yes."

"Why?"

His tone is stern. "For safety."

"When were you gonna tell me?"

"Never. You don't get a say in that, silly girl."

"And you didn't watch me tonight?" I demand.

"Was there a reason why I should?"

"Um, Kai mentioned you may've been jer... Nothing. Never mind." It's stupid that I feel a pang of disappointment. *So stupid.*

"What have you been doing with Kai and Logan that you want me to see?" He's teasing me now, I know it. He must've watched us, and now he's trying to embarrass me.

"You don't even want to eat with me, so mind your own damn business," I huff. "Please just tell me why you're here. What do you want?"

He clears his throat. Clearly, he's here on business. *Good.*

"We killed Camila. But you figured that out already, so we now have one more reason to kill you. We won't, unless you betray me in any way, in which case I won't hesitate to pull the trigger. You said you read stuff about us, so here I am. What information can you give me?"

"Why would I betray you if you're protecting me?" *Arrogant bastard.* "Anyway, what do you want to know?"

"I don't know what you know. Tell me everything."

"Everything? Pffft! Ask me about names, places, locations. If I've seen it, I'll tell you what I know."

He narrows his eyes like he's evaluating me. "Okay. 57th and Savak Street."

"I presume you want me to tell you information connected to the mafia? Because I know shitloads of information about that street."

"Naturally."

"I saw an article. There was a drive-by shooting last November 5th, at eight in the evening. Three criminal organizations were involved–the Delgados, the Vitalis, and the Slavs, which is Milan's mob. There was an extortion going on at the time and the Delgados and Vitalis did a drive-by and killed ten of Milan's men. Milan returned fire and killed three men from the Delgados and two Vitalis. The mobs acted independently. But the article finished with a question about if the Delgados and the Vitalis had been working together."

"And?" He must know the answer, that's why he's asking me.

"And what?"

"Did they work together?"

"The journalist was killed three days after publishing the article," I retort. "But you knew that already."

"OK. Guns, and Ireland."

"There was an arms deal that went south. The Delgados were running the deal, and it ended when they killed seven of the Irish gang members."

"That's public knowledge," he snaps. "Give me something I don't know."

"There were ten members of the Irish gang there, and three were left alive to spread the news about the Delgados and their bad practice," I continue. "The Delgados' profits dipped after that deal and the Slavs took up dealing arms with the Irish.

"Milan still buys a small number of guns from the Delgados, and their requests act as a decoy. He's the new arms dealer on the streets of New York. He managed to bribe the law enforcement agencies, and the controls at sea and ports have decreased, giving Milan's syndicate an easy ride by leaving ample space for the global circulation of weapons.

"The Delgados are just there to be harassed by the police because officially, they're the ones supplying arms to the city. Which tells me that the Delgados never killed those Irishmen in the first place. It was the Slavs."

Orion takes notes on his cell. When he finishes, he looks up and fixes me with a stare. "Good girl."

His dark eyes are boundless, deep, and somehow inviting. I want to stroll down the forbidden path and let the wolf find me. I don't know if it's me, or if he's doing something. For some strange reason, I find myself blushing.

"You should be proud of yourself, Maisy. You've been a good girl tonight."

"You don't know that," I blurt out. I'm not going to allow him to get to me.

He cocks his head to one side. "I don't?"

My face burns. He waits patiently, watching me as I become increasingly embarrassed. One of his hands is relaxed on the arm rest, while the other cups his chin as he trails his index finger across his lips.

I avoid looking at him as he stands up and sits next to me on the bed. His hand, the one bearing four large silver rings, lands on my thigh, and with the other he pinches my chin, pulls my face to his, and fixes his eyes on me. They're so black, the color of rebirth, connecting me to something raw and intense.

"I promise you, you've been a good girl. I *know*." The last words are whispered ominously, and his hand starts to slide up my thigh but stops way too soon. He pats me on the leg like I'm a little girl. "Get some rest. You've had a long night."

He moves to get up and is halfway to standing when I grab his arm and pull him back down.

We stare at each other. He doesn't move.

"Kiss me," I say boldly. I don't know how else to tell him I want, no, *need* him.

He closes his eyes for a moment and sucks in air. I'm sure he's as affected as I am but dammit, he controls himself much better.

He takes me by the wrist and kisses the back of my hand. "You've been up all night. You must rest."

I hold his hand and tangle my fingers with his.

"Maisy..."

"How did you know I was up?"

Black fire fills his eyes and it's pulling me in, absorbing me into the tornado raging inside him, angry, violent. His nostrils flare. "You just don't give up, do you?" He looks down at his hand as it lands on my thigh again. His fingers dig into my flesh and move up toward my core, leaving a red trail on my skin. I swallow hard. The moment his fingers reach my panties, his large hand is cupping my cunt, and with the other he grabs my neck, pushing me down onto the bed and pinning me to the headboard. His hand around my throat tightens to an almost unbearable level.

For a moment he watches me as I feel my eyes bulge, before he dives for my lips. I'm powerless to do anything except moan when he devours me with his tongue, kissing me violently and sucking on my lower lip. The muscles clench in my lower belly and I find myself becoming hazy, gasping for air as I anxiously cling to his hand at my neck.

"My touch will both console you and devastate you, Maisy," he mumbles against my lips as he chokes me.

I nod, still trying to breathe.

He growls, and roughly shoves his entire hand under the band of my panties. My arousal surges. I melt under the sudden flash burn, and open my legs for whatever's coming.

He cups my folds in his hand and squeezes me in such a way that I try to wiggle out of his grasp, but then he slides two fingers inside me and at the same time bites my lip, holding it there, sucking it between his teeth. I taste a hint of copper in my mouth and moan. His fingers feel so good, but my lips are bleeding and it's... different. I try frantically to kiss him back, but I'm pinned to the headboard by his huge biceps and solid body, looming over me and consuming my reality, and it's impossible. He's playing with me, chuckling as he sucks on my lip, and finger-fucking me into oblivion. I'm becoming hazy as my juices gush.

"You like this?" He smears my arousal over my nub. I nod wildly and buck into his hand. "Enjoy it while it lasts, Maisy, because now that you're in, the mindfuck I got planned for you will split you in half." He groans against my lips. "And if that doesn't, I will."

"Orion..." I'm on the edge of the abyss, about to fall into some sort of liquid void, when I sense my waves crashing on the shore. It's started, and I think I'm dying from lack of oxygen, but somehow, I know I'm flying.

"I think you've had enough for today," he rasps, and releases his grip on me. I desperately suck in air. My panties feel empty as he removes his hand and then licks his fingers right in front of my face.

Deprived halfway to heaven, I'm panting and almost in pain, but he knows this. He's a raging bull under a cloud of rain, cooling off, but his fire's too strong to be quenched. I don't really believe he'll go.

But when he chuckles, it's clear.

"Good girl, Maisy." He gets up and leaves my room.

Oh my dear God. I hate him. I hate him for making me this fucking deprived. I'm not waiting for him to come back.

Without wanting to lose my high, I reach down into my panties and run my middle and index fingers up and down my wet folds. I slide them inside then drag them out, taking my arousal and smearing it all over my nub. My hips start moving as I think of Orion. I lick my lips. I want him to do everything and anything to me. Nasty, terrible things. And I'm there, the waves of pleasure crashing because I was already so close, but it's a different high altogether. I open my knees and thrust my fingers inside while my other hand rubs my clit.

Eager to draw it out, I take my hands away and pull down my cami top, making my breasts pop out. I pinch my nipples, one then the other, and as my whole body responds to my tender but raw touch, I moan. Arching my back, I tug my nipples harder with both hands, needing something hard between my legs and spreading them wider. My hand flies back to my panties, rubbing determinedly, while I continue to pinch my nipples, way beyond my pain threshold now. It hurts, and I squeeze them harder, at the same time thrusting my hips back and forth against my fingers.

My orgasm builds up faster than I can control and, feeling the explosion coming, I whimper. Ripples of pleasure come forth, devastating my body.

The waves start crashing over me when the door opens and Orion walks in with a tray of food. He's looking right at me but I-just-can't-stop-

"*Orion!*" I gasp quietly. Our eyes lock as I cum so powerfully that my hips buck into my fingers and my staccato moans fill the air. I ride the waves to the end, all the way to heaven while his eyes burn into me.

My heart is leaping in my chest as I come down from my high and finally stop rubbing, my eyes still locked on his.

His voice takes on a new, darker tone. "Did I not say you'd had enough for the day?"

He did. But my body *ached*. I had to do something about it. I look at him and, as if he hasn't said anything, slowly bring my fingers to my mouth, tasting myself.

He closes his eyes for a moment and sucks in a breath. He's either annoyed, or horny. I still can't read him. "Clearly you haven't felt the consequences of not playing by my rules. Soon, you will. I promise."

He turns and leaves me with wet heat pooling between my legs, again.

What consequences?

ORION

That damn alarm doesn't stop. It's as if it's waiting for me to enter the bathroom before it turns on. Why the fuck I use it, beats me.

I jump out of the shower to turn the alarm clock off, the still-running water spraying all over the floor. I find the deafening culprit that's ramping up my morning irritation, turn it off, and head back. My cock's painfully hard, a solid rod of morning steel, and as I walk I feel the weight of it slapping left and right. I know what it wants: Maisy.

I last saw her two days ago, touching herself, a big no-no in my world. I don't play easy. Kai and Logan can give her that. With me, it's painful, bare, and raw. Without that I don't feel it, and she certainly doesn't get to feel it either. Still, that didn't stop her dirty, wanton eyes carving her name on my cock.

For the last forty-eight hours I've been under a spell, trying to decide whether to just go and fuck Maisy or jerk off. Just remembering her eyes on me as she was masturbating keeps my cock alive. Kai and Logan enjoyed her and maybe it's childish, but I want her now. I've been holding off from jerking and my balls ache badly.

When I asked if they used protection, I nearly lost it when Logan said, "She's clean, brother."

My question was aimed at Logan rather than Kai, with good reason. Kai knows me better than anyone. He knows I'm worried for Maisy, and that I'd never let anything happen to her while she's under my protection.

I may kill her, yes, that's a clean cut for me, but I'd never mess up her life. Also, she makes my cock twitch every single day, which means at some point I'll have to pay a visit to my doctor.

Also, I know Kai's clean, since he hasn't had sex for more than a year. But when I asked Logan, after his *She's clean, brother*, and me yelling profanities at him as to what I really meant by asking him, he responded with, "All done."

Now that was surprising.

Logan's usually the one who complains when he has to do an additional sexual health check, which we do only when we're fucking the same girl, but of course, none of those girls were Maisy. Which tells me Logan's growing up. It makes me feel good, seeing him becoming a responsible man.

I finish my shower, though before I turn off the water I pump my cock a few times, waking the animal inside me.

With the towel wrapped around me, I go to my desk. My cell's lit up with a message. I read it, and my blood boils immediately. The animal that woke up just a moment ago is now seething.

I dial Kai's number and wait for him to pick up.

"Yup."

He's not going to be too cheerful when he hears my news. "We gotta talk. Urgently. Call Logan and meet me here. Now."

I don't give him time to respond. This is non-negotiable. I cut the call and get to dressing. I choose my shoes first, black, just like the three-piece suit in front of me. Some may find it boring, but it keeps me focused, organized, and in control, whereas my tats, rings, and bracelets remind me of who I am. In my world, I cannot be seen as anything but in control. That's my external persona, something I've learned practicing law.

Which reminds me as I tighten my tie, take my holster, place my gun in it, and secure it under my arm, that I'm angry, and I'm not breathing properly.

I go down to the kitchen. My breathing isn't settling, my cock isn't twitching anymore, and Maisy is nothing but a name. I pour myself a cup of coffee but then, incensed, I slam the cup against the wall. The coffee splatters all over the kitchen floor, the cup in dozens of pieces.

I step over the broken crockery and pour myself another.

The sensors outside my house ping Kai's arrival on my cell. He probably rode his motorbike like a lunatic. I should've thought this through before asking him to show up at mine immediately. But had I told him over the phone, he'd have reacted in his usual impulsive way. One day, his lack of control may cost him his life.

He rushes inside my house in full bike gear, and as he enters the kitchen he spots the mess on the floor. "What happened here? Is Maisy okay?"

"Grab yourself some coffee," I mutter. "Let's wait for Logan."

Kai understands me and knows not to ask any more questions until Logan shows up. He's the one who feels the most out of the three of us. That's why the thing with Natasha hurt him so much.

He pours himself a cup of coffee and leans against the table. He pulls up a chair with his boot and rests his foot on it.

My cell pings with Logan's arrival at my house. He hasn't gone home yet as he closes for business at midday. He rushes in too, dressed in a three-piece suit like mine, except his is stained in two places and all scrunched up from dealing with 'business' behind the doors of his strip club.

"What did you do, fly here?" Kai asks him.

"I was in the neighborhood. There was some fuck-up with Bobby, I had to bail him out. I sent him home and I came here," he explains as he pours himself a coffee.

"Okay, we're here." Kai's impatience is evident. "What is it?"

They both look at me. It's rare that I'm this enraged and silent at the same time.

"Did you do your due diligence on Maisy as I asked you to?" I eventually demand.

"Orion, we rely on *you* to do proper research on anyone. You're good at it." Kai shrugs. "Just like I'm good at killing people in the ring. I wouldn't ask you to, would I?"

"Very well. Let's not waste any more time, then." I read from the report on my cell, sent this morning by the PI who does this stuff for me. "Maisy Roy is actually Melissa Roystein, a genius from Princeton, NJ, with a photographic memory. At the age of twelve her IQ was recorded as 155, and since her mother was already dead and her stepdad was a gambler, he sold her to Milan the Dog for a period of four years." I look at them. "Yes, literally *sold* her."

Kai's hands clench into fists as I talk, and Logan's wicked eye tic comes on, the one that appears just before he kills someone.

"She's a genius? I knew there was something special about her," Logan mutters.

Kai shakes his head in disbelief. "She was sold like a slave. I'm gonna kill that motherfucker!"

"So she knew of him before. Huh." Logan gets it first. "She lied to us."

"She was doing his books for four years, although she may've been doing something else for him too," I continue.

Kai's still in protective mode. "Do you think she had a choice at that age?!"

"At the age of sixteen, she's sent back to her stepdad but runs away from home," I say. "Next, she pops up on the radar four years later as a tenant in Jerry Trialow's building, where she offered to help him in exchange for her rent." I finish and look at Kai. "What are the chances of her going back to work for the same guy?"

Kai looks away; disappointment, anger, hurt, betrayal–everything is clear on the man's face. He finally responds with a growl. "Get her here. Right now! If she's lying, I'll kill her myself!"

It breaks my heart to see him hurt, but nobody lies to us and lives.

Logan and I look at each other. Kai doesn't need this. If he kills her, it'll be Natasha all over again. Guilt and remorse would follow him everywhere for another year. Poor guy just can't get a break.

"Are you sure?" I ask.

"Just bring her here!" he orders through his teeth.

I go up to her room, knock loudly a few times, and open the door. Maisy's in bed, the TV remote next to her. She's lying on her side, facing away from me, her knee bent and her ass pointing right at me.

To my cock: stop making uninvited appearances!

She lifts her head sleepily and rubs her eyes.

"We need you in the kitchen. Now," I order. I don't even wait for her to look at me. I leave the door open and leave.

Five minutes later, we hear footsteps on the staircase, and she walks into the kitchen wearing a cami top and panties; her face, pure bliss. She looks at the floor, at the broken pieces of my cup. "What happened in here?"

Her eyes question me, but I don't give in to her wily ways. I just glare at her, so she flutters her eyelashes at Kai and Logan, smiling. "What is it?"

She sounds so innocent. I could kill her just for that.

Kai takes a chair and places it between the three of us. "Sit down."

"Kai, what is it? Logan?" She sits down slowly, like she's biding for time.

Kai towers above her, arms crossed over his chest, his feet apart. "You lied to us."

Logan approaches and he, too, looms over her. Their egos are hurt, and she needs to see who's in charge. "We promised we'd keep you safe. And this is how you repay us?" His voice is gruff. This is what he sounds like before he slits someone's throat.

I step up too, and narrow my eyes at her. She's getting pure venom fired at her from three directions now. "I gave you the chance to tell us the truth, and now? I'd hate for my kitchen to be a mess again."

She remains glued to the chair, craning her neck to look up at us, her eyes wide, looking petrified that these may be the last moments of her life. "Everything I said was the truth. Everything!"

"You didn't tell us you used to work for Milan, did you now?"

Her eyes well up but she tries to hold it back, frowning. Her chin wobbles until she can't contain the tears any longer.

"Are you still working for him?" I persist.

"That was not *working*," she chokes out. "I was held there against my will."

"Doing what?" Kai asks, but judging by the tone, he really doesn't want to hear the answer.

Maisy's eyes slam shut and more tears bubble beneath her lashes until they overflow and roll down her cheeks. She wipes them away with her hand and looks at us. "I was *twelve!* Do you know what it's like to lose your virginity to an old, disgusting guy?" she blurts out, and I notice Kai's fingers curling into a fist. "To be raped, to be totally at the mercy of that animal?"

She turns to Logan, then to me. I have no problem looking at her red eyes, rosy lips, and flushed cheeks. She can cry all she wants; in fact, I may want to keep her in this state for longer.

"I never lied to you. I just didn't tell you some painful facts about my past," she insists. "I had to work for him, run his books, and if I hadn't run away, that stamp on my back would probably have been there years ago."

"And yet you went back to work for the same guy?" I have to be ruthless. Cold. I want her like this, terrified.

"Do you think you scare me, Orion?" She raises her voice as she cries harder. "You don't! You got nothing on what I've read and seen of what's going on with the Slavs. Yes, I went back to work for him, because there's a tape of me doing unspeakable things that I'm trying to get off the streets. But you know what? I got Jerry killed, and his wife too. What a fucking wonderful person I am. Getting people killed to get to what I want. Same as them, vile filth. When Milan found out I was still around, he sent Camila to take me to Zed, the pimp. She wanted me to see what it's like living the life of a whore so I'd beg to work for Milan again. I ran away from Zed that night and came straight here. When I saw Camila enter your house I had to go after her. She was the one recording the videos. I was gonna torture her, take her eyes out, cut her tongue out–I don't know what you mobsters do when you torture someone, but I was going to fucking *kill* that bitch!" She's sobbing as she stands up and pushes us away from her. "Now I'm going to my room. Feel free to kill me in there, so you don't mess up your fucking kitchen!"

She runs up the stairs and I hear the slam of her door.

I want to roll my eyes, but I can't even get myself to do that. This is what fucked up looks like. This is the reason why I want order in New York. Why I want the syndicates working together. Kai and Logan regard me; I know we're all thinking the same thing.

I shake my head. Milan will fucking die and the Slavs will cease to exist, that much I know. But I also know that we need a plan. *One step at a time.*

I do know that the thought of Milan raping Maisy makes me want to skin him alive, and I need *someone* dead today. "Isn't Zed a pimp in your jurisdiction, Logan?"

"Yes, the fucker is." Logan straightens up and takes the blades out of his pocket.

Kai looks ready to go, the four-finger metal ring on his hand already.

"We're killing someone today, and it's not gonna be Maisy," I say.

They nod, and we depart.

MAISY

My whole body is shaking. My heart hammers in my chest and I can feel my pulse in my head. They're behind me... Any second, they'll burst in and kill me. I deserve this. I got people killed. I lied to these three men, when all they did was protect me and look after me.

I'm waiting for my judgment, my punishment, and as I do I realize they never mentioned Rosey, my sister. It's like she doesn't exist. We were *both* sold to Milan, the *two* of us! And yet, there's no talk of Rosey. It hurts. Apart from me, there's not one human being alive who will make her existence real. If I die, she dies too. Wherever she is.

Anxious of what's to come, I lie down on my bed and let go, sobbing into my pillow. Why did my mother die on us and leave us in the hands of that man? I miss Rosey. I miss my partner in crime, my twin. I used to feel her being alive, like she was still close to me, and then one day, it just stopped. I wonder if it was because we hadn't seen each other for so many years. I miss her so much, and now I won't ever get to see her again. It's over. I won't live to see the day. Instead I'll die here, in this bed.

Orion will only have to change the sheets. I won't fight, so there'll be no mess for him.

I must have dozed in bed, and as I turn onto my side I feel cold metal on my cheek. I open my eyes, startled. Orion's sleeping next to me, wearing a black hoodie, sweatpants, and sneakers, all muddied up and dirty. His face is cut in a few places and he has a reddish bruise on his jaw. His body's facing me and his hand, the one with all the rings, is resting on my pillow, palm down. That must be what I landed on in my sleep. His knuckles are red and swollen.

I lift my head, confused. I was to die this morning, but he's here, yet I'm still alive.

I sit up quietly and, not knowing what to do, go to the bathroom. If I'm to die now then I'll be ready. I wash my face, brush my teeth, and look at myself in the mirror. The words my mother would often say to Rosey and me come into my head: *"This is it, girls. This, right here, is your life. And it's going to go however you believe it will."*

Those words have always given me hope to not just accept where I end up. I hope Rosey remembers them too.

I take the hairbrush with me and walk back to the bed. I sit down next to Orion, start brushing my hair, and lean in closer to check out his neck tattoo. He usually wears a buttoned-up shirt and tie, but this time, in his hoodie, I can see more. There's a scar that the tattoo covers and I'm trying to make sense of it.

His husky voice sends vibrations through me. "What are you doing?"

I immediately jerk upright as he opens his eyes. "Nothing. I was wondering when you were going to kill me."

He cringes in pain as he sits up. "Is that why you're brushing your hair? To look pretty before your death?"

"Just get it over and done with, Orion. I'm sick of waiting."

Orion massages his red knuckles. Seemingly becoming aware of his muddied clothes and the dirt they're leaving on the sheets, he shifts his feet off the bed.

"Why are you in my bed? And why am I still alive?" I demand. I hate feeling like every moment will be my last.

He regards me for a moment and sighs. There's a slight annoyance in his eyes. "We agreed to honor our promise, Maisy. We'll help you get those videos and get Milan off your back. You've been through enough already."

"So you're not mad that I didn't tell you the whole story?"

"Kai and Logan aren't. I'm still undecided. Pissed, more like. But I tell you now, if there's anything else from your past that you're still keeping to yourself, so help me God, I'll be the one that puts a bullet through your head."

"I never lied to you, Orion." *Just a little white lie.*

"You omitted pertinent information."

"We're not in a court of law."

"If we *were* in a court of law, you'd be charged with perjury. And there'd be consequences for your actions!"

I roll my eyes, annoyed.

He eyes the dirt he left on my bed, and gets up. "I'll bring you fresh sheets."

"I can wash these. I want to do something useful around here."

"Suit yourself. You'll find everything in the basement. I'm sure you remember where that is."

I think of him exercising in his basement, and seeing the boxing ring and gym, but I don't remember a washing machine. "Thank you."

"We'll talk more when I'm back."

CHAPTER 6

MAISY

I spend the rest of the afternoon in Orion's basement. The washing machine and the dryer were hard to find. I had to turn all the lights on and literally check behind every door, and there are at least five doors downstairs: changing rooms, most likely for when they box in the ring, plus bathrooms, a cleaning closet and so on. Once I found the laundry room it was easy. Surely there's someone else doing this for him because judging by the plethora of detergents, he wouldn't know where to start. It screams a woman's touch. A pang of jealousy overwhelms me as I wonder who that might be.

Once the washing machine is on, I go back to the main basement room and check the last door to see where it leads. This room has one small yellow dimmer light. Once I turn it on, I wait for my eyes to adjust and push on, feeling brave enough to nose about a little. You get to learn a lot about someone by simply seeing their most hidden rooms. Especially the ones in their basement.

One side of the room is exposed brick with iron cuffs hanging from the wall, with chains attached, and some sort of metal contraption hanging from the beam overhead. Knowing this is a mobster's house, I don't want to think about what goes on here, because if I look closer, I'm sure I can see blood on the wall. In the corner, there's a desk and a flimsy chair. Just like in the movies. But this is no movie. The smell's real, too, and a little too disturbing. A big, scary furnace is in one corner, not in use.

The washing machine suddenly makes a loud whirring noise and I jump. I spin on my heel and run out.

I get back to the machine, which has just finished its cycle, and move the wet sheets into the dryer. Without the need to wait around, I head back to my room; I won't be in this space any longer than I have to be.

I walk back through the gym and up the staircase. The moment I set foot in the hall, I hear someone in the kitchen. But it's too late. I'm already here and now I'm staring at an elderly woman cleaning the kitchen floor and collecting up the pieces of broken crockery.

The basement door closes behind me with a slam. She clearly hears it, but doesn't even raise her head.

"I'll be out of here in five minutes," she says.

"I… I could actually use the company?" I say nervously.

She doesn't respond. She finishes with the floor in five minutes. Deliberately or not, she turns her back to me, tidies up, and leaves.

And that was that. *Strange.*

With the kitchen clean and my belly empty, I open the fridge to see if there's anything to eat. Chicken, lettuce, and some dressing; enough to make a chicken Caesar salad.

I start preparing it, and realize I'm salivating. I can't remember when I last ate. After this meal, he'll need to buy more food, since I've made use of everything in the fridge.

I decide to make a plate for Orion too, it's the least I can do for not killing me last night. I cover the one for him and leave it in the fridge, and take my plate at the table to eat.

Clean sheets. Roof over my head. Full stomach. How long until this ends, I wonder? How long until they find out about my sister, and then kill me, no doubt?

I must've dozed off because a knock on the door jolts me from my slumber.

"Get dressed and come down to the kitchen," Orion orders. He doesn't ask. He never asks.

I remember finishing my food, taking my sheets from the basement and making my bed. Since my body always wants to rest when my stomach is full, I took a shower, got dressed, and... I suppose I fell asleep.

I rub my eyes and look at the time: three in the morning. I shouldn't be keeping these crazy hours just because they do. With messy hair and in my cami top and panties, I get up and go down to the kitchen.

Orion's in his suit, minus the jacket and tie, and is wearing the holster with his gun. His sleeves are rolled up, tats showing on his forearms, and those rings–it looks like they never leave his fingers. Looking hot, as always. My insides clench at the sight of him. He's making pancakes, despite the weird time of night, looking fully engrossed in the job.

"Hello," I yawn.

He turns to me, his eyes running down my body. "Didn't I say get dressed?"

"I am dressed, and it's three in the morning." *Who makes pancakes at three in the morning?*

"Suit yourself. Sit down, we're having pancakes."

I walk up to where he is, heading for the coffee pot. "Is there any coffee at this hour?"

His eyes fall to my breasts. His tongue darts out of his mouth and he licks his lower lip. “I’ll bring it over. Go and sit down. I have questions for you.”

“Okay.” I blink at him and sit on a chair at one end of the table.

Orion pours me a cup. “Sugar or cream?”

I shake my head. “Neither.”

“Here.” He passes it to me.

“I saw someone cleaning the kitchen earlier,” I tell him.

“Leila. She works for me, cleans the house, helps with whatever I need. Did she see you?”

“She did. Or at least she knew I was here. Didn’t say a word to me.”

“Five years ago, I helped get her son out of jail and she wanted to help me in return,” he says. “She turned out to be the most trusted person on my payroll. Not interested in anything or anyone. She comes, does her job, and leaves.”

“Was she the one that bought my clothes?”

“Yes.”

I roll my eyes. “Figures.”

“Why’s that?”

“Can’t you tell by these granny panties that I wear? She’s old.”

Orion seems to be biting back a smile as he takes the pan and flips the pancake. “Tell me about July 15, 2019.”

I look away, trying to remember. “I got nothing. Nothing connected with any of your crime syndicates in New York. Apart from random facts, the only note I remember seeing is about a mobster from Miami.”

His eyes flicker. “Go on.”

“John Lopes, tortured and killed in Miami after a state-wide syndicate meeting. Among the gruesome stuff done to him, someone cut off his balls. That was underlined in red.”

Orion has a notebook next to the pan and as he writes, he forgets the pancake, which starts burning. “Fuck!” He catches it in time and flips it quickly.

"I can help if you want." I stand up. "You need your hands to take notes."

"I'm good, thank you. Stay where you are," he orders, and I sit down again. His next question is more of a statement. "The letter addressed to me."

"There were too many letters with your address on. When I think about it, it's as if someone's been taking your mail. Have you noticed that happening?"

"Yes, a while back."

"Okay. Um, a court case from seven years ago. As a public defender, you represented the state versus Logan Vitali over the murder of the owner of the local store. You made so many errors that the case was thrown out of court. It's why you lost your job as a public defender."

Orion takes notes, skillfully flipping pancakes at the same time.

"But the letter from your mother, I got nothing," I continue. "I never got to read it as it was sealed and in a box. I only glanced at it. Hm, who's Lisa Carte?"

He turns to me. "Why?"

"I saw her name among your mail. But it was part of a different document. Is she your mother?"

"My sister."

"What I saw wasn't clearly written, quite a lot had been redacted, but it was about Christmas Day last year," I recall. "Something happened or was about to happen and afterward, 'she' had to be killed. They kept referring to her as 'she' in inverted commas, and in another document it said 'she' wasn't a threat any longer and was to remain alive, according to a psychologist."

Orion stops writing and leans on the kitchen counter with his hands, his head low and eyes closed. "The name of the psychologist?" he asks through clenched teeth.

"Sigrun Jones."

Orion curses under his breath, a long, juicy line of words that leave my mouth hanging open.

"Are-Are you okay?"

He doesn't answer. Just adds two pancakes to a plate and passes it to me. He puts the maple syrup, strawberries, and whipped cream on the table. "Here."

"Aren't you eating?"

"No." He sits next to me.

I blink. "What was that all about?"

"Some fucked-up shit you don't need to worry about. What else you got on my address?"

"Um, activities that you're involved in, door-to-door services and deliveries of essentials for disadvantaged neighborhoods. That was surprising to read. Also, the boxing club. It was noted in detail about what goes on in there, basically illegal gambling, fixed boxing matches, special parties. I wondered even then, um, what *are* these special parties?"

He cocks his head. "You couldn't guess? Come on, genius, don't dumb yourself down for me."

I shrug. "You could still tell me."

"It's sex parties. But you knew that already, didn't you?" he chuckles.

I meet his eyes and pick up the can of whipped cream, squeezing some into my mouth. Some of it dribbles onto my chin. *I did know that. I just wanted him to tell me.*

He wipes the blob off my chin with his thumb and uses it to deposit the cream back into my mouth. As it lingers there, I wrap my lips around it and suck it clean. He pulls it out, picks up his coffee, and takes a sip.

"You do this all the time," I accuse him.

"Do what?"

"What you just did. Start something and... don't finish it."

"Did that turn you on?"

I nod.

"Who made you squirt cream into your mouth?"

I shrug.

"Was that not done to provoke me?" he asks.

I nod again, not looking at him.

"Maisy, there will always be consequences for your actions. Especially if you act like that."

"Like what?"

"Like a brat."

"What do you mean?"

Orion sucks in a breath. "Let me ask you: did you enjoy our last encounter?"

"I did."

"And when I left, I said you'd had enough, didn't I?"

I nod.

"Do you also remember the pain you felt when I left?"

I nod.

"And then you did what you did. If you're not playing by my rules, that's all you'll get to feel."

Our eyes are locked as I squirt more whipped cream onto my tongue. He watches me stuffing my mouth full and his lips curl up at one corner.

"I must say, I love your courage."

I smile and gulp down the cream, then pour maple syrup onto my pancake, rolling it up and biting into it. As I do, the syrup squirts onto my cami top, a few drops rolling down to my bare thighs.

"Oh no!" I yelp. I try to swipe it up with my fingers and lick them at the same time. "This is delicious."

There's a beat before he moves or says anything, but his eyes become darker with each moment.

"You missed here." He lowers his head and laps up the maple syrup from my cami over my breast and sucks my nipple through the material. I hum, enjoying the moment, but he finishes too soon and pulls back. "Eat your pancake like a good girl, Maisy."

"Or else?"

He closes his eyes and inhales deeply. "Or else..." His hand reaches under the table and lands softly on my thigh. His warm touch is soothing, and slowly it wanders up. His fingers reach my panties and I stare at him, feeling needier by the second. "...you get nothing." He removes his hand.

I take another bite of my pancake, watching him as I chew and swallow.

"Keep eating."

I finish quickly, almost choking on the last bite.

"Are you done?"

I nod and grin.

"Before we continue, you should know what kind of consequences I'm talking about."

I've forgotten about everything. I only stare at him like I'm under a spell.

He pulls my chair closer to him so we're face to face, and hooks his fingers into the hem of my cami top, clearly intent on taking it off. "Good girls get everything. Bad girls get spanked."

I lift my arms as my cami is slipped off my body, leaving me sitting on the wooden chair in my panties only.

"Place your legs on either side of the chair, and hook your upper arms on the backrest. I want to see your titties perked up for me."

I assume the position and with my arms behind the back of the chair, my back arches and my breasts are in his face. He's staring at my body as I bathe in his power, engulfed by his presence. The pads of his fingers trail along my collarbone, moving south and stopping at my nipples. A soft pinch, and he starts kneading them as I move into his hand. I want more of it. I'm desperate for his touch.

"Stay still, darling." His half-closed eyes stay on me, his lips quirked at one side. As he lifts his chin, he pinches my nipples hard. "*Yesss.*"

I whimper. My legs spread wider on the chair as he holds my nipples between his index fingers and thumbs and tugs them, taking my body with him. Then he releases me, allowing me for a split second to feel at ease, before he slaps me hard on the sides. First one, then the other.

I moan. My feet are now on tiptoes, my body arched toward his. I want to get up; I want to climb him like a monkey.

"If you move, you go back to your room."

I close my eyes and sit back as I was, and he continues with the torture. The pinching turns into slapping and then tugging, harder and harder, yanking them, striking them with greater intensity, tormenting me. I moan again. I think I'm in pain–no, I haven't decided yet, because this is too sweet to be pain. I'm immobile–I wouldn't want him to stop and send me back to my room–but I'm loud.

I open my eyes to meet his obsidian gaze, now alive from pelting my skin, from watching me writhe on the chair. The throbbing sensation in my core is building. My juices have surged and soaked my panties, and my clit needs just a flick for me to come undone.

"I see you're enjoying this, Maisy." His voice reverberates through my body; it's deadly and hot all at once.

I swallow, moistening my dry throat. The pain in my nipples makes me groan long and loud. "Yes," I pant.

"And you haven't moved, like I told you." A sharp pain shoots from where he pinches harder still, and I whimper and roll my hips on the chair.

My mind is lost. Every nerve ending in my body is awake. The throbbing doesn't stop and my nipples hurt like hell, but at the same time pull a string of desire down to my core. It's too much.

"Come here." He releases my nipples and leans back in his chair, making space for me on his lap as he chuckles.

I'm feral at this point. I get up and sit in his lap, straddling him, right over the huge protrusion in his pants. His fingers dig into my flesh as he claws at my hips, stilling me.

"You are so beautiful."

I lick my lips at what's to come. *Finally.*

My breasts are right in his face and he leans in, inhales my scent and sucks one, then the other. They're too sensitive but he's gentle, his hot tongue soothing them. I shudder beneath his touch. His movements are slow and loving, and after sucking them he pulls back and blows on them. I throw my head back, surrendering to him.

I run my fingers through his hair and lift his head, pressing my lips to his as I grind on his steely cock. He kisses me hungrily and I moan into his mouth, wanting more, wanting all of him. He devours my mouth, deepening my desire as I reach between us to unbutton his vest and shirt. I manage to undo half the buttons and slide my hands inside to stroke his pecs–*so fucking fine*–all the while expecting him to finish the job himself. And free his cock, too. *Surely it's painful as it is.*

But he doesn't do anything except devour me, suck my bottom lip, bite me, and wait on me to do the rest. So I do, and go back to fully undressing him. I take off his vest and shirt, then work to free his erection that's already poking from the top of his underwear, shining with precum.

When I finally get to wrap my hand around him I notice he's as big as Kai and Logan, with a small addition: a thick, steel ring at the top of his penis. A Prince Albert piercing. I look down at it and grin.

He snickers. "I take it you had someone with this piercing before?"

I shake my head. "No."

"Why the grin then?"

"I read about it." I run my tongue over my teeth and he pulls me to him. His lips latch onto mine, giving me yet another taste of his addictive masculinity.

I fist his cock at the base and squeeze his shaft on every upstroke, determined to make him lose control, to make him feel the same urgent need wreaking havoc on my body. He groans, dipping his head to bite my nipple between his teeth while his fingers play with the other.

"Do you have protection?" he asks in between bites.

"I don't," I pant, "but I'm clean, you said so yourself."

“Hey!” He slaps my breasts two, three times, making me jump. “Are you gonna just blindly believe *I’m* clean?”

“If you say you are, I believe you,” I purr.

“You’d believe me, huh?” He slaps my breasts at the sides now and I feel a rush of wet heat. I think I’m losing my mind.

“Logan and Kai talked about you,” I tell him. “You wouldn’t do anything to me on purpose.”

He points across the room. “There’s a condom in that drawer. You want to ride me, you got to be a good girl and go get it.”

I jump off him and run to the drawer. There are hundreds of condoms inside. I’m not used to doing all this work to fuck someone. Usually guys are more than happy to do the ‘admin,’ so to speak, in order to fuck. But he has a way of asking me.

He’s looking at me and fisting his cock with a smirk on his face. I run back and straddle him again. As I do, he tears at my panties and throws them aside. “You forgot to take these off.”

There. That’s the madness I want to see when someone wants to fuck me.

I pass him the condom, wishing, no, *expecting* him to do the rest of the work before we actually get started. Seriously, I don’t know how men do this. My mind is incapable of thinking right now.

“You wanted to ride, so ride me, darling.”

Doing errands for him is the last thing on my mind but I’m beyond making sense. I quickly tear open the condom and roll it down his cock, maddening desire surging through me.

“Good girl, Maisy.” He sucks my nipple and bites me again. I whimper and hunch over as I pull my nipple out of his mouth.

I have no comprehension of the world at this moment, only of all-I-want-to-do-right-now, which is to ride him. That’s my sole aim. I lift up and try to get him in my cunt as he watches me, looking smug. He’s big, and I may not be able to do this by myself, so I lower onto him slowly, but there isn't any give. And it's painful. I try nevertheless. And my frustration, my need, grows even more.

"Easy, Maisy, easy, girl. Breathe."

He digs his fingers into my thigh, and with the other hand positions his piercing at my entrance. It's cold even through the condom, but with my heat, not for long. He glides it against my arousal, up and down my folds.

"Now, take a deep breath, and... exhale."

As I do, he watches his cock pushing into my opening. I shudder, but not from pain. The hard steel of his piercing hits a tender spot that makes my insides pulse wildly. He pauses there, seeming to test the depth.

"Mmm, there you go," his voice low and rough.

My juices gush as he enters me to the balls. It burns, but those are the best burns, sweet and slow.

"Now, show me how you ride."

I waste no time. I begin to ride him, easy at first, and as I become adjusted to his girth, my ass cheeks clench and stay tight each time I raise my hips. My movements are slow and measured while I'm still being stretched but soon, as I ride him harder, my hips start to swivel sideways and I rub myself on his base. I hold his shoulders and tilt my head back as he sucks my nipples, tearing my insides with pleasure and making me fully surrender to the moment.

"Go up to the tip and back in, deep, to my balls. No half-job, Maisy. This is for me, not you."

I try again, doing better, but it's much harder as I'm doing all the work. I can see I'm getting to him, though; his head falls back and he groans. Suddenly, with urgency, he dips his head and sinks his teeth into my shoulder, leaving marks.

"Your sweet pussy's so hot, so tight... Don't think I don't feel you squeezing me," he chides.

His fingers dig into my hips, and he lifts me up and pounds me hard against him, primal grunts escaping his mouth as he moves. I'm not sure if it's the piercing, but I'm propelled into frenzied rotations of my hips, chasing my dose of ecstasy. I run my fingers through his hair and pull him hard to my lips. We kiss hungrily and I moan as he plunges deeper, more forcefully into me.

The next time he lifts my hips he raises me up to the table, and makes me sit there as he takes off his pants and underwear. His body is perfection: six-pack, tats on both arms and the whole left side of his torso from his neck down to his thighs, a thick silver bracelet and watch, together with the rings still on both hands.

With his arm he sweeps the plates onto the floor, breaking them in the process, and pushes me down onto my back. He climbs on top of the table, one knee planted and one raised, his foot firmly pressed against the wood for leverage. He lifts my legs up and pushes them back, my knees stopping close to my head. I'm twisted like a prawn, my cunt high in the air, in need of him.

Orion leans in and inhales deeply. "The nectar of the goddesses," I hear him murmur to himself before he starts lapping up everything I've created, fast, like I'm going to deny him the right. He holds my legs firmly in place while I moan loudly each time he thrusts his tongue inside my cunt and swirls and sucks my core. His sounds of appreciation are loud as he laps at my clit, and just as I'm easing into his rhythm and edging toward release, he pulls back and, just as fast, slides his cock back inside me.

"Oh, *fuck!*" I cry out.

It must be the piercing, because *oh dear God on this earth*, I'm in heaven. He enters me to the balls each time. His thrusts and growls are not connected but come one after the other. I whine out loud when he leaves my pussy empty, gaping, and he spits on it before slamming into me again. I whimper from the intensity, and he does the same again, but this time when he spits on my pussy, he slaps me there too.

"Do you want this, Maisy, to be a little whore for me?"

Every nerve ending I possess is trembling as I enjoy the pain of the slap. *His words, what they do to me*. He slaps me, again and again. My moans grow louder.

"I know you like this, you little slut," he grunts as he thrusts into me again. "Don't make me cum so soon! Fuck, your tight cunt will get it from me!"

He's out, pumping his cock and controlling his eruption, all the while spitting on my cunt and slapping me, harder each time. I gasp for breath. I'm there, almost coming, but I'm empty, and he only slaps me again.

"You're going to cum for me, on five. Clear?"

"Yes," I breathe.

He briefly rubs my swollen clit before he starts counting down.

"Five." He slaps my cunt, his hand landing on my whole mound that's up in the air. He thrusts inside me twice and pulls out, grunting.

"Four." And again, another hard slap, and my legs shake where I lie.

"Three, be a whore for me, show me you can." Another slap stings me but gives me the push that's going to get me there, and he thrusts three times before he's out again. I'm reduced to whimpers, long and loud. It's upon me, I feel it.

"Two." His palm comes down on me violently, with an intense burn and an extra oomph that takes me over the edge. But instead of his cock in my cunt, I get his fingers in my ass.

"One!" I see his mouth move, but I can't hear him any longer. He slaps me one last time and this is it, my peak. I begin to erupt so hard that my whole body is convulsing, when he suddenly flips me sideways, then thrusts into me until I fall to pieces under him, moaning and gasping at every touch, shaking violently.

"You ready for my cum, whore?"

"Yes..."

"Yes, what?"

"Please, I want your cum," I cry.

"Open wide." His cock is out, the condom's off, and he fists himself roughly. He lifts me to a sitting position and I open my mouth, still on a high.

"Wider!"

I flatten my tongue beneath his cock and he spurts into my mouth and face, six or seven times. There's so much cum, and I take all of it in. Heat swells up again in my core as I lick my lips and swallow every last drop. I dip my head and run my tongue over the length of him.

"Fuck, yes, Maisy!" He stares down at me, in all his glorious dominance, and wipes the jizz from my cheek to bring it to my lips. "You missed this."

I lick his fingers as one more spurt of semen coats my neck, and he takes it to my lips again. "And this."

He leans in, grabbing hold of my hair with one hand and my neck with the other, and presses his lips to mine so powerfully, it's as if he wants to take his jizz back.

"I'm gonna have fun with you, you little slut," he mumbles against my lips, then straightens up above me and slaps my cheek twice. He tilts his head back. "*Fuck* yes!"

He gets down from the table as I collapse backward in a puddle of cum, sweat, shame, and praise. A mess.

Our eyes lock. I'm sated, and ruined, and yet, I want more of him.

He must read it all on my face. "Are you okay?" He presses his lips to mine and chuckles, then kisses my forehead. "Perhaps you need an ice pack."

Perhaps I do.

I lift myself up, probably too soon, and it takes me a minute to see clearly. There's mess on the floor: broken plates, and spilled syrup and cream all over.

I'm still flying high, my pussy pulsating like a live entity between my legs thanks to the orgasm he just gave me. I look at Orion, who's already listening to messages on his cell.

His face darkens. "I gotta take this in my office. I'll come to you once I'm done. You okay in here?"

"I'm more than okay," I purr, and watch him collect his clothes and walk out. I get off the table slowly, avoiding the shards. It stings between my legs as I slowly walk upstairs to my room.

Taking a shower in this condition is an experience. With my body so roughed up, the water droplets are sharp, pricking my skin where I've been bitten, pinched, or slapped. I wince in pain multiple times, and have to keep dodging out of the way.

I have never lathered my body so slowly, so exhaustingly slowly, and I end up leaning on the tiled wall and letting the steam engulf me.

Once I'm done, I put on a new pair of panties and a cami top and get into bed. Being woken in the middle of the night for whatever that was that Orion gave me was hot.

I once read of a special place on Earth for sated girls. Now I know it's real, and fuck me, I'm in it.

CHAPTER 7

ORION

I'm still not over Maisy lying to us, although having shot my load all over her face just now *(fuck if I'm not hard again)*, I'm beginning to think of several ways to forgive her. My cock twitches the moment she crosses my mind. She's ours. That much is true, and there's no going back from here. We've marked her for good.

I can't believe I was going to kill her and miss out on that sweet little genius cunt of hers, and the rest of her killer body. Plus, having her on our side tips the scales in our favor which is always good; it gets us closer to what we want to create.

Kai loves her company and acts giddy around her, like a kid. His focus in life up until the moment he met her was torturing and killing people. Dead on the inside, the guilt he felt prevented him from having fun. Which is always good for his syndicate and sometimes us, but not for him. Little did he know his dick would start making decisions for him once again. And Logan, fuck, he initiated the health check, and did it by himself–that says a lot.

I, too, booked an appointment with my doctor. I'm heading there tomorrow morning to get it over and done with. I'm clean, I know, but getting a full-blown hard-on each time I think of her begging for my cum is not conducive to my work, my wellbeing, or my cock, and searching for condoms is the last thing I want to be doing when she's on top of me.

With her in my thoughts, my cock refuses to sleep. She didn't stop me from spanking her titties or her sweet, juicy cunt, or even say anything about me calling her a slut. Taking that on takes courage. Or stubbornness. Couldn't tell which. What I could tell was the arousal it invoked in her each time I called her by that name. *Fuck me if she's not my perfect girl!*

I texted Jonah, my right-hand man, to meet me tomorrow. That fucker is the only one who knew about Sigrun, my niece's psychologist. The message he left on my cell was not what I wanted to hear. He stuttered once, not twice or three times. Just once. That's a bad sign. He's lying. I left Maisy in a puddle of cum and sweat on the table just to call him. Fucker! She'd better still be there when I get back.

I've been calling him for the last half hour, but he's not picking up. I hate his pathetic games so much that I'd rather peel someone's skin off by hand for hours than watch a grown-ass man blatantly lie for one minute.

I put the speaker on to hear his cell ring while I walk into my bedroom's ensuite and run the shower. I don't want to wash Maisy's scent off my cock and body, but that damn condom was in the way and it's that feeling I want to eliminate.

Jonah's cell goes straight to voicemail yet again and I cut it off. "Fucking asshole!"

I make sure I have the holster with my Colt still in it, then enter the shower. I don't take it under the water with me, of course, but it has to be within reach, always. I've killed more men when I least expected it than when I actually planned to. Go figure.

The water descends on me when I turn it on, and I realize the only reason I'm not in a murderous rage is Maisy. *Fuck!* My cock's hard again.

I lift my head toward the water stream and snicker. Reminiscing about what went on a short while ago. Am I fucking *daydreaming*, like some cunt? Huh. I guess I fucking am. I'm addicted to her and I don't give a damn.

I'm miles away, deep in Maisy's cunt, when something outside gets my attention. My sixth sense works overtime, and when it tells me something, it's usually right, and that's bad. Not for me–I'd kill whoever's there–but this time, for Maisy. If she's still in the kitchen, she has no chance. My blood boils to dangerous levels. Someone will be sorry they woke up today.

I see a shadow under the door as whoever's outside gets nearer. *Fools*. They're just about to enter my bathroom, so I grab my Colt and as they're standing outside the partly open door, I slam it straight into their face. I hear a loud thud. Whoever's there did not expect me.

I swiftly pull open the door, aiming straight at–"*Maisy?!*"

Maisy's lying on the floor of my bedroom, unconscious. I kneel down next to her and take her head in my lap. "Maisy! Maisy! *MAISY!*"

She doesn't respond as the water from my hair and body drips onto her. I check her breathing. "What the fuck are you doing here?" I shake her body and slap her face until I hear a small moan of protest. "Hey! *HEY!* Maisy!"

She blinks and tries to sit up, but wobbles and falls into my lap again. *Thank God!*

"What happened?"

"You snuck up on me." I soften my voice. It's not her fault I live on the edge of murder and mayhem. "I nearly killed you."

"Nothing's changed, then?" Her eyes are closed but I see her lips curve upward.

I can't help but smile at her sense of humor. "You think you're funny? Wait 'til you see the bruise on your eye tomorrow." I pull her hair to the side, away from her face. She opens her eyes and looks at me. She's had a shower, and is now dressed in her usual pair of panties and a red cami top. I wish she'd wear something else around the house. It's driving me nuts. Nobody can concentrate with her dressed for fucking all the time. "What are you doing here, Maisy?"

Her dark eyes have hazel specks dancing around in the irises. It's like looking into a void, one that absorbs me and allows me to just be. There's no past or present, just this very moment, being immersed in her gaze.

Now I'm certain. She's my new obsession.

"You said you'd come to me. I showered, and then I thought you'd changed your mind, so I wanted to wish you goodnight before I dozed off. I'm sorry." She bats her eyelashes at me.

"I got held up by some shit that's going on. I'm the one who's sorry." I take a pillow from my bed and place it under her head. "Don't move. Let me get dressed and I'll take you back to your room."

I get up and pull on my gray sweats and a t-shirt as she watches me.

"Orion, what's that?"

Her finger's pointing behind my back. I know what she's pointing at. Hence the reason why I never let anyone in my room, unless they know what they're getting themselves into. But it's too late now. Maybe this is the best way for her to find out, off her own bat.

I look back at the central feature of my bedroom: my St. Andrew's Cross, an X-shaped wooden frame mounted on the wall with restraint points on each of the four arms. My toy. True, I haven't played in a while because there just hasn't been anyone I've connected with lately, but after my day with Maisy, fuck me if I'm not going to ask. Just thinking of her being tied there, spread-eagled and restrained for my pleasure, makes my balls ache.

"What, that?" I better not scare her. I've imagined her tied to that cross way too many times. "You don't know?"

She lifts her head, cocks it sideways, trying to make sense of what she's looking at. And she does. She's a smart cookie. A sly smirk appears on her face as she rests back on the pillow. "Oh, you think I'm asking about the St. Andrew's Cross?"

"You're not?" My eyebrows shoot up and I tilt my head. "Maisy Roy!"

She loved the spanking, the name calling, the countdown, the control–why didn't I put two and two together?

She grins. And I grin too. She knows the name of it? Fuck me. She's the one. I know it. *Little slut.*

"I'm asking about the thing next to it. The chair... or bench? At first I thought it was for lifting weights, but then I saw the restraints at the base and yeah, actually, I think I know."

"That's a spanking bench," I say, watching her intently. "Have you been on one yet, Maisy?"

She goes back to the little slut I just fucked and shakes her head. Even that makes my cock stir. I'm hard again. *Fuck!* Will I ever be able to have a conversation with her without being in cock-pain?

"Maybe I'll show you one day." A beat passes and before she can say anything, I add, "If you're a good girl for me."

She locks eyes with me, looking a little embarrassed, and nods faintly. At this very moment, something becomes as clear as day to me. I want to dive into Maisy's abyss, search for her in the black void, then pull her up from the depths and take her back down again. Until she can't take it any longer, and she doesn't know if she's lost or found. Until I save her. Or she saves me.

I lift her up into my arms. She's so soft, small, and fragile, and she smells so good. This must be the feeling that got the other two hooked, looking after someone in a world where nobody knows about them and for that reason, they can never be destroyed.

In our world, women are tokens that we play with.

That's the curse of the Cartes, the Delgados, and the Vitalis. We can never have a normal life. We were brought up in this world to rule over the weak, extort, kill, torture, and hold the power no matter what.

That's how I met Kai and Logan. When I was fifteen, my father took me to a deserted factory and told me I was to make my first kill there. Who was I supposed to kill? He'd heard that Mickey Delgado was going to take his son Kai there, who was thirteen at the time. Lorenzo Vitali had heard the same thing; Logan was fourteen. So they pitted us all against each other. We found out later they'd laid bets on us.

We were just boys who wanted to have fun, to play. Not kill each other. It was then when our brotherhood started. We did make our first kills, though. Had to be done. We found the closest man on the lookout for each one of our families, and we killed them. My father never questioned me after that day. I told him, *You wanted me to kill someone, and I did. Be specific next time about who you want dead*. I felt so proud of how I'd screwed him over, which is maybe partly the reason I chose to study law. The devil is in the details.

Maisy's smiling at me as I carry her down the stairs to the second floor, where her room is. "I can walk from here," she purrs.

"You're not heavy," I say, and take the last few steps before I lay her down on her bed and prop her pillow up. "Comfortable?"

She nods, but scrunches up her nose as she touches her cheek and cringes in pain. I think the door slammed her good–well, *I* did. She's lucky she's alive. I was only going for incapacitating the enemy, not for the kill. That's the definition of lucky.

"Let me bring you an ice pack."

I head downstairs to the kitchen and, after carefully maneuvering through the shards and the sticky mess on the floor, I reach the freezer and grab the ice pack. Then I head back up to her.

I help her secure it in the right place. "Here, hold it."

"Ouch–it's cold!" she protests.

"Ice is usually cold. Didn't they teach you that in school?" I scoff, knowing perfectly well how smart she is.

"O-ryon," she mutters in a small voice, "you're always out at night. What do you do during the day?"

"I'm here, having meetings, or in the courtroom if there's a case on." The moment my guard's down, she does something like this. *What am I to think now? Why's she questioning me?* I pick up the remote and point it at the TV. "Let's see what's on."

I search through Netflix and steal a glance at her. I would've thought she'd be tired at nearly five in the morning, but her eyes are following mine and there's still a wicked spark in them.

"How about a drink? Do you want to drink something?"

"You mean alcohol?"

"Yes. What's your go-to drink?" I ask.

"I love champagne."

"Oh, you do, huh?"

"I know it's extravagant, but I can't drink any other alcoholic drink. It's the only one that doesn't give me headaches. But trust me, I haven't had it a lot. It's expensive."

"When was the last time you had a glass of champagne?"

"Can't remember. A couple years ago."

"I have champagne in the fridge, as a matter of fact. Do you want me to bring it up?"

She just gave me the fucking of the century, so I'll do anything to make sure she's relaxed and sleeping for a while. There's too much on her mind, always thinking, calculating something. She needs a break.

"I don't know, it's way too early. We should go to bed, Orion."

I hear one thing but I see another; there are fireworks in the black pools of her eyes. Dark, dirty thoughts that only a man under her spell can see.

"Just one glass." I jump off the bed and head down to the kitchen again. This time, I move some of the broken pieces from the floor so I can walk freely. I collect two flutes from the glassware cabinet and take the champagne from the fridge. I have to laugh. This is so fucking *normal.* Yet my heart contracts in fear. And I don't get fearful, ever.

As I carry the flutes upside down, I don't see the kitchen counter and I somehow shatter both glasses against the side.

"Fuck!" *Why am I nervous?* I take another two flutes and hurry back up. The kitchen's a mess and I'm not touching it. I'll get Leila to sort it out. She always does anyway.

Maisy smirks when I return to her. "What else did you break?"

I roll my eyes at her. I'm annoyed at myself, having let my thoughts derail me. "Just ignore it. Here, hold these." I pass her the flutes as I open the bottle. It makes a loud 'pop' sound and she claps her hands.

I present her the bottle. "Dom Perignon, Miss Roy. Would you like to taste it, or shall I just pour?"

She grins. "Just pour, please."

I fill both flutes to the top, hand one over, and clink them together. "Bottoms up!"

As I drink mine I watch her taking a small sip, her eyes full of joy. I could watch her drink champagne forever.

"Oh, this is very good. The one I had last time was bitter."

"This is the best, Maisy."

"Anything that counts as 'best' is actually quite subjective."

"I assure you, Dom Perignon *is* the best."

She giggles. "Would you say you're tasting the stars right now?"

She's extra attractive when she's being sassy. Dom Perignon was the monk who invented champagne, and upon having his first sip he is said to have exclaimed, 'Quickly, come here! I'm tasting the stars!' The whole world knows that.

"Don't you start with your smart mouth, Maisy." I press my lips to hers and she offers me an easy, tender kiss. Those are rare for me. There's little need for softness in a rough world.

"My smart mouth? What do you mean?" She drinks up, smiling with her eyes.

I cup her chin and lift her head. "Why are you afraid to tell the world that you're smart?"

"You must know why. Now *you're* making yourself dumb for *me*."

I want her to be free. We all want to help her live her life, for we can never have what she could have. "Yes, I do know. Just, don't hold back with us. We'll never use it against you."

I clink her glass again and we both take a few more gulps.

"I don't even know how that feels," she mutters.

I refill our glasses, finishing the bottle. The flutes I have are the only ones in the kitchen, and they're usually for my enemies. Especially large, basically, to get whoever's drinking, drunk, and fast.

"There's always a first time for anything," I say, and raise my glass. "To being the smartest person in the room."

She drinks to that, looking lost in thought.

"I think we need another bottle." I don't wait for her to respond, I just get up and go downstairs to the kitchen again, forgetting there's glass all over the floor. I step on a few small shards, but luckily I'm not cut. I pick up the second bottle and take it back to Maisy's room.

I open it without much drama and fill her glass again. Mine too. I decide to try to get her out of her head. "You said last time you had a drink, the champagne was bitter. Where was that?"

"Um, it was at this house where I was giving math lessons to a ten-year-old boy called Terry. His big brother was there, and at first, I thought he liked me because he sat with us and kept talking to me."

"How old was the big brother?" I regret the question as soon as I ask it. I don't want to know about other people flirting with her.

"Twenty-nine. Halfway through the lesson, he sent Terry out, opened a bottle of champagne, and we drank and talked for the rest of the afternoon."

"And?" I'm grinding my teeth now.

"And, that's it."

"Did he try to do anything?"

"No. He was a drunk. He needed someone to drink with."

I exhale the breath I've been holding. My mind goes straight to a drive-by with a semi-automatic where anyone having filthy thoughts about Maisy gets sprayed with bullets.

"What about you?" she asks. "When did you last have champagne?"

I take the bottle and top up her almost-empty glass, then mine. "Let me think. Ah, yes. Almost ten years ago. When I was eighteen. Kai, Logan, and I got together and went through seven bottles of Dom Perignon." I chuckle. "That was a fucked-up night."

"What's your go-to drink, then?"

I cock my head to one side. "You don't think it's champagne?"

"Haha." She punches my arm playfully. "Tell me!"

"Why don't I bring you a glass for you to try it? I drank champagne for you. You'll drink McCarthy's single malt whiskey for me. Deal?" I offer her my hand.

"Deal," she laughs, and we shake on it.

I head to the kitchen yet again, and this time I pick up the broom from the corner and sweep the broken plates into a pile, making some space for me to pour the whiskey.

I take two tumblers from the glassware cabinet and pull the whiskey bottle from the bottom drawer.

"So, that's where you keep your alcohol," comes Maisy's teasing voice.

I didn't even notice her come in. Fuck! *Am I drunk?* She certainly is. "Mind the shards, Maisy." I point at the few I missed when sweeping.

She doesn't have the ice pack with her, but instead is sporting a big lump on her cheek that's yellowish in color. She giggles and totters around, bumping into me and wrapping her arms around my waist to steady herself.

I turn to her, hungry for her kiss, and see her eyes suddenly go wide. She releases me and her eyebrows shoot up; she's gaping at someone behind me. I reach for my holster, which stupidly I forgot upstairs. Being drunk, I wouldn't have time to shoot anyway.

I turn to fight whoever's there, and see Lisa, my sister, standing frozen in the doorway. Her mouth's hanging open as she stares at us. At the mess in the kitchen. At us again.

"What the fuck are you doing here?" I snarl. She should fucking know better than to turn up unannounced.

"I came back. I told you I'd be back in the morning." She's not even blinking. Still shocked at the sight, I suppose.

"Fuck! Is it seven already?" I check the time. Goddamnit, I've never gotten this ridiculously carried away.

"I'm Lisa..." She's obviously curious, but I don't fucking care.

"I'm Maisy," Maisy giggles, and I could bend her over my knee and spank her until she can't walk for being so foolish.

"No," I interject, raising my hand, and then point my index finger at my sister. "Lisa, there's no one here, is that clear?" I glare at her; she knows in our world there are no second chances.

Lisa nods silently, not looking at Maisy.

"I need you to say it."

"There's no one here, Orion."

"Now leave," I order. "We'll talk later."

Lisa leaves just as she came, quietly. I turn to Maisy, whose cheeks are wet with tears.

"*No one?*" Her voice wobbles, but those big, dark, wet eyes tell me she wants an answer.

My sister won't say a word–I trust her with my life–but Maisy's life is in more danger if Lisa knows about her. And she doesn't need that. She's had enough grief in her lifetime, and I will not put her through more.

"Go to your room and do not leave, no matter what!" I command.

She starts to sob and runs upstairs to her room. *Why the fuck can't she understand the danger of people seeing her?*

MAISY

Racked with pain, I run to my room. I can't stop the tears, however hard I try. Maybe it's the alcohol making me so emotional. I'm 'no one?' Of course I am. *Stupid girl, who did you think you were to him?*

I slam the door shut. A sickening feeling stirs in my gut and makes me want to vomit. I'm nauseous, and I sense the bile rising up in my throat. That's when I know it's time to run to the bathroom. I'm just reaching the toilet when I barf everywhere, almost missing the mark.

There wasn't much food in my belly to start with but it still stinks and I retch again, my gut contracting and forcing everything out.

I'm on my knees hugging the toilet, dizzy. The vomiting stops but I don't move from where I am. Dropping in and out of consciousness, I lose sense of time.

I'm not sure how long I'm here–I may have dozed off–but suddenly the cool porcelain touches my forehead. My head jerks, and the cold jolts me into alertness.

My stomach has calmed, although the anxiety's still there. I try to get up; with the alcohol now out of my system I have more strength but my legs are numb, and pins and needles obliterate my body for a few minutes. After massaging my legs for a while, I finally push myself to my feet and step into the shower, fully clothed. I wash the vomit from my hair, my cami top, and my arms, but the pain still lingers. Typical, it's the one thing that would stay longer. I turn off the shower, take off my clothes, and wrap a towel around my body.

I walk gingerly out of the bathroom. For some reason my brain has detached from my skull and with each step I take, a pounding vibrates inside my head and through my body. All I want is to lie down and nurse this stupid hangover.

I reach the bed and go to lie down when I nearly squash a little girl, who looks no more than five years old. She's on my bed, propped up on my pillow and staring at me.

"Oh, God! I didn't see you there... I nearly crushed you!" I force myself to laugh, trying to get a smile out of her, but her face is expressionless. She's somber, looking at me like death, not a peep of childlikeness in her eyes.

I sit next to her and smile gently. She seems to have no intention of talking to me and with my headache, I'd rather just curl up next to her on the bed.

I give it a try anyway. "I'm Maisy." I raise my hand and start counting out the number of letters in my name on my fingers. "M – A – I – S – Y. Five letters. How many letters does your name have?"

She looks at her fingers for a second, then raises three.

"Three. Can I try to guess your name?"

She looks away, as though uninterested in any interaction, but I spot the twinkle in her eyes.

So, I persist. I'm not sure where this little girl came from, but she's the distraction that I need. "Is it... Eva?" No reaction. "Maybe it's Eve? No. Zoe? Ana? Lia?

Kay?" I throw my hands up in the air dramatically. "Okay, I give up."

There's an infinitesimal smile on her lips when she glances at me, but she quickly looks away again. She's amused, at least.

"Okay, I got two more names, and it must be one of those two. It *must!*" I giggle. "Is it... Ivy? No. Okay. Right. Right. This is it. Are you ready? It's..." I make a drum roll sound on my thighs which draws her eyes to my hands, then back to my face. "It's Mya! Ta-daaa!"

She flashes me the biggest grin ever, her eyes shining, and she nods, looking dumbfounded that I guessed her name. Lucky for me, I did.

"Now, you must tell me how old you are. Come on, I guessed your name."

She lifts her hand and spreads all five fingers in front of my face, still grinning.

"Five?! Oh God, you're *big!* And you got a great name. I love it! I'm Maisy, and you're Mya. M and M."

Her guard seems to be down now, and she laughs.

"Have you had M&M's before?"

She nods.

"I love M&M's, the peanut butter ones especially." I rub my tummy. Although if I'm honest, I can't stand to think about food right now.

She shakes her head, becoming serious again.

"What, are you allergic to peanut butter?"

Her eyes widen and she nods again.

"That's okay." I scrunch up my nose. "You're not missing much. It's just peanuts wrapped in some artificially colored candy. Meh." I try to play down how amazing M&M's actually are, but she must see through me because she laughs again.

"Mya! Mya! Where are you?" a voice is calling. Mya looks at the door.

"Who's that? Who's calling you?" I ask.

Mya just looks away and crosses her arms over her chest. Her face goes back to being vacant. *Poor child. She reminds me of Rosey.*

Someone knocks softly on the door, and I know it's the woman who's been calling Mya.

"Come in!"

Lisa, the woman who I saw earlier, is standing in the doorway, and on sight of Mya she runs to her. "I'm so sorry, she's shouldn't have come here. She's never like this."

"It's not a problem. We had a chat, she's lovely."

Shock fills Lisa's face. "What?"

"Um, I'm sorry," I say defensively. "I didn't know I wasn't supposed to talk to her."

"You *talked* to her?"

"Sort of. She told me her name's Mya, she's five years old, and she's allergic to peanuts. I think that's not so bad." I wink at Mya.

"But, how? She hasn't spoken a word for nine months, since Christmas." The woman reaches for my hand and shakes it. "I'm Orion's sister. I'm sorry about earlier. Orion's very particular about who I talk to and can or cannot see. Please forgive me, and him. He's only trying to do what's best for me. And you, I'm sure."

His sister, Lisa Carte. I remember. "Yeah, he's a little OTT," I scoff.

"Mya, say something, sweetheart." Lisa strokes Mya's face. "You talked to Maisy here a moment ago. Why won't you talk to your mom?"

"Um, she didn't actually say anything out loud," I admit. "We played games and she participated." I look at Mya and smile. Her eyes smile back at me.

Lisa evidently notices. "She's never been like this with anyone. I guess you're special to have Mya talk to you."

"Nah, she only played my games. It was fun, right, Mya?" I playfully pinch her arm and she gives me a shy smile.

Lisa's eyes well up. "I haven't seen my child smile for such a long time. You don't understand what this means to me. Thank you! Thank you so much!" She lunges for me and gives me a big, crushing hug. I'm not sure what to do so I just sit there in her embrace, looking at Mya and rolling my eyes jokingly. Mya continues to grin at me.

The last person who hugged me like this was my mother, ten years ago. I don't know how to react. I'm detached, and impassive. Because if I give in, I'll be crying for hours.

"My hair's wet, you'll get soaked," is the only thing I can think of to say as she holds my towel-encased body and the water from my thick curls drips onto her clothes.

"I'm sorry, I'm always emotional." She pulls back and glances at her wet top, then at my hair. "You have beautiful hair. Trust me, I'm a hairdresser."

I get excited. "Then you must have a hairdryer lying around somewhere? Actually, would you mind cutting my hair, maybe? Nothing fancy, just up to my shoulders. It's too long and I'm trying to change my look, if you know what I mean."

"What do you think, Mya? Should I cut her hair?" she asks her daughter. Mya's face remains blank, but she nods. Lisa starts crying and embraces her. "Then I will, sweetheart. I'll give Maisy the best haircut there is." She peels herself away from Mya and sniffles. "But first, you're going back to your room. And promise me you won't go out again."

Mya silently gets off the bed and starts walking to the door.

"See you soon, Mya," I say softly.

She turns to me and opens her hand as if to wave, but without raising it at all. I spot it, though.

"Um, Lisa, do you have an Advil, too? I have a terrible headache."

"Of course. I'll bring it over later."

CHAPTER 8

ORION

I'm late. If any of these fuckers in here mention anything, I'll kill them on the spot. Pain rattles around my skull, both from the champagne, and from being reckless with everyone's lives.

I've been late only once–when I had to deal with the murder of Lisa's husband–but everyone knew about that. When someone's late and there isn't a known reason, people start talking. *They better not say a word.*

I keep the agenda short, let people talk quickly, and we focus on the matter at hand: the Slavs. They're a continuous headache to me. To us. Milan suspects me of foul play with his wife, but he can't prove that Camila actually came to my house that night and attended the meeting. Lucky for me, she had a mind of her own and he knows that. We took her back at La Toya's within half an hour and set it up so it looked like she was banging her bodyguard when they were killed. And with the Slavs not knowing Milan was to meet me, I'm in the clear. Still, they continue to leave their shit in our backyard, which takes me weeks to clear with the cops. I bet it's done on purpose, but I also have a feeling that someone on the inside's helping them.

I scrutinize everyone at the table, one by one, while playing with the tumbler of whiskey in my hand. My hangover is from the champagne, not the whiskey, which right now I need like water. *Anyone* in here could be a snitch. And they'd kill me in a flash only to take my place. They all respected my father, Willer Carte–or as they knew him, Willer A La Carte. He got his nickname from allowing people to choose how they died. But he's fucking dead now, and no one gave him the option to choose his own death. Fucking cancer.

Jonah jerks me out of my hangover fog. "Orion, I think we're done."

"And you're all still here? Get to work, fuckers!" I snarl.

It takes twenty minutes to walk from the club to my house, and instead of taking the car, I decide to go on foot. I need to clear my head. I notice Jonah following me from a distance, smoking as he does, but he doesn't bridge the gap between us. The fucker wants me to get inside my house before talking to me.

I reach my door and turn, staring at him as he draws near. I'd rather not have anyone in my house right now. I want to check in with Maisy, since I left her in tears. Something I often do with her. "Did you want something, Jonah?"

"Yeah." Jonah nods at my house. "Do you mind if we go inside?"

I groan, exasperated. "Make it quick, I'm busy."

I enter and he follows. We head straight for the kitchen, where Leila's cleaning up.

"What the hell happened in here?" Jonah's barbed voice is riling me.

"None of your fucking business. Now, what do you want?"

"You know, you've been very guarded lately. Your mind's in a different place, and everyone's noticed. I see the kitchen in a mess, you're not letting me in, a few weeks ago you freaked out when I went upstairs... It's as if you're hiding someone." He narrows his eyes at me. "Someone that shouldn't be here."

He did not just say that. I march across the room and tower over him. He's bold, I'll give him that, because the fucker stares right back at me, defiant.

"Fuck. You," I bark.

"Why don't I just go upstairs now and see if anyone's in?" he counters.

Rage unlike anything I've ever felt floods me. "Do that and you're a dead man walking, I promise you."

Garry, our youngest member who's barely over eighteen, walks in. *The fuck?! Since when is my house open to everyone?*

Lucky for him, he's new, and doesn't know the rules yet. I should lock that damn door, though.

Seeing Garry in my house seems to encourage Jonah, who starts walking backward toward the kitchen door. He must stupidly think I won't shoot him.

Garry looks confused. "What the hell's going on?"

Jonah turns and runs upstairs, and I follow. He heads straight to Maisy's bedroom. I want to catch him up and smash his head in, but no matter what happens, I'm the one with the power here. As such, I must be composed. I know that much. He'll pay later, anyway.

He enters her room and a few moments later I stroll up to the open door. He's making apologetic noises and raising his hands, protecting himself from the angry words and blows of my sister, who's hitting him and yelling.

"You fucking *idiot*, Jonah! Did you think you could just get in my bed and fuck me?" She kicks him, right in the balls. "Has my brother not done enough for you?"

That must've hurt. I laugh to myself.

"Arghh! I'm *so* sorry, Lisa, no... I mean, I didn't know you were using this room. I'm sorry." He tries to dodge her next hit, but no one can escape Lisa when she's in a fury. Even I couldn't when I was young. When she's mad about something, everyone takes cover. Jonah should know that. He's been around my family for years.

"Get out! *OUT!*" she yells, pointing to the door.

He's holding his crotch as he limps past me. Garry has appeared and helps him get back to the stairs.

That kick to the balls was what he deserved. And not enough.

"I see you don't need any help, sis," I say, but as I go to close the door, she points to the bathroom.

"She's in there," she mouths.

I nod, appreciative. Though she didn't listen to my order in the first place, seeing that she saved Maisy, I won't say a thing. She never listens to my orders anyway. That's why I made her say it earlier, but what was the point? She's as stubborn as my father was.

I walk downstairs, trying to decide Jonah's fate. He's had his run with the Cartes. He can go and fuck himself wherever he wants now.

Growing more enraged, I stride quickly to where he's sitting in the kitchen. I pull out my Colt, twist the silencer on and press the cold barrel to his forehead. I unlock the gun, and there it is: the crying, and the begging.

"Get up and go," I snarl.

"Don't kill me, please. I'm going, here. Please. Don't kill me." He backs out of my house onto the street. I stay right with him, my index finger on the trigger and the barrel stuck to his head.

"Run, Jonah."

Jonah starts running, and I know he's heading straight for the club. Great. I bet he'll wait for me there, with enough supporters to stand against me. *Let's see who wants to die today.*

I get back to the club in no time. There are few people standing outside, their eyes cautiously following me as I march in with the gun in my hand.

"Why did you come here, Jonah?" I yell. "When I said run, I meant anywhere but here. There's nothing left for you with the Cartes anymore!"

Jonah pops up from where he was crouching behind a table. "Don't do this to me, please, O-Ryon... The Cartes are my life, I served your father. He respected me!"

I can tell from his eyes, he knows death draws nearer for him.

Lucky for me, the boxing club is nearly empty this time in the morning, but even so, the few familiar faces that happen to be in here, hold their breath. The club is where we meet, drink, or fuck. We get rid of our differences in the ring. Not with guns. That's my one rule. But here I am, aiming my Colt directly at this asshole in front of me.

They all know me. They know what I'm capable of doing. As much as I want to stop the bloodshed, he went over my head and intruded on the one thing I never give out for free: access to my personal life.

Outside the back exit, he trips and falls backward.

"Run."

"Please don't kill me, please. I'll run, but–"

"Three – two – one."

He finally sees the depth of shit he's in and starts running for his life. Of course, he's not fucking getting away–the rage inside me will only be tamed when I pull the trigger of my trusted Colt. I aim for his kneecap and fire. He screams and falls.

"Get out of here you piece of shit! I don't want you disturbing the neighbors!" I yell as he drags himself out of my sight.

I go back inside and everyone exhales the breath they were holding.

Garry's already arrived and is fidgeting at the bar. A whiskey tumbler rests next to him and he offers it to me. He knows what calms my nerves. He's lucky he's a fast learner.

~

For the few days after the shooting, I was pestered constantly about the reason why Jonah was banished. If he was a snitch, I should've killed him, so everyone wondered why I left him alive, but few dared to ask me.

It was simple. I never trusted him. The moment I questioned him about Sigrun, he showed his real face. I knew he was lying to me, but his involvement in the murder of my sister's husband, Tom, was what triggered me in the first place. Things that Maisy mentioned.

Shooting him was not the best decision I've made, I know. Him running to Maisy's room triggered my rage, and therefore, my decision was made by my cock. Nobody is to mess with my girl. Even now I feel it in my body, that protectiveness that will never cease to exist with Maisy around. She's like my drug, and I'm a fool for thinking I have control. I don't. It just takes longer for someone to get to me.

In any case, I've messed up. Now I'm a bigger target than before. People talk, and I see more of them coming to the club. Every night in the last three nights, my dozens of surveillance screens stare back at me, showing me at least a hundred people in the club at a time, instead of the usual twenty. It's good for business, they say. But something's going on. Someone's leading this coup and I'm going to find out who. And with too many people at the top of my street, it's too risky for Kai or Logan to come to my house. We talked, they wanted to come see Maisy, but I don't want to draw any attention to her at all.

Last time I saw her, I yelled at her to go to her room. If my sister wasn't around, maybe all of this would've been over by now, but she was and she saved Maisy. Out of the three of us, Lisa saved the day. Go figure.

I thought of apologizing to Maisy, but to what end? I'd do the same thing again if I had to. We were drinking, not thinking of the consequences. And there's always a consequence to any action we take. And so I stay in my office, working until late.

My phone constantly rings. For some reason, there's shit happening at every location where we have people working. There's a snitch inside the Cartes and

I've got to figure out who that is before they cause any more damage.

~

A light knock on the door of my bedroom disturbs me. I look up, already vexed. Today it's only Maisy and me at home, although most days Lisa and Mya stay with us too. When there's something happening, I want them in the safest place, which is here.

If that's Maisy, and by the sound of it, it is, why the fuck is she here? But I cannot take enough precautions. I pull my gun and point it at the door.

"Come in."

The handle jerks down and Maisy pushes the door slowly ajar, her heavenly body revealed with the dark hallway behind her. She's in her panties and cami top, nothing new there. But she looks different. High heels. *She's wearing high heels.* As if my cock wasn't twitching enough, now I have an instant semi.

"Maisy." I suck in a breath, searching for words. Her hair's different too, shoulder-length, with hazel highlights among the dark. It looks like even the sun wants to play with her. "You should know better than coming here."

"I haven't seen Kai and Logan in a while, and you, you yelled at me last time I saw you, said I'm nobody, and you're always working and, I'm bored. You said I'm supposed to help you but you're not using me at all. I'm not used to not doing anything."

I push my leather chair back with my legs and stand abruptly from my desk. The screech visibly startles her. "Have you thought about *why* I'm not coming to see you?"

She shrugs. "I fucked everything up for you."

She's regarding me with those dark eyes; if only she knew how she affects me. I went out of my way for her sweet pussy–even saw my doctor and got myself checked out for her. And she thinks I can't stand her?

"Maybe I'll go." She turns her back on me and now, I truly see her.

Her shorter hair, revealing her elegant shoulders; her perfect round ass; her legs, elongated by the heels.

I will fucking fuck her until she can't walk in those shoes.

"Is that why you put those heels on?" She stops. *She better*. "To come and tell me you're bored? And then go? Who gave you the heels, anyway?"

She looks back at me with a sneaky smile, her eyes sparkling. "Your sister."

I saunter over to where she's standing and curl my hand around her waist, pulling her to me. I move a few strands of hair, revealing her shoulder, and nuzzle my face into her neck. My eyes drop shut and I breathe in her scent. That scent is enough to give me life for the next hundred years. My hand moves up to encircle her neck, gently, but with intent. The slight pressure is enough to compel her, and when I finally meet her eyes, though she continues to look at me boldly, the profound desire inside them makes me want to keep her forever.

"I haven't given you shoes on purpose. I don't want you to leave this house."

"I wasn't going to leave."

I take her with me a few steps and rotate her around so her butt is pressing against my desk. "You're damn right about that. But did you think you'd come wearing heels to my office and get me to fuck you?"

"The thought had crossed my mind," she purrs.

I hook my fingers around the band of her panties on either side of her hips, lowering myself to a crouch as I slide them down.

She lifts one foot, then the other to remove them.

"I know what my little slut wants," I whisper against her skin, and pepper her thighs with kisses, skipping her pubic area as I rise back up.

Immersed in her body, I lock eyes with her as my hands glide over her shoulders, thumbs hooking into the straps of her cami–taking them partly down, but not fully. I love to see my girl uninhibited and needy.

"Sit down, slut."

She takes a small step back and sits on my desk. Her pussy's on heat, her nipples hard, and my cock's bursting out of my pants.

"Lie back, put your heels on the desk." She follows my orders. "Yes, just like that."

Fuck! It's a sight I'll want to remember. I pull my cell from my pants and take a photo. For a moment, I see the alarm in her eyes. "Don't worry. It's for Kai and Logan. I want them to know what they're missing."

I put my cell away and unbutton my pants. My cock springs out; he sensed Maisy was in the room with me and has been fighting for his freedom since she appeared.

I stand between her legs. "Are you ready, Maisy?" She thought she was coming here to play with *me*, and I cannot let her have it her way. I pump myself a few times before teasing her slit with my piercing.

"Um, we're not using condoms?"

"Not anymore, darling." I move up and down with the glans, making her arousal gush. The temptation is real. I just want to fuck her.

She tips her head back and moans, rolling her hips down, trying to engulf my cock, but I don't let her. I just stand here, playing with her silky folds, sliding my piercing up and down and over her clit.

Her hips buck. "Orion, *please...*"

"You want me? You do?" I rasp. I remain at her entrance, teasing her with the head, and then repeat, going up the whole length, up to her clit and down, then pump my cock. Fuck, her cunt's so sweet.

I press my glans against her ass and her heels lift off the table, her knees coming close to her head, giving me full access. *Sweet little whore. She'll do anything to get my cock in her.*

I pull away and relish her yelp of frustration. "Nuh-uh, heels on the table."

She goes back to the same position and this time, she slides down on me. With her arousal dripping, my cock is practically tricked into it. Fuck, she's got a cunning little pussy.

"Orion, please," she purrs again.

She reaches for my cock, but seeing all the juices between her legs, she seems to decide it'll be much easier for her to get herself off. And that's what she starts to do. Yes, that's what I want to see. Another fucking sight I never want to forget.

I reach for my cell, take the photo, and put it back again. "You're so wet, darling."

She makes another frustrated noise, pinching her nipples as she chases her high. I could easily slam my dick into her and fuck her to oblivion, but this is much more fun. Did she think she'd come here for a fuck, and I'd just serve it up to her? Ha! She'll have to work for it.

"You want to cum, Maisy?"

She mutters something, whimpers, and I see her just about reaching orgasm, climaxing. I move her hand from her cunt and put my cock under her fingers, leaving it to her to decide which road she'll take. I groan as she starts pumping me but she isn't giving up, and tries to push my cock inside her. "Let me," she whispers.

When I don't let her, she whines and starts rubbing herself again, so I move her fingers from her clit with my piercing. I offer the head to her and she bucks as I rub my cock against her swollen clit, which practically makes me cum.

I feel my balls tightening so I step back for a second. "Fuck, you're making me feel so good. No one makes me feel this fucking good, slut."

She moans again. Her frustration at not knowing what's coming next is evident. I will not waste any more of her juice. I push open her thighs, kneel down, and dive in; my tongue, like a swirling torrent, enters her cunt and I literally bite into her. I suck at her silky folds, lapping up everything she has to give me.

"*Orion!*" she screams, her orgasm crashing down on her.

I hook two fingers inside and finger-fuck her as I suck her nub, enjoying her whimpers and the sight of her lost, floating. With my other hand I take the arousal from between her legs and rub her ass, then push my finger inside. "Let that whore come out and play."

I live for this moment, when she's bucking, wild, her soul exposed as I finger-fuck her in her cunt and ass and suck her clit. She grips my head, screaming and jerking while I suck every last drop of her cum.

Her whole body shakes as small, broken sounds leave her lips. Coming down from such a high takes time. I stand up and pull her in for a kiss. Her mouth needs consuming. She's limp, her legs hanging off the desk, her arms still weak from her orgasm.

"We're not done yet, darling. Heels back on the desk." I help her lift her feet back up, and her glistening pussy is calling my name again. I brush two fingers around her entrance and continue down to her ass. She takes it, and even tries to push down on my fingers.

I take my hard-as-steel cock and push in, my piercing rimming her slowly. She moans and I try again, and again; each time she allows me to go deeper, gushing so much from arousal that it drips to just the right place, soaking me as I stretch her. Her ass is going to be the death of me. She's bravely taking me inch by inch, and she gets to halfway when I see the whore coming out to play again. Her pupils dilate, her nails claw at my arms and her long, whining moans make me slide the rest of my cock in with ease until I'm balls-deep.

"There you go, slut... I own your ass now!"

I grab her ankles, lift them up, and start pumping her deep, hard, letting out a grunt each time I do. *Fuck, this little slut is gonna make me cum so fast.*

She's rubbing herself as I slam into her, gasping like she's flying up to cloud nine, right where I am. "I want you to cum inside me," she breathes.

"How much do you want my cum, slut?"

"A lot."

"Do you crave it?"

"Yes–I do–I want it," she stutters between thrusts.

"Do you dream about it?"

"Every day. I haven't stopped thinking about your cum," she whimpers. She's starting to come undone. Her whole body's vibrating.

"Your sweet fucking ass squeezes me so good." Electrifying, staccato moans fall from her lips and I increase the pace. Her back arches and her head falls back.

But she's not getting my cum today. "Maybe another time."

I withdraw as I speak and, untouched, my cock spurts. I look at it glistening, hard, the veins pumping as the first rope shoots across the middle of her stomach. The second and third land at the crack of her cunt, dribbling down her gaping entrance and over her ass.

I growl, long, loud, animalistic. Still gripping her ankles. "Fuck... I want you to be my slut all day every day, Maisy."

"I want that too," she purrs.

I button up my pants and go to the other side of the desk to lean down to her gorgeous face. Her hair's stuck to her sweaty forehead. She's the epitome of a muse.

"You did good today, coming here with the heels on." I kiss her. "But make sure you leave them on my desk when you go."

Maisy cups my face, holding my gaze in her bottomless eyes, pleadingly. "I want your cum..." She takes one of the sperm ropes from her stomach and licks her fingers. "...inside me."

"Maybe one day. You'll have to keep coming 'til then."

She grins, flashing her teeth at me. I sit back in my chair and look at mess I made of my paperwork. I cannot think straight with her here, she's such a distraction.

She props herself up on her elbows to regard me. "Shall I go?"

"Yeah. I'm busy."

She gets off the desk and picks up her panties. Puts them on and heads for the door.

“Aren’t you forgetting something?”

She stops, takes off her heels, and drops them on my desk.

CHAPTER 9

KAI

I haven't seen Maisy since the day we killed Zed and I miss her like crazy. I find myself grinding my teeth when she gets in my head. I just want to sink my cock, inch by inch, into that sweet little ass of hers and pound her indefinitely. This obsession I have with her is the one thing that keeps me sane in my world.

Killing has never been easier for me, especially killing the people who messed with my girl. That day was fucked up. A true challenge, I might say. We expected five people tops, but there were more than twenty in Zed's pissy apartment. All men, armed and ready for a fight. They were expecting someone, that was obvious. The firearms they had were out of their league; they clearly didn't know how to use them, but thanks to my four-finger metal ring I put quite a few to sleep before they could even find the unlocking clips on their guns.

Storming in wearing balaclavas, we annihilated everyone in there. This could never be traced back to us. Of course, Logan wanted to snap Zed's balls off, but we managed to pull him away. He's extremely persistent if he sets his mind to something, so we watched him like hawks all night.

And today, again, the killing never seems to stop where I am. I've been up from four in the morning, going through my books. Something's not adding up–either people stopped buying guns, or someone's stealing money. And I know it's not the former. The signature of Rocco, my number two who's in charge of the cash, has been showing up on each slip with the money missing. Coincidence? I know it's not. And if that wasn't enough to get me angry, I was called by Dewei as a backup to help him with some personal shit. Some ex-boyfriend's back and he's not liking it. The *fuck!* That personal shit nearly killed us. If I hadn't had my right hook ready, that animal would've torn my body in half with his sawed-off shotgun. I smashed his face to a pulp, then shot him. At that moment of life or death, all I had in my head was this craving for Maisy. As if nothing else mattered but her.

But we had to put her through shit to see if she was lying. It turns out she both was and wasn't. That's the moment we entered the gray area. We've avoided gray areas all our lives, and now, none of us have the guts to end it. Being among the three most dangerous mafia heads didn't scare her. She stood up for herself. She keeps doing that.

So I'm going to help her. Fuck Orion and fuck Logan. I don't want her to suffer. I want to help her, and I want her to stay. I want to see if she'll stick around once she's done with us.

I spend my time riding with Rocco, Dewei, and Buzz, talking about Camila's death, the wanted girl (Maisy), and the sales of our guns that are going down, and I think I got a lead. Someone said they saw Camila at the studio close to my club a while back. If she produced Maisy's video in there, then that's where Maisy and I are going. That's the quickest and easiest way to go about it. If the studio has Maisy's video, they'll recognize her and then I'd make sure she gets it. One way or another.

Maisy. I haven't seen her in close to a week and I want nothing more than to have her on the backseat of my BMW K1600. I'm sure she'd be willing. I even got a helmet for her. If I really think about it, this would be good for Maisy's wellbeing. Both Orion and Logan would agree. They'll do everything to keep her comfortable. Saying that, I've been calling Orion all day, and he's not answering his cell.

I rev my bike once as I approach his house, wary of my surroundings. I've done this so many times, but one can't be too careful. Revving could cause problems, but at least I'll have time to speed off.

The way is clear and I park my bike under the shrubs, remove my helmet, and climb up to the window. Maisy's in bed, in her cami top and panties, watching TV. What a sight to behold. I could sit here and watch her for hours.

She jumps when I knock on the window. Seeing it's me, she immediately relaxes and smiles. My baby girl's had a haircut, and I'm smitten. The shoulder-length hair suits her so well, and highlights, too. She's never been more of a woman in my eyes than she is now. I'm overwhelmed by my desire to claim that barely-clothed body of hers. That face. That child-like smile that's mine, right now.

She opens the window and I'm still looking at her in awe. "Come in, someone might see you," she purrs.

I jump inside and immediately touch her hair. "Wow." I cannot stop myself from sounding like a teenager, when only a few hours ago I smashed in someone's skull. I was feared. I was ruthless.

"You like it?"

"Well, I didn't know you could look more beautiful than before, which leads me to believe that men would ogle you even more now, so I'm not sure."

"It's only you three that look at me. I haven't seen another living soul for quite some time." She takes a deep breath. "Kai, I know I messed up by not telling you everything about–"

"It's fine. You didn't mess up. I got you." I'm not going to let her apologize to me for having a fucked-up life. She did lie to us, though. *Why am I willing to look the other way for her, but would skin anyone else alive?*

"I didn't lie to you, I just didn't–"

I stop her again. "Don't apologize."

Impatient, I press my lips to hers and she offers me a sweet, long, unhurried kiss. I pull her body close to mine, and as I kiss her, she moans into my mouth. Her delicate fingers run through my hair, then down over my pecs and around to the back. She grabs my ass and pulls me closer.

"Kai, I missed you so much," she mumbles, sucking on my bottom lip.

This is all I need. I peel off my leather jacket and pick her up in my arms. She wraps her legs around my waist as I pin her against the wall. My cock is rock-hard, having cried for her every day, and now, as I grind into her panties, her body sandwiched between the wall and me is mine to do what I wish with.

I'm devouring her mouth as I unbutton my jeans and free up my cock. I fist it a few times and rub it against her panties. Without a moment to waste, her arms are over my shoulders and on my back, clawing with her nails, pulling my body close to hers with urgency, and she moans again into my mouth.

I hook my fingers into her panties and rip them, my cock finding her opening easy as I run it up and down her slit, and I edge inside her, an inch at a time as she moans. I know my baby girl wants me in one go, and I groan, lifting her by the butt cheeks and stretching her as she takes me. Her sweet pussy is so tight, she'll make me cum before I want to, so I don't give her any time to adjust to me and spear her fully.

"Take-every-inch-of-me," I growl, like an animal.

Using the wall for leverage, I begin to pound into her, hard, fast, feral. Wordless grunts tear from her throat as I slam into her, intent on expelling all the air from her lungs. Each thrust into her cunt is rough, ruthless. I will wait no more; she's here, she's mine. Too soon her grunts become staccato as I pace myself to her rhythm, but it's too late for me. She's milking me with her screams.

"Kai! Oh my God, *Kai!*" She unravels under my body and I lower my head to her shoulder, releasing a loud, guttural groan as my seed empties into her and her cum gushes down my cock.

"I needed you just like this. Hard, raw, and wet," I mumble against her lips before kissing her.

Out of breath, still panting, she grins. "That-was-the-*best!*"

I lift her up and slowly slide my cock out of her, then lower her down.

She passes me a tissue. "Here."

"I don't need one." I wink at her and button up my jeans. "I love your cum on me."

"Me too," she chuckles, and sweetly presses her lips to mine, humming against my mouth.

She turns and opens the closet, pulling out a new pair of panties that she puts on as I wrap my arms around her body from behind and kiss her neck. She leans into me, and our eyes land on our reflection in the mirror.

"You're beautiful, Maisy Roy."

She turns back around, her head burrowing into my neck. "Kai, you make me feel like a giddy teenager."

I see something on the side of her face in the mirror, and nudge her away from me. "What's this?" I pinch her chin and turn her face sideways, revealing a yellow-colored bruise above her cheek.

"Orion–"

"*Orion* did this?" He *said* he wouldn't go all the way with Maisy. "The fucker!"

"Kai, I'm okay. It was an accident."

"An accident? Huh!" I'm annoyed, but all I can do is rake my hands through my hair.

"He thought I was someone else, so he slammed his bathroom door in my face."

"His bathroom door, as in inside his bedroom? He took you there?" I knew it. *I knew it.*

"No. I went there to wish him goodnight."

"And? Did you see, um, his room?"

"Yes," she giggles, which reassures me. "I saw the cross. It's okay. I'm okay. He didn't hurt me, I promise."

I look at this woman and I want to grab her and run away with her to a different world. One where all of us live our lives like gods, enjoying her body.

If the cross didn't scare her, we have her for good. Not everyone can handle Orion's intensity. Yet she laughed about it. Maybe Orion's met his match.

"Still, that doesn't mean I'm not mad."

"I'm sorry," she purrs.

"I think I should be apologizing to *you* for not taking you out of here sooner." I wink at her. "How about we go for a ride?"

Her eyebrows shoot up. "A ride? Where?"

"There's a studio I want to check out for your video recording. After that, we'll go for a ride with no destination. How does that sound, baby girl?"

Concern settles over her face. "Does Orion know?"

"Don't worry. I left a message for him."

She grins. "I'd do anything to get out of this house and smell the fresh air."

"Good. Get dressed." I slap her ass. "There's nothing quite like riding a motorbike. Your legs wrapped around me, your body pressed against mine, your hands holding onto me. Fuck, I'm going to have to fuck you again if you don't hurry!"

Maisy rummages through her clothes, pulls out a t-shirt and jeans, and gets dressed. She looks at her feet and sadness clouds her face. "I have no shoes."

"It's not a problem, we'll get you some on the way."

"What about people seeing my face?"

"You'll have your helmet on, plus you have a new haircut now, so I wouldn't worry that much."

MAISY

I cannot contain my excitement as we walk out through the front door. I turn back to see it closing behind me. To see how it feels. I've been cooped up in Orion's house for so long that it's strange to be leaving it. Orion doesn't want me going out, but if Kai's found a studio that may have what I'm looking for, then we're going there.

Behind the shrubs, Kai pulls open a curtain of greenery, showing off his bike like it's on the red carpet or something. His chest puffs up with pride as he regards me.

"I love it!" I exclaim.

Immediately, I'm handed a helmet. "This is yours."

I try to make sense of it and he's more than happy to assist. "Here, let me help you." He neatly tucks my hair beneath it. "Who cut your hair?"

"Lisa. Orion's sister. She's lovely."

"Shame about the kid, though," Kai mutters. "She witnessed her father's murder and hasn't spoken a word since."

Little Mya's communication, or lack of it, makes sense now. She's been through hell, having looked in the eyes of a murderer and survived. That could be worse than dying, having to deal with the fear and terror after the fact. No wonder she's so withdrawn.

My head's now snug inside the helmet, and he taps the top. "There. You're ready."

"And they couldn't find the killer?"

"They will. Trust me."

Kai's fixing his riding gear as I observe him. He looks vicious, intense, macho, but deep down, he's really a sensitive guy. I know this because when I'm with him, he knows what I want. No other man has ever been able to read my wants. Not Orion, or Logan. They're special to me in a different way.

"Kai, why haven't you asked me yet what Milan has on you?"

He shrugs. "If you know something, I know you'll tell me."

I roll my eyes theatrically and raise my voice inside the helmet. "I have a lot of information in my head, but I can only recall it if you ask me specific stuff, otherwise my head's like an encyclopedia of relevant and irrelevant information."

He fits his own helmet on and reaches to press something on the side of mine, then does the same to his own. "Now you don't have to shout." His voice is coming from inside my helmet.

"Wait, you can pair our helmets?"

"I just did." He laughs. "You could tell me what you know about my father's death. He died two years ago in a car accident. Mickey Delgado was his name. He was on his way to meet me when the brakes gave out and his car crashed at 150 miles an hour."

I look inward, through the scramble of words and images I get in my head when I'm searching for something. "I remember seeing a newspaper clipping of his last photo, taken on October 5th, just before he got in the car. He had a lot of journalists tailing him, right?"

"The fuckers. Half of them were on the force. They wanted to get something on him."

"Yeah, then that's not important information. You would've known if anything was amiss by now," I tell him. "Okay, let me think. I read seven or eight emails in a thread between Milan and a woman from later that day. Her email handle was 'shedevil6,' so I assume it was a woman. She was upset that your father died. In one of her emails she wrote 'I never meant for this to happen' and Milan wrote back, saying 'Well you have, and you did. This is now your shit. You stepped in it, and you'll be smelling it for the rest of your life.'"

"Did Milan order the hit?"

"I don't know. She sounded like she made a mistake and was asking for advice."

"So, the woman killed my father? You mean to tell me this was a spat with one of his hookers? And what the fuck does Milan have to do with it?" Kai mounts the bike and gestures with his head for me to follow.

"I don't know." Climbing behind him on the bike, I lean in and wrap my arms around him. There's a big protrusion at his back that jabs into my stomach. "What do you have here?" I lift his leather jacket and see a gun tucked into his jeans.

"Let me move it." He immediately takes it and places it in a compartment at the front. "Now you can get closer," he chuckles, and lowers my visor.

My body is glued to his torso even before the bike's revved up. In jeans, with a black t-shirt stretched over his pecs and abs, and a leather jacket on top, he's such a sight. Too sexy if you ask me, when he's in full control, straddling this monster of a bike.

My eyes drift down to the ground, where I spot a dark liquid under the bike. "Hey." I point it out with my index finger. "I think your bike's leaking."

"Don't worry about it, baby girl." He closes his visor and laughs. "You'd be leaking too if I rode you this hard."

I don't have time to respond. I'm not prepared for the sound his motorbike makes when he ignites it, and it shakes me to my core. With a loud blast, we thunder off.

Our ride starts with the sun shining on us, but it gradually disappears behind some gray storm clouds. After the cold wind has been washing over my body for a while, I begin to shake. I wish I had more clothes on.

"I'm cold, Kai." I try to mold my body against his and take some of his heat.

We stop at the traffic lights and without a word, he gets off the bike, takes off his leather jacket, and gives it to me. I don't complain. I just try to relax my jaw and stop my teeth from chattering.

"Better?"

I nod. His jacket is big, heavy, warm, and smells of him.

He hops on the bike again and we ride for another twenty minutes through the streets of NY. What a feeling it is to be out, and free. Kai nods to at least five people on our journey. They must recognize him by the tattooed arms and bike, but nobody knows me. The joy of being invisible.

After a while we slow down, I presume because we've reached our destination, just outside an old building in a rundown area of town. It has one metal door with a sign that reads 'Studio' hanging above it, the opening hours written underneath.

Kai turns to me. "Shall we wait a half hour for it to open, or shall I just go in now?"

He's waiting on my response, but his cell on the handlebars is flashing repeatedly with a message.

I point to it. "Your cell."

He leans forward and reads it, then checks the time. "Let's wait for them to open. I have enough time to sort this out." He does a U-turn and we zoom off.

"Where're we going?" I shout.

"My club. Don't worry, it's gonna be fine. Nobody'll know we're there."

My heart's in my throat as we drive through the wide entrance. Bikers are all over the place, most of them tinkering with their own bikes. Some are listening to music, some smoking dope, some just lying there with a girl next to them. Nobody really pays any attention to us. *Maybe this will be fine, as Kai says.*

At the far end is a swinging door where people are coming in and going out, and as they do a bar inside is revealed, where everyone seems to be enjoying themselves, even at this time of the day. We pull up at the opposite end, away from the bar and next to an office. A tall, lanky man sees us through the glass and comes out. His nose is crooked and his tiny, squinty eyes are too close together. He's unsettling.

Kai parks the bike but leaves the motor running.

"Stay here, I'll be right out." He's talking to me without looking at me, scoping out the place instead. He gets off the bike and heads toward the office. "What's so urgent that you needed me back right now, Rocco?"

He's gone, and I'm left alone, sitting barefoot on his bike. What was I thinking? Staying out for even one minute could take me back to square one. Kai did not think this through. *Is anyone looking at me? Fuck.* Anyway. I look different now. Just as I try to steel myself and say 'fuck them' in my head, a tap on my shoulder startles me.

"Hey, what's up?"

I turn to see a petite girl with short blonde hair and piercing, serpentine eyes. Her black vest reveals a lot of skin, covered in tattoos from her neck down to her arms. I can't see her legs as she's wearing greased-up jeans, but I'd bet the tattoos go along her whole body.

I pull my visor open and shrug. "Not much."

"That's Kai's jacket you're wearing, right? He rarely takes that thing off. It must be nasty on the inside."

"It's not, actually," I reply, and glance over to the office. Kai's sitting down with the man and talking.

"Where are your shoes?"

"I lost them."

"What are you, size seven? Here, have mine." She takes off her sneakers. They look too expensive and unique for anyone to part with: red-and-white striped, with a strange insignia hand-stitched on them.

"A-are you sure?" *She's a lifesaver.* We don't have to stop to buy shoes anymore.

"Of course, I got plenty." She too looks over at the office. "What's Kai doing? Working?"

"Yeah."

"And you? All alone here? Come with me. And take your helmet off, I'm sure everyone'll want to meet you."

"Um, I was told to stay here, actually. I'm sorry."

"Oh, come on. Kai's not gonna be back for a while. He probably told you to stay here and he'll 'be right out.' Well, if you do, you'll end up waiting on him for hours. Trust me. I know."

That's what he said, exactly. If he's like that, what a prick. I remove my helmet slowly and observe her reaction. There is none. She's nonchalant, which puts me at ease. I place the helmet on the bike in front of me and lift my feet one after the other to put the sneakers on.

"I'd rather not go anywhere. Kai told me to wait for him here," I repeat. More for myself than for her.

"Don't worry. Let's grab a drink then come back here. I'd hate for you to be alone–there are pervs in the vicinity." She looks around at the few people who are staring at us. I wouldn't want to be near them either. "What's your name?"

"Um, Em." It's all I can think of on the spot. I should be playing defense, I know, but she seems such a sweet girl.

"Right then, Em, come on." She reaches out a hand to me.

I'll have to either take her hand now and get off the bike, or be rude and leave her hanging after she's given me her shoes and invited me for a drink. I throw one last glance at the office. Kai's in there by himself, deep in paperwork.

"I'm Natasha, by the way," she adds, and now I'll be borderline insulting her if I don't take her hand.

"Nice to meet you, Natasha." I shake her hand, and lean on her as I hop off the bike.

"Likewise."

Walking inside the bar makes me nauseous. My senses are attacked by the blaring music and the smell of alcohol. The place itself is not that big. There are wooden floors, with tables positioned in a random pattern. People probably just move them as they gather here. The bar's on the right side of the room, spanning the length of one wall, with two bartenders pouring drinks. The other side has the street entrance, but the tinted windows don't allow much natural light to come in.

"Listen up, everyone!" Natasha yells at the bikers in here. There are about twenty of them, most with a beer in their hand. "Kai's brought this lovely girl on his bike today!"

"Did he, now?" a sleazy, bearded older man jeers. He instantly gives me the creeps.

"Her name's Em. Shall we make her welcome?"

"Heyyy! To Em!" All of them cheer and raise their drinks.

This is a bit too much. I didn't expect it. I didn't even *want* it. Low-key, that's what this outing was supposed to be. And suddenly, it's not.

Natasha helps me take off Kai's jacket. "It's hot in here, you don't need this."

"Sure."

Those who didn't have drinks approach the bar, and the bartenders begin to pour like there's no tomorrow. Why's there a big deal about meeting me? And it's like there isn't any monetary system in place at all. It's a free-for-all.

Someone hands me a drink, a shot of something. "Here's one for you, Em!"

I'll have to drink this, even though I don't want to. "Cheers." I gulp it all down. Yuck. I *hate* vodka.

There are gathered around me now, and all of them want to clink my shot glass and drink with me.

For some reason, I'm hearing alarm bells. "Sorry, I can't drink this anymore."

Natasha laughs, then pinches my chin and opens my mouth while the bartender manages to pour more vodka down my throat before I pull away.

I manage to jerk out of her reach. "Hey, what the hell are you doing?" The alarm bells are in full siren mode now.

"You're gonna need it!" Natasha jeers, and pushes me into the crowd. My heart pumps erratically while the fear grows more potent. I lose my balance, and whoever I land on gropes my ass as they help me up.

I'm confused and shaking. *What the hell's going on?*

"You're gonna have so much fun, Em," a bearded man with no front teeth says mockingly, and grabs my boob.

"What the *fuck?!* Let go of me!"

Natasha saves me. "Dewei, keep your ugly hands to yourself." *Thank God.*

I think it's over, but then I hear her next sentence.

"Let's take off her t-shirt first."

My heart thumps in my chest and tears prick my eyes. I feel sick, like my head will explode from the tension. Here I am again, like a petrified deer surrounded by hyenas. I ran away to avoid this.

Someone behind me grabs the neck of my t-shirt and tears it in half. They all pull on both sides while I struggle to fight them off. I am left without a top on and I cover my breasts, frozen in fear.

"Check out her bazookas! Shotgun!"

People yell and jeer. I try to run away, but they've formed a circle around me and are pushing me from one person to another to do what they want with me. Fear coils tightly around me as I realize how useless I am, how powerless to fight back. *There are too many.*

"Let me go," I whimper as two girls grab my arms and lift me, while the man who was with Kai earlier hooks his filthy fingers into my jeans and panties and takes them off, even as I kick him.

"Make sure the sneakers stay on. It's my initiation gift to her!" Natasha yells.

Kai must be around. He must be close. "Kai! Help! Kai!" I scream gutturally. I'm not giving in, not today, not ever.

"Cover her mouth!"

A girl rips up a tablecloth and tries to tie it across my mouth. A few of them restrain me while I bite and kick, but I'm overpowered. The courage is sucked out of me like a vacuum when the girl headbutts me, incapacitating me for a moment, which gives them enough time to bend me over a table and tie my arms and legs to it. I choke on the terror penetrating every pore in my body at the horror I know is coming. “Please, God, I don’t want this, please, God, please,” I hear myself muttering.

“How many can your sweet little pussy take in one go, Em? I bet all of us!” someone behind me sneers. “We need someone at her head, to check her holes thoroughly if she wants to become one of us, right?”

Their words send chills down my spine. I hear laughter. Girls like me are *helping* them. They are pushing them into this, watching the show, seeing me helpless.

I’m tied to a table. Perhaps it would be best if I just closed my eyes, but I can’t. I look back once last time and raw panic sets in, my heart thundering. *This is it.* Everyone has undressed and they’re pumping their cocks. I give one last pull on the restraints, trying to tear my arms and legs free, shaking like a live wire.

I cry, I beg, and end on a sob. “Please, please... don’t.” My words don’t make sense. They come out unintelligible through the gag that was put on me.

“You knew our initiation rites. You got to be taken for a test drive by everyone in here, Em.” Natasha’s smug voice makes me sick. “Or maybe Kai forgot to tell you. Shame. Don’t worry, you’ll get over it. We all have.”

She nods at someone behind me and just as I feel his fingers dig into my ass cheeks, I hear a gunshot, followed by a thud on the floor.

I lift my head and look back. *Kai.* I start crying in relief, the sounds muffled by my gag. I want off this table.

He glares at everyone, crazed, a rabid dog. Totally unpredictable in his nature.

Panicked, hushed whispers rise from the group. They turn to each other with fearful eyes.

Natasha looks shaken. “Y-you killed Rocco.”

“Isn’t the rule, whoever brings a chick here gets to fuck her first?” Kai demands.

They're all silent. I'm crying. I don't want to be a part of this. I just want to go home.

"Right. So what the fuck d'you think you're doing to her?"

Silence.

"W-we thought you already fucked her."

"Everyone who touched her, step up." Kai's cold, calm voice is scaring even me. "If you groped my girl today, step *up!*"

A man steps forward.

"What did you do?"

"I grabbed her tits."

Kai points his gun at him and shoots him between the eyes. His body drops to the floor with a dull sound.

"He can't do that!" someone whispers.

"Who took off her t-shirt?"

"I did, but I didn't–"

BANG! Thud.

"And her jeans?"

Silence.

"Her. Jeans," Kai repeats.

I hear people stepping forward. Another two shots follow.

There's muttering behind me. "Someone should stop him."

"And finally, one last bullet for the person who brought her in here."

"Natasha! Natasha!" I yell through the gag, but the words don't come out clear.

I look at her. Everyone else does too. She's standing next to me, shaking, tears running down her cheeks.

"That was me, Kai."

Bitch. Kill her!

My cheek is pressed to the table, tears drenching my face, and I watch Kai raising his gun to her forehead and pressing the barrel between her eyebrows. *Shoot!*

But he doesn't. He hesitates. "This is it. I don't owe you anything anymore. We're even now."

He lowers his gun just as a loud spray of bullets shatters the windows and rains down on everyone.

While everyone takes cover, Kai starts untying me, but twenty men with balaclavas run in with baseball bats, smashing everything in their way, and Kai takes a hit. They run past me and the last one grabs me by the hair to look at my face, and, I'd recognize those eyes anywhere.

"Maisy!"

My replying cry is muffled, but he hears me. It's Orion.

He unties me, removes my gag, and lifts me into his arms while his people break and shoot everything in their way. I sob uncontrollably in his arms, clutching at him and wailing.

"I got you. It's okay." He takes me out and puts me inside a car. I don't let go of him. I'm hanging onto his neck, tightly, unable to stop crying.

"They were going to... They were going to..." I stutter.

"But they didn't."

My sobs become violent.

"It's okay. Shh, it's fine. I'm gonna fucking *kill* Kai when I see him," he mumbles.

I must've fallen asleep in his arms because I sense him peeling himself away from me, but I don't want to let go. I open my eyes to see we're in my bedroom.

"Let me remove these abominations of sneakers you got on." He unties my shoelaces. "Where did you find them? In the trash?"

"Someone gave them to me. She tricked me." I look at them, and an image suddenly unscrambles in my head. I remember something. I've seen them before. I reach out to take them, but Orion throws them behind him.

"Those sneakers, I think... I think I know who killed–" I start.

"I don't wanna hear it! Now, let me get you dressed, please."

I never get this with Orion. He's usually mad at me for something. Even now, he should be upset with me, but he's not. He puts panties and a cami top on me while I sniffle and watch him.

"There, your favorite outfit." He smiles sadly and strokes my face. "Why did you leave, Maisy?"

"We were going to a studio, a place that potentially could have my video recording," I tell him. "Kai thought if I went there they'd give it to me without hassle, and all this would be over." I wipe away the tears that are spilling over my lashes. "Also, he wanted to take me for a ride on his bike. I haven't been out, Orion."

"I want you to go out for a ride too, with Kai and Logan and me, but we can't do that right now."

He's right. They're looking after me, and they know best.

"Lie down next to me, please."

CHAPTER 10

ORION

It had to be done. I told the Cartes about Maisy, the wanted girl who was at the Delgados' club. She has too much information on Milan to let her go just like that. We had to get her, and I didn't have time to plan anything else considering I saw Kai's text when I did. At least he told me he's taking her. Getting there in the nick of time was pure luck.

She lies next to me, her small arms wrapped around my body and holding me close. My cock's twitching but right now she needs me protecting her, not fucking her.

Turmoil seems to be raging inside her. Her shoulders still shudder from time to time, and every now and again she starts crying, then reaffirms her grip on me, and I retaliate with a stronger hold on her.

When I'm certain she's fallen asleep in my arms, I pull out my cell and text Kai. That motherfucker nearly got her gangbanged! He's an idiot–didn't he know he wouldn't be able to live with himself if that happened?

WTF?! I text him, and wait. This is always unnerving because no matter how much we plan, there'll still be one moron who wants to pretend to be boss, then messes things up.

My cell rings and I try to peel myself off Maisy so I can get up.

"No, no, stay," she moans.

"I'll be back, darling. I got to take this call."

I manage to get off the bed and leave her room to take the call. "You better have a damn good explanation for what happened!" I snarl.

"Is she okay?"

"No thanks to you!"

Kai sighs, sounding pained. "Thank God!"

"What the fuck made you take her from my home, you asshole? We talked about this before–why do I have to keep repeating myself over and over?!"

"You can talk," Kai mutters with a sharp intake of breath. "The bruise on her face? You're still into that shit?"

"THAT was an accident! You fucker, I can't believe you went there!" As much as he's riling me up right now, something's off. He's usually more of a fighter. And his breathing's uneven. "Kai!"

"Yeah?"

"What's wrong?"

"I'm bleeding. One of your assholes shot me."

"How serious is it?"

"The shoulder."

"You'll live. You deserved it, too."

"Fuck you."

"Fuck you too! Get it sorted and get over here!"

I cut the line and see a message from Logan waiting for me on my cell. *I heard about the shootout at the Delgados. I'm on my way.*

The front door's unlocked. Just get inside, I reply.

I go back to Maisy and she's still lying on the bed, her eyes open and her hand reached out to me. She patiently waits until I lie down next to her and she nestles snugly in the crook of my arm.

She looks at me with sadness in her eyes. “Do you think Kai did this on purpose?”

I almost crush her in my embrace. “No, Kai’d do anything to protect you. He’s just a little reckless.”

She nods. “He killed five men, those that ripped my clothes off.”

“They had an easy death. If it was up to me, I’d torture them one by one.”

“He was about to kill the girl, Natasha, but told her letting her go was the last thing he’d do for her. He couldn’t pull the trigger.”

“She’s as good as dead,” I say. “I’m gonna kill her for you.”

“I don’t want that.”

“I do.”

“Is Kai okay?”

“Are you seriously asking me that question? He nearly got you gangbanged!” I snap at her. “Once you go through that hell, you never go back! *Fuck*, Maisy!”

“I’m sorry. I was just worried for him.”

“Just don’t mention his name for a while, please.”

The closed-circuit camera buzzes on my cell: Logan’s in my house. He soon knocks on the bedroom door and as he enters, I get up to greet him.

“Logan.”

“Orion.”

We have a specific way of shaking hands when something significant happens; it’s almost as if we’re saying, *we still got each other*. Logan puts his hand on my shoulder, the brother I never had, reading me, and I let him because we can’t talk openly in front of Maisy.

I’m aggravated. I press my lips tightly together and shake my head. Logan glances behind me and sees Maisy. She’s sitting up, looking at us.

“What’s wrong?” She asks.

“Nothing’s wrong. In fact, look at you!” Logan chuckles. “You cut your hair shorter, and highlights too, wow. Are you trying to join Kai's Motorcycle Club?" He takes a seat next to her on the bed.

Maisy's eyes fill with tears and she's crying again.

"What did I say?" Logan looks at me, surprised, then embraces Maisy. "Calm down, sweetheart. I just meant you look gorgeous."

I sit in the chair facing them and shake my head again. This is way too fucking soon. "That shooting you heard about? Kai took her to his club and Maisy almost got gangbanged."

A tic immediately appears in Logan's left eye, a scary one. It shows up when he's planning someone's death. "Almost?" His voice is muted.

I hate repeating it, for Maisy's sake, but he needs to know. "She was naked and tied to a table."

"*What?!*" he thunders.

"I got there in the nick of time. That was what the shootout was about."

"Did they see you?"

"No, but the Cartes knew who we were extracting from there. I had to do it, Logan."

"They know about Maisy? This changes everything."

Logan takes off his suit jacket and shoes, lies next to her and immediately she cuddles up in the crook of his neck.

"Where were you, Logan?" Her croaky voice is breaking, like she's hurt.

"Working, sweetheart. But I missed you like crazy."

"I missed you too. I thought you were mad at me."

"Me? I could never be mad at you." He ruffles her hair. "Are you okay? Do you want to tell the doctor what happened?"

She shakes her head and strokes his chest, seemingly lost in thought.

Logan and I look at each other for a moment too long. What happened today could've been a disaster. She seems vulnerable. The three of us are like wolves, protecting what's ours, yet we exposed her to the most dreaded thing we all want to eradicate in our world.

I want to distract her, to stop her from thinking about today. "Are you hungry, Maisy?"

"No."

I don't succeed in diverting her attention, but just seeing Logan and Maisy lying on the bed in front of me feels like enough. I want to lie next to her too, and soothe her, but I would never take that away from Logan. He deserves all the love he can get. As a baby he was dropped off on the doorstep of Lorenzo's house, and once the DNA test was done, that was it. He was prepped for the life of a mobster. Lorenzo made him work with whores from the age of ten, and any love he got was always bought or sold. It's the same even today, thanks to his strip club.

From the day we first met, in the factory, his father made him kill people with his bare hands. But nobody really knows what a compassionate guy he is. Although to learn that, one has to go with him on a killing frenzy, which we have too many times, and see that the days of remorse that follow for him are the most painful. Neither I nor Kai can reach him then.

What a doctor he is; once, he said, he gave an oath, but it means shit. That was the moment I saw the real him. He despises all of this, just like Kai and I do.

Ever since Maisy, that scary tic of his comes only when he talks about protecting her. She placates him in the most unusual way, and that works for him.

Logan's stroking Maisy's shoulder and kissing her head. It's time for me to leave. She's in good hands.

I stand up. "I got something to deal with."

"Orion, please, I need you," Maisy purrs. I know she does, but Logan can give her more right now.

"Let him be," I hear Logan say as I head out. "He needs to release all that anger somewhere."

He's right. I'm heading to the gym. I'll have a tough time controlling myself around her until she's okay. But when she is, I'll fucking put her in her place.

I close the door behind me. He'll give her what she needs. I'm too angry to think.

LOGAN

Goddammit. Kai's always been the one who thinks the least about the consequences of his actions. He thought joining the MC would distance him from the mob life, but it actually propelled him into it even deeper.

Every real biker knows our faces are weathered as we stare down evil. Our hands are tough and our arms strong, to keep things safe. We are that way to protect those who need it the most.

Noble words he started to live by, until Mickey, Kai's father, changed all that. He took the mob inside his MC. He thought his son was a genius considering most motorcycle clubs dealt with guns, and the fact that he was boxing, well, a few fixed matches at a young age and Kai became the new God. No thoughts or anything. And since he's the youngest, we've always looked the other way when he'd show up and say he'd done something stupid... but this has gone too far.

If anything were to happen to Maisy, out of the three of us, I'd be worried most for Orion. Because I can't see anything within that man. He's a wall nobody can knock down. Kai will most likely kill everyone and everything out of anger, but Orion, *fuck*. Orion will implode. I've seen him go crazy at his worst, when his father passed away from cancer. He didn't even like his father, but the fact that he didn't have control over his death, his life, was enough. He was looking for someone to blame. Those months were critically dangerous for the three of us. Kai and I couldn't reach him, and we didn't know if he'd turn his back on us, spill all of our secrets. He didn't. Instead, he started murdering people all over New York. We'd find snitches in pools of blood, their eyes gouged out and faces smashed in with a hammer. We'd find bones half-burned in sulfuric acid. We'd receive neatly-packed dry meat for dogs, only later realizing he'd chopped up bodies into small pieces and stuffed their remains into bags. And we don't even know the half of it. Finally, we managed to get to him and beat the grief for his father out of him.

Today's been tough. If he saw Maisy tied up and naked, he's seen that she's breakable just like anyone else.

The thought makes me determined to deduce if she's okay. "Sweetheart, were you hurt?"

She shakes her head, looking lost in thought, but I pinch her chin and raise her head to make her look at me. Her highlights bring out a different shade in her dark eyes. I'm beguiled.

I press my lips to hers and she responds. We kiss softly, but she ends it all too soon, and rests her head on my chest again.

"It's okay. You're in shock, that's all."

"I'm not."

"I'm a real doctor here, did you know that?"

She nods. "You guys keep forgetting. I have a photographic memory."

"We don't forget, we just don't put that much importance on it. You're so much more than your genius mind."

She flashes her teeth at me in a grin. I get the impression no one's ever said that to her. "Well, I've seen your medical record from during your residency," she says.

"Where?"

"Jerry's place. He was the sort of record-keeper for Milan."

"Sneaky fucker. Why would he have that? What use is it to him?"

She shrugs. "There were many documents with your name in there. One was from a DNA facility."

I sit up. This is getting serious. *My DNA?*

"It said 'positive match.' And it had your name on it, Logan Vitali. That's all."

"Maisy, why didn't you mention this sooner?"

She looks apologetic. "You didn't ask me."

"Anything else?"

"Lorenzo Vitali–was he your father?"

"Yes."

"And he's in the adult industry?"

"Yes, why?"

"Because I read someone cut off his... you know what. It's how he died. Bled out."

I raise an eyebrow. "In Milan's files?"

"Yes. Who took over from him?"

"My cousins," I lie. I can't tell Maisy the whole truth, it would kill her. My cousins run the adult industry operations, but they report to me. No matter how much I hate that side of the business, none of the fuckers would let it go.

"So they could have my video?"

I see now. Clever girl. "I assure you, sweetheart, Milan's our sworn enemy. There's not a chance in this world that we'd have a video of you. Or that he'd give it to us."

"Sure. Does the name Bobby Saunders mean anything to you?"

"Yes, it does."

"It was in the same pile where your father's name kept appearing. Bobby Saunders and Maurice Het."

We cut Maurice's balls off for being a snitch. And then, of course, we fed them to his dogs. His trusted pit bull terriers tore him apart. It's what we do to snitches.

"They're on Milan's payroll," she adds.

"Wait, what?"

"Maurice Het and Bobby Saunders are on Milan's payroll."

"That's not possible. Bobby's my right-hand man, my blood. He sleeps in the same room as me. I trust him with my life."

She blinks at me, incredulous. "You sleep with a man?"

"I'm serious, Maisy. How sure are you of this? Is it possible that you've made a mistake? Got the names confused?"

"I'm certain, Logan. I'm sorry."

I'm starting to see that Maisy's more valuable to us than we originally thought. I mean, even without her photographic memory she's worth more to me than anything, but now I see why Orion was so intent on keeping her safe, keeping her here. "Do you know for how long?"

"No. But the date on the document was April last year."

"What else?" Suddenly the urge to know more, to know everything, overwhelms me. But I clock my addictive streak awakening instantly, and stop myself. "Actually, no, don't tell me anything else. I want you to rest and forget about today."

"It's fine, I'm okay. In the same box as the documents, there was a small yellow teddy bear with the label 'Baby Logan Moros Vitali.' Is Moros your middle name?"

"Moros? Not that I know of. I don't have a middle name. I never met my mother, and my father wasn't really a talkative guy, especially about shit like that."

Huh. *A teddy bear?* That must've been mine. I must investigate this. The identity of my mother has tormented me my whole life. I've searched for her all over NY and beyond, and now suddenly there's a bear with my name on it? And why's Milan been collecting stuff on me?

"Did your father have a girlfriend, or wife?" Maisy asks.

"Everyone working at the strip club was his girlfriend. And if they weren't, he'd break them and make them. He was cruel in that way."

"He raised you by himself?"

"There were too many women around when I was growing up. None the motherly type."

Maisy presses her lips to mine, kissing me tenderly. I wasn't looking for pity, but I respond; I need her love, her touch. Everything she offers, I want. She's someone worth living for.

I pull back from her magic, and smile at her. "Come, sit up."

"Why?"

"I want to take your top off. I'm going to give you a massage to get you to relax."

She's looking at me dubiously. "I'm not sure, Logan."

I hook my fingers under her top. "Trust me, no sex. I want to relieve your stress, and I want to do something for you. I feel useless."

"You're not. You're lying here next to me."

I bat my eyelashes at her. "For me?"

With playful exasperation, she raises her arms and I pull her top over her head. Her breasts bounce as I free them up, spying those sweet nubs I want to suck on and never let go, but I remind myself it's not about sex.

"Lie down on your stomach, and stop flaunting your boobs in my face or I'll have to do something about it," I chuckle.

She giggles and lies down as told. "And my panties?" she purrs.

"They're definitely staying."

She turns her head toward the window, away from everything. I wonder if it's a sign that she wants to be cut off from reality. "I'm not sure if this will help me," she mutters.

"You'll feel much better afterward, and that's all we want to achieve."

Sitting next to her, I run my hands up from the base of her spine, letting my thumbs glide along the vertebrae. A hum escapes her lips. I repeat the movement a few times and then trace small circles around her shoulder blades, applying pressure.

She moans each time I do. I like to think she's expelling her worries. When I'm useful to her, I'm a man. Shame my father considered me useful only when I killed, and thus created a pattern that's, well, not good for people. I'm glad I'm not like him, though. My kills are with a blade: clean-cut, fast, invisible. By the time you realize I've cut you, you're bleeding to death.

"Was the doctor right, sweetheart?"

Her pillow swallows her groan as she nods into it.

My hands go down her legs, smartly skipping over the panties. I massage her all the way from her buttocks to her feet. I then take one foot in my hand and begin to rub her sole with my thumb.

I move up her leg from her ankle, and work my magic on her butt cheeks using the right amount of pressure, massaging the muscles there. She's stiff. She must've gone through hell today.

My hand slides between her legs, focusing on her inner thighs. I use long, circular motions from the backs of her knees and along her adductor muscles. She continues to moan softly as I massage her.

My fingers sporadically brush her panties, and with each light touch her sounds come out different, deeper.

I place my palms on the backs of her thighs and knead upward, my fingers sliding under her panties over her buttocks, and as I do her ass lifts under my touch.

"You're enjoying this, Maisy?"

"Yes." She looks back at me, pushes herself up onto her hands and arches her back, sliding one knee aside, opening up to me.

I snicker. This girl can't make me harder than I already am. "I'm not finished. Turn onto your back."

I help her roll over and start with her legs, my fingers going up to the space between her thighs, then back down again. Her eyes are locked on mine but her breathing is what gets me, her breasts heaving, her nipples already hardening.

Between her legs is a wet patch on the material of her panties. The final straw for me. This beautiful creature wants, no, needs, no, *calls* me to fuck her. There's clear evidence.

"Your panties are ruined." I gently run my fingers over them and she smiles at me. She takes my other hand and guides it to her breast, using my hand to knead herself.

My eyes close. I'm loving every bit of this, and before she changes her mind, I pinch her nipple and give it a soft tug.

She is gorgeous as she lies there. I lean in and suck the other nipple, then pepper her with kisses from her neck up to the edge of her earlobe. Her fingers rake my hair and she pulls me to her, eyes locked with mine, absorbing every particle of my existence.

"I need you," she whispers.

I feel my lips quirk. "The doctor agrees, sweetheart."

I press my lips to her and devour her mouth, our tongues tangling in a rushed dance. I cup her breast in one hand and knead it gently before squeezing her nipple, tugging it again and making her bite my lip. *She loves that.*

I hook my fingers under the waistband of her panties and peel them off. Everything is so smooth, like it's been choreographed since a long time ago. She opens her legs and pulls me between them by my collar. I kiss her as I shrug my shirt off my shoulders, then pull away to lift it over my head.

Hungry for touch, we kiss again, our bodies pressed into each other. She's hurrying in her own way, but I take my time. This thing she does, when the moment she's horny, she rushes in as if someone else will take her place, is not good for her.

"Hey, breathe," I whisper.

I fix my position between her legs and unzip my pants. My cock is hard as a rock and I fist it a few times as I dive into the black pools of her eyes. She's holding me safe as much as I am her. This is pure heaven. I brush my cock along her arousal, sliding up and down and over her clit.

"Logan," she breathes.

She uses her hips to try to move down on me, but I want to tease; it's what I love, to see her desperate. But I'd rather be inside her than out and too soon I give in, thrusting slowly into her, stretching her as I move, filling her beautifully, inch by inch. My head drops to her shoulder, feeling every part of her as I enter her to the hilt and growl into her neck.

"Stay inside me forever," she whispers in my ear.

I place my elbows on either side of her head and hold her face in my hands. We stare at each other as I thrust, pulling out to the tip and entering her to the hilt in a rhythm that gradually picks up speed.

With each accelerated thrust, I pound her harder and deeper. My need, my craving for her, is raw, and I hear myself grunting in between her staccato moans, and the faster I move the closer we are to erupting into our own fireworks. That's what spending time with Maisy is.

"*Logan!*" Her orgasm erupts, and collides with mine.

I bury my head in her neck and growl again as I ram our bodies together, over and over, emptying my balls inside her cunt so many times over.

I hold her in my arms with my cheek pressed to her neck. When our panting eases off, I lift myself up onto my forearms and regard her face: glistening with sweat, celestial.

I push back a lock of hair that's stuck to her face. We kiss, and then she turns her head to the side. I follow her eyes. Orion's in the chair, wet-haired, in a black t-shirt and sweatpants. He's been in the gym, and it appears to have taken at least some of the anger out of him.

She reaches out a delicate hand to him. "Come."

Orion cannot handle emotions, but Maisy is so good with him. I lift myself off her and she turns sideways to Orion. Her hair is sweaty; she's gorgeous. I could look at her forever. Orion's under her spell, too. He just stares at her.

I meet his eyes. "She needs you," I remind him. I want to give Maisy everything in this world.

I get up and peel off my sweat-soaked pants fully, then head for the shower.

CHAPTER 11

MAISY

I sensed him entering the room, his eyes hooded, watching me like a ghost. Everything he does is twisted. He saved me, took me back to his house and looked after me, and now I see anger and anguish pointed at me, which earlier was reserved solely for Kai.

My mind's a swirl of emotions, good ones trying to push the bad ones away. I don't feel guilty about going for a ride with Kai. But how could I have been so stupid to let that bitch trick me? Kai didn't shoot her today, but he will once I tell him I saw the sneakers she gave me in the last photo of his father before his death.

Something else came to play today. Once I realized who Logan's father was, and his involvement in the adult industry, I connected the dots. Milan's got information on him. I only hope Rosey's never been part of their films. Although, judging by what was going on at Milan's, I have to check. Someone's bound to recognize me if I show my face there.

My thoughts are interrupted by Orion's stare. It's as if he knows what goes on in my head. "Don't look at me like that, I'm sweaty." I run my hand down my neck, over my breast and to my tummy. "And sticky, and–"

"You're beautiful, Maisy. You know that," he states matter-of-factly.

I needed to hear that. But why do I feel there's something else on his mind? I pat the space next to me. "Orion, come here, please."

His face is dead serious. He looks away briefly, then resolutely locks eyes with me. "Maisy, I'm going to say something now and you better listen carefully. What you did was inexcusable." His voice is thick with unbridled anger. "You acted reckless and immature!"

"I'm sorry," I barely whisper, and lower my head. I'm aware of what I did.

"Do you understand how much it takes for us, for *me*, to protect you?"

He stands up, and in two strides he's towering over me. Cupping my chin with his hand and pulling me up to stand, he makes my neck crane as I look up at him.

His jaw's clenched, he talks through gritted teeth. "I-am-really-angry-with-you. Because of you, Kai was shot. Today could've gone in a different direction and it's all-fucking-because-of-you. Do you get that?"

I stare at him. He's scaring me–he looks just like he did the first time I saw him, like I'm his biggest irritation. I try to jerk my chin out of his hand but he's holding me tight. The tears in my eyes come uninvited. I'm hurt, and I feel my chin wobble.

He pushes me away, looking pissed. I fall back to the bed.

"I'm sorry. I didn't want anyone to get shot today. If you're so angry with me, you should've left me there."

"Maybe I should have. You'd probably enjoy the gang bang!"

I wince at the painful words. I narrow my eyes and stand up, getting right in his face. I'd punch him if I could. "And maybe I'd finally find a place where I'd be truly protected."

Orion watches me silently, giving no response. Just an obsidian black glare shooting arrows at me.

"You know what, why don't I just get out of here so I won't be your problem anymore?" I shout, and start hauling my naked ass toward the shower. I was in such a blessed state, and now I feel like I'm back to day one, when he was thinking of killing me.

"Oh, no. You're not going anywhere, darling." His words ooze menace. "Now that the Cartes know about you, it's gonna be a different story. And also, until I get everything I need from you, you're not gonna see daylight."

"And THERE IT IS!" I yell through my tears. "The reason why you keep me in here! ALL OF YOU are the same! Every single man in this world–the SAME!"

Storming into the bathroom, I bump into Logan coming out, rubbing his hair with a towel. I push him away and slam the door between myself and them.

"Maisy?" Logan's obviously confused, but Orion said what he needed to say, on all their behalf.

I turn the water on and get under the shower, lifting my head toward the spray and closing my eyes. My face, my hair, my body are rapidly drenched and before I know it, I'm choking back sobs, then bawling in loud, gut-wrenching cries.

The shower door suddenly opens and through the steam I see Orion in his t-shirt and sweatpants, his eyes burning with black fire. Before I have time to say anything his hand lunges at me, encircling my neck and pushing my face flat against the tiles.

"First, do not walk away from me, ever."

Orion whispers the words in my ear before sinking his teeth into my earlobe, so sharp I think he must've drawn blood. I whimper in pain. He presses his large, muscular body over mine, a wall of hot flesh, flattening me on the cold tiles. His clothes are wet, but through his sweatpants I feel the steel ridge of his erection pressed firmly to my ass.

"Second. Whatever I say, goes."

"Screw you! You don't own me, Ori–Ow!" He sinks his teeth into my shoulder, again drawing blood, no doubt leaving marks.

"Third, never talk back."

I struggle against his weight, trying to push him off, but he's like a wolf, holding his victim secured in place before taking another bite. I look back at him, and see he's pulled down his sweatpants and is fisting himself.

"And never, ever, ever"–he grabs the back of my thigh and lifts my leg up–"compare me with all those that used you," he growls, as his cock finds my cunt and is shoved deep inside me.

"Because-they-never-fucked-you-like-I-have!"

The veins in his cock rub against my insides, his piercing penetrating me deep as he ruthlessly slams into me, over and over.

Why is my traitorous body enjoying this? I cannot contain my grunts, the air expelled from my chest each time he claims me. And when they become staccato, he growls and shoots his load inside me before pulling out. Frustrated by my lack of orgasm, I moan as my hips search for friction–I'm close. From behind, he wraps his arm tightly around my waist and the other hand reaches down, between my folds.

"I'll never let you go. Not because I *can't*," he hisses into my ear, swirling his digits around my core as I roll my hips, "but because I'm in too deep." He slips two fingers inside me and my legs buckle, but he holds me tight as I cry out. "We all are."

He's rubbing my clit with his thumb now as he finger-fucks me, and I'm thrown over the edge. My body jerks as I cum, and my arousal gushes over his hand. All the while I hear his voice. "I've fallen in perverted lust with you, and Kai and Logan adore you, obsessively. Whatever it is that you're doing to us, please, stop it."

I turn to him and wrap my arms around his body, and he does the same. For some inexplicable reason, I'm becoming addicted to this man. *How can someone be hurting in so many different ways?*

"For the record, I'm still mad at you." He kisses my head. "But not kill-you mad, just fuck-you mad."

I crane my neck to look up at him and chuckle. "Take off your clothes, you're soaked."

He strips off and stops the water while I get him a towel. We didn't have to go through all this heartache if we were going to end up fucking. Which we always do. Though I don't necessarily enjoy his hurtful words that get us there.

I leave Orion in the bathroom and walk back into the bedroom. Logan's on his cell, sitting in the chair. I wrap my hair in a towel, find my t-shirt, and grab a new pair of panties.

"Is everything okay? What happened to your face?" he asks, looking up.

"I was being pushed against the tiles a little too hard," I titter, and glance at Orion, who's exiting the bathroom stark naked. The tattoos spread over one side of his perfect pecs, abs, and arms are on full show, and all he's wearing are the rings on both hands, the ones he never takes off.

"Oh, you were, huh? Come here, you little minx." Logan pulls me into his lap and I sit down, giggling.

Orion cuts his fun off. "Let her rest, Logan."

"Why, if she's game for it?" Logan continues to tickle me and I laugh louder.

"Logan." Orion gives him a look. "We need to talk."

"Come and lie in bed with me, Logan," I purr.

LOGAN

"Get some rest first. I'll come as soon as I can, I promise." I kiss Maisy's forehead and cup her face, locking eyes with her. "I'm here, and I'm not going anywhere, sweetheart."

She nods, and I head out after Orion. She's the most important thing to me, showing me a semblance of what my life could be like.

"I'll meet you in the kitchen," Orion announces, not turning back. "I'm gonna put some clothes on."

"Sure."

I follow the stairs down and go to the kitchen. Orion doesn't keep me waiting for long. He's changed back into a black t-shirt and sweats when he enters the room in silence.

First thing he does is reach for the whiskey, pull out two tumblers, and pour. He brings them to the table, the bottle too. He downs one glass and pours another shot.

"Is it that bad?" I ask.

"They know about her." His voice is solemn. Fuck knows what's going on in his head. He's always the one who can see three, four steps ahead. And now he's worrying me.

"Yes, but we won't let them do anything to her," I insist.

"Logan, there are snitches among my men. That much I know." He pauses for a beat. "She's told me a lot. Do you remember the Savak Street drive-by?"

"Yes, and the journalist was killed after reporting on it."

"We know it wasn't you or Kai. And we never questioned it. We didn't want anyone to doubt you, right? But actually, it was the Slavs."

"The *fuck?*" I sputter.

"And the problems Kai got after the shootout with the Irish? The arm deals that went rogue? Kai swore he didn't kill them."

"Yeah, what about it?"

"Well, there were ten Irishmen there and not seven, as we originally thought. Apparently, three were left alive to go home and tell their people about what the Delgados did. We know Kai. That's not him! He doesn't leave one witness alive. That was Milan!" Orion looks furious. "And what happens after? The Slavs take over the arms deal with the Irish and the Delgados are left to deal with the police."

"Fuck, man. Does Kai know?"

"Not yet. He's like a bomb waiting to go off. I don't know what he'll do with it. We need to make a plan before telling him. Not just show up, spray bullets into thin air and hope for the best. What's Maisy told you?"

"Quite a lot. Bobby Saunders is on Milan's payroll. I'm still trying to recover from the shock. I'm inventing new ways to torture the fucker."

"Bobby–as in your right-hand man? Is she sure?" Orion asks.

"And why the fuck does Milan have a copy of my residency record, and my DNA? Maisy knows a *lot*, and she's only just now sharing information with us. She knew about my father, and his involvement in the porn industry."

"I wondered when that would come up. Did you tell her?"

"I told her the truth," I tell him, "that my cousins run that side of the show now."

"Logan, this is deeper than we thought." Orion takes a moment before talking again. "Milan has a letter from my mother."

I'm confused. "What d'you mean?"

"Wendy wasn't my real mother."

I'm in shock. I thought we shared everything. "How long have you known?"

"Long. I didn't know what to do with the information, so I parked it."

"How come you never told us?"

He shrugs. "Willer told me a long time ago, when he was drunk. It was a one-time thing, and that was that. No matter how much I pressed, he avoided answering my questions. I thought nothing of it 'til Maisy mentioned it. I mean, what's this letter about? And why the fuck does Milan have it? Everything suggests that he's preparing something."

"Yeah, he sure is. We got to be ready for him. Is there a plan?"

"Not right now. We got to deal with Kai first. He's shot. It had to be done, the fucker. Any other man would be dead by now." Orion looks down when he gets a notification on his cell. The CCTV app blinks and the live feed of his front door camera kicks in. "Wait, someone's outside."

He tilts his cell so I can get a better look. Both Orion and I watch a motorbike approaching. The person's riding it with one arm, slumped on the handlebars. It's not Kai's bike, but I'd recognize his style anywhere.

"Shit, that's Kai!" Orion exclaims.

We both jump and run to open the door for him.

"Kai! Are you okay?" I grab him and he collapses into my arms. "Get the bike before it lands on us, Orion."

Orion grabs the bike and takes it to where Kai always parks it behind the shrubs. No one can find it there. Especially if it's not Kai's.

I lift the visor on the helmet, but can't make out his face from all the blood. He's seriously messed up.

"Come on, buddy, easy now." I help him inside, taking him straight to the living room, and lay him on the same sofa we put Maisy on when she arrived. I remove his leather jacket and he moans in pain. He's lost a lot of blood. His gunshot wound isn't patched up. He has cuts all over his upper body, the shirt he's wearing bloodied and torn.

"Let me take your helmet off." I try to pull it off as Orion enters.

"I'm sorry, I really am," Kai mutters.

"About what, Kai?" I've got to keep him talking, since I'm not sure how hurt he is.

"About Maisy."

The helmet is fully off and I'm startled by the sight. He's been beaten to a pulp. I don't know how he rode here as both of his eyes are nearly shut; his lip's cut, and there are numerous bruises all over. Anger boils inside me. *I'm gonna kill whoever did this to him.*

"Don't worry, she's fine." I'm trying to sound unaffected but I can feel my eye twitching, a dead giveaway.

Orion's not hiding anything. His voice exudes anger. "What *happened* to you?"

"They jumped me. I killed five of them, those that touched her. After the shootout, they jumped me."

Maisy suddenly shows up like a ghost at the doorframe.

"Kai! Oh God, what happened?" She runs to him and wraps her small arms around his wide shoulders, ignoring the bloodied shirt.

He nuzzles her neck and starts apologizing again. "I'm so sorry, Maisy, I didn't mean for that to happen."

"It's fine, don't worry, I'm fine. Please, Kai," she peels herself off him and studies his bloody face, but doesn't cringe. "Let Logan check you over. *Please*."

Kai raises his head and finds Orion, his face contrite. "I need a place to lay low for a few days."

"You'll stay here," Orion says bluntly. "It's safe. The Cartes know I have Maisy and nobody'll dare come here." He's ready for everything. That's why we follow him.

All of us are worried for Kai. It's clear. In silence, Maisy stands up and steps back, allowing me to examine him. Orion wraps a hand around her waist and pulls her to him.

"This is all my fault," she breathes, and leans into his chest.

I look at her. Orion cups her cheek and she cranes her head to regard him.

"None of this is your fault," he tells her. "Okay?"

"So why does it feel like it is?"

"This is our *life*, Maisy. Whether you're here or not, we deal with this kind of shit every single day." He winks. "Don't think you're so special."

She smiles and pushes herself onto her tiptoes, kissing him softly. Kai's watching them as a semi develops in his jeans.

I smack his cock. "Hey! Focus here, bro!"

MAISY

Orion's eyes are filled with concern. "Maisy, I hope you understand the situation I put you in. You'll have to meet the Cartes and for that, you got to be ready. I don't want anything happening unplanned."

I nod, and chuckle. "You're gonna have to buy me more clothes. And panties. I have no more of those, since you guys keep ripping them apart."

"I'll tell–"

"Please, not Leila!" I'll die before I wear panties like those again.

He smirks. "I was gonna say Lisa. I asked her already to get you some."

"And shoes," I say.

"And shoes."

"And dresses."

"And dresses."

"And coats."

"Whatever you need, darling." He kisses my forehead and I smile, wrapping my arms around his buff body.

I should be feeling guilty for having something else on my mind, but I'm not going to think about that right now.

"What do you need to remove the bullet?" he asks Logan.

"Nothing. It's gone right though. I just need to patch him up and give him some antibiotics. Probably stitch a few of the cuts, too."

"I'll get your kit." Orion places another kiss on my head and leaves me be.

I lie on the sofa next to Kai and hook my arm around his waist. He's almost unconscious but he clutches me immediately, and takes my hand to his lips.

I'm scared for him. He got *attacked*. Can he even go home now that he's killed so many of his own people? "Is he going to be okay?" I ask.

"Yes. Come here, let him rest." Logan's patting a place on the floor, next to the sofa.

I go to him and sit in his lap, nestling snugly in his arms. I want to be held. To be certain that I'm fine.

"We got to get you more clothes, you're freezing." Logan rubs my arms to warm me up and I nuzzle my face in his neck.

"Just hold me, please."

I stay like that for a while, enjoying Logan's scent. I want all of this to be over, and Kai to be fine, but it's not going to happen. The Cartes know about me. That's all I'm thinking about, and Logan knows it. He understands me so he just holds me in silence, stroking my head.

When Orion shows up with Logan's kit, he takes over from Logan, reaching a hand out to me. "Come on, Maisy, let's go."

I don't ask questions, just allow him to pull me from the room.

"Are you okay?" he asks.

"I am."

"Are you hungry?"

I nod and as we enter the kitchen, I spot five takeout bags splayed across the table. "You already ordered?"

"I got Logan and Kai to feed, and they don't eat like you."

"What did you order?"

"Chinese, Thai, pizza, little bit of everything," he says, and starts opening the bags.

"Oh! Pizza!" I exclaim. I'm craving junk food. I open the pizza box and there it is, cheesy tomato and pepperoni, staring right at me. *Yum*.

"Watch out, it's hot," Orion warns.

"The hotter the better." I take a slice, gobble it up in one go, and take another. My mouth's dripping with grease but I don't care.

He passes me a napkin, smirking. "Eat properly. You're not a child."

I take it and as I wipe my mouth, I become aware of something happening. I glare at him and feel my mouth burning, more intensely as the seconds pass. My ears begin to grow hot and my eyes burn, most likely turning scarlet.

Orion starts full-on laughing. "I told you it was hot. You should start listening to me."

"I can take it," I sniffle. My nose is running now but I bite into another slice anyway, this one smaller.

"Don't." He takes the slice from my hand. "You're not proving anything to me."

"Orion, give it to me!"

"Only if you're sure."

"I am. I want it hot."

He watches me wiping my nose with the napkin and shakes his head. "Here. Enjoy it." He hands back the hottest slice of pizza I've ever had in my life and picks up a box of noodles. "Maybe these'll do you good. Finish your mouthful and I'll let you have some."

I chew and swallow my pizza, wiping my tears afterward. Not waiting for another moment to pass, I open my mouth and wait for Orion. He picks up some noodles with the chopsticks and as he lifts them to my mouth, he leans in and kisses me, flicking his tongue against mine.

"Let me take away that hotness you have," he chuckles.

"Your kiss is soothing it... Please, more."

He pulls back instead and feeds the noodles straight into my mouth. I hope they'll alleviate the sting of the pepperoni. "Nobody made you eat the pizza, Maisy. It's your own fault. Open wide now, I got more noodles for you."

I finish the next mouthful and open for more as he continues to feed me. *Yes, this really is what I need.*

He pushes one of the boxes in front of me, together with the chopsticks. “Here, feed yourself,” he grins.

“No need to be so stingy,” I chuckle, and grab my box of noodles.

Logans walks in and sits opposite us. His eyes land on the pizza box and he reaches for it. “Where’s the rest of my pizza? Who ate it?”

I haven’t seen Logan hangry before.

“Maisy.” Orion points at me with his chopsticks. *Traitor*. “She’s responsible.”

“If it makes you feel any better, I wish I hadn’t eaten it,” I admit. “My mouth’s on fire.”

Logan curses me sweetly. “You deserve every little tear and sting, sweetheart,” he says, and takes a slice of hot pepperoni.

“How’s Kai?” Orion asks.

“He’ll be fine. He’s hurting because of Maisy mostly. What he did. Or nearly did to you.” Logan regards me.

“But nothing happened, I’m fine,” I protest.

“Yeah, it doesn’t work like that. Especially with him.”

Orion’s cell flashes with a notification. He opens up a video and mutters to himself, “Lisa.”

In a short while, Lisa shows up in the kitchen with shopping bags.

I’m happy to see another woman in the house. “Lisa! Come and join us.”

“Hello everyone.” She spies the food on the table and playfully snickers. “Any pizza left for me, Logan?” She probably knows Logan’s love affair with his pizza. I wish I knew before taking a slice.

“Uh-Uh. No way.” Logan disregards her jeer and responds like he means it.

“Ha-ha, you’re such a greedy asshole,” she laughs.

“At least you asked. Maisy here didn’t.”

Lisa sits down next to me and drops the bags on the floor. “These are for you, Maisy.”

"Me?"

"Yes, Orion asked me to get you some things for going out."

I grin, overjoyed, and jump into Orion's lap and kiss him on the cheek. "Thank you, Orion!"

"Well, you needed it. Now you have no excuse to be walking around practically naked," he chuckles.

"Thank you, Lisa."

"Don't mention it."

I jump off his lap and head to wash my hands in the sink. "Let me just do this, and I'm out of here."

I tip the shopping bags upside down on my bed and shriek with joy. "Yes! Black lace panties, so many of them!" *Thank you, Lisa!*

She got me jeans, shirts, a coat, a few dresses for all occasions–a whole new wardrobe. And bras! I haven't worn a bra for a long time. A lace one, too.

I quickly get dressed in lace panties, a bra, jeans, and a long-sleeved black top, before heading back down to the kitchen. I walk in grinning.

Logan laughs. "Who's this girl, Orion? I don't recognize her with so many clothes on."

Lisa nods approvingly. "You look great, Maisy."

Orion's eyes are twinkling. He's looking at my jeans–and my boobs. He can tell I'm wearing a bra.

"I *feel* great, Lisa. Thank you," I reply, feeling smug.

CHAPTER 12

KAI

How stupid am I? Orion's right. I'm an idiot. An idiot who doesn't think. Why did I think she'd be safe with me? I'm the fucking head of the Delgados, that's why, but they still had the guts to challenge me. Rocco got what he deserved. *Everyone* got what they deserved. You mess with my girl, I'm gonna fuck you up.

I have no remorse for killing any of them. I probably should've killed Natasha too, but that stupid guilt always creeps in. I'm not sure what I would've done if the same thing happened to Maisy. I get PTSD when I dwell on how close Maisy was to getting gangbanged–something I couldn't save Natasha from, and have been feeling regretful about ever since.

I deserved the bullet, and the beating afterward. But fuck, they *knew* I'd been shot, and that's why they jumped me. Had I not been, my fists don't speak words, they just slay. And nobody would've stood a chance.

The very moment I get better, I'll show those motherfuckers what it means to lead a mutiny against me. All of them!

These thoughts rove constantly in my head, not allowing me to sleep, which I've been trying to do for some time. Logan patched me up pretty well, including a few stitches, and now all I'm waiting for is my body to heal. Meaning, I can only lie here, in the darkness.

I hear Maisy's sweet voice. "Kai? Are you awake?"

"Yes, come in." I turn the table lamp on. *Huh. That's new.* "Hey, look at you. You got clothes on."

"Everyone keeps saying that, but not for long." She pulls her top off and presents her perfect breasts, supported by a black lace bra.

I raise my eyebrows at her. "New underwear, too."

"Yes." She kneels on the floor next to the sofa where I lie. "How are you, Kai?"

Even in the dim lamplight, I manage to lose myself in the depths of her eyes, wide and dark. When I look at her soft, rosy lips, I know I'm looking at the most beautiful girl in this world. *My baby girl.*

She cups my face and waits for an answer, but it's me who should be asking that question, not her. I place my hand over hers and bring it to my lips, kissing her fingers.

"Kai, nothing happened. Okay? Nothing. Please don't beat yourself up about it."

"I'm not. I just can't wait to go back there and crunch every skull with my fists, that's all," I snarl.

"Well, how can I make you feel better?" she purrs.

"You have to ask?"

"But, um, you can't do *that*. I'll hurt you."

She thinks I can't manage the pain. Huh. I'd do anything for her plump lips to wrap around my cock.

She's trying to think of a different way to 'help' me when the door opens and Orion and Logan walk in. "Thought we heard someone talking in here."

"Maisy and I are deciding what she can do to make me feel better," I say.

"I can think of a few ways." Logan chuckles and winks at Orion. "Orion, what d'you think?"

"Yeah, I can think of a few ways, too."

Maisy blushes. The shy smile on her face is so innocent.

"Whatever you have in mind, Kai cannot move. And I won't hurt him." She starts unbuttoning my jeans. "But I *will* make him feel better."

"Not right now, you won't." Orion's words hang in the air, and Maisy's deft fingers stop their work, her eyes locking with his. *Dammit!*

"Let him stew in his own precum for a while." Orion sits in the chair opposite the sofa and pulls down his sweatpants. "Come here, darling. Put your sweet little mouth on me, and show me how sorry you are for leaving my house without permission."

She looks at me, then slowly walks on all fours across the room to where Orion is. Her body is beautiful, like a gazelle's, her ass raised as she crawls, her back arched, her mouth open. Logan looks as bewitched by the sight as I am.

She reaches Orion and lowers her head into his lap, giving him a few long, wet licks from his balls up to the head. *Fuck!*

A grunt rises from the back of my throat. That long wet lick was meant for me. My cock protests, and I don't waste any time in taking it out and pumping it with my hand, my fingers wrapped tightly around it. "Fuck you, Orion," I mutter.

Logan has taken his cock out. He's pumping it too and smirking at my frustration.

I have the best seat in the house as Maisy takes Orion fully into her mouth, throat-deep, then pulls out and swirls her tongue around the tip. Desire surges through me and spirals down to my balls, drawing them up tight. *Fuuuck... why isn't that* my *cock?*

"That's it, Maisy, that's a good girl," he moans. "Show me what a good little slut you are."

She bobs her head, sucking him; he tangles his fingers in her hair, gripping her tightly as he sets his own pace, fucking her mouth, hard, with louder grunts each time, pulling her flush against his groin. Her husky groans and wet pops resonate around the room.

Logan kneels behind her and reaches around to unbutton her jeans. He pulls them down to her knees, revealing black lace panties.

I groan again.

"Lace panties, Maisy? The doctor approves."

She moans in agreement around Orion's cock.

Logan pulls them aside and runs his cock up and down her slit a few times before sliding inside her, giving her no time to adjust to his size. "That's it, Maisy, take it all in," he grunts.

Maisy whimpers and now her focus is behind her, and what Logan's doing to her–clawing her hips, thrusting to the hilt. She releases Orion's cock from the suction with a full-voiced groan. The goddess moaning in front of me is a sight to behold.

Orion cups her chin and pulls her down onto him again. "Is Logan's cock too big for you, slut? I don't care. Take it, and finish the job in front of you."

She takes him in and sucks with renewed gusto.

"Show me how good you are sucking my cock." Orion presses Maisy's head down. It appears to stop her intake of air. She chokes for a good few moments before he growls and lets her breathe.

She bobs up, her eyes glossed over, gazing at him as a strand of saliva connects her mouth with Orion's cock.

"That's my gooood girl." He snickers and slaps her face, once, twice. *Fuck, I'm gonna cum just by watching them.* He growls louder and thrusts roughly into her mouth a few times before he stills inside of her with a deafening groan.

"Oh yes, Maisy, yes, you're doing great, sweetheart," Logan mutters as Maisy comes up for air, and her hips start bucking. She must be close to climax.

"Logan!" she breathes.

"You're all fuckers, y'know," I say. I start jerking, but it's difficult when I'm in pain. Hearing her loud whimpers and seeing her body shake as Logan empties his seed inside her is my rapture. And yet, I'm hard as a steel rod, and suffering.

Logan pulls out and slaps her ass a few times. "Now you can go to Kai," he tells Maisy.

My beautiful baby girl! She grins and walks to me on her hands and knees and *fuck yes*, that's all I wanted, her lips on my pulsating cock.

MAISY

Now I've received permission to suck Kai off, I lower my mouth to his lap.

"Perk your ass up as you suck his cock, Maisy," Logan jeers. "I wanna see your dripping cunt."

"Who says I'm gonna suck him?" I wink at Logan and give Kai a swirl of my tongue before I take off my jeans fully, get on the sofa and plant a knee on either side of him.

"Oh, fuck, you little cunt!" I hear Orion say. I'm happy I'm getting him hot again.

I position Kai's glans at my wet entrance and moan as he slowly stretches me. I can feel every vein of his rock-hard cock inside my cunt. I start riding him, perking my ass up as I slide up, and inward as I take him in.

"Baby girl, just be careful, please," Kai begs. "I can't move a lot."

"Don't worry, Kai, you won't. I'm doing all the moving. Is this good? Does it feel good?" I go up and down, swiveling my hips and bracing myself against the back of the sofa. The sound of his groans is giving me much-needed assurance that I'm doing a good job.

Orion gets to his feet, his cock swinging left and right, and stands next to me. "Come here." He pushes my head down on his cock again. I start bobbing, riding Kai at the same time. "You're a little whore, Maisy, you know that?"

He pulls his cock out of my mouth and positions himself behind me, his knees landing next to mine on the sofa so both of us are straddling Kai. Before I can say anything, Orion pushes my body down onto Kai and I'm more than happy to oblige. I press my lips to Kai's and kiss him passionately. He may be in pain, but he devours my mouth like there's no tomorrow. The level of horny can be tasted. I roll my hips up and down as we kiss and gasp for air, and I feel Orion's hand flat on my lower back, holding me down.

"Don't move, now." Orion takes my arousal and spreads it over my ass, pushing in one finger, then another, and my whole body awakens. I whimper, I moan, I bite Kai as I kiss him and Orion holds me still.

"Shh, it's fine, you've done this before, baby girl," Kai mumbles against my lips as I buck in panic.

Orion fixes his pierced cock at my ass and pushes in, little by little. My bucking seems to help him; I adopt his rhythm of taking him in deeper, and out, until my body is full, and his cock is in to his balls.

"There you are, slut, I knew you could take both of us!" Orion hisses.

Kai moans, though I'm not sure whether it's from pain or pleasure.

"Are you okay, Kai?"

"Yes, yes, I am. I'm so close, but I'm fucking okay."

Orion grabs my hips, clawing deep with his fingers and starting to dictate the rhythm. With Kai thrusting from beneath me, my body begins to lurch and surge with an electrifying zing. I hold onto the sofa and close my eyes, trying to swallow my whimpers and let myself fly on this cloud of decadence.

Someone's cupping my chin and by the time my eyes are open there's Logan, pushing his cock into my mouth. I take him in too. I want to please all of my men, forever.

"Fuck, Maisy, you're so beautiful!" Logan groans.

"Who knew this cum whore would do such a good job for us?" Orion states as he slaps my but cheek, and continues to thrust into me as Kai does. They alternate their entry to my kingdom and with Logan's cock in my mouth, the heights they take me to remind me I'm going to crash down harder than a full speed freight train running over me.

"Look at me, Maisy. Your eyes, on me. I want to see my little slut coming."

I open my eyes and gaze back at Orion as I convulse and jerk from the hit, whimpering. Logan's cock is in my hands and I'm jacking him, my eyes locked with Orion's as he pounds into me. I hear Kai's shout when his hot cum spurts inside me, and I squeeze his cock with my pussy as my cum gushes. Orion's next, his growl unmistakably gruff and his nails at my hips drawing blood.

Logan's roar is last. "Open wide, show me your tongue!" I obey, and his cum shoots directly down my throat, some ropes of semen landing on my face. I wipe them off and lick my fingers.

Logan collapses onto the floor in exhaustion, and laughs. "Maisy, you'll be the death of us!"

Judging by the look of Kai, that might be somewhat true, despite his orgasm. "Pull up, please, both of you. I'm in pain."

Orion lifts me off him and Kai's cock drops onto his stomach. Orion bites my neck as his cock slides out of my ass.

"I don't want to ever leave this house, Orion," Logan huffs. "I'm perfectly happy being here, eating and fucking our girl."

"That's a thought, right?" Orion gets off the sofa and helps me to do the same.

"Oh, man, if only."

"I'm sure that's possible?" I purr. "We could always go somewhere on vacation, the four of us? There's also tonight. You could sleep with me tonight?"

Orion puts an end to my enthusiasm. "No. No one's sleeping with you tonight."

I pout. "Why?"

"Kai needs rest, and I need Logan to stay with him. He's been shot. That's not something you just dismiss."

"And you?" Kai asks.

"I won't sleep with Maisy, don't you worry about that. She needs rest too. Tomorrow night she needs to go to the club, so I need her fresh and alert."

I cross my arms over my chest. "You're a real party pooper, you know that?"

"As least I'm a responsible party pooper." He slaps my ass. "Go. Go before we fuck you again. That sweet pussy's unquenchable."

~

The sun shining through the window wakes me. I try to hide from it under my pillow, but it's too late. I'm already awake.

I blink a few times before my eyes fully open. Judging by the height of the sun, it must be noon. And someone's been in my room. It's neater. Towels have been folded and placed on the side. My cover isn't scrunched under me and between my legs as always, but is draped over me instead. I turn to my bedside table and there's a breakfast tray, as well as cream and strawberries. I sit up, yawn, and lift the tray onto my bed. Famished, I start eating.

Today is the day. It must work as I planned it. Kai's in bed, Logan will leave if he hasn't already, and Orion rarely comes to see me during the day. If I'm right, Lisa should be here.

A light knock on the door startles me.

"Good morning, beautiful." Logan walks in and kisses me on the forehead.

I smile at him through a mouthful of egg and bacon.

"I just came to give you a kiss before I go. I'll see you later."

I nod. "Mm-hmm."

"Is everything okay?"

How am I different to any other day? And how does he know that today, I'm withholding something? From everyone? I swallow. "Sure. I'm starving, that's all."

"Okay, sweetheart." He kisses me on the lips and leaves.

I wait until he's out of the door before I start getting ready. If I'm to pull this off, I need to do it early in the day.

I take a shower, put on a sleeveless, knee-length black polka-dot dress and white sneakers, nothing flashy, and head downstairs to the kitchen.

"Good afternoon, Maisy."

Yup. There she is. "Hi, Lisa. Good to see you. Coffee's already made?"

"Yes, there's plenty." She pours me a cup and passes it to me.

I take a sip. "Thank you. Is Mya around today?"

"She's at school."

"Oh, yes. Silly me, of course she's at school," I laugh. *Am I laughing too much?* If my calculations are correct, nobody should notice I'm gone. *So why am I nervous?*

"I see the clothes fit?" Lisa's scrutinizing the dress she got for me.

"They do. I'm so happy you went shopping. My other clothes were bought by Leila and–"

"Say no more. Haha, poor you."

"Yes, exactly that!"

"At least I've dressed you up a little now," she laughs.

"Yes, thank you!" I touch her arm, wanting her to know how grateful I am. "I really appreciate it."

"Then I've done what I needed to do. I filled the fridge, too. Let me quickly go to the bathroom and I'll be on my way." She checks her watch, then shoots out of the kitchen.

When the way's clear, I take her cell and order an Uber to take me to Lorenzo Vitali's business address, which I remember from seeing in Jerry's box. I request the Uber picks me up from here and drops me back all in one go.

I hope by the time my Uber arrives, Lisa will be out of the way and Orion will just think she's come back having forgotten something, and if I'm lucky, he won't check his notifications for the security camera.

I get an instant text back: the Uber will arrive in ten minutes. I quickly close the app and put the cell back down just as Lisa returns from the bathroom.

"Okay, see you soon, Maisy." She waves.

"See you later, Lisa."

I stay in the kitchen with my coffee and wait. Ten minutes is a long time to spend hoping nobody else will turn up, or hoping the car won't come early while Lisa's still outside. Which will ruin everything.

But somehow, I manage to remain calm and quiet. I'm doing this, no matter what. Once I find my sister, I'll tell them about her. Doing this today is the only way it will work.

I leave the house in exactly ten minutes and pray I won't be stopped by Orion. *Please God, let him think Lisa's come back for something.*

Outside, I run to the car and get in.

The driver looks confused by my stealthy entrance. "Uber for Lisa?"

"Yes, thank you. Please, could you hurry?"

"Sure." No questions asked, he drives off. After a while, he glances at me in the rear-view mirror. "I'm supposed to wait for you, right?"

"Yes, I won't be long."

He shrugs. "It's your money."

"Thank you."

I'm enjoying being a backseat passenger in New York, watching people running around like headless chickens, missing their lives altogether. But as we drive, the sights go from lively and colorful to gray, derelict, and abandoned.

In a short while, we drive around a very tall building, and stop at a neon sign that's flashing pink *Crew Entrance,* with a black door underneath.

"This is it?" My eyes are fixed on the view through the car window. This place reeks of mafia and murder.

"Yes."

"Thank you. Um, you'll wait for me, yes?" I plead as I open the door halfway.

He must know I'm doing something I shouldn't. "I'll be here."

I exit the car and stand in front of the door. With a deep breath in and out, I knock. Loud. Confident. *I'll be ten minutes. In and out. No longer.*

A big, square-shouldered guy unlocks the door from inside and peeks through the narrow opening. He checks me out from top to bottom as I gather the strength to speak.

My voice cracks. "Hi, I'm here–"

"Get in," he orders, and opens the door wider. "Go straight down there and take the first door on the right. Someone'll come get you."

"S-sure."

As I walk along the long, dark hallway, the dim red light makes me feel like I'm in a horror movie. I wonder if this was a mistake. Nobody knows where I am, and that's how people disappear.

When I find the first door on the right, I reach for the handle with a sweaty palm, my heart pounding in my throat.

A bright, empty room greets my terrified eyes. What a difference. On three sides are glass walls through which I see stairs, offices, and possibly boardrooms beyond. Everything looks clean and corporate. I'm shocked. I was expecting a seedy little studio where they shoot adult films.

Now all I need to do is find the videographer, that's all. I know that once he sees me, he'll remember Rosey. That's all I want at this stage. Proof that she's still around. Then I'll head back to Orion's and tell them where to look. *That's all.*

The door behind me opens and a fat old man with a beard enters. "I was told you're here. Let me see you." He grabs my arm and turns me around.

"Excuse me? I–"

"We'll call you in five. Be ready."

And just like that, he leaves. *Who can I talk to in here who'll actually stop and listen to what I have to say?* The office space is full of people working, and nobody's batting an eyelid over me being here.

A young woman in panties and stilettos walks in. Her boobs are big and jiggle as she moves. "It's your turn, cutie. With a rack like that you may get a permanent gig on set."

"My turn for what?"

The seedy old guy pokes his head through the door. "Come on, I don't have all day!" He disappears again.

The woman next to me is giving me advice. "If this is your first time, don't worry. Just think of something you like and it'll be over in a half hour."

I frown at what she's insinuating, and run out to follow the old man to get an explanation.

When I reach him, he stops and points at my feet. "These sneakers, can we change them?"

"No, I like them," I protest.

"Fine. You'll lose all your clothes in the first ten minutes anyway," he mutters.

"Wait, no. Listen to me, I want to ask you something." I hurry after him and we enter another room with glass walls, this time with a bed in the middle. From here I can see through to one other cubicle in the line, being used. I stop, my mouth dropping open. *Yes, this is the right place.*

The old man keeps talking. "The scene is, you're studying at home, and your frat buddies come over and start playing with you. Remember–"

"No, I'm not here for that. Um, look, I'm here for... Do you know Rosey? Have you met someone that looks like me?"

Finally, he stops for a split second and looks at me. "...Yeah, I thought you looked familiar. It was you, right? But that was a while ago, one or two years back."

"That was my sister!" *Yes! Thank you, God!*

"You're twins? That's what we need, twins! Where's your sister now, sweetie?"

"I'm looking for her, too!" *He's going to help me. I know it.*

"Well, when you find her, I'll have a job for you two. Double pay. People love videos with sisters," he says nonchalantly, while checking his camera. "Stop moving, and stand next to the bed. And, roll!"

"Wait, no! I'm not part of this, you got it all confused."

The door opens and men start coming in. There are at least six of them, and the last one closes the door. They surround me and start groping me as I scream.

"Let me go! I'm not here to shoot porn! I told you, I'm looking for my sister!"

Thankfully, the men stop, but they look confused.

The guy with the biggest beer belly steps forward. "What are we doing, Ronnie? Is it frat buddies or kidnapping?"

"Frat buddies, yeah," the old man, Ronnie, responds, looking through his camera as though I never spoke.

The beer belly turns to me. "Hey, let's get this over and done with. Don't make trouble."

"What trouble, asshole? I'm not an adult actress!" I need to leave this shitty place, and I try to get to the door but the square-shouldered bouncer's there, and picks me up like a rag doll. I start kicking him, screaming and yelling, trying to get everyone's attention.

Surely someone will do something! This is not how I thought my outing would turn out.

Everyone's listening now. They begin to raise their heads, one by one. Even the people in the boardroom are staring at me.

"Let me go! Let me out of this place!" I yell.

The bouncer holds me over his shoulder as the beer belly and the rest of the pricks exit the room. "Where do you want her, Ronnie?"

"Leave her here, and put one–no, *two* of those special patches on her lower back, somewhere she can't reach them," Ronnie tells him. "I don't have time for this nonsense," I hear him mutter to himself as he leaves the room too.

"Okay, boss."

"Fuck you! Help! Help me!" I yell as the bouncer lifts my dress and sticks something to my back.

"Huh. Look at that. Your stamp's still visible. You should be grateful. Porn pays better than whoring."

He thinks he's the good guy here! I try to reach back to whatever he's put there, but it's impossible. Plus, he has his arms locked around me. He holds me in place and starts counting down from twenty, ignoring my screams.

By the time he reaches eleven, my strength has dissipated and I ease off. I'm fine, there's no need to fight anymore. Why did I complain, anyway? They're good with me. And as he holds me, I become aware of his touch. God, I *melt* into his touch.

"Two, one." He releases me and I moan in frustration.

"No, don't let go. I need you, I need your touch."

"Yeah, you all do on that drug." He yells to someone, "Ronnie, she's ready!" A happy little smile forms on his face. "Have fun!"

His body, *oh God, he's so powerful*, and his hands, how they caressed me... But he's gone, and I see fat Ronnie, and *fuck, he'll do too*. I grin at him, and pull my dress up as I get onto all fours on the bed. "Hey you. Come over here."

CHAPTER 13

LOGAN

What in the fucking hell of Satan? *What the fuck?!! Is that* Maisy *in the recording studio?*

I glance at her two, three times, trying to look indifferent. Then four.

Blinking slowly, my fingers clasped, elbows on the table, I do everything in my power to sound aloof. "Who's that girl?"

I'm sitting in the boardroom, attending a meeting I wanted to end five minutes ago, though now I'm thanking my lucky stars I didn't.

Everyone at the table is uninterested. My cousin Vince, who's running the gig, peeks at her. "Which one?"

"Some new chick."

My self-control is usually great. Now, with Maisy, it seems like I have none. I shoot up onto my feet, drawing everyone's attention, as twenty-two members of my family are now staring at me.

"Has she been checked? She's screaming. I thought we didn't force girls into porn anymore."

“We don’t, unless they scream. Haha!” Vince laughs.

“For fuck’s sake, Vince!” I push out the chair behind me, the screech visibly startling everyone, and leave the boardroom.

I hear a few grumbles of “Come on, Logan, we need you in here.” They all want to go and spend time in a seedy booth with their stripper whores. What they always do, and always did when my father ran this place.

I stride down to where Maisy is, and I still cannot believe my eyes. If I don’t hurry, it looks like Ronnie’s going to fuck her and that’s not good. I’m gonna have to cut off his cock and kill him.

He sees me approaching angrily but doesn’t stop, even when I storm inside. But why would he? They’ve always shared these girls. I must remind myself to fire everyone who worked with my father.

I grab his arm and pull him back, away from her. “What the *fuck* are you doing?”

“Don’t be such a spoilsport, Logan, wait your turn.”

Funny, he thinks I play by Lorenzo’s rules. He’s looking at her hungrily and has already unzipped his pants, though he’s struggling with the top button under his big stomach.

“You better fucking stop what you’re doing because you’ll end up with nothing below your waist. Zip up, I don’t wanna see your ugly wiener. Now...” I point to Maisy on the bed, moaning and touching herself under her dress. “Has she been checked?”

Ronnie grumbles, but does what I tell him. Once he’s dressed, he heads over to the camera, and the blinking red light on top switches off. *The fucker was recording himself.* “She must’ve been if she’s here. It’s not up to me to check, y’know.”

“Has she been given something?” I don’t even look at him, just press my lips together because I know what’s going on. I can see it. She’s been drugged.

During my father’s reign, women didn’t have a choice. Or a voice. Those who ended up within his vicinity for whatever reason and were pretty enough to be fucked, but didn't want any part in adult filmmaking, were medicated to get them horny. All that stopped when he died, and Vince swore to me on several occasions he's not doing that anymore. *Asshole.*

"Yeah, two doses."

Maisy's eager eyes lock with mine and she inhales, her whole body beginning to undulate. She's high. "Oh, you. I want *you!* And your big cock!" She rises up on her knees, coming closer.

I got to get her away from here. She may start talking, and that's another ticking bomb I don't need. "She must be tested first," I say.

"Well, *you* test positive for being an absolute God in bed!" she giggles in her sweet voice, her finger pointing at both of us.

I grab her by the upper arm and lift her dress to check her over, and remove the two patches they've slapped on her. Fucking Vince. He *swore* to me. And if we're not stocking up on them, where the fuck does he buy them? Orion's right: there are too many snitches among us. I know my books, my income and outgoings, my profit. Nothing of this sort appears on them, so who's paying for this drug? And why am I not being told about it? My blood's boiling for so many reasons; I could explode right here.

I pull her up roughly. "You're going to my office to be checked, right now." I've had enough of her lies. I should leave her here to rot. Dammit, *why* have we all fallen for this trickster?

"No, no, I wanna stay, they told me I'm about to play with ten men!" she whispers, sluggishly. "*Ten men*, Doctor! I'd hate to miss that."

I ignore her words. If I didn't know she was drugged, this would've been the last straw for her. But seeing that she is, I can't leave her here. She's depending on me. And my men will tear her apart.

I drag her across the floor while people go about their business, everyone ignoring me apart from Vince who's watching me from the boardroom. I shoot him a look and shake my head.

We reach my private office, the place where I check all my patients in the privacy of four solid walls, and sit her on the chair. "Maisy! What the fuck are you doing here? I thought we said no more lies!" I want to sound angry, menacing, but I hear the plea in my voice. *I hope to God she has a good fucking reason for being in my studio.*

Maisy looks at me with those dark eyes, the hazel specks around the pupils making her even more enticing, and with all her effort–which I know is all of it, because this drug doesn't take prisoners–she takes a deep breath. "I must find my twin sister. Rosey." And that's it, she's lost again.

What did she say?

"Logan, I can't talk. Please, fuck me, or I'm not sure what I'm gonna do. I need someone." Maisy's sweating profusely, her nipples hardened under her dress, and she's touching herself again.

"Your *sister?* Maisy, you have a sister? Fuck, girl, why are you doing this to me? You thought you could just come here and ask about your sister? What about the recording of you? Please tell me that's not a lie!"

"It's not. But I must find my sister, too. She was taken by Milan when we were twelve, and he told me if I worked for him, if I did what he asked, my sister would be spared, but he lied! That fucker *lies!* He made her a prostitute, he made her take part in adult films, and all this time I thought I was helping her..."

I'm listening to her talk and if I could, I'd kill her myself. All these lies–why did she keep so much from us? We wanted to protect her, and we are, but she's in too deep now. I take a needle from the cabinet and give her an injection in the buttock. It will help the drug dissolve in her body within a couple of hours.

"Fuck, Maisy."

"Logan..." Frenzied, she grabs my top and pulls me to her. "There's a taxi waiting for me outside. Take me there. Please."

"Where's it taking you?"

"Back to Orion's." She lunges as if to kiss me, but I keep her at bay.

"Right. Okay, you go there, yes?"

"Yes. Logan... if you knew about Rosey, you wouldn't have wanted to help me... help *us*."

I'm just furious she never trusted me in the first place. "I *would've*."

I grab her arm again and we leave my office, me dragging her out and back through the red-lit hallway. "Right now, I just hope Orion doesn't find out you're gone. If he does, this is our last goodbye."

"Don't tell him, please. Please," Maisy begs as we get outside, and I see the car waiting. I open the door for her.

"She had something to drink, but she'll be fine. Here." I give the driver a couple hundred dollars. "Look at her, or talk to her, and you're dead. She'll tell me if you do. But she'll try you. So be strong if you want to live." I throw a blade at him. It lands neatly on the seat between his legs, a few centimeters from his crotch. His breath catches, and he nods.

I pull my cell out and take a picture of him, just in case, then send her off.

Going back to the meeting in the boardroom, enraged and with a twitching eye, I begin to wonder if I've been too lenient as head of the Vitalis. My father got his dick cut and died. That was his thing. But why on earth we continued with the adult movies... *Fucking Vince.*

I enter the boardroom breathing hard through my nose. Everyone seems to notice my twitching eye.

Vince is standing. "Logan, glad you could join the meeting again. As I was saying, we're not sure if you're suitable to lead the Vitalis." His two brothers, sitting on either side of him, nod and make noises of agreement.

Little does Vince know, his words are coming at the wrong fucking time for him.

I regard everyone else. Not one person has the guts to look me in the eye.

"Right." I take the blades from my pocket and swiftly throw them one by one, each landing in the necks of the three men, tearing them open. Blood starts spurting from their throats and everyone else in the room shouts in disgust.

"Come on, Logan, I just bought this suit!" Uncle Jon shouts, taking cover from the gushing blood.

Bobby also jumps back to save his clothes. "We've told you, not the neck! It's too messy."

The glass walls grow red as Vince and his brothers clutch their necks and choke on their own blood, before finally succumbing to their deaths. *Too easy if you ask me.*

"Anyone else think I'm not suitable to lead?" I ask quietly.

I look at those remaining as the blood drips from me. I bet I'm a sight to remember. That was my kill, and I'm proud of it.

"I thought so. Now, sit yourselves down. I'm not finished."

I roll my neck, feeling the muscles popping, then crack my knuckles. This is my world now. I've been too lenient for too long, not wanting to imitate my father. But in order to survive, one has to take charge.

"The shithole you see behind you"–I point to the porn studio–"is gone. We're not doing that anymore. You want to fuck a girl, go get yourself one! I'm not here to be your pimp. For years, the Vitalis made capital investments in the pharmaceutical and healthcare sectors. Why the fuck do you think I qualified as a doctor? My father started the strip club as a front for the adult industry. But that's where it stops. I don't want us involved in that anymore. Starting right now."

"Hear, hear," Uncle Jon exclaims. "I see you've grown some balls, Logan. Big, like your father's. Haha!"

Others back me with noises of approval, but I notice Bobby doesn't do shit. He just stands by the door. *Fucking snitch.* I should've killed him, too.

"Bobby, what d'you say?"

"Sure, whatever you want, Logan."

"That's right. This is my kingdom now, so don't you fuckers forget it!"

I leave, and all I can think about is that I have to check for a tape of Maisy's sister, hoping I never find it here. I head straight to the videographer's room, where the archive is. Ronnie's editing something and on seeing me, he stands up in alarm. He clearly saw the blood-stained glass.

"That girl that was here earlier. Do you know her?" I snarl.

"I think so, yes. She looked familiar."

"Try to find what we have on her. Search under the name Rosey or Maisy."

I cross my arms and tower over him as he sits back in the chair and starts searching through files on the computer.

"Um, this might take a while, Logan."

"I have time," I snap.

The process is lengthy and from looking at him, I think I'd do a better job. And faster. He finds a file, opens it, checks the girl's face, and closes it, all while I watch over his shoulder. There are lots of Roseys, but only a few Maisys.

"Ronnie, think smarter, or we'll be going through these files for years. When was the most recent one made?"

"Let me see. Hmm, it wasn't made here, just edited here. Less than a year ago."

"Put it on."

The video starts, and the first thing I see is Maisy smiling, unnaturally, at the camera.

"There! That's her! Give me the file–now!" I growl. I'm not letting him look at her a second longer.

He downloads it to a memory stick and passes it to me.

"Where else do we keep these files? Are they on a cloud?"

"Nowhere. Only in here. This room's protected from fire and flood."

"So we don't have any backup?"

"Vince couldn't afford the backup. He told me too many times."

"Delete this file from the system," I order.

He turns to me, looking shocked, as if he's forgotten that my father's dead and I can decide his fate. "We don't do that."

I don't say a word. I just cock my head and stare at him, putting my hands in my pockets. Lucky for him, he remembers his place. And what's in my pockets. Lucky for me, he doesn't know I have no more blades in there.

"Um, sorry, Logan. I... forgot. Please, don't kill me. Here, it's deleted."

"Try searching again."

He searches for the file, and cannot find it.

"What about the other Maisys in the system?"

"They're from a few years back." He opens the next file and we see a short blond girl. The next one, a redhead. He opens them all, one by one. Our Maisy does not appear again.

"Okay. Thank you."

"Any time, Logan."

I exit the archive room with the memory stick in my pocket, and head straight to my penthouse. My impenetrable fort up in the sky. My father was a control freak, he conveniently set up the strip club together with the offices and the studios in the same building as the penthouse. I need to change and wash off the blood before heading to Orion's.

I still can't fucking get that she asked me not to tell them. And why I'm even considering it is beyond me. *I shouldn't feel guilty we found her video in my studio.*

She came to my club–that's on her.

We drugged her–that's on me.

She lied to us about her sister–that's on her.

We found her video in my studio–that's on me.

Fuck this! Is there any way out?

ORION

The Cartes are eager to meet Maisy and I don't like it one bit. I don't want people looking at her, let along greeting her and shaking her hand. She's too special for that. I'm wary and extra-vigilant since I told them. No one should dare think of trying their luck with her.

It was easier when no one knew about her, but then again, with Kai being so reactive, this was bound to happen. We wanted him to get back to how he was, to start living again, and now that he has, I remember how uncontrollable and intense his dramas tend to get.

But back then, we didn't have Maisy. And being addicted to someone like her, I could never imagine not having her in my house again.

Even Lisa likes her, and Lisa never liked any girl I hung around with. She got Maisy's clothes without argument; I just asked her and she showed up an hour later. And filling my fridge without asking personal questions is unlike her. So she's on board with Maisy, too.

This morning, she was smiling. There must be some improvement with Mya having gone non-verbal, going by Lisa's mood, which is a mirror to her soul. She was also singing in the kitchen earlier.

I check myself in the mirror. Tailored three-piece suit, shirt, tie. My lucky rings, bracelets, and a watch. Shiny black shoes. Nothing's changed in the last half hour. I've been fully suited and ready to pick up Maisy for our meeting. Still, with time on my hands, I head to Maisy's room to check on her. I don't want her wearing anything too revealing. The Cartes are jackals; they'll circle around her until one of them takes a bite.

Outside Maisy's room, I stop and check myself. *This is it.* Considering all the activities we've been doing, I wouldn't want anything to happen to her.

I knock and don't wait for her to respond before I enter. "Maisy?"

She's not here, not even in the bathroom.

I go down to the living room to check if Kai's seen her. He's been sleeping all day, not once asking for Maisy, which is good–it means his body can heal. He's in physical pain and he knows, like a true athlete, he must recuperate. He ate three times today, so he should be getting better by tomorrow.

I enter quietly, and the first thing I see is Maisy's body, undulating like a goddess. One knee on each side of Kai's head, her dress pulled up, scrunched between her fingers. Head tilted back, eyes closed, she's sitting on Kai's face, rolling her hips as if in slow motion, and moaning quietly. If this isn't the best sight I've ever seen in my life, I don't know what is.

Kai is downing her arousal, his groans smothered by her cunt as I stand here and watch in awe. I lean against the doorframe, my cock twitching. She's never sat on my face but when she does, I'll eat her forever. She tastes so good.

But this vision is different. There's no sense of urgency like she always has when she's horny. This is just her, taking her time, enjoying each sound Kai makes.

"Maisy, I hate to stop you from doing this, since you look like a sexual deity, but we got to be out in a half hour, darling," I say.

She doesn't respond. Kai just growls louder, taunting me. He knows I wish I was in his place.

She opens her eyes. They're wanton, no hazel specks visible, just that black abyss I want to dive into. I've never before seen them like this, so enthralling. She rolls her hips, smiling seductively at me as she does. "You're next, Orion."

That rasp in her voice, I believe her. A true temptress. If I was anyone else, I'd drop everything and wait in line like a puppy with its tongue out and tail wagging. But I'm not. Though my cock wishes I was.

"Maisy, that's enough. I need you to get ready for tonight. I told you how important this meeting is." The urgency in my voice is clear, but she's unperturbed. Her head tilts back again and she picks up speed.

Kai's hands wrap around her thighs and I can see he's putting in the extra work.

I take a different approach. "Kai. *Stop*."

He tries to move her off his face but she moans in frustration, and fixes herself properly back where she was. I wouldn't be able to resist that myself, and I bet he sticks his tongue deep inside her because she starts making unintelligible sounds.

"What the fuck's going on?" I demand.

Kai taps Maisy's thighs and lifts her up. She scrunches her nose and pouts at me, not happy at all.

"I don't know, to be honest," he admits. "I was sleeping all day, haven't moved at all, and an hour ago Maisy walks in and doesn't say anything, just sits on my face. And of course, am I stupid enough to not give her what she wants? I'm *not!*"

"Why are you talking like that?"

"I've been doing this for an hour. My jaw hurts and my tongue's swollen but Maisy, oh, my beautiful Maisy," he takes her hand and presses his lips to it. "She's my femme fatale. She hasn't cum yet. She just enjoys the ride, so to speak."

Maisy's sitting on the armrest, looking spaced out.

This is unlike her. "Maisy, are you okay?"

She looks at me, grins, and jumps up, trotting over and wrapping her arms around me. She cranes her neck to flash her teeth at me. "Yes." Then, she presses her cheek to my chest and shakes her head. "No."

I decide to take charge. "Kai, we're going."

"Come back once you're done," he says. "I want to know how it went."

I close the door behind us as Maisy hangs on to my body for dear life.

"Hey." I try to get her to look at me but she won't. "Maisy, what's wrong?" She burrows deeper into my chest. She must be afraid she'll end up back in Milan's hands. "Hey, don't worry, they won't hurt you. Let's go to your room and get you changed. I'm not sure I like this dress. And your panties? I bet you left them with Kai, didn't you?" I chuckle.

We get to her room and I help her get the dress off, then open her closet. "Let's see what Lisa got for you."

I'm going through the dresses when she pushes in front of me and chooses the skimpiest one there is, a bodycon minidress with open shoulders and deep cleavage.

"Maybe not this one. I want them to talk to you, not look at your body."

"Orion." She tilts her head up at me. "I want to wear this dress." There are those wanton eyes again, and I want to slap some sense into her. Those eyes are *ours*. No one else should see them.

"Out of the question."

She cups my cock and squeezes, knowing perfectly well it'll grow in her hands in a matter of seconds. And, there it is. I got a hard-on and I'm about to go to work.

"I'll wear it for you, but they won't know that," she whispers to me, and winks.

I step back, removing her hand from my cock. She's not making much sense but I can't be arguing over this. We shouldn't be late.

"Very well. Dress up, put some heels on, and"–I take in the radiant glow she has from sitting on Kai's face–"um, and maybe don't look so pretty. I'll be downstairs."

She nods happily. "I'll try."

I pace nervously about the kitchen. This must turn out like I planned, and not any other way. I check my watch. We should've left by now, but she's still getting ready.

Finally, I hear the clacking of heels on the stairs and then Maisy shows up in the kitchen.

She's one hell of a sight. Black heels elongating her legs, her dress way too short for my liking, low cleavage, bare shoulders. Strangely, she's left her hair messy, but it goes with the bright red lipstick. That lipstick can stay on my cock all night after we get back.

In fact, she's ready to be spanked. And then fucked. Not to attend a meeting.

She smiles. Those eyes are different, raw, lustful. "I'm ready for you," she breathes. She's fucking me in her mind, that's clear.

"We're late," I chide her.

I take her hand and lead her out to the car that's waiting for us. Garry's in the driver's seat and once we're in, he sets off. Our eyes meet as he glances at Maisy in the rear-view mirror one too many times.

"Keep your eyes on the road, Garry, if you want to still have eyes by the time we get there," I growl.

He looks uncomfortable and nods at me via the mirror.

Arriving in no time, he parks the car and gets out to open Maisy's door. He's either too young or he just doesn't know what to do. He spots me through the window and at the sight of my face, runs to my door instead and opens it.

I exit the car and go to Maisy's side to open her door.

There are a few members of the Cartes standing outside the club and they all stare as Maisy's legs make an appearance out of the car, the rest of her nearly-bare body following. I turn to them in a relaxed manner, but they know what that means. They scatter all over the place like cockroaches.

Def Leppard's "She's Too Tough" is playing as we enter the club. I place my hand on Maisy's lower back and meet her eyes, which are still wild and needy. Was she always like this? Is that why we can't get enough of her? Maybe her not getting release with Kai is messing with her head.

I look around the club and every single person is looking at her. I'm gonna kill someone tonight. "What's the matter, you've never seen a girl before?"

I wait for an answer. They resume drinking and talking, all of a sudden making more noise than before. I choose to ignore them and head for the boardroom on the second floor, up a narrow staircase. I direct Maisy there, allowing her to walk in front of me.

"You okay?" I ask.

She turns to me, her hands raking through her hair, sliding down her neck, then cupping her breasts. "Orion, I need you. Badly."

"Maisy, not right now, darling. I need you to focus."

The door at the top of the stairs opens before we get there. It's Uncle Leo who greets us, and I cannot protect her from his greedy glare. "So, this is the woman we saved yesterday!"

Maisy reaches him and he pulls her to him, kissing her on both cheeks.

For fuck's sake. I shouldn't say anything. But I'm petty when it comes to Maisy. My two other uncles are behind Uncle Leo, seemingly competing over who's going to perv on her the most.

They kiss her, and I've had enough. I pull her to safety, out of their grasp. They shouldn't be enjoying her this much.

As we enter the boardroom I'm quick to point to a padded leather chair at the head of the table "Maisy. Sit here." And as an additional precaution, I sit next to her while the others sit at the opposite end and along the sides with plenty of space between Maisy and them.

"Uncle Leo, Uncle James, Uncle Colletti, this is Maisy Roy. She's the girl we got from the Delgados."

Maisy waves sweetly at them. "Hi."

The two perfect mounds on her chest, rising with each breath she takes, is where their eyes land. She flicks her hair to one side and touches her fingers to her collarbone. I can't make her out. *I know she wouldn't flirt with them, but what* is *she doing?*

My father's brothers are overweight, wheeze when they breathe, all smoke cigars, and are the perviest men there are. They're family, and they follow my lead, but I wouldn't put it past them to kill me in my sleep.

Uncle Leo takes a sip of whiskey and quirks an eyebrow. "Maisy, Orion tells us you're special," he begins, a suggestive edge to his voice. *Of course.* "What's so special about you apart from, um, what we see in front of us?"

She laughs uncomfortably and twists in the chair, her breasts jiggling too much for my liking. *What is* wrong *with her today?*

"Uncle Leo, please mind your language," I warn him.

"Okay, okay." He takes a long drag of his cigar, stalling for time. I fucking bet he's imagining all kinds of filthy things about her.

Maisy looks at me to check if she's okay to respond, and I nod. *Good girl.*

"I have photographic memory, Uncle Leo. That means whatever I see, I remember. It's forever etched in my head." She ends with a wink.

Uncle Leo looks flustered and I stare at her, shocked. *She'll get spanked for that wink, little brat.*

"Oh, is that so?" Uncle Colletti asks.

"I worked for Milan the Dog for a number of years and I've seen quite a lot of the stuff he has on all of you," Maisy drawls.

Uncle James's eyebrows rise and he shifts uncomfortably in his chair. "What did you do for him, Maisy, apart from, um, you know?"

He just had *to go there.* "Uncle James, Maisy's a genius," I growl, feeling the need to defend her. "Milan hired her to run his books when she was still underage. I don't want you insinuating she was his whore. She wasn't."

"Oh? And you were there, were you?" Uncle James asks mockingly. *Always testing me.* He turns to his brothers. "Or maybe he tried this little angel's pussy last night and now his smitten cock's doing all the talking for him?" The three of them burst into laughter.

I've seen them do this too many times, and I'd often join in too, except this time I want to slit their throats and skin them alive. Maisy laughs too, but the way she bites her lip is what riles me the most. I'd slap some sense into her first before I shoot the other three. I don't usually show what I feel but right now, I have issues hiding my pettiness.

Maisy places her hand on my thigh and it glides up, reaching my cock, and strokes me over my pants. *What the fuck? Is this supposed to calm me down?*

"Do you want to know what I know? Ask me. I dare you. Give me a date, a name, or a location, and I'll tell you what Milan has in his files," she purrs.

She then leans in close to whisper in my ear. "I need you to fuck me, right now."

My eyes land on her legs. She's spread them in her chair and is rolling her hips. Her body's undulations are detectable only to me as her eyes meet mine and she winks again. "Yes, *now*."

I become aware of Uncle Leo's voice as I'm trying to make sense of her behavior. "Okay. Maisy. Tell me what you know about Christmas Day last year."

That was the day when Tom was killed. We're still looking for the killer. Although it was one of us who gave him away. So much has happened since, but my sister had it worst. Mya has not uttered a word since that day.

My uncles gulp, looking transfixed by the glide of Maisy's tongue across her top lip as she thinks.

"Maisy..." I warn.

My cell buzzes in my pants and I pull it out, reading the message under the table.

URGENT: Maisy's had two doses of the banned patches, you know the ones I mean. She should be coming down from it in the next hour. I'll fill you in tonight. L

Banned patches? *BANNED PATCHES?!*

"FOR FUCK'S SAKE!" I bellow, startling everyone. I look up and notice they're staring at me. *I'm no better than Kai. Totally out of control.* Quickly, I wave my hand dismissively. "Dry cleaner ruined my shirts."

Uncle Colletti ignores me. "We're waiting, Maisy."

Now, everything's as clear as day. Spending time with Kai, her behavior makes sense. That need in her eyes, I see it–I know how much it hurts. Why couldn't I see it earlier? Was I obsessing over Maisy that much that my perception of how I do things has changed?

Let's start with who gave her this patch.

We tried those stickers once on a girl we hooked up with. Forty-eight hours later, we all agreed they were bad news. The girl was prepared to do anything with anyone and we just couldn't control her. When we thought she was done, she went home and ended up fucking the pizza delivery guy, then a bunch of her neighbors for the rest of the night.

"Hmm, Christmas Day last year... I remember." She takes my hand and places it between her legs. "I remember seeing a few emails about a job being done."

Uncle Leo leans in. "Who were these emails from?"

She sits at the edge of her chair and rests her breasts on the table. While everyone's ogling her, open-mouthed, she spreads her legs more, one on either side of the chair. No one but me can see her under the table.

"The email correspondence was between Milan and someone else, who at the end wrote 'Don't ask for my help again. I could be made.'"

"What was the job?"

I don't make out who asks the question because I'm under her spell, watching her playing everyone.

"Um, let me think," she says breathily.

For fuck's sake! I'm going to pound that cunt the moment we're alone. There's a rage inside me I must keep under control, because I soon discover she's not wearing panties; her arousal is spread between her thighs and her cunt is brimming with juice. I press my fingers over her sleek lips and slide to her clit, swirling slowly, and she *ums* and *ahhs* until I pinch her.

"I got it!" she exclaims, just as I slide two fingers snugly inside. She moans, making out as though she's thinking. "Hmm, no, that wasn't it. Let me think again." On the second go I insert my fingers to the knuckle, and do so a few more times.

"Mm-hmm, mm-hmm, yes. *Yes.*"

They're not sure what's going on as I've turned sideways to them so I can watch her. "Maisy, they're waiting on you," I remind her.

"Someone died," she says. "Got killed. But there was an unplanned element, and this was what the email correspondence was about. Can you give me a name so I can cross-check it with whatever else I have in my head?"

"Good girl, Maisy," I whisper. Her eyes lock with mine as I rub her swollen clit. Her licentious eyes undress me, reminding me how dangerous this drug is as I continue to satisfy her craving.

"No–let's not give her names just yet!" Uncle James exclaims. I turn to him, surprised by his anxious response. "Maybe she's trying us out and digging for information," he adds.

"Ask me anything, Uncle James."

Maisy's fuck-me voice has lured my uncle into her trap. "I will, yes," he replies. "Um, what does Milan have on us, the Cartes?"

I jerk two fingers inside her once again, crook them, and massage her g-spot.

"Mmm, yes. Yes. He does have a good hold on–"

"Tell us!" he yells, interrupting her enjoyment.

Looking exasperated, she sighs. "I came across a document explaining the whole establishment. The boxing club, which is your front, here, this boardroom, usually twenty people in it, um..." I swirl around her nub a few times. "...The gambling, special parties, et cetera." She speaks rhythmically, bouncing slightly on my fingers as she does. "You also provide loans, not at the usual high-interest rates, lower than the banks offer." I pick up her rhythm and jerk my fingers to it, all the while registering my shock at how much she knows. "For every honest entrepreneur at risk of having to close their restaurant or store, there's a Carte mafia family member, ready to take over the business or offer a cash injection in exchange for shares. Basically, you've established yourselves for both 'protection' and extortion. *Yes!*"

She finishes with an exclamation and the others look at her strangely. "I told you, I know everything," she adds.

"Okay, so you know quite a lot about us," Uncle Leo reiterates as I continue sliding my fingers inside her and rubbing her swollen nub on repeat. "It's clear Milan was involved in Tom's murder last Christmas. He had an inside man. But he wasn't close enough to Tom to know he'd have Mya with him that day."

"I can't hold it in any longer," Maisy whispers in my ear.

Uncle Leo demands full attention, as always. "Are you listening to me, Maisy?"

"Be a good girl and cum without a sound," I murmur in her ear. "Can you do that for me, my little slut? Come on. Not a peep." She lowers her head as I turn to them.

It's time I take over the conversation. "Maisy told me that she remembers seeing a document that stated Mya was supposed to be killed. Whoever wrote it knew about Mya's psychologist."

Maisy holds her head in her hands and lets out a long moan, her body tautening almost imperceptibly.

"Is she okay?" Uncle James asks.

"Headaches," I respond. "So basically, it was an inside job."

Uncle James slams his fist on the table. "The *fucker!* I'll skin him alive when I find out who he is!"

Uncle Colletti looks deep in thought. "Do you know more, Maisy?"

Now she's had her orgasm, Maisy takes a deep breath and looks up at them, practically glowing. But all I'm thinking about is when the next wave will hit her.

"Tons," she yawns, "but I'm tired now. Headaches and all. I'll send you information via Orion if that's okay."

Uncle Colletti sounds concerned. "Yes, Orion, take her to bed."

Fucker. I know he can't wait to go and jerk off. "Very well. See you tomorrow. Sorry this was such a short meeting," I say.

"Maybe we can come to your place in, say, two weeks? Where Maisy's more comfortable?"

Uncle Colletti knows perfectly well I do not host people at home. Unless I must.

"Nah, we don't need to bother them," Uncle James says.

Him helping me screams red flags for miles.

Now Maisy interjects. "That's a good idea." *What the fuck? It's* my *house!*

"Okay, we'll talk, sure," I concede.

I help Maisy up and see where she was sat is a damp patch in the shape of her cunt. Fuck. That's the first time I've ever wanted to lick something off a chair. They'll see it too. *Fuck!* This is actually my fault.

I pull a handkerchief from my breast pocket and wipe the chair.

"She got a little sick," I say, by way of explanation.

On the drive home, while I'm fighting with reason, Maisy falls asleep with her head in my lap. Who gave her the patch? Has someone been in my house? Surely not, or I'd have seen them. Has she been out? She knows better. Whatever the case, something tells me this little angel's been lying to us. *Again.*

But what was I expecting? Of course she has, she's a genius. None of us stand a chance against her but right now, she's in too deep. I won't give her up, even if she's my prisoner for life. I pull her chin to my face and kiss her hot, feverous lips. She must be going through hell with this drug.

“I’ll keep you for myself, darling,” I whisper to her, “and no one will find you, not ever.”

CHAPTER 14

LOGAN

I pace angrily back and forth in the living room. Kai's brow, dipped with concern, is adding to my stress. I filled in the details for him and told him about Maisy's little trip, and what could've actually happened had I not been there. And the whole chain reaction afterward. Although I'm not sorry for that. What I omit to mention is, dammit, that she has a sister. I can't get myself to say it because it's one thing for her to blindly chase what's stopping her from becoming a teacher, and another thing for us to know that she looked in our eyes and lied to us at the very start. She's doing all this for her sister. Her fucking *sister*. She's ruined everything.

Kai's hurting more than his wounds do, and he's only aware of half of what I am. I couldn't bring myself to tell him. In a really stupid–and *smitten*–and selfish way, I'm not prepared to lose her. They'd shoot her the moment they found out.

Let's just see this video and then peel back the mysterious layers of Maisy's life. *How did Orion miss this? A fucking* sister! *She could've told us, stupid, stupid Maisy!*

The front door opening tells us it's judgment time. We glance at each other and head into the hall. Orion's there, waiting.

He's holding Maisy in his arms, and she's sleeping. An angel in disguise. We exchange somber looks, and as if she can see us together, she moans, so sweetly.

She is so precious, and at the same time, so deceptive and cunning and so many other things that I don't know which Maisy is the real one.

"Let me take her to her room." Orion disappears with her up the stairs, not waiting on our response.

Kai and I head into the kitchen, and stand awkwardly like teenagers who've been stood up for prom. The foreboding silence is what gets me. I dread Orion learning the news and I know Kai does too.

"How're you feeling?" I ask him.

"Better." That's all I get from him. Although, I can read his thoughts, which consist of killing everyone and everything in his way once he's good enough to get back to work. And Maisy's just adding to his misery.

Orion runs back down the stairs with loud thumps, enters the kitchen in big strides, and walks straight up to me. His face is red with anger, and fire spews from his eyes. He grabs me by the collar and pulls me to his face. "Where the *fuck* did she find the banned stickers, you dickhead?" he snarls through his teeth.

I'm not sorry for much in my life; in fact, I celebrate just about everything I've done, but this part, this stupid drug, for that, I'm sorry. And there's no going back. I invented the patches when I was studying medicine, all to please my father, and of course he was ecstatic. He loved it. He got my research and with it the patches were easily reproduced. I hated it and I hated myself for it. When he died, we stopped using them. I was fucking *promised* we weren't using them anymore. And I believed it.

I instinctively pull my blade from my pocket and press it against Orion's neck. "First tell me how the fuck she managed to leave your house, asshole!" I roar back.

He leans into the blade, knowing perfectly well it'll draw blood if he gets any closer. "She *didn't!*"

I ease off and put the blade back in my pocket. "Oh, but she did. She came to my club, entered through the back door, nearly did a scene with ten frat boys in the film studio, and fought like hell, enough to be given two doses of the banned patches. Had I not been there and seen her, this would've been a very different conversation."

Orion looks bewildered. He pulls out his cell and opens his security camera app. He then goes through his notifications for the day, one by one. He stops at a video where Maisy enters a car and watches it on repeat a few times before he says anything.

"I can't believe it. I thought Lisa forgot something. I didn't even look."

"And when she came back? How come you missed *that*, Orion?" Kai's accusatory words are biting.

Orion fast-forwards to the next notification on the cell and we see the postman outside, smoking. After a few minutes, Maisy is shown returning in the same car. He stares at the screen, then raises his eyes to mine, furious. "Why would she go to yours?"

"She knows my father's involvement in the adult industry. We talked about this. She just wanted to find the video!"

"Stupid girl!" Orion growls.

"Actually, she's a genius, man." Kai's been following our conversation, and since he's unable to punch his way around this, he's using his head for once. "She knows all of our addresses, where we live, where we work. She probably knows a lot more about us than we know about each other, and she's focused on one thing. God knows what else she has in her head."

"If she was a genius, she wouldn't have been so stupid!" I snap. "Still, I guess there was some good in her coming to my club. Her little excursion got my cousin

Vince and his brothers killed. The situation was perfect, it made it easy. In five seconds, I changed our entire business model. No more adult videos at Vitali's."

"Maisy's extremely valuable," Orion says slowly. "That much we know. But if we don't help her get the video soon, she'll do something else stupid and it'll be too late. Fuck, do we want to be heads of families who prey on young women? Gangbangs at Kai's, six dead. Porn films at Logan's, three dead. I dread to think what my family's plan for Maisy is once she's served her purpose. Why the fuck must I fight for this, to keep her safe? We'll stand against Milan with the Delgados and Vitalis and stop this once and for all. And as for Maisy, she's gonna get it when she wakes up."

I nod. "Very well."

Orion seems more forgiving than usual, and I'm not sure if I should be afraid that he'll make a stupid mistake because he's starting to think with his cock, like us, or if I'm actually happy I'm not going to have to fight him to save Maisy's life. Especially after the information about her sister comes to light.

Both Orion and I look at Kai, waiting on his response.

"I'm game," he says. "The Delgados are dead anyway, or at least half of them will be when I go back."

"When you tell them about the Irish, the rest of them will want to join you too," I laugh.

Kai's confused. "Irish? What about the Irish?"

"Now is not the time, Logan! The fuck?!" Orion snaps.

"What about the Irish, Orion?" Kai presses.

Orion huffs, looking pissed. "Kai, Maisy knew about the Irish incident. We now know for certain it was Milan, who, after assuming the identity of the Delgados during the arms deal, killed everyone except the three he left alive. He sent them home to spread the news that it was the Delgados. So the arms deal went to the Slavs."

Kai's jaw tightens, his blue eyes narrowing and darkening. No light will be getting in there anytime soon.

His hands curl into fists. "And you weren't gonna tell me this?"

"Not while you were wounded," Orion says calmly. "But I'm trusting you not to react irresponsibly. Right now, you're shot. Take this all in and make a *plan* for once, you fucker." He puts his hand on Kai's shoulder.

This won't really make any difference, knowing Kai. Whatever's in his head will happen. Not yet, for sure, but once he's better.

Kai chuckles darkly. "Ride or die, baby."

Orion smirks. "It's always ride or die with you. How about ride and live, for a change?"

I observe them while my head whirls. I have to come clean eventually. Besides, now's the perfect time to ruin everyone's mood.

"There's one more thing."

Orion's cheerful expression darkens. *How is it that he knows what's coming? I could've had good news. I don't, but...*

I pull the memory stick from my pocket and hold it up. "I got Maisy's video recording." *And she has a sister!* No. I'll give it one more day before I tell them about the sister.

"You found it?" Orion flashes his eyebrows.

"Mhm. She doesn't know about it."

Orion and Kai look at each other, and Kai immediately reacts with his cock. "Let's watch it."

"What do you think, Orion?"

"We need Maisy's permission," he says. "Tomorrow morning, when she wakes up, we'll ask her."

What a bunch of perverts we are. *Trustworthy* perverts. Who just want to fuck her nonstop.

"I'm sleeping with Maisy tonight," Kai announces, as if he's called a shotgun.

"I'll join you," I say. *I'm sleeping with her too.* "Orion?"

"You think I'm letting you hog her? No way. But you'll sleep on the floor. Give her space in the bed."

"I bet *you'll* sleep in the bed with her," Kai mutters.

"Last time I checked, that bed was mine. But no, I'll just wish her goodnight. And make sure you stay on the floor," Orion laughs.

ORION

The fuckers insisted on sleeping in Maisy's room, but they get the floor. I got them pillows, at least, but fuck me, right now all I can hear in the darkness are their low rumbles as they sleep.

I lie next to Maisy and stroke her face. I should be angry at her for leaving on her own, and I am. But looking at her sleeping gives me hope that there could be peace in this volatile world of ours, and everything lightens.

"Mmm, Orion," she murmurs, and snuggles closer. I pull her to my chest. Her skimpy dress is still on, so she's practically naked as I pull the blanket over her body. This tiny woman has invaded my mind; she's all I think about, day and night. She's a worthy opponent, too. Maybe that's why I'm so obsessed with her.

Sleep evades me. Instead, I stare into the darkness, my thoughts saturated with what's coming next now that we have her video. Will she leave? Has she had enough of us? How can I reprimand her for leaving? Losing her is not an option. Not for Kai, Logan, or even me. She's still to serve the Cartes. But wouldn't that be forcing her, just like before, into working for the mob? And then we'd be no better than Milan.

~

I never intended to fall asleep in Maisy's bed, but I guess I did, and now with the sun so bright, I'm up very early. The sun, as well as my unrelenting cock, where all my blood cells gather each morning for a meeting. This is the reason why my bedroom's preferred. My dark curtains keep me shrouded in darkness and my cock is duped into thinking it's not yet time for that meeting.

My eyes land on Maisy. She's pushed her ass against me and I'm spooning her, my arm draped over her waist. My shirt's crinkled and my pants have seen better days. My cock is up-close and personal with her ass. I stroke it once, then push it down. *Now's not the time.* She's asleep, as everyone else is. Although, thinking about Maisy's video, I want to wake everyone up.

I check my watch. She's slept ten hours. An executive decision is made. That's enough sleep for her. "Psst, Maisy," I whisper. "Hey, beautiful."

"Mmm, I'm tired," she mumbles, and opens her eyes, drawing me into the abyss of those dark irises I'm willing to die for. Then she smiles and turns to me to snuggle against my chest, just like last night.

"Maisy, we have news for you."

"What news?" She asks with her eyes closed.

I can feel her warm breath through my shirt. I speak louder. "Logan, Kai, you up?"

Maisy opens her eyes again. She seems alarmed, and regards me from the cocoon of my arms. "They're here?"

Kai and Logan mutter something, enough for me to proceed.

"Do you think Maisy would like to hear our news?"

Maisy's eyes search for Kai and Logan and find them on the floor. She sits up abruptly. "Logan? What's going on?" Her voice is trembling. She must be remembering what transpired yesterday.

"Hey, Maisy," Logan yawns, and gets up to sit on the bed next to her.

She's about to say something, but Kai interrupts.

"Hey, baby girl, you're forgetting about me?"

"Of course not, Kai. Come here."

The love she has for us is something none of us have seen. Maybe that's another reason why we're so infatuated.

I sit up too, to admonish them. "Ahem! Have you all forgotten that she got in a shitload of trouble yesterday?" We got her video, but we're also mad at her for leaving. She'd have ended up with a few more movies on her resume had Logan not found her.

"*You* must've forgotten, because last time I checked you held her all night and cooed 'Wake up, beautiful' in the morning," Kai fires back.

I deserve every bit of his ridicule.

Logan stifles a laugh. I turn to him, then Kai, ignoring the jibe. "Kai, don't get on the bed. Everyone up. I'll make the coffee."

Logan follows. "I'll join you. I'm dying for a cup."

"Maisy, get dressed. We'll meet you both in the living room," I order and as I leave, her voice sounds taut when she says, "S-sure."

Kai's "Hey, baby girl, how're you feeling?" quickly follows.

Logan's been awfully quiet. The behavior of a guilty person. He knows that–he's not stupid. Usually, it's because he needs time to process. But process what? I know he's not the one who gave Maisy the drug. For that, I'd swear on my life. Whatever it is, it'll come out, I'm sure.

I sit at one end of the sofa and Logan sits at the other. We each have a cup of coffee in our hand. I lean back and rest my left ankle on my right knee. Logan, in a nearly identical position to mine, seems to be lost in thought. We don't wait long for Maisy and Kai to arrive, and while Kai's clothes are all wrinkled from yesterday, Maisy's like a breath of fresh air in jeans and a white top.

They enter with an arm wrapped around each other's waist. Kai's kissing her head, and after spying the two cups of coffee on the table, they pick them up. She accepts one last kiss to the lips, and Kai peels away from her and sits between me and Logan on the sofa. He leans back, knees spread apart.

I can see the turmoil raging inside Maisy. Clearly sensing something's up, she sits on the chair facing us.

"You look like you finally found the guts to kill me." She smiles bitterly. "Let me at least have my coffee first."

"Why would we want to kill you, Maisy?" Kai asks.

"Because of what I did. Look, I'm sorry–"

"Maisy, Logan found your video recording," I announce calmly.

Her eyes widen, as if she never actually trusted we'd do this for her. *So much disbelief in there.* I'm starting to question everything she's ever told us.

"Where is it? Show me! *Show me!*"

I hold up the memory stick in my fingers.

"I knew it! I fucking *knew* it!" She jumps and turns to Logan. "See, Logan? It was there all along! *I KNEW IT!*"

"Sit down, Maisy," I continue. "We're going to watch it."

"Can I... Can I watch it first?"

Of course she can't.

"Surely you remember having sex before." Kai reminds her we are the ones that want to see her video.

Not sure why it's important at this stage. Either we're the biggest perverts in the world, or it's a case of finders keepers. *No, scratch that. I didn't mean it like that.*

"Maisy, the reason you're with us is because of this video," I say. "Now that we got it, we want to see its credibility."

"You don't trust me?" She raises her eyebrows indignantly at me, as if all this time she's been a loyal, honest person. *She hasn't.*

"Well, you did go on your own to Logan's club, after I told you to stay put."

She narrows her eyes at me. I bet she's trying to think of a different tack. "Why do you want to watch it–to jerk off to it?"

Kai and Logan look as thrown off as I am. I shake my head in disbelief. "Really, you think that's why? I'll tell you why. We want to see who's in it, and kill them. That's all." From the corner of my eye, I see Kai and Logan nodding.

She looks at us, hundreds of new strategies running through her head, I'm certain, but she gives up and sighs, dejectedly. "Go ahead. Watch it."

Without missing a beat, I walk to the TV, inject the memory stick into the back, pick up the remote, and go back to my seat.

The TV's set up sideways to Maisy, but even though she can turn to see the screen, her eyes are trained on us.

I press play and lean forward, resting my elbows on my knees.

The film starts, and we see Maisy in stockings, black lace panties with a slit through them, and a matching bra with the cups slit open and her nipples poking out. She's wearing a collar, and she's being led by someone. We can't see his face. My blood boils just at the sight of someone having put a collar on Maisy. *My* Maisy.

Two guys walk in, unclip the collar, and take her to the bed. And it starts. The full-on sex starts pretty quick.

The three of us sit in silence and watch, barely breathing. All of us have a full hard-on but none of us dare touch ourselves. We have honor, after all.

At one point, our heads all tip to the left to better see the position she's in and check out her face, as well as one of the guys who's now slamming into her quite rough.

"Oof!" we all exclaim at the same time when he misses her cunt as he's pounding her. *That must've hurt.*

Kai's had enough. "Nuh-uh." He crosses his arms over his chest, but his eyes don't leave the screen.

Our heads now lean to the right, nearly upside down, trying to figure out what Maisy's doing with the girl who just showed up.

"Ahh," Logan and I get it at the same time, and chuckle.

At this point, I realize why Kai's frowning. I don't believe it, but it's there, right in front of me. Evidence. Maisy has lots to explain. I glance over at Logan, who locks eyes with me and shakes his head. I nod. We've seen enough. I point the remote at the TV and turn it off. The room is in silence, except for Maisy's foot tapping on the floor, something she's been doing for some time.

She bites her nails. "Well?"

"Are you nervous, Maisy?" I ask.

"I'm not."

"You're biting your nails. You can't tell me you're not nervous."

"Okay, I am. A little. What did you see?"

I shake my head in disappointment. "I was hoping you'd tell us."

She looks at Logan. Him, and no one else. Like she's asking, *begging* for something.

He shakes his head too. "Don't look at me, sweetheart. I can't help you."

"Come, sit next to us. Let's continue the video." I reach out a hand to her. Even in the moments when I should be speechless, I can talk. But no emotions come out of me.

She sits in my lap, and I press play again.

My eyes are on her, and as the scene is unravelling in front of us, she watches but through squinted eyes, closing them at some points, then opening them again.

When I see a closeup of her on the TV, I freeze the video. "What's the matter, Maisy? Can't look at yourself?"

The three of us wait until she opens her eyes fully, and her whole being *stops*. As if the life has left her body. The stillness is eerie.

She stands up slowly and, as if under a spell, walks to the TV. She reaches out with her hand and strokes the face on the screen.

The face that is not hers. Similar, but not hers.

"Maisy." I say gravely.

Kai's voice is dark. "When will the lies stop?"

"Just be honest," Logan adds softly, concluding the reprimand. If we can call it that. *We've turned into wimps, I see.*

When she turns to us, we see tears roll down her cheeks. She's looking at the floor as she starts talking, her voice somber.

"This is Rosey, my twin sister. I haven't seen her face in eight years. My father sold us both to Milan when we were twelve." She raises her eyes to Logan. "When was this made?"

"A few years ago."

"In your studio?"

"No."

I'm sick of her lies. *And now this?* "Was there *ever* a video recording of you in your apartment?"

She looks at me, then lowers her eyes again.

"Thank God," Kai mutters. I shoot him a look and narrow my eyes in irritation.

"And were you ever raped by Milan, or was that a lie too?"

She looks at me from under her hair. Her obsidian eyes are flooded with tears, rivers flowing down her face. Yes, he raped her. Why is it that instead of being furious with her, I just want to kill Milan? What is she doing that stops me wanting to skin her alive for lying to us yet again?

"We should've killed you five times by now. And for some unfathomable reason, we haven't. Why did you lie to us, Maisy?"

Those dark eyes are like space, glittering from tears but so lonely, I can feel the hurt myself. "Would you've helped me if I told you I was after Camila that night because she took my sister eight years ago and made her work in porn?"

We look at each other. Of course we wouldn't have helped her. It's clear as day. And yet, I still ask. "Why do you think we wouldn't help you?"

"Because I know." She wipes at the tears with the back of her hand. "I'm smart, remember. You told me not to dumb myself down in front of anyone, and I won't. I look at the odds. Statistically, people are eighty percent less likely to help two damsels in distress than one. I didn't want to take that chance."

Huh. I can't help but smile at her reasoning. My chest aches so bad for what's to come, but I can't show it in my face. *Stupid men. That's what we are. Fooled by a cunt.*

"You've put me in a very awkward position, darling. The Cartes know about you, which means I never get to fulfil my wish and cut that pretty little throat of yours, even though I want to badly."

"I'll help you with Milan," she says. "I said I will. That hasn't changed."

"Has anything changed at all, Maisy?" I ask.

"The fact that now there are two of me, not one."

Kai's not looking at her. But I can see he's thinking, for once. "Is your sister smart like you?"

Maisy shakes her head. "No. But I promised myself I'd find her."

All of us stare at her. I can't believe she's not seeing the weight of the situation she's in. I cannot kill her, because I put my fucking head on the line for her, and she's not even acknowledging it? She's not even seeing that all this is over.

"Will you help me?" she breathes.

"You sent us on a wild goose chase," I snap. "You put us in danger, nearly got yourself gangbanged, killed, a few times, mind you. We killed about ten men because of you, and now you want us to do the same thing for your sister? Lies after lies after lies. When will you learn? Lying doesn't get you in our good graces. I could throw you over my knee and spank you right now, I'm so mad! No. The answer is no!" I stand up to make my point. "You don't care for anyone but yourself. You're selfish, and all we are to you is protection that you get to fuck whenever you want."

"That's not true! You think I wanted to fall for not one but *three* of the worst possible humans on earth?

Mafia heads that share the same job description as the most hated, most despicable man, Milan the Dog?"

"HEY!" Kai shoots up and she recoils. He'd never hit her, but I put my hand on his shoulder just in case. He's hurting. "We are *not* like Milan!" he spits through gritted teeth. "But if we're all the same to you, and you can't see any difference"–his disappointed eyes land on Logan, then me, and he throws his arms up in surrender–"then why do we bother at all, boys? Let's just kill her."

"Kai," she reaches out to touch him, but he brushes her off.

I want to strangle her. And love her. And strangle her again.

"You sleep with us a few times and you think you know us, Maisy? You don't," Kai responds.

"I know when I'm with you, Kai, you're the one that knows what I *want*," she declares. "When I'm with you I'm Maisy, the teenager. I've never been just a careless teenager, and with you, I am. I *fly* with you, Kai. And I know that you fly with me too." She looks at me, her eyes still teary. "You, Orion, you know what I *need*. And in a stupid, perverted way, I'm always in your vicinity, or craving it, hoping to *get* in it. Diving into the darkness with you is enlightening, and I like it. *We* like it." She's my void, true, but I don't want to look at her dark gaze right now. "And you, Logan, you get me, you get the woman inside me, you know what my body demands of me, even before I do. You were the first to promise me I'd be safe and that's because you want to take care of me, to look after me."

The silence is unnerving. I sense my face hardening in a way that's terrifying for her, darkness closing in that could easily swallow her whole.

She wipes away her tears again and heads to the door. "Never mind. I know I'm not worth it."

"Maisy," Logans calls out, and she stops but doesn't turn. "All this love you feel is worth nothing without your loyalty."

Her shoulders shake. A sob catches in her throat but she doesn't make a sound. Then she exhales loudly and in a small voice, says, "I'll be out of your house in a half hour."

"Where are you going?" Kai asks. For a moment I think he'll run after her. But he doesn't.

Maisy leaves the room. We hear her sobbing, the sound gradually fading, leaving me infuriated.

"She's not leaving our world this easy," I growl under my breath.

Logan turns to me, his chest all puffed up like he's ready to defend her. "What are you doing, Orion?"

"Logan, please remind me what it is that we always do in these situations. You have to, because you've clearly forgotten."

"Orion, we've been through this. We are not killing her! And I don't want to hear that anymore. Maisy's ours. Whether she likes it or not."

"You think I don't want that?" I retort. "But she must see the consequences of her actions, and the impact she leaves on this world. On us. If we don't punish her, she'll learn nothing. Come on, you know that."

"She must know she's made a mistake," Kai interjects calmly, "but Milan's after her too."

"I haven't been taken for this big a fool since second grade!" I exclaim in frustration. "She's playing us with her little cunt and none of us have the strength to end her."

"I don't want to end her." I say.

"Me either," Kai agrees.

"Then she must learn her lesson. And if she dies in the process, it wasn't meant to be."

CHAPTER 15

MAISY

I run away, choking on my sobs. *My love is worth nothing without my loyalty?* I've *been* loyal. What more do they want? My life? He probably just meant my love is worth nothing. That, I believe. My heart is torn by this new, raw pain. I've never had a man in my life who didn't want to use me in some way. But I made sure it was always tit for tat. I knew this was how it would end, and because of it, I'm in control. *I'm in control.* My plan was to find Rosey, that's why I came to this house. That's what's been driving me all this time. Had I not taken things into my own hands I'd never have found out that Rosey's alive.

There. More proof that the only way to succeed is by myself. But somewhere along the way, *they* happened. I feel them crawling under my skin, like flesh-eating bugs I can't get rid of. All three of them. I hate this feeling of dependence. Of addiction. Did I think it would last? No. But it's been going on for longer than I imagined. I got caught in their trap. *Their* trap. I'm the smart one, I am a genius, I have the brains to think clearly and to push them away and yet, I didn't. I waited. For what? They were the ones who said *my love is worth nothing*. My love is worth as much as they're willing to give back. It's no illusion, it's clear as day. Just like I know men exist to use women, the three of them used me and discarded me like a piece of garbage. And then said my love wasn't worth it. I predicted this. A long time ago.

As I wipe from my cheeks the tears spilling freely from my eyes, I enter the kitchen.

Lisa's kind face greets me. "Maisy! Are you okay?"

I snort. "Um, Lisa. Good morning. Yeah, I'm okay. It's... nothing."

She raises her eyebrows. "Nothing?"

I manage a little smile. "Orion helped me find my sister, Rosey. I don't know exactly how I'm going to get her, but I will."

"You found your sister? That's wonderful, Maisy."

"Um, I'm not sure if you saw, I used your Uber account yesterday," I sniffle. "I'm really sorry. I have no money, but Orion will pay you back."

"Yes, I noticed. Don't worry about it." She passes me a tissue.

"W-Would you mind giving me a ride to a friend's house?" I shouldn't ask her, since I don't want them knowing where I am. But all I want is to leave this place, and the memory of it.

"Sure. Does Orion know you're going?"

"Th-that's over." I try to choke back another sob, but it's too late.

"Come here. I'm sure you'll work things out." Lisa hugs me and I bawl on her shoulder, letting it all go.

It's cathartic, and it feels like I'm back in time. No one has ever held me like this except for my mother. I miss my mom. *I miss my mom*. There, I said it. *I can't always be the strong one, Mom. What if* I *need someone to lean on? Like today? Then what?*

I sense someone entering the kitchen and Lisa shooing them back out. The last thing I want is for anyone else to see me crying.

"I'm sorry." I peel myself off her, wipe my eyes, and check if anyone's around. "I'm not usually this blubbery, but I guess finding Rosey got to me."

"It's fine. Don't worry."

"Would you mind if we go now? Is that okay?"

"Now? Sure. Are you ready?"

"I'll just get my sneakers."

I head upstairs, dreading I might meet one of them on the way. Or am I hoping? They let me go without trying to stop me. Brutal. Nevertheless, I meet nobody on the way.

I look around my room. This was my safe haven, the first place I wanted to call home since my mother died. But nothing in here is mine. Not even the clothes on my back. I'm not dwelling, that's for losers. I put my sneakers on and decide to leave a note for Kai. There's one thing I never got the chance to tell him.

Dear Kai

I know where I saw Natasha's sneakers. Red and white stripes with a handstitched insignia. Check the NY Times on October 5th, the last photograph of your dad entering the car. You'll see them in the bottom left corner. Out of all the paparazzi, why would Natasha be there unless she was the one emailing Milan?

Maisy

Lisa dropped me off at the home of Kirstie, my high school friend. She came to New York for college, and she's now living with two roommates who go to the same college as her. I haven't seen her in years and I've never been particularly close to her, but she's the only person I know who's living anywhere near Orion's place. I didn't want Lisa to have to drive for hours, and I didn't even know where else to go, but I was sure once I got to Kirstie's I'd regroup, and manage on my own. They won't be looking for me. They don't even need me anymore. Orion's uncles met me and they got what they wanted, at least enough to start asking the right questions.

When Kirstie appeared at the door her hair was still golden, although not shiny anymore but matt and dull, matching her pasty skin. She used to have the glossiest hair in my school. I guess life happened to her too. Her round, wide-set blue eyes were glazed and as I expected, she didn't recognize me at first. Given the smell of marijuana coming from her house, I could've been anyone to her. She hugged me, let me in, and asked me to stay as long as I wanted. What a pothead would usually say, which works in my favor. I knew I could count on her becoming who she is today, thanks to her parents' divorce.

And now I'm back to square one, lying on a dirty mattress and crying my eyes out. Kirstie's roommates didn't even bother greeting me. Just like her, they were out of commission, munching on something in the kitchen as I walked by them. Just as always, I'm an insignificant bystander.

~

It's been two weeks since I arrived here. I've slept on the dirty mattress, under blankets with holes, washed my underwear twice, and tried my best to get dry under the hairdryer. My face has broken out in zits from the dirt in this place, my hair's becoming matted, like Kirstie's, and I even took marijuana a few times.

Maybe that's why I cried every night. I tried regrouping, but I was afraid to set foot outside. Milan's men will find me the moment Orion's or Logan's snitches tell them I'm gone. Milan knows I have nowhere to go. *Nowhere to go.* Homeless, unless I go back to him. Did he know this was how I'd end up? He must have.

Or maybe I cried because of the invisible knife stuck in my chest that I cannot take out. Kai and Logan didn't come looking for me. Lisa would've told them where she left me, although she didn't see Kirstie's house. I walked two blocks for that reason. So actually, they *don't* know where I am. As for Orion, if I see him, I know he'll be after his kill.

As I lie awake in my bed at night, inhaling the lingering pot and feeling indifferent to the world, my favorite pastime lately, I keep hearing a motorbike in the neighborhood. I always hope it's Kai, coming to save me as my knight on shining bike, but I'm not that lucky. The motorbikes would come and go. Not one would stop.

I wish they'd show up and ask me to go back. I'm stupid, I know, but my heart tells me one thing and my genius mind another. And while I've been waiting, I've been fading out of their existence, like a withered flower. Would they even remember me, or has someone else taken my place in their bed already?

If Milan comes knocking on the door, I'll probably give my life to his service again now that I'm certain Rosey's alive. But even he's forgotten about me. And nothing has been happening. Just the four of us getting stoned. Which I'm beginning to enjoy. My sluggish, emptied mind is a treat. Kirstie and her roommates have stopped going to college altogether because they noticed the security cameras in the auditorium where they take the exams. Until this is sorted, they'll stay at home, being paranoid over their privacy. Too much pot does that to your mind. But who cares? This feeling of indifference is mine now, and I won't give it up.

Did we not share something special? Or was I too arrogant to see what was going on? They absorbed me, wrecked me, ripped me to pieces and left me completely numb.

Kirstie's loved having me around because I try to tidy up the place as much as I can, but her slobby roommates make it damn hard.

To thank me, and to keep my spirits up, she's promised me a party in my honor, tonight. According to her roommates I'm dampening the mood in the house, apparently, and people coming to the house to get doped up have had bad trips because of my energy.

A few of their friends are coming over. We'll have beer, and hang. Maybe that'll help me forget the world of the Cartes, Delgados, and Vitalis. I'm history anyway.

The first thing Kirstie told me about the party was that I'd have to change my clothes. I bet her roommates said something. I wish they'd talk to me, but they're always stoned and staring absently at me when I try to make conversation. I've been in the same clothes for two weeks straight, and I know I reek. But all Kirstie gave me were a few short, flowery dresses to choose from. I hated them. I *hate* them. I'd never wear something like that, but I got to wear something. So here I am, in a god-awful short, frilly, flowery blue dress, a beer in my hand and Kirstie next to me, proud of how I look.

By ten o'clock, the music blares through the open windows and the house is filled with not just a few of their friends, but at least thirty of their frat buddies, judging by the jocks arriving. First thing they do is light a joint, and after a few puffs plaster big grins on their faces and try to move their limbs to the rhythm of the music, failing terribly. I'm not for this type of shit. And when two frat boys stare at me and smirk, I don't have any intention of acting my age.

"Psst, Maisy, *look*." Kirstie nods her head toward them. "They like you. Maybe it's finally time to forget whoever you're crying over."

One of the guys has the audacity to join us, and he hooks his arm around my waist. I try to move but he's faster, planting a wet kiss on my cheek.

"Ew!" I push him away but he just laughs it off.

"Your friend's pretty, Kirstie! Is this the one that needs a good fucking?"

"Excuse me?" I'm shocked, but then I get it. "Kirstie! How could you?!"

"Oh come on, you'll enjoy it!" She slaps my arm, not remotely apologetic because she's high on God-knows-what, and walks away. I'm left with two men who are ogling me repulsively. This is what I'm trying to get away from constantly and yet, somehow, I always end up in the same position.

I try to cover the tremble in my voice. "I'm not interested. Please move along."

The second frat guy grabs my wrist, holds it above my head, and checks me out fully. "You must be Maisy." The way he smirks is revolting, and when he wraps his other hand around my waist, he forces me flush against his front. I sense the swelling in his slacks as he grinds into me.

"Get lost, fucker!" I raise my knee sharply, aiming at his balls and bingo, I got them. He shrieks, the sound drowned out by the music, and he falls to the floor in pain. By the time his frat bro realizes what's happened, I'm running, hoping to lose myself in the crowd.

Where the fuck am I going to go? Stupid me. I have zero protection here, and those who I thought were helping me actually are not.

I check behind me but can't see them, so I allow myself a breather in the kitchen, to calm my terrified heart now thumping in my throat. I drink a glass of water, spilling half onto my dress while doing so. I look around for a towel to dab at my chest and spot four frat boys smoking weed in here, quietly gawking at me with the same look in their eyes as the other two. I don't even take my chances this time. I run outside onto the lawn, and I intend to keep running, as far as I can get. *It's back to the streets for me, I see.*

I'm halfway across the lawn when I hear them.

"There she is! Get her!"

They seize me before I can take two more steps. I'm captured by their claws and dragged to the hedge while I kick and scream, but only for a little while. One of them grabs me from behind and clutches me tight, covering my mouth. The other man lifts my dress, and all this is getting too close to home. I feel nothing but blind terror. I cannot allow myself to be hurt again. Never.

I can't see it, but I hear a belt unbuckling as my legs are spread and held open. There's a painful burn on my skin from my panties being torn, my eyes are wide open in terror, and I see a cock being pressed between my legs. The pounding of my heart sets a rapid pace the moment I see his face, the scariest of all. A sickening scowl, set firmly in his narrow, sinister eyes. *This is it.*

I close my eyes and take a deep breath, expecting the hell I remember like it was yesterday. They can rape me, but I'm in control of my mind. *I'm in control. I'm in control. I'm in control.*

"What are you doing, man? Come on, get on with it!"

I open my eyes in time to see the guy in front of me nodding to someone behind us. My captor turns around, taking me with him, and under the streetlight I make out three shadows standing too close. In an instant, a spurt of hot, metallic-tasting liquid sprays over my face, and I'm dropped to the ground as a gurgling sound fills the air.

I can't see clearly. I wipe my eyes and can just make out both frat guys falling to their knees and clutching their necks, but the streetlight's too strong for me to see who those three, sinister shadows belong to. *This is it. My time has come.*

One of them grabs me by the arm and I recoil, kicking him and trying to get away. Ignoring my pleas, he pulls me up. The streetlight hits his somber face–a face I know.

"Maisy." He's incensed, his sharp, obsidian eyes making him look mad, heartless. He inhales through flared nostrils and looks down at my dress that's still bunched at my hips.

I breathe a sigh of relief, although the smell and the stickiness on me is nauseating. "Orion, h-how did you find me?" Pulling my dress down, I see I'm covered in blood. "Th-they killed them."

He's wearing an impeccable three-piece suit and black leather gloves, but I can just about spot the bracelets on his wrists. He's looking suave, perfect.

Definitely not dressed for this low-key frat party. *Where they've killed two men already.*

"Thank you," I say.

"I didn't come here for your thank-you," he snaps back.

He still hates me. "Then why did you come? Why did you bother saving me?" My voice trembles, tears brimming under my lashes.

He's as cold as ice. "There's a meeting tomorrow with my uncles. They want to hear more about Milan."

"I'll come tomorrow." I suck in a breath, hoping a sob won't come out. "This is where I'm staying now."

"This is where we *let* you stay. But that shit's over now. Especially after what just happened. See that car across the street, with the tinted windows? Get in."

I look over at the car. The two men with Orion are heaving the frat boys' bodies into the trunk. I glance back at the house. The party's still going strong. Someone's throwing up on the lawn. Nobody would've been any the wiser had I been raped. Maybe Kirstie called them for that reason only.

One of Orion's men opens the car door for me. This battle is lost, and fighting is futile. I want to leave this god-awful place. But more importantly, I want to go back to them. Into my safe, clean haven.

Orion walks beside me as I take slow steps across the street. He reaches the car first and waits on me to get in. He thinks he's mad at me. It's actually the other way around. *Does he know that?*

"Get in." Nothing, no pleasantries. Just that cold voice.

I get inside, and he follows closely behind. Sitting beside me, he exhales sharply and looks out of the window as we drive off.

"Do you know what you are, Maisy?"

"What?"

"You're a selfish brat, that's what you are!" He locks eyes with me. "You know you can never win with men like us, so you're testing us relentlessly to see if we can be manipulated. I bet that's a challenge any genius would like to take on!"

I lick my lips. There is magic in his eyes: dirty, dark, beautiful magic. Magic I've missed.

But he's still yelling at me. "All you want is our power, and to be overwhelmed by it. You want to play, to succumb, to end up right where we want you, but always with a personal agenda in the background. And all because of some fucked-up childhood."

How can I tell him he's right? Being with predictable people for so long, almost all of them on Milan's payroll, made my life monotonous, indifferent. But when I met them, not one but *three* mafia heads, that was a challenge and then some. I gave them my all, played full-on, and they made me feel alive, worthy, and loved. They made me work for what I wanted. I was saved, in every meaning of the word.

He cups my chin and pulls me to him. "Well, my little slut, I'll know how to behave with you from now on."

I'm staring at him, my lips parted, as if taken by a strange force. He sees my need, he always could. I shift forward, begging for a kiss, but he laughs mockingly.

"You don't get to choose when to kiss me ever again. *I* do that. If you don't listen, you get punished. I bet you'd love that."

I nod, and he raises his eyebrows at me. My chin is released and a slap lands on my face.

"Like this? You like this? You do, don't you?"

My open palm lands on the leather seat next to me for leverage as Orion's smacking me, hard enough to hurt but hot enough for heat to pool between my legs. I can only stare at him, my chest jumping with every slap, and I whimper each time. My breasts jiggle, threatening to pop out of my dress.

His eyes land on them and he cups one, pinching my nipple through the material. I moan and bite my lower lip. *God, I needed this.*

"Fuck!" He stops himself and adjusts his cock in his pants while I'm left panting, arousal gushing between my legs. My need for him is greater than I thought.

"I missed you, Orion," I whisper. "I missed all of you."

There's a moment when I see *my* Orion, but it's gone in a flash. The car has stopped, and the door's now opening. Without a word, he's out, leaving me to run after him like a puppy.

Orion doesn't want me anymore. He's just taunting me. They brought me back for the meeting, and to taunt me. To taste my own medicine.

"Deal with the bodies and go home," he orders the driver. "I won't need you again tonight."

It feels like it's been months since I left. Only now I realize that I missed the smell of the only place that ever resembled home. And Lisa's embrace. And them. *Us*.

Once we're inside, Orion heads straight for the kitchen counter. I follow. He takes the whiskey out and one tumbler.

"I want a drink too," I breathe.

"I don't have champagne." He pours whiskey into his glass, not looking at me.

"Whiskey, then."

"It's not for you." He downs the glass.

"And it is for you?"

He takes out another tumbler and fills both glasses. He raises his and downs it again.

I take my glass, sniff it, and remember it's vile, and too strong, but I need something that'll knock me out. I pound it like he does. *Bottoms up*.

"Go and clean yourself up," he orders. "You stink of weed."

KAI

I've been living in hell for two weeks straight. And I made sure everyone around me knew it. *We let her go.* Two fucking weeks. She could've been murdered at that pothead's house.

All this time, I didn't see it: she was living at Orion's on borrowed clothes and borrowed time. She didn't have any certainty with us, and we messed her around at our end of the deal. I know we did. We focused on spending time with her, fucking her, and satisfying our wants, completely forgetting about the video. Goddammit, she kept secrets from us for no reason other than statistics. *My genius baby girl.*

And even leaving the way she did, she wrote me a note. Gave me another piece of my puzzle.

Naturally, I followed up the information. The *New York Times* photograph from October 5th, about the same time as Natasha and I started seeing each other, does indeed show her striped sneakers in the corner. *She was there.* That was hard to take.

I called a meeting that very same day. I nearly died at their hands, but I'm still the head of the Delgados and something must be done to stop Milan. And those responsible for the death of my father. Orion begged me not to do anything stupid but he knew I wouldn't listen. I do stupid things all the time.

Instead of arriving at the agreed time, I got there a few hours early to teach them a lesson. Nobody messes with Kai Typhon Delgado and lives. The four people who jumped me got what they deserved. I didn't give them an easy death, though. I made sure the four-finger ring on my fist turned them into pulp. And then, I made it known I was there.

Once all of them gathered, in silence, they realized who was missing. Their eyes opened wider, and they listened. Huh. It was easy for them to listen once they saw I was back to my murderous self.

First, I told them about the Irish. And how the Slavs tricked them. Everything made sense to them, including why our profits were low. Rage and disgust were among the main emotions on show as I was talking, but I didn't stop there. I moved on to the second reason why I came back.

"I know who killed my father."

My words resulted in an eerie silence. Everyone held their breath, waiting on me to expose the culprit. All of them except Natasha, who stepped behind the bar to make herself a drink.

When I showed them the photograph from the day my father died, I asked them to see if they could make out anything familiar. They all passed it around and as they saw it, their eyes landed on the bar, and on the person standing there, drinking and looking anxious.

She knew I knew. The ring around her was closing.

"This is all bullshit, Kai! How do we know *you* don't work for Milan the Dog?" Natasha asked tightly.

"Are those your sneakers, Natasha?" I asked, utterly calm. Although everyone knows the weather around me is usually this calm before a real Typhon comes on. *Such an apt middle name they gave me.*

She tried to defend herself. "So what if I was there that day? Other people were too!"

I told her I knew that the leak in the brakes was meant for me, and that was fine. I wasn't mad about that. What really incensed me was that she went to Milan the Dog to complain about the mistake she made. A *mistake*. Killing my father was just a mistake to her. Anyway, it meant that she'd been working with the Slavs all along.

"And here I was feeling guilty about what happened to you when you joined the Delgados," I scoffed.

"I was gangraped by everyone in here!" she screamed in anguish. A fake, theatrical performance that looked good on her. Which got me triggered. The only time I lost my nerve.

"You knew what you were getting yourself into. You *knew!* And you were fine! I *wasn't!*" I yelled.

She flung a bottle of rum across the room at me, scarcely missing the heads of a few others, and ran. I nodded at Niko and his brother to get her since they were closest to the bar. She still managed to get away, but there's no place she can hide that I won't find her. I had a different priority that day.

Finally, I told the others about the idea of joining forces with the Vitalis and Cartes against the Slavs. Whereas before I wasn't sure about this, I now stand one hundred percent behind the idea.

Some of my esteemed mafia members spat when I mentioned the names of our arch nemeses but I continued nevertheless.

"...If we want to fuck pussies, make money, and ride, we can do that. But not without joining the Vitalis and Cartes. Together, we can eradicate the Slavs. Which is our number-one priority at the moment."

Silence fell while I was giving my speech, knowing perfectly well most of them were afraid to do anything more than spit.

"I won't mention you fuckers wanting to kill me because those that tried are no longer among us, God rest their souls. You all know me as someone who's reactive. I don't *think*. I *do*. Well, now, I've had time to think. And this makes sense. I've already spoken to Logan Vitali and Orion Carte."

I stopped there and observed them, waiting for a reaction before I continued.

Niko piped up. "Who destroyed our bar last month and put Jeff in hospital with broken legs? Who kidnapped your girl? If it was them, how do you expect us not to retaliate?" he asked.

"I wouldn't be surprised to find out it was the Slavs. Milan the Dog wants her. She's some sort of genius, that you pricks were gonna gangbang." I change the tone from accusatory to professional. "There'll be a meeting at some point between the heads of the three families to see what we can do. But be aware, Milan the Dog has snitches everywhere. And he's been killing us, slowly and methodically."

Their nodding heads gave me the approval I needed. Though maybe half of them were hoping I get killed in the process.

Once that was over, and life went back to normal, my favorite pastime was to ride past the house Maisy was staying in. I daydreamed over the idea of being an ordinary man, coming back from work, going home to my girl. I lived an alternate reality where I got both the girl and the life I wanted.

And it wasn't only me. The three of us safeguarded the perimeter of the house daily. The only person coming in and going out of their place was the piece-of-shit drug dealer. We monitored Maisy's whereabouts closely, but she stayed in. She smoked weed. She did nothing. She was becoming a pothead. Without money, clothes, a phone, anything really, she was becoming nobody. Maybe that was her plan.

Where would she have gone if her friend hadn't let her stay? And what kind of fucked-up person is Kirstie anyway, letting in anyone off the streets? Orion had investigated this Kirstie Stones. She and Maisy went to high school together, but nothing else. No connection since.

How we'd dealt with Maisy felt wrong but I wish she hadn't lied to us *for the second time*. She must face the consequences, although I don't know what those are because she's still alive. And we're still guarding her like rabid dogs.

Maybe she'll remember that a clean room, clean clothes, and a private bathroom was preferable to that filthy pot-smoking dump. But would it make a difference to her? She looked skinny and pale smoking weed at her window, with messy, tangled hair and clothes she hadn't changed in days. She was radiant before.

~

Tomorrow is the day the three of us officially meet. Publicly, for the very first time. Orion's uncles are meeting him at noon, and we'll meet later.

After a long day of work, hard grafting, punching, and maybe a tiny bit of torture (the asshole was asking for it), I take a quick get-the-blood-off-me shower and ride to Orion's to discuss tomorrow's meeting. There's a chance that we won't be alone and we have to make sure there isn't a glitch in our communication.

As per usual, I leave my bike behind the shrubs and enter his house. He'd have seen me approach and left the door open for me. I head to the kitchen and see a half-bottle of whiskey on the table. I take a tumbler, pour myself a shot and bring it to my lips, instantly becoming warmed by the spice and full-bodied smoky undertones. I treat my taste buds to a second and take a third with me, crossing the room to sit down on the corner of the table. I take my leather jacket off and hang it on the chair, and put my booted feet on it.

"You're here." Orion strides in from behind me in his usual smart-looking attire. I don't know how he does it, or Logan.

"I got Maisy," he announces, sounding annoyed.

I leap to my feet. "She's here?"

"Hold your horses, Casanova. Sit back on your ass."

I realize I'm overreacting and sit down. "Why did you get her? I thought the plan was to leave her there for longer."

Raging, he pours himself a shot. "Why do you think? She puts herself in these situations where men end up dead."

I stare at him. "You had to kill someone?"

He nods angrily. "Of course. They were gonna... Yes. I killed them."

"Well, you did what you could, I'm sure. Cheers."

We clink glasses and down them in one go. Orion pours us another one.

"Logan?" I ask.

"He should be here any minute."

Speak of the devil. He walks in as Orion takes another tumbler, fills it, and hands it to him.

"What are we celebrating?" Logan asks.

"Maisy's here," I grin.

His eyes twinkle. "Why so soon? I mean, not that I care."

"There was a problem," I reply. "Orion got her out just in time."

We clink our glasses and drink up. I notice Logan looks buffer than usual. "Have you been working out, man?"

"Of course I have. I'm ready for war." He sits on the other corner of the table, his foot on the chair.

"The Delgados know about our meeting," I say. "What about the Vitalis?"

"They know too," Logan confirms. "All of them want to take down Milan. They're willing to play until Milan the Dog is down."

I turn to Orion. "And the Cartes?"

"They're game too. Not sure until when, but bottom line is we understand the need to take Milan down. And we will."

ORION

Torture. Hell. Daydreams. Rage. That's how my time went by. I hated everything about it because too often I caught myself daydreaming about sinking my cock into her cunt as I gazed at my cell, at the few pictures I took of her naked. I never showed Kai or Logan those pictures. I didn't want them to get distracted. Or mess with them. That sweet little cunt we've allowed in our lives had too much power over us.

The letters she wrote to me about the food she had when she stayed in her room, I re-read those too. Fuck knows why I kept them. She loved strawberries. And cream. Each time I'd think of the word 'cream' a vivid flash back would come to me of her squirting whipped cream in her mouth, and the activities that transpired that day. Little manipulative cunt.

I also drove too many times around the house she was staying in and had to be held back from going and killing everyone in there. Garry, the only person from the Cartes I trust, supplied them with quality marijuana, because I didn't want her taking a bad trip. Although even now, I'm not sure how much she smoked.

But she had to learn the lesson of being on her own, unprotected. I wanted her to appreciate every fucking little thing we've been doing for her. It was either that or kill her. And that's out of question.

I'm still reeling from today. Had I not been in the area, Maisy would've been raped. Again. How many times now? For fuck's sake. Aren't there any other women in this world? Everyone wants ours? Well, tough luck.

At least our heads and not our cocks were full of blood and oxygen while she was gone. We dealt with our business like the men we are, not giving a shit about anyone. Merciless. Logan managed to get rid of the porn studio in his club. It only took him two weeks to implement the changes. You can tell when someone's sexually frustrated and needs a good fucking. His eye would twitch daily, with everyone wondering why and petrified of the consequences. It turns out the cause is only a full nutsack.

Kai's back in charge of the Delgados, not that I ever doubted him. Although he does have a new adversary now. He won't stop until he finds Natasha. Milan's snitch. Mickey Delgado's killer. I wonder whether Milan wanted to kill Mickey and not Kai, as they think. Removing a worthy adversary from the equation would leave him dealing with the son. And now with the sons of the opposing mafia families ruling, whatever made him think it would be easier? I love it when people underestimate me.

Saying that, we underestimated Maisy a lot. She told us she's a genius, and yet we ignored that part as if it doesn't make up a lot of who she is. Of course she wants a challenge. Who wouldn't? I'll give her the biggest challenge yet. All she needs to do is come up with good information tomorrow, because persuading my father's brothers on the idea of joint attack was damn hard. Maybe I was too hard on her. Hmm. She saw in the car what she does to me, and her eyes were begging me to take her. *Little fucking slut.*

"Tell Maisy to come to my room." The throb of my cock puts urgency in my voice and makes it deeper, a dead giveaway.

Logan knows what's about to happen. "Your room? Orion, come on."

"Logan, if we're to get past what she did to us, this must happen. Besides, you'll see how much she loves it."

Out of the three of us, Logan's always been the caring one. The most respectful. Women adore him, but that doesn't mean he doesn't enjoy playing the bad guy too. He loves to rough it up, but has to be certain everyone consents. Which, of course, they do. I'm not an animal. Well, unless I'm specifically requested to be.

"Kai?" I ask.

"I want her to see who we really are," Kai says, "and what she did to us. Although, Orion, you won't hurt her that bad, yeah?"

I can't believe he's questioning my fucking process. "Hurt her? She's gonna be begging for more, and you'll be there to see it. Just send her to my room. I'm gonna prepare." I head upstairs to my bedroom. *It's fucking playtime. And way overdue.*

The St. Andrew's cross is standing tall, prepped. It's been ready for her since the day she saw it, but I won't restrain her there. It's going to be the breeding bench for her, padded with leather, with knee rests to get her ass at the right angle for her punishment. I grin as I wipe it clean. She'll be using this beauty for the first time today. The wooden frame's sturdy enough to withstand her squirming, and if she moves a lot, which she won't if I restrain her arms, I could use the bench's other attachment points for proper restraint. I don't know, rope, chains... maybe even cuffs.

I take off my vest and tie, unbutton my shirt, and roll up my sleeves. I'm going to have a fucking good time today.

CHAPTER 16

ORION

I glance around the room for a final check, just as my ears prick up at the sound of movement outside. I hear a timid knock. *She's here.*

Out of the drawer of my closet I pull a thick leather belt, and loop it around my hand before I open the door. Instantly I feel the pull.

Maisy's looking at me with those dark eyes that feed my obsession. The dark circles under them make her look deprived, like she'd do anything for a slice of bread. I doubt she ate anything good in the last two weeks. I'm furious at her for not looking after herself, because deep down I sense my fear and helplessness. And I hate it.

Her wet hair's resting on her shoulders, soaking her t-shirt. There are already two wet patches over the mounds of her breasts. Her nipples poke through the now translucent material. She hasn't bothered with a bra. She's definitely lost weight. Her jeans are barely holding up on her hips.

For a split second she glances behind me. She can see the St. Andrew's Cross from her position, and her eyes glint. But it happens so fast it could be me hallucinating, as my cock thrusting balls-deep into her cunt is all I can think about.

"Kneel," I order, pointing to the floor.

She hesitates for a moment but obeys me, kneeling just outside my bedroom door, and cranes her neck to look up at me. Fuck, those eyes. Debauched, hungry. *Mine.*

"I'm gonna show you what we do with girls like you in here."

She just stares at me as I wrap my belt around her neck and feed it through the loop. "Walk with me."

I turn around and pull on the belt. She hurries behind on all fours as I tug her on the short leash, most likely constricting her air flow. She doesn't complain, though. *I bet there's enough arousal between her legs to take the three of us at the same time.*

We reach the bench and I crouch down in front of her. She's panting, her sweet breath intoxicating me even when she's leashed, her eyes diluted as if I've fucked her already. She's messing with her own mind too soon. My fingers tangle in her hair and I pull her to me.

Her mouth, partly open, yields under my pressure. She offers me her lips, and I give her a hard, still kiss and inhale all that she is. Every moment she was missing from my life, I get back now. I pull her lower lip between my teeth and bite her, drawing blood. A little warning of what's to come.

"You see the breeding bench over here, Maisy? I'm gonna tie you to it and use your body as a cum bucket." I mutter the words against her lips as her eyes dart to the side. "As my whore, you'll do anything I want you to."

Visibly eager for a full, deep kiss, she lunges at me, but I hold her in place by her hair.

"You want that, slut?" I whisper in her ear. "The three of us fucking you and using you as breeding practice so when the time comes, we can do a good job and breed a real woman, multiple times… and have *her* babies, not yours, you fucking whore!"

She freezes for a millisecond, hurt filling her face. Good. Excellent. She's jealous. *Fuck me. I see what gets to her.*

I press my lips to hers and claim her mouth fully, selfishly, in my own way taking everything she has. But it's a bittersweet moment for her. She's doubting my love. *That's where I was, all this fucking time, thanks to her lies.*

I stand up and pull on the belt, taking her to her feet, and then remove it. "Take off your clothes." From the bottom drawer of my desk, I take out a leather harness and hand it to her. "And put this on."

I need to be able to hold on to something while slamming my cock into her cunt. The plan is not to touch her in any other way today. As she follows my orders I unzip my pants, relieving the tension from my cock.

She starts undressing and her scent hits me like a ton of bricks, something like orchids, enough to put a whole army under a spell. As she pulls her t-shirt over her head the material catches on her breasts a moment before they drop, abundant and bouncing freely in front of me. Irresistible. As for her jeans, the moment she unbuttons them they fall to the floor and I see she's not bothered with panties, drawing my urgent attention to her cunt. Fully shaved. I suck in a breath as precum seeps into my pants. Did she do that today? She better. *She better!*

"Fucking cunt!" I adjust my cock in my pants. *She did this on purpose.*

A frown appears between her brows as she picks up the harness, her diluted pupils sharpening while she makes sense of how it works, and where to put her arms and legs.

Maisy dons the harness and her breasts jiggle as she does. I'd give anything to put them in my mouth and suck on them. With the harness on, she turns her back to me, waiting to be buckled. No words are spoken. *Good girl.*

I tighten the straps over her shoulders, her waist, and around her thighs just under her butt cheeks, being careful not to touch her skin. As I deftly fasten the buckle across her back, I lean in close to her ear. "You're gonna lie face-down on the bench and be quiet, understood?"

She turns to look at me, as if she's not understanding what I'm asking her to do. Her obsidian eyes show fear, helplessness, panic, but so what? That's the idea.

I quirk an eyebrow at her. "Anything you want to say, whore?"

Maisy's anxiety is obvious. She's been bound before, but not like this. She exhales and lowers her head, her eyes downcast. She shakes her head in response.

She climbs onto the bench and lies down, cringing when her stomach touches the cold leather. Wasting no time, I secure her left wrist by strapping it tight with the leather cuffs at the base. I do the same with the other. The bench narrows slightly at the far end, allowing her breasts to overhang on the sides as her upper body is pinned to the leather.

I walk around her and admire her spread legs, straddling the bench with her ass and cunt open for me. I strap in both of her ankles with the leather restraints on each side, and pull a lever to position her ass higher. *Fuck me. She's open for business*. Finally, I secure her torso by buckling the leather restraint across her waist.

Now she's secured firmly in place, I stand over her and assess her position. I want perfection, though, so I fix the harness better on her body, along each strap, letting her stew in the anticipation. She looks away as I tether her and with each fastening pull, she gives off a small whimper.

I'll go easy. I don't want to break her, but in a way, I think she wants this. I intend to enjoy myself. I glance over at my desk where the second drawer's open, holding all my tools ready to be used. My eyes land on the leather spanking paddle, one side flat and the other with rivets for scratching, and the two-layered paddle with the word 'slut' on it. That one's tough to take, but I'm gonna make her my slut today no matter what.

I take the paddles from the drawer and leave them on the desk, directly within her eyeline. I didn't expect to see panic in her eyes, and yet there it is. She's practically stopped breathing, taking small, shallow breaths that are barely enough to keep her alive, as if I'm going to kill her.

I stroke her head and lean close to her ear. "If anything's too much, just say so and I'll stop. Deal?"

She nods and inhales deeply, squirming on the bench as if testing how much room for movement she has while restrained.

I take two nipple clamps from my drawer, each with a small lead weight in the shape of a heart, and reach for one of Maisy's nipples, playing with it between my fingers before pinching it. She hums as I tug on it and with the other hand, without letting her notice the swap, I place the clamp on it. The moan that struggles to come from her is bravely swallowed down as I force an uninvited feeling of arousal into her body. She turns her head and her pupils, wanton and diluted, follow my every move. Now that she's tied to the bench with a clamp freely hanging from her nipple, I know any minute movement she makes will go straight between her thighs. Her ass somehow looks more raised than before. *Little slut!* I attach the other clamp in the same way.

There's one last step before I let loose. I connect my cell to the speakers and put on Sisters of Mercy's "More" on repeat. That first chord blaring on the speakers drives me to open a brand-new bottle of whiskey that's neatly stashed in my drawer with a few tumblers. I planned to drink this every night she was gone, but then I realized my plan was shit. So, I made a better one. This one right here, now. I pour myself a generous amount and drink it neat, welcoming the burn that slides down my throat. The fire in my mouth demands more and I pour myself another. With my whiskey in hand, I pick up the paddle from the desk and go to Maisy.

The chorus kicks in as I drag the cold rivets of the paddle up her legs to her ass cheeks. She flinches at the cold touch. Maybe she thinks that's what she's getting, but then I turn the paddle over and smack her, hard.

The lead weights move, and her mouth opens without any sound coming out. Her moan comes a beat later, heavy and deep. Her head turns to the side, her lustful eyes opening slowly and landing on me. In her infinite darkness, I see dazzling stars. She looks powerless and yet so powerful, as if she's absolving me of any wrongdoing. I continue dragging the paddle over her, grazing the skin of her back and gliding back down to her ass cheek where I smack her again, the smooth side up. Then, I do something unplanned: I dig my teeth into her ass, leaving a mark.

I needed that. I won't apologize.

She jolts, then whimpers, her nipples tugged by the weighted clamps. She attempts to still her body but it's impossible to stop the movement of the weights, swinging in circles like little crystal pendulums. That's what's getting to her. I run the paddle rivet-side down to the other leg, from the soles of her feet up to her ass where I land on her skin another perfect smack.

I turn the paddle, then surprise her by dipping the handle between her legs. It's slick with her arousal when I retrieve it. *Now, how did I know that would happen?*

"Hey, slut, I don't remember saying you could enjoy this." I smack her harder on the ass. "I didn't, did I?" Another smack lands as she cries out, and I rain on her skin at least ten more strikes of the paddle, losing myself in the sweet, red welts that develop. Her arousal is glistening and leaking onto the bench. Her moans vibrate through her body.

I stop to take a breath as the music blares *I want more!* and realize I'm taken to a different dimension when I'm with her.

My whiskey needs topping up, and as I set the tumbler on the desk, the open drawer catches my attention. The glass butt plug is calling my name. I wasn't going to use it, but fuck me, she needs it. I pick it up.

"Suck on this. All of it." I push it into her mouth to warm it up and make it wet, and she obeys. "Mm-hmm, that's enough." I take it back and gently press it into her ass.

She tugs on her restraints, squirming, but when I start rimming her she gives me a small whimper.

"Yeah, I know you like it. Easy now, my little whore, easy. Just relax." I push it in fully and she bucks and shoves until she adjusts to it. I imagine her losing her mind as every nerve in her body awakens.

"We gotta loosen up your ass, bear with me now." I pull it out, then start edging it in again. "There, is that better? Good girl." I slot the plug in and praise her some more. I'll be fucking praising her forever if she keeps doing such a good job taking that butt plug. *Her ass couldn't be needier if it wanted to.*

"*Goood* girl." I pull it out again, and reinsert it.

I leave it there, turn to pour myself more whiskey, and as I pick the tumbler up, I see Logan and Kai have entered my bedroom and are watching me. I didn't hear them over the music. I lower the volume slightly and smile, pointing my index finger at them.

"Fuck her, but do not touch her," I say quietly, so Maisy won't hear. "Use the harness. Don't suck her clit, or rub it or do fucking *anything* else. If you can't manage that, leave. I want her to understand her position. I want her to leave this room resurrected, and with a need that will never, ever be sated unless we say so."

Kai's already surveying my open drawer and has the flogger in hand. This is not his game but he's always a willing participant and apprentice, for whatever his date wants.

Maisy still doesn't know they're here; her eyes are closed, and she's facing the other way.

Kai runs the fringes of the flogger over her body and starts to flog her, although not hard enough for my liking.

She recognizes that it's him immediately. "Kai..." she drawls, opening her eyes.

The love she has for him is so pure, but the frustration is clear: she wants to feel something, and in one step I'm there, smacking my paddle hard against her ass.

Her eyes roll backward and she moans, her whole body trembling and her ass perking up. Kai raises his eyebrows at me and I nod, leaving him to it. His powerful arm takes a mighty swing and he strikes the flogger against her back. She jolts on the bench and gasps, arching her back as much as the restraints allow.

But that's it for Kai. *Always the one thinking only with his junk*. He unbuttons his jeans enough for his cock to spring out and suddenly he's behind her already.

He strokes himself, preparing for the inevitable. "What's this bite mark on your ass, baby girl? Did that hurt?"

"What can I say? I like to bite when I'm horny," I chuckle.

"If you get past the canine, you're hungry, not horny," Kai retorts.

"Hungry for *her*. Yes." I finish my third whiskey. With the song now on its fourth play, I sing along and pour myself another, offering one to Logan. He dismisses me with a shake of his head, standing with his feet slightly apart, arms crossed over his chest. He looks like he can't decide if he's mad or horny.

"Look at you, baby girl." Kai looks captivated by her, watching the arousal dripping down her thighs. "I want to lick it off your legs, but I really shouldn't ruin it."

He slides his cock up and down her folds and she bucks backward, trying to move against her restraints. She's forgotten about the heavy clamps; they start to swing and she's there again, flying, trying to focus.

"Is this what you want? My cock inside you?" Kai's gripping the back of her harness as he teases her but he clearly can't do it any longer. He slides inside her and he's a goner. "Ohh, yes... *Yes!* Did you miss me, baby girl?" He's lost in her pussy, grunting as he thrusts into her. "Good girl, Maisy, that's it, oh my God, how good your little pussy takes my big cock, how wet you get from me, yes! You're a fucking–"

"Cum bucket," I finish for him. I take a black felt pen and write the words across her ass. "She's our whore, Kai. Our whore to do whatever we want with."

Logan's stroking himself already. "I can't wait to fill this whore with my cum."

I walk around the cross to stand in front of her and pinch her cheeks. "Open wide, cum whore!"

Maisy takes me in, sucking and humming as if her life depends on it while her body jerks upward like a rag doll in time with Kai's thrusts.

Fuck, I better last longer than a minute. I tangle my fingers in her hair and push my cock to the back of her throat, holding there for a few moments while she gags. I stop her air flow and dig in deep, entering heaven for a moment, then release her. I could keep doing that for eternity, but I want eternity with her too. A few threads of saliva connect us as she takes a gulp of air.

"Eyes on me, slut!" I command.

"More" continues to play on the speakers as Kai holds her tighter by the harness at her hips and bangs her even harder.

"Fucking-slut... Get-ready-for-my-cum. Ahh!"

He shudders violently and pulls out, growling as he jerks whatever's left over her pussy and ass.

"Your turn, Logan!" Kai slaps her butt cheek, spreading his cum all over her, and suddenly Maisy's sucking like a world champion. *She's desperate.*

The way her pleading eyes watch me, I just want to reach between her legs and let her explode. "Mm-hmm. I know you want to cum, slut, I do. Just keep sucking." I take her jaw in my hand and pinch her nose with the other to let her fly, using her for what she's here for, and after ten seconds, I let her breathe again. Her desperate gasps for air are raw and needy and make my cock that much harder.

Logan grunts and I look up. He's already fucking her.

"Yeah, sweetheart, take my cum like a true champ, all of it," he mutters. "We'll be here all night, filling you up until you can't walk." He slaps against her cheeks each time he thrusts. Maisy's moaning, whimpering, and talking gibberish. *She better not be orgasming*. Logan doesn't stop; what he's doing to her pulls at the harness yet she's held firmly in place.

I hold her head as I slam into her throat a few more times, making sure I stop her breathing every so often; she needs the high. *She's here for us, not herself.* When I pull her head up to look at me, I slap her face a few times.

"What are you, Maisy?"

She's struggling for breath. "I'm... I'm..."

"Say it, you fucking whore." I slap her again, and again.

"I'm a cum bucket..." she moans.

"Do you want to be a cum bucket?"

"Yes, yes, I do. Please, I do, I want your cum," she whimpers as her body jolts again and again to Logan's rhythm.

Fuck, I'm too close. I want to cum in her cunt.

Logan yells, spewing curses as he erupts inside her. "Fuck, you whore, you know how to milk me good!"

"Move!" I order Logan. He slaps her ass once and makes space for me.

I step behind her and, grabbing hold of the harness, plunge inside her like a lunatic who's been denied his cure. My piercing makes her suck in a breath. "God*damn*, that feels so good! That's it, slut!"

I ram into her and as I do, I reach around her and take off the nipple clamps. She wails loudly and jerks backward toward me, which tells me she's so fucking close, I know, right in her subspace, but I won't let her get there.

"Please, I want to. I want to..." she begs in a frail voice.

"Not this time, whore! You gotta earn your place among us!" I slap her ass. She's too tight; I won't last long. "Fuck, that's it, fuck, *goddamn*, you're so fucking wet for me." I lean down and bite her shoulder. "You want my cum, slut? Come here." I hook my leg beneath where her ankle's restrained, giving me deeper access. "Oh fuck, *yes!* Take my big cock like the true slut you are!"

I cum inside her with a growl, and I keep ramming as my cum spills, taking what's mine, what she's taken away from me for two weeks. But still, I'm losing control, this urgent need wreaking havoc in my mind. Still angry, I pull out, pick up the double-sided 'slut' paddle and smack the word hard against her ass.

"Fuck, yes! Now you're branded!"

Maisy shrieks, then gives me a drawn-out moan. Her head turns and her eyes land on me, hooded and hungry, her ass raised, every inch of her pleading for release.

Kai's ready to go again, already stroking himself. After a two-week drought, our balls are heavy with cum meant only for her.

"Who's for sloppy seconds, boys?" I ask as I play with her butt plug before slowly pulling it out.

"You need to ask?" Logan snickers. "I'm just gonna press shuffle. I'm afraid we'll hurt her if that song keeps playing."

I lean down to address Maisy. "You want this?"

"Yes," she pants.

"You think you do, but it'll be worse," I say softly. "Just say if you can't go on, darling."

She just bats her eyelashes at me.

I laugh and step back. "Kai, she's all yours." I reach for my whiskey, and see Logan stroking himself to another stealthy hard-on. When I look back at Maisy, I know I too will be ready when the time comes.

"Yeah, baby girl. It says 'cum bucket' right here, so let's make you a good one." Holding her by the harness, Kai dips in and out of her backside.

"Kai, please, just touch me." She moans.

Her ass is stretched and he enters her deep, fully, and starts to pump into her. She's dripping with arousal, no lube required, and whines as Kai loses himself in her, growling all too soon and stilling inside her. As he pulls out, some of his seed slides out of her asshole.

"Fuck, that was uncontrollable. Her ass is so tight. She squeezed me on purpose." He slaps her butt and steps aside for Logan.

"Let me take her. I've dreamed of her asshole for days." Logan pushes into her gaping ass. Kai's cum clearly doesn't bother him as he proceeds to ram into her.

"Logan, Lo-Logan, I can't anymore. Please..." she pleads.

"Oh, sweetheart, you can't? Well, I can, so as long as I can, you'll be my sweet little cum bucket today." He accelerates the tempo, shouting out loud as her body jerks on the bench with every stroke. "You brought this on yourself!"

I'm ready to go again. Logan sees me and steps away so I can slot between her legs, lining up directly with that ass that's been waiting for me.

"Orion, I can't. *Please.*"

"Yes, whore?" I slap her buttocks and enter her forcefully a few times before pulling back. "Kai, Logan, remove the restraints on her arms and legs." They do as they're told and I unbuckle the belt around her waist. "Help me turn her on her back, I think she's had enough."

Maisy's totally gone. She whimpers and trembles as we roll her over. I immediately lift her ankles onto my shoulders and slam back into her ass. Her head tilts and falls back, and seeing an opportunity for release, Logan positions himself at the end of the bench.

"Oh, fuck!" he exclaims as his cock pushes into her mouth. With his hand on her throat, he drives into her as I continue slamming her ass. Kai sucks on one of her nipples as he finally gives her what she wants, and starts rubbing redemption into her swollen clit. It's at that moment that we experience the room move. Maisy wails and screams in one long, loud sound before she explodes. She starts to shake, squirting so much liquid as Logan cums in her mouth, and I don't last much longer. She drags me down to my jail, the best place on earth. I go still inside her, inside my perfect cum bucket, and her legs spasm for a full minute. When I pull out, a few remaining ropes of jizz spurt all over her sticky cunt.

We're still panting as we stare at Maisy lying on the bench, an overstimulated mess with her eyes closed and muscles contracting. She's leaking, drooling, sweaty, sticky, covered with red welts: a fully-surrendered-to-whatever's-happening mess.

Kai's in awe of her. "Fuck. This was one fucking session I'll never forget."

I tuck away my cock and button up my pants. Logan and Kai follow suit.

"Most women wouldn't last this long. She wanted to please us." Logan kisses her forehead. "My sleeping beauty."

Kai kisses her breast. She jerks; too many stimuli.

I take a towel from my closet and wipe her cunt and ass clean of all the cum. "Let's get you in a nice bath, Maisy." I pick her up in my arms and carry her to my bathroom.

Logan's one step ahead, already running the water in the tub.

I put Maisy in the rapidly-filling tub, and gradually she opens her eyes.

She looks at all of us and smiles. "I need you. *All* of you," she breathes. "Kai, your beautiful, innocent loving makes me believe in love where heartache doesn't exist. You make me feel loved."

That's exactly who Kai is: a free spirit who loves without conditions.

He kisses her hand. "You *are* loved, Maisy."

"And Logan, there's something about you that awakens the woman inside me, the mother, the protector."

He raises his eyebrows at her. "The protector?"

"I don't know what it is, but I didn't know she existed until I met you."

Logan kisses her on the lips. "I'll always be here."

Her eyes land on me. I have no words. No words to express my love for her. *I'm a lawyer, for fuck's sake. I should always have words.* She's the best thing to happen to us, ever. I don't need her to say anything to me, she's said enough. She's got Kai and Logan, and I don't matter in the grand scheme of things.

"Orion."

"Shh. There's no need to say anything."

"I want to. What you do to me, Orion, is free me up from my jail. My curse. My ever-recording mind that I couldn't ever stop unless I was drugged. Your way is my way."

This is a moment where the penny drops for me. Nothing can ever be the same again. *I love her.*

The water level coming up to her breasts reminds me to turn the faucet off. After I do, I take her hand and kiss it. "I know. But please, please, no more surprises."

She nods.

CHAPTER 17

MAISY

My body is sore. I have the word 'slut' marked on my ass and it fucking hurts each time I move. A reminder of what went on, which, if someone asked, I wouldn't be able to put into words. I was sucked into a vortex of hedonism, that's what it was. Orion, Kai, and Logan sent me to heaven instead of punishing me. Or so I think. I experienced it as an absolute nirvana, and I'm not sure if it's because I smoked dope for two weeks straight, or because they know I'm a perverted, deviant, sex-deprived girl, or maybe they did it on purpose, because what happened last night is so deeply engrained in me that I crave more of it every time I think of it. They've got me hooked on endorphins I cannot say no to.

I'm forever grateful they took me back. The pain of being away from them was unbearable. It's not that I wouldn't survive on my own–it's just that I disappointed them, that's what got to me. I'd endure anything to redeem myself. But I don't know... This didn't feel like penance, but the discovery of a newfound thirst I can never quench.

Huh. Last night at Kirstie's, I'm trying to remember if I've always been predisposed to getting raped, or did that happen after my life got tangled up with the dark lives of three New York mafia heads?

Either way, watching Orion killing those frat fuckers felt good. Even though I was scared, it's fucking great seeing people get what they deserve.

I turn over in bed, and the pain in my ass cheek shoots directly to my brain. I frown and open my eyes. I remember getting dressed for bed in a cami top and black lace panties, and Logan spreading some kind of ointment on the broken skin of my butt.

I spot the tray of food next to me. Now that I can see it, the smell of toast and eggs suddenly fills the room and makes my stomach growl. God knows I haven't eaten properly in days.

I stretch out my arms, content to be back in my sanctuary. I sit up and lift the tray of food onto my bed, immediately stuffing a loaded forkful into my mouth. I'm *famished*.

The orange juice tastes like the oranges have been freshly picked and squeezed mere moments ago. I gulp it all down in one go, freshening my mouth.

Without anyone here to see me I'm free to pig out, but as I get started I suddenly look up. A small hand is pushing the door open, and Mya's cute face makes an appearance.

"Oh, it's you! Come in. Join me." I don't stop eating. As long as there's food on my tray, I'll be eating.

She closes the door softly and walks up to me, her eyes getting bigger as she draws closer. She looks petrified.

"Are you okay? Is everything alright? What happened?"

She looks back at the door, then her eyes roam around the room like she's searching for a place to hide. I hear Lisa calling her from outside.

"Quick, get in the closet," I tell Mya. "I won't tell her where you are."

Mya jumps inside and closes the door behind her just in time before Lisa walks in.

"Maisy, I didn't know you were back!" She looks shocked to see me. "I'm so sorry for barging in on you like this."

"It's fine." I wave it off and take another big bite of toast.

"I was looking for Mya, as she's been coming in here while you were gone. Have you seen her?"

"Um, no," I gesture silently toward the closet. "Why are you looking for her?"

Lisa's eyes widen and she nods. "Oh. Um, my uncles are coming in ten minutes and Orion told me to get Mya and stay in my room. He doesn't want us downstairs when they visit. It's... It's complicated."

Shit. Ten minutes?

"Okay. If I see her, I'll tell her to go to your room and hide in there until they leave. Will that work?"

"Yes. Please tell her that," Lisa says, then mouths 'thank you' to me.

"Sure. Bye, Lisa."

Lisa closes the door, and at almost the same time, Mya opens the closet, as if she couldn't wait to get out.

"Is that why you were hiding? You didn't want to see your uncles?" I ask.

Not looking at me, she nods.

"Has any of them hurt you?"

She shakes her head.

"Has any of them hurt your mommy?"

She shakes it again.

"Okay. Has any of them hurt your daddy?"

Her eyes flick back to me at the speed of light. Her pupils dilate, and she freezes. Almost stops breathing.

"How about we play a game, Mya?" I ask carefully. "Why don't you go to your room, real quickly? You have ten minutes before they show up, and you can hide in there until they leave. I'll make sure they come and go as quickly as possible, okay?"

She shakes her head again. No wonder; she's terrified.

"Okay then. How about I get dressed and take you to your room, and then I'll go and tell them to leave. Deal?"

She nods.

I stuff the last piece of toast into my mouth before putting the tray aside and getting out of bed.

While I wash my face and brush my teeth, Mya chooses a short navy-blue dress for me. I put it on, brush my hair, and apply some pink lip balm. I then offer her my hand. "Shall we?"

She holds my hand tight in her small fingers, as if she's ready to face the world. We leave the room and walk across the landing in the direction of her bedroom when I hear Uncle Colletti's voice from the bottom of the staircase.

"Maisy, is that you?"

He's looking up at us. I stop, and Mya doesn't let go of my hand. "Give me a minute, Uncle Colletti!" I call. "I'll be there shortly."

Uncle Leo pushes his brother aside. "Let me see her... Maisy!" he grins. "Oh, Maisy." *Perv.*

Uncle James shows up behind him too. He doesn't say a thing, but his eyes move from me to Mya and she squeezes my hand so hard, it hurts.

Orion shows up from behind me, and instantly shields me with his body. "Why the fuck is Mya with you? And what are you wearing?" he hisses.

"Mya chose my dress. And I *love* it." I look at her and smile. "I'll take her to her mother. See you in two minutes." Orion grunts and I lead Mya up to the top floor where her bedroom is.

Lisa's sitting on the bed waiting for us, but judging by her fidgeting fingers, she's nervous. "Mya, where were you?"

I get down onto one knee, putting myself at Mya's eye level. "Don't worry, sweetie. We're not going to let anything happen to you."

She jumps into my arms, hugs me hard, and breaks down in sobs.

"Wh-what happened?" Lisa asks anxiously.

"It's okay, Mya," I whisper. "You squeezed my hand when Uncle James showed up his face just now. Is that the man you saw when your daddy was killed?"

She nods, and whimpers on another sob.

"Shh, don't worry. I promise you, he'll pay for what he did. Your Uncle Orion's the best uncle in the world." I peel her off me and look her in the eye. "He's never going to let anything happen to you or your mommy."

She points to me.

"Yes, and me, of course," I add.

Lisa's crying silently, tears rolling down her cheeks.

"Do you want to give your mommy a hug for looking after you all this time, and keeping you safe?"

She nods and runs into her mother's embrace. More sobs. My own eyes burn and go glassy.

I have a job to do now.

"I'll talk to you later. Stay here 'til I come and get you," I say to Lisa, and leave.

As I head downstairs, my heart hurts from everything Mya has been through. Particularly the trauma of seeing her father killed. That redacted information now makes sense. He was going to kill Mya. The 'she' who had to be killed. Yet again, Milan managed to fuck up another young life.

In the kitchen, I find Orion has arranged the chairs so he and I sit at the far end of the table and the three uncles are facing us.

I smile sweetly and sit next to him. "Hello, everyone."

Uncle Colletti's first with the compliments. "Maisy, you look fresh."

"I just woke up, actually. Is there any coffee, Orion? I can get it."

I'm half-standing when he stops me.

"Let me get it for you." He jumps up, pours me a cup, and brings it back to the table, where he immediately becomes curt and to the point. "Now, let's talk. What did you want to know?"

"Tell us what you have on the Delgados," Uncle James says.

Orion and I look at each other. "She's here to talk about what Milan has on us," he says.

Uncle James seems to be looking for a fight. "The fuck she is."

I remain silent.

"Tell us what we can use to get to the motherfuckers!" he demands.

"Uncle James, the Slavs are your biggest enemies," I remind him. "They're conspiring to work against you, and both the Delgados and you should focus on removing them from the picture. Judging by what I know about the Slavs, you're in imminent danger."

"You work for us now, little girl," Uncle James snaps. "We saved your cute little ass, and gave you the freedom to give your little pussy to everyone in here if you want to, which you probably have already, so don't get smart with me, you hear me?"

Uncle James is a fucking idiot.

Under the table, Orion places his hand on my knee, reminding me that he's got me.

"I'll tell you what I know, how about that?" I suggest. "What I know for certain."

"Start talking."

"When I saw you two weeks ago, you asked me about Christmas Day last year. I told you that someone got killed. And I mentioned an email thread between Milan and someone else."

Uncle Leo leans in. "Yes?"

"Fuck that!" Uncle James interrupts. "We don't wanna know about that. Tell us about the Delgados!"

"Actually, James, we do." Uncle Colletti's low, somber voice embodies authority.

Uncle James scoffs, making sure everyone's aware of his discontent.

"Now, when I think about it, the last line in the email to Milan was 'don't ask for my help again. I could be made.' I think I know who that was."

Orion turns to me. "You do?"

"I know, because it was all about something unplanned: Mya, looking into the eyes of her father's killer." I stare hard at Uncle James.

Uncle James says nothing, but retaliates by holding my gaze with a scowl, not saying a word. Just breathing heavily.

"What?!" Orion thunders, leaping to his feet.

My eyes don't leave Uncle James. Everyone can see what's going on.

"Uncle James, you got *one-fucking-minute* to come clean!"

He looks nervously at his brothers. "You believe this whore?"

They watch him in silence.

"Uncle James, you killed Tom," I conclude.

The glares from his brothers make him repent immediately. "I-I did what I had to do. He was asking too many questions–"

"You killed Tom, in front of Mya?" Uncle Colletti asks softly, with a composure that scares me.

"She wasn't supposed to be there! For fuck's sake! I should've killed her too."

Orion pulls his gun from the holster so quickly I don't have time to blink. With his chin raised and his arm extended directly ahead, he fires three muffled shots between Uncle James's eyes. The man's head sags and drops to the table, as if in slow motion.

Uncle Colletti and Uncle Leo look at the limp body between them with contempt. Blood is starting to pool on the table. "We didn't know, Orion."

Orion places his gun back in the holster. "This meeting's over. We're meeting the Delgados and Vitalis at the club to discuss the Slavs, tonight. There better not be any trouble."

"Sure. See you then." The two remaining uncles stand up, look at their brother's body on the table, and spit on him.

Orion watches them leave with his cell at his ear. "Garry. I need a cleaning crew in my kitchen." He ends the call and looks at me. "How did you know?"

"Mya told me."

"Mya?" His eyebrows shoot up. "She hasn't said a word in almost a year. To anyone."

"She talks to me."

"To you? Does Lisa know?"

"Kinda. Can we please go? There's a dead person on the table. I can't look at it."

"What, him?" Orion pulls his gun again and shoots him three more times in the head. "Fucking traitor."

"Orion!" I gasp.

He slots his gun back into his holster as if nothing happened. "Let's go to Lisa's room."

We find Lisa and Mya in bed, talking to each other in whispers. Mya's eyes land on me and she exclaims, "Maisy!"

Orion freezes in the doorway. He looks at Mya, then at Lisa. "What the fuck?"

"Language, Orion," Lisa warns, though her voice trembles. "That's Mya's new best friend."

I kneel down by the bed to talk to her. "Hey, Mya. You know how I told you about your cool Uncle Orion?"

Her big blue eyes shift to Orion. "Mm-hmm."

"Well, he just made sure that horrible man downstairs is sent to forever land–never ever to come back."

"You did?" she asks him.

"Yes, kiddo. Come here." She goes to him and he takes her in his arms. "You've grown so much. I missed your voice."

"I missed your voice too." She grins and wraps her arms around his neck.

Orion closing his eyes and visibly melting in her embrace is the best thing ever.

"I promise nothing will ever happen to you again," he whispers.

ORION

"The art of profit is based on exploiting need, and no one perfected that dark art better than my father," I decreed in the boardroom to an audience of Kai, Logan, and two additional members of each of their families, all looking at me impassively.

"And my father," Kai added curtly.

"Yeah, let's not forget about Lorenzo, either," Logan interjected, as if this was a competition. "He loved to fuck, but he was fucking smart!" His relatives nodded approvingly.

I ignored them. "With his great business acumen, he invested in a number of companies that have turned out to be very relevant to the COVID crisis: multi-service businesses such as catering, cleaning and disinfection, industrial laundries, transport, funeral homes, waste collection, food distribution–and health," I continued. "All of these sectors have been fundamental during COVID, which worked out great for us. I'm sure your fathers did the same, and you both have something you're working toward.

"However, now that we've found out Milan was out to get us all this time, the mess the Slavs kept serving us for too long cannot be ignored any longer. It's the perfect time to join forces and attack.

"Our relationship, if I could call it that, shouldn't last long. But it sure will serve as a foundation for the future, providing it's successful. I therefore propose we strike Milan's HQ, get access to his safe, where all the important documents on us are held, take what's ours, and go our separate ways. We don't have to pretend to be friends here."

I vividly remembered Maisy telling me the safe was what we needed. There should be three boxes in it, one on each of our respective families. Everything she'd read was placed in there. All the evidence of crime, snitches, profits, scams, and more. But selfishly, I wanted this for no other reason than to get my hands on that letter from my mother. *Why the* fuck *would Milan have a letter from my mother at all?*

"How do we know you won't do something stupid? Like, pull the gun on us mid-heist?" one of Logan's people asked with a scowl.

"It's always our own division that destroys us. We've been on the verge of extinction and we survived, all of us, too many times. I'd have to be stupid to do something like that. One thing we all know is that there's too much animosity. The family we each belong to is important, but it's also about the honor and loyalty and character of the family members. I believe Kai and Logan have that." As I concluded, both Kai and Logan nodded so everyone would know they agreed.

"So, do you believe the same about me?" I asked.

Logan stood up and offered his hand. "I do."

I shook with him and nodded.

"Yes." Kai got to his feet and offered his hand too. "You may be many things, but you're loyal, Orion." I knew he meant it.

Their family members rose and we all shook hands, sealing the plan tight.

As for executing it, we didn't waste much time. We knew Milan had snitches everywhere; heck, we knew about Bobby from the Vitali family and so, officially, we said it would take place in a month's time, when in actual fact we did it within mere days.

Two days from that meeting, fifteen of us–five from each family–were in Milan's house. In and out. He figured something was going on when we took an expensive painting from his house, one that he shouldn't have had in his possession in the first place, and left it outside the Interpol HQ, leaning against the sign saying *The Stolen Works of Art Database*. We dropped him in the shit, needing him to be focused on something while we were sifting through the information he had on us and making sense of it.

Initially, he didn't know we infiltrated his safe. We didn't take a lot, mostly just the three boxes Maisy had told us about. Of course, we went through everything, including a bunch of old DVDs, each with a photo of an underaged girl on the cover. That made us sick. I would've left them there if I hadn't seen Maisy's face staring back at me from one of the covers. A scared-looking little girl sitting in the corner of a dingy gray room, with short hair and dark circles under her eyes. That's what I saw first, the abyss in her eyes. And then I decided I was taking them all, so I shoved the DVDs into my box and we left.

We went our separate ways, each with our own box. We had to go through the important documents, the money, the snitches, and our own personal shit before passing it on to everyone else.

~

It's been three days since I've seen them, and Kai and Logan are due to come over today. I'm sure Milan knows what happened by now. Interpol contacted him the next day, and he's bound to have joined the dots. And if he didn't, I bet one of his snitches told him.

But if Kai and Logan do what I did, there won't be any snitches left. Among the rest of the stuff in my box, there was evidence on three snitches. Fucking *three!* Not one or two. *Three!* That very night, I drove to their homes and killed them in their sleep. Game over. Why would I bother talking to them?

Actually, there were four if we count Uncle James, but it was Maisy who flushed him out.

Are they now more afraid of me? I fucking hope so. Only loyalty will keep you alive with me, they know that.

As for Maisy, I've given her some normality in her life. She's been cooking and making herself useful around the house. Lisa took her out shopping, and Maisy's even taken Mya to kindergarten a few times. Of course, they had a bodyguard following them but still, it's the thought that counts. It's as if my life is back to how it was (naturally, it's much better with Maisy being around), but then I look at the box in my office and remember what's in it.

Maisy's been asking me about the DVDs. She's seen what's in the box and was eager to find out what's on them. Knowing her, she must know already. She's been trying to manipulate me in the most innovative ways, but it hasn't worked so far. At least, I think it hasn't. She's a challenge to keep around, alright.

Kai and Logan agreed we should share the information with Maisy together. And so, we will.

CHAPTER 18

MAISY

"Hey."

I enter the living room with my hands in my pockets. Relaxed. Happy. Plus, Kai and Logan are coming today. "Are they here yet?"

"I'm sure when they get here, you'll know," Orion chuckles.

"Maisy!" Two thunderous sets of footsteps reach my ears. The door opens wide and it's them. "Maisy!" I'm lifted with Logan in front of me and Kai behind. They hold me in their arms and bury their heads in my t-shirt, sniffing me.

"Oh *fuck*, I missed your smell!" Logan shouts.

"Mmm, yes!" echoes Kai.

"Put me down!" I scream, laughing and trying to drop to the ground.

They oblige but Kai doesn't let go, instead burying his head in my neck, peppering me with kisses that turn into nibbles, and grinding into my ass. Logan follows, pressing his lips to mine, holding my hips and rubbing against me from the front.

"I take it you missed me, boys?" I grin.

Orion laughs. The sound is intoxicating.

"I know I missed you." I wrap an arm around each of their necks and pull them close. "Hey, horny fucks, how are you?"

"Mmm... horny!" Kai replies, playfully nipping my cheek.

"Guys, come on," Orion says. Everyone ignores him. "Maisy! Come here."

I manage to peel myself away from them and take Orion's hand.

"Can you see me now?" he asks them. "Or are your cocks still looking at Maisy?"

"You've had her for a week, come on!" Kai argues.

"You came here for something else. Focus."

Logan tries to get serious. "Right. Right."

Kai adjusts his junk in his jeans and rubs his face. "K, I'm good. I'm good."

"Sit down." Orion gets comfortable on the chair, and I sit on the armrest while the other two take the sofa opposite us. "What's the update?"

"We've heard about the Carte snitches," Logan starts, "and what you did. Three! Wow. Good on you."

I heard about Orion killing someone in the middle of the night, but of course, that was expected. I knew what was inside those boxes. I'm just glad I didn't have to tell them everything myself.

"Yeah. You?" Orion asks.

Logan nods. "One. Bobby Saunders. We knew about him, though." He catches my eye.

"Did you kill him?"

"I couldn't. He's like my older brother. I knew he was a snitch for a while, and even then I wasn't sure what to do with him."

"Don't leave it open," Kai warns. "You gotta make the cut."

"I cut his balls off. Sent him to Milan. That's me being generous."

Orion turns to Kai. "And you?"

"Out of the four that jumped me a few weeks ago, who I killed, three were snitches," Kai reports. "I killed those bastards before I even knew how much they deserved it. What worries me most is the personal stuff Milan has on us. Our everyday conversations, every single thing I've taken part in, from a motorbike sale to a racket I took from the Gianini restaurant. That's bad, man."

They all nod and exchange glances. Nobody says a word. Everyone's in their own head.

"You know, I know what's in those boxes, too," I remind them. "Orion, did you read your mother's letter?"

I can tell he's prepared himself for this, as if he knew it would come up. He pulls a letter out of the inside pocket of his suit jacket and throws it onto the coffee table.

"I couldn't. Fuck knows what's inside, or who wrote it."

Kai leans forward. "What's this now?"

"In short, Wendy isn't my real mother. Nobody knew. Nobody except my father, who never said anything about it."

Kai's shocked. "The *fuck?*"

"Yeah. So now I have this letter from my 'mother' that was at Milan's for God knows how long, and I don't think I want to open it," Orion concludes gruffly.

"Logan, did you find the teddy bear in the box? Was that yours?" I ask.

"The bear was there, and I found my original birth certificate stuffed inside it," Logan says. "Although, the name of my mother had been crossed out. I could only read a few letters of her first name–Ebe."

Orion looks sympathetic. "Sorry, man. I know finding your mother means a lot to you."

"Yeah. But hey, there's more. I got a middle name now. You know what it is? Moros."

"Huh. Moros. It suits you," Orion grins.

"Does it? It means 'the hateful personified spirit of impending doom, who drives mortals to their deadly fate.'"

"Fuck!" Orion laughs. "What's yours, Kai?"

"...Typhon," he mutters.

"What?" Orion and Logan gape at him before breaking out into laughter. "Typhon. That's weird. Crazy."

"It means destruction! So keep laughing, assholes. I could destroy you like *that*," Kai quips.

"What about you, Orion?" I ask. "What's your middle name?"

"Luckily, I don't have one. Although I haven't seen my birth certificate yet so I can't be sure."

I nod toward the table. "Maybe it's in the letter."

He shakes his head and reaches forward to pick up the letter again. He tears it open and I watch him pull out an actual birth certificate, as well as a note. He reads the note and flips it back onto the table. It lands with the words facing up.

'*I'm sorry. Mom.*'

Orion doesn't flinch, his walls as impenetrable as ever, but he's still clutching the birth certificate. I gently take it from his hand and read it.

"Oh my God, Orion, you *do* have a middle name!" I exclaim.

"It's probably Devil or something," Logan snickers.

"It's Keres." I look up at him. "Fuck, I know this one. It means death. Boys, you lucked out with your middle names. Keres–death, Typhon–destruction, and Moros–impending doom."

Kai smirks. "That's basically our lives. Fitting for all of us."

"Orion, here." I pass the paper back to him. "You can finally see who your real mother–"

He cuts me off. "Maisy, there's more important things we wanted to discuss with you today. Not that. It can wait." He flips the birth certificate back onto the coffee table.

"Oh?" I ask.

He takes out a small box full of DVDs from behind his chair and sets it on the table. "We found this in Milan's safe."

"What is it?"

"Videos. Of girls."

I look at Logan, Kai, and back at Orion. They're all regarding me somberly. "Doing what? What do you mean?"

"There's one of you in here."

"Of me? What about my sister?"

"I didn't check. I just saw your face and took them all."

I drop down to my knees next to the table and rummage through the DVDs like a mad woman. The DVD featuring my face is on the top, the picture of me from back when I was twelve years old. Reaching the last one, I see Rosey's. It's from that first week with the Slavs, when they took us.

"Do you know what's on it?" Orion asks.

They're waiting for me to speak. But they know before I tell them.

I push myself to my feet and sit down on the sofa, between Kai and Logan–right where I'm safe, where I can remind myself I'm a world away from that day. I pull my legs under me and close my eyes. In darkness, I can say the words. "That was the week we were taken to Milan's place. Maybe ten of us. And he... he raped us. One by one. Maybe that's what's on it."

"He's a dead man walking," Kai spits out.

"Are you okay if we see what's on it?" Orion asks.

I pretend I don't hear him. What should I say? Yes? I'm not okay. But they'll watch it anyway.

"Maisy?"

I look up at him. My past has finally caught up with me.

I try to look indifferent. "Do what you want. I'll go and grab myself a drink."

LOGAN

I wait for the door to close so Maisy doesn't hear me. "Do you have a DVD player?" We aren't going to watch someone being raped, but we must see what's on it.

"Yes. My father kept one in the attic. It's behind the TV now," Orion replies, and passes me the DVD. "Put it on."

I slot the disc into the old machine and as we wait for it to start playing, I read the back cover out loud. "'Maisy, twelve, child prodigy.'"

The video starts playing and the three of us watch in horrified silence. It's her. Maisy. She's too young, too naïve, and she's being coerced by a vile old pedo, Milan. He reaches her in the first few minutes, and I pause the DVD before we see something we can never unsee, which will probably do more damage because acting on impulse never ends well.

It's not that I can't watch it. It's that I don't want to.

We glance at each other. "She was telling the truth about this. Do we want to see it?" I ask.

Both Kai and Orion shake their heads.

"Check Rosey's DVD," Kai suggests.

Orion goes through the box and finds the DVD with Rosey's face. He hands it over and I take a better look at her features. I see the resemblance. They're twins, but not identical.

"'Rosey, twelve, doll,'" I read from the back cover.

I remove the disc and as I do, a small note flies out. We all reach for it just as Maisy walks in holding a bottle of water. The note lands on the floor, clearly readable to the three of us.

'*Dead, suicide.*'

Orion snatches it and crushes it in his hand.

"Did you see me?" she asks coolly, her chin a little raised. *No one will ever take away her pride.*

"Maisy, we're not gonna watch it," I reassure her.

"Good. And Rosey? I want to see her video."

We regard each other in silence. She doesn't have to be strong in front of us. That's why we're here. So she can let go. This couldn't have been easy on her.

"Are you sure, darling?" Orion wraps his arm around her waist and pulls her to him, and she immediately finds a home in his chest.

She shrugs. "I don't know. If it connects me with her, then yes."

"It won't." He kisses the top of her head. In a few strides, Kai and I reach them and embrace her too. The three of us surround Maisy like a human shield.

"Nothing will ever happen to you again. Nothing," Kai mutters.

She cranes her neck to look up at us and smiles, her eyes glazed with tears. "I know."

MAISY

They still haven't figured it out, but they will eventually. Right now, they're dealing with the Slavs. Milan found out about his safe and what was taken from it: the three boxes and the DVDs. His main concern would be the DVDs, anyone could figure that out. Especially after Orion sent the box to the police last week.

I told him not to do it because we could use them as leverage, but he didn't agree with me. He knows Milan has someone working for him in every police station in New York and beyond, but he thought this would at least give them time to regroup, to plan. Because for some reason, Milan is still managing to cause them complications.

Every day, something and someplace are attacked by the Slavs. Simultaneously, the Cartes, Delgados, and Vitalis are being targeted by Milan's devious plans. They don't say anything directly to me but I'm around, I spend time with them, and I hear the worry. People are getting killed, tortured. Bobby, the snitch Logan couldn't kill, is now working for Milan. He's the one who told him it was all three of Kai, Logan, and Orion who were involved in the heist. Natasha, Kai's ex, is also working for Milan. And he must've caught on that it was me who's been rattling his cage. *Fucking bastard.* But that won't deter me. I'll find my sister no matter what.

With my boys next to me, I'm invincible. They're smart. There's already a plan to assassinate Milan, with the promise it won't be before he sings like a canary of my sister's whereabouts.

I couldn't protect her that day from Milan, but everything I did after, I did for her. Milan promised me as long as I worked for him, she'd be taken care of. That didn't do her any good. Now I know better. Now I'm playing my cards right, with men who I trust and love.

With Kai, Orion, and Logan, I've found my place, my home. I don't know how we'll work out, but we have so far. I'm still at Orion's and I love it here, but there are other options. Kai's talked about his beach house in Long Island. His secret place. Nobody knows of it but us and it'd be a great place to take a vacation. Logan told me he lives in a penthouse and would love to take me there. Orion and Kai aren't invited, of course–because of the security and cameras, and his whole family living in that building–but I am. And I'd love nothing more than to be treated like a princess in his tower. The problem is, with Milan's retaliations, the mafia families are back to hating each other and Orion's plan is farther away than it ever was. There was a failed attempt to join forces when Milan declared New York belonged to him, and that the

Cartes, Vitalis, and Delgados were to leave the city and never come back.

Milan figured it out. He saw through them. He knew all this time they were together as allies, and that's what he wanted to expose. The idea was they'd kill each other and let him rule. But when they attacked first, I told them, *Be ready, be prepared. Milan's a sneaky fucker. He has information on every person in New York and can make whole buildings disappear, not just people.*

As long as they played safe, and looked twice behind their backs, I was happy. Sleeping with the three of them, all of us sharing my bed, is a hedonistic pleasure I've learned to love, and crave. One important thing we all had to remember in the past three weeks was to tell Lisa when we'd be 'together,' as she's run into us once already. She's petrified Mya may see something she shouldn't. Rightly so.

We've been locking the door since that happened.

~

This morning, after one of my wildest ever nights with my boys, I wake up alone in bed.

I know they had to go, each rushing to his own family when the message came on their cells. Milan has done something again, this time big. They wouldn't tell me what. I didn't want to know.

They shot out in a hurry and left me naked in my bed, the door still slightly ajar, and now the aroma of freshly-made coffee reaches me and is what actually makes me get up. It smells divine.

I hear someone shuffling about downstairs in the kitchen, making noise. Maybe Orion asked Lisa to make me something to eat. I've told her so many times I can make food for myself. And for everyone else. She doesn't need to cook for me, or do anything for me any longer. *Orion just doesn't listen.*

I head down in my cami and panties. Lisa's seen me wearing skimpy clothes plenty of times before. I was woken up too early, and coffee is what I need.

Following the scent into the kitchen, I head for the coffee pot. The fridge door's open, concealing Lisa behind it, who must be deliberating on what to cook for breakfast.

"Good morning." I pour myself a cup, take a large gulp, and cringe at the bitterness and smoky flavors that attack my taste buds. *This coffee is vile!*

I look up to see a man's hairy hand holding the fridge door, closing it slowly to reveal the person standing behind it.

I freeze. My heart pounds in my throat. The cup I'm holding slips from my fingers, but the loud crash when it hits the floor doesn't even make me flinch. *I–am–dead–already.*

"Good morning, Maisy." The barbed, nauseating voice I hoped never to hear again. His fat, rounded physique has become more revolting, his thinned hair combed to the side. The greasy face is the same. It's always been his signature look.

My worst nightmare, Milan the Dog, is standing in front of me. I'm locked in place, pinned by his narrow, bloodshot, amber eyes with dilated pupils that glow with triumph. Although, he never used to have dark circles under his eyes. We must've been giving him a run for his money. Exhaustion is what I see in his face. But what scares me most is the creepy absence of emotion.

"Surprised to see me?" His raised eyebrows suggest doubt, albeit false.

How did he get in here? Will Orion storm in and save me? Where are Kai and Logan right now?

I blink a few times. Then blink some more. Insecurity and anxiety take over my every pore. He has me cornered.

"Milan," I whisper. More to myself, than to him.

"Rosey made me come. She said you've been looking for her." He takes a sip of his coffee and regards me closely for a few moments. "She's alive, you know that, right?"

After what seems like staring at me for an eternity, he continues nonchalantly to pour me another cup while carefully avoiding the broken one on the floor. "You must try the coffee I made. What you've had here's below par, don't you think?"

"R-Rosey?"

"Yes. Your sister." He passes me the cup. "Take it. Drink."

"Where is she?" I demand, ignoring the offering. It's my right to know where Rosey is.

He shrugs, and sets the cup down again. "Rosey? In my house. She's perfectly fine. In fact, she wants to see you."

"Stop lying, you piece of shit! Where is she? I want to see her!" I take a step forward, wanting to threaten him, although I know that could happen only in my dreams. But the fact that I'm in Orion's house gives me strength.

"Great, because as I said, she wants to see you too. And I'm more than happy to send her your way. For good, this time. Except," He takes a swig of his coffee and swallows, his Adam's apple bobbing disgustingly under the wrinkled skin of his neck. "It'll cost you. And if you can't pay, I'll kill her."

"You do that, and I'll kill you myself!" I try to spit back with venom, although I don't even believe myself. My threats are weak. I'd do anything for Rosey.

"You'll kill me? Haha. Please, sweetie. Check yourself."

"Milan, please, I haven't seen Rosey in years. Please." Uninvited tears fill my eyes and roll down my face, out of my control. She's so near I practically feel her, and he's doing the same thing as always, blackmailing me. I take another step, this time to grab his arm, to plead my case, to show him the pain in my heart. "Please, don't kill her. I'll do anything. *Anything*. You know me."

"Tomorrow, at noon, be at Gianini's on 34th and 6th Street. Make sure the Delgado, Vitali, and Carte heads are with you. Park at the back, inside the alleyway."

"Wh-what are you going to do?" The words taste like tar on my tongue as I suddenly realize what's he asking me.

"Bring them with you, and don't worry about the rest. I'll send Rosey to you. You can go wherever you want with her, I don't care. I hear she's saved quite a lot of money, too, so your lives could actually work out."

Rosey saved money, for us? I know her. I know what she's been thinking. I'd do the same. Gianini's, that's one of Kai's places. He talked about it before. *Could I do it? For Rosey?*

Milan checks his watch and leaves his cup on the kitchen counter. "Our time's up, my little rat. Until tomorrow."

"Wait, can we talk? Milan–" I start, but he's out the door, and I'm left in the kitchen and the silence is buzzing too loud in my ears.

My heart is in my head, beating so fast I think it will explode.

I sit down at the table, trying to think through all my options. But there are none. It's either them, or Rosey. And I came here for her. She's my family. She's my everything. They've become my family, too... but who am I without Rosey? No one. One half of a human. And who am I without Orion? Logan? Kai? A broken soul.

"Maisy!"

Orion's guttural voice startles me. I jump, and wipe my tears hurriedly.

"I'm here." I get down on my knees and start collecting the broken pieces of the cup off the floor. "I dropped my coffee."

"Thank God! The connection to my security cameras wasn't working. Glad you're okay." He sees me kneeling on the floor and chuckles. "I'll have to start charging you for the cups."

"It slipped," I say sweetly.

He sniffs the coffee pot. "Did you make more?"

"How'd you tell?"

"It smells different. Can I try it?"

"Sure. Please do. Although I'm not sure I like it."

I watch him from the floor as he pours himself a cup and tastes it. His face contorts, but I know he's trying not to make me feel bad. *I don't like Milan's revolting coffee either!* I want to shout.

"It's... not for me, darling."

I push myself to my feet and throw the broken shards in the garbage. "I don't like it, either. Here, let me pour it down the sink. I'll make a fresh one."

I take the pot and stand at the sink, waiting for it to empty. Orion wraps his arms around my waist from behind and presses our bodies together. I lean back into his chest, allowing his scent to overwhelm me. Maybe that'll help me decide. I'm torn. I can't see myself not being with him, and yet, the mere mention of my sister awakens the fighter inside me. I *will* save her.

"Mmm, last night was amazing. You were divine. My goddess," he mumbles against my skin, nuzzling my neck and gently grinding his bulge against me.

"Yeah, and then you left me. All of you." I force a chuckle, and move away from his arms. "Let me make the coffee."

He tilts his head to look at me. "Are you okay?"

Now is not the time to scrutinize me. I add a few scoops of his coffee to the filter. "I think my period's coming on, that's all. I'm a bit moody."

"Sure. If that's all it is." He kisses me and slaps my ass. "I have to go. I only came to check on you. I see you're perfectly fine on your own."

"Yeah. See you later."

~

All I've been doing today is thinking, planning, and avoiding Orion. I had a good ten hours before I saw him again, and they were too short because my brain not only went into overdrive, it got jammed. Pacing up to the top of the stairs and down to the basement, over and over, with my head down and mind racing, trying to make sense of it all. Yet, I still couldn't figure anything out.

All my life I knew what and who I was after. Kill Milan, find Rosey. Not necessarily in that order. I woke up with that thought, I went to bed with that thought. All my life, up until the moment I met Kai, Logan, and Orion. They complicated my life. They made it better, but instead of having peace of mind, I'm bewildered. They were supposed to protect me, help me find Rosey, and then... and then Rosey and I would be on our way to Mexico. Or somewhere farther, where nobody would find us. The way things are now, I have my boys on one side, and Milan and Rosey on the other.

I could have threatened him with the DVDs, but they were stupidly given to the police. I could've gone to the media and exposed him. There are always one or two journalists willing to risk their lives for fame. Why didn't Orion listen to me?

Orion got back an hour ago and he was ready to play, saying he wanted to get ahead in our game before Logan and Kai join us later tonight. He and I have played from time to time, not full-on sex, but he'd tease me, degrade me, praise me, and by the time Kai and Logan would join us I'd do anything to get their love. Who would've thought that words like those would rouse the needy, deprived little girl in me?

And I didn't want anything more than to have sex with him tonight, but seeing Milan up close and personal has put me off. I must figure it out. I could never follow through with what he's asked me to do. Betray my boys? Never. *But could I, for Rosey?*

So, I denied Orion. He didn't like it, but put it down to my imminent period. I even complained of belly cramps. Had to make it believable.

When I rejected him, I withdrew to my room and I'm still here. I'm too agitated to sleep, though. Later on, I hear Kai and Logan arriving, checking in on me as I pretend to sleep.

If only I knew what to do.

CHAPTER 19

ORION

She said no. *No.* And she was asleep when Kai and Logan got here. That's never happened before. Not wanting sex when the three of us are here. I'm not convinced it's because of her period. She's had periods while here and that never stopped her. Could it be that she found out about her sister? I doubt it. I burned that piece of paper, and neither Kai nor Logan would tell her. She was restless all night. I know she barely slept. And for the couple of hours that she did sleep, she sobbed a few times. I had to tighten my arms around her body, and only then she would calm down.

Her short breaths on my chest told me she was awake. Something's torturing her. Or maybe I'm just a paranoid man who's been betrayed too many times.

Whatever it is, when she finds out about her sister, she'll be crushed. We discussed last night what the best way to do this is, and agreed we won't be the ones to tell her. Once we find Milan, he'll have to come clean one way or another. Which will give her an opening to kill him, and when she does, it will be a revenge kill, thus eliminating any guilt that would come afterward. To get revenge for herself, for her freedom, for her sister. To claim her life back. Because without that, guilt will ruin her life.

I stayed up almost all night. Lying next to her without doing anything, it's hard. I was hard. I *am* hard. Logan's sleeping on her other side, having snored for most of the night. For him, as long as his body's touching Maisy's, he sleeps like a baby. At some point in the night, they were holding hands. She was definitely awake then.

The first ray of sun falls on her face, and suddenly she frowns. Her chin begins to wobble and she buries her head against my chest. Her shoulders shake with silent sobs.

"Shh, you're just having a bad dream, Maisy," I whisper. "It's okay. We're here."

Kai sits up on the floor and looks at us. I shake my head at him, willing him to go back to sleep. I don't want her to wake. Not when she's like this.

Logan opens his eyes and rolls over to face us, covering her body with his, practically breathing down my neck. I hope it will calm her but her sobs grow louder, and now she's full-on crying.

Logan whispers in her ear as he holds her tight. "Hey, Maisy, shhh, we're here. It's just a dream, sweetheart."

Realizing we're all awake, she stops for a moment to wipe her eyes, but it does no good. Her shoulders continue to heave and she gives in, covering her face and just sobbing.

"I'm sorry, I'm sorry, I'm... I'm so sorry–" Her voice falters.

"Maisy, you were dreaming." I pull her closer and kiss her forehead. "Wake up."

Kai sits on the bed and all three of us look at each other. *Is this just her period? No way.*

"Hey, baby girl, come here."

The moment she hears Kai's voice she crawls into his arms, still crying. "I'm sorry, Kai."

"What for? It's only a bad dream. Don't worry, baby girl, I'm here. We're all here. You know we'll never let anything happen to you. You know that, yes?" He lifts her chin as tears streak her face.

She nods, and more tears roll down like rivers. "I'm sorry. Yes. I had a bad dream."

She wraps her arms around him and remains like that for a while. Her breathing eases off. All of us are exchanging glances, worried for her.

"I don't know why I cried. I think I love you so much and I don't want anything to happen to you." She looks at us through red eyes and wipes her tears dry. "That's all."

"*Is* that all?" Logan raises his eyebrows at her and laughs, and all of us join in.

She smiles, too. "Can we go out today, the four of us? Like, for lunch? Is that possible?" she asks sweetly, looking at Kai. Of course the fool will do anything she wants.

I catch Logan's eye. It would be dangerous. But not unheard of. People know the three of us have met already, and we were fine. No one got killed. It was a good meeting, everyone agreed. This could be seen as the second official meeting.

Instead of responding, Kai looks up at me. "I can arrange it at Gianini's. But we all have to agree to it."

"I'm game," Logan says, and strokes Maisy's arm. "I'd love to take you out, Maisy. You deserve it."

"I think she does. Gianini's makes the best pizza in the city. And I kinda own the place. Well, nearly." The arrogance in Kai's voice is considerable. *She's already ours, no need to show off,* I feel like telling him.

"Very well," I concede. "I'm not gonna stop this if you two are up for it. We'll decide later what story to use."

"Nobody'll know, Orion. The Gianini family will look after us. They have no other option."

"Even so, we'll keep the lunch to one hour. Say, one o'clock?"

"Twelve. I don't want to eat too late," Maisy says matter-of-factly. A little *too* matter-of-factly. *Why is it that I always cast doubt on her?*

I shake it off, because I'm certain this is it with her. There's nothing else she could be hiding. And I better get used to it, get used to having a woman around with all her mood swings, her requests, her desires.

"Twelve it is." I lean in and press my lips to hers. She responds with a soft hum and leaves Kai's embrace for mine, shuffling over his and Logan's legs and wrapping her arms around my neck. *Fuck, this girl is everything we've ever needed in our lives.*

"I love you." She looks at me. "And I love you, Logan." Her eyes fall on Logan, then Kai. "And you, Kai. I love you, too."

Logan strokes her cheek. "Maisy, what brought this on?"

She shrugs. "My nightmares. Come on, all of you. Give me a hug. I need you."

11.45PM

Kai's making excuses for her. "Any minute now."

The three of us have been waiting for Maisy in the kitchen for almost twenty minutes. We were supposed to leave at eleven-thirty. Knowing the traffic's terrible, we should've left on time. But Maisy's still getting ready. I don't know what kind of person she is when she's getting ready, but I know some of the women I went out with were fucking terrible.

Today is special for us; we're going out with her for the very first time. A date. Huh. My stomach overturns when I think that word. It makes me sick. But she's ours. There's nothing more to it. We'll wait for her as long as it takes.

The sound of footsteps coming down the stairs makes us all stand up.

Finally, the door opens and she enters. I don't know what we were expecting. We're all nervous in our own way, and because of it, none of us dressed in anything special and we're wearing what we always do: Logan and I each in a three-piece suit and tie, and Kai in his leather jacket and jeans.

But Maisy, oh dear fucking God! Maisy is something else. Bright pink heels, baby pink bodycon dress wrapped around her killer body, makeup–she's enough to slay you with. *And those lips*. I stare at them as if I'm under a spell, imagining them wrapped around my cock. *Fuck!* I fix my hard-on in my pants, leaving it some space to grow.

"You're gorgeous!" Kai exclaims as he adjusts himself similarly. *He has the same thoughts as I do.*

Logan laughs and kisses her cheek. "Maisy, sweetheart, let's just stay home and fuck."

Her eyes land on me and I take a deep breath. For some reason, I can never breathe properly in her presence. Not after I made peace in my head with the fact that I'm not letting her go. *Ever*.

"You're mine to fuck after this. *I'll* be taking that dress off." My eyes lock with hers. "Got that, boys?"

"Only if we watch," Kai grins.

"Do whatever you want. But she's mine to play with." I walk over to her and cup her face. "Aren't you, my little slut?"

Her eyes glaze over, her pupils dilating. She's there, in her subspace, in an instant. Her bottom lip's pulled between her teeth, and her cunt is wet, I know that for a fact.

She nods and blinks a few times before she clears her throat. "I'm hungry now," she breathes.

I study her face as I tower over her. My cock's bursting in my pants. I can't fucking *wait* to have my way with her. "Let's go. The sooner we get there, the sooner we'll be back."

She turns and leads us out of my house and straight to the limousine that's been waiting outside for twenty minutes. Garry's behind the wheel. He's the only one I trust. Anyway, he thinks this is a business meeting.

The four of us climb into the back of the car. Maisy chooses the seat behind Garry and we sit opposite her.

I press the button next to my seat and address the driver. "Garry, just get us there as soon as possible."

He nods in the rear-view mirror as I switch off the comms and lean back.

"Thank you for coming with me. You truly are something." Maisy laughs sadly. Her mood seems as dark as her eyes. Indecipherable. I wanted to see her happier.

"What do you mean?" I ask.

"I've never been out on a *date*-date."

"You got the three of us today. Ain't that something?" Logan drawls.

I narrow my eyes at her. "What about the boyfriend you told us about?"

"I was never taken out on a date." Her eyes are fixated on her shoes, her response filled with dejection. But in an instant, as if she's just woken up, she smiles. "Thank you. I know how much is at stake if anyone sees us."

Something's off. "Hmm. A lot," I reiterate quietly.

Kai plays down the seriousness of our situation. "Nobody'll find out. Chill."

"Hey, um, your middle names sure are funny, right?" Maisy asks suddenly. "What were they again, remind me? Keres, Typhon, and...?"

"Moros!" Logan exclaims, and pulls out his blades. "Yup. Impending doom. That's me."

Maisy seems to be trying to change the subject again. She bats her eyelashes at us. "Does the name Rebecca Trellis mean anything to you?"

Rebecca Trellis. "Should it?" I ask, knowing perfectly well where she's heading with this. She saw my birth certificate. I read it too. Rebecca Trellis was named as my mother. Who she was to my father, I'm yet to find out. The moment we get back from lunch, I'm calling my PI. Why I never knew about her is a mystery I plan on unraveling.

"Nope, not at all," Logan interrupts.

"I remember seeing an article–"

"Maisy," I warn, cutting her pretense short.

She's afraid to look at me. Her eyes are downcast, her shoulders jerk faintly, and now I can see tears rolling down her face.

"Maisy?" Kai reaches for her, but she pulls away from his touch.

"What's wrong, sweetheart?" Logan cups her chin and tilts her head up.

Instead of seeing love, exactly what we have for her, there's something else in there. Something terribly wrong. Her face is twisted into a grimace from the silent cry nobody expected. Her head shakes from side to side, and when she catches her breath she lets out a wail.

"You better start talking," I order.

"I'm sorry, I'm so sorry. I really am." She gasps for air again, having finally sobbed it out. She's a blubbery mess. "I love you. Why would I do this? I love you all. I'm so sorry."

We don't move, just stare at her. Waiting.

Please, God, as much as I don't believe in you, don't let another lie break me because I swear to you, I will kill her right here. And you don't want that.

"Milan... Milan made me do it. Milan was in your kitchen yesterday."

My blood boils at her words. My cameras cutting out, that was him.

"When you all went out, he–"

"*Milan-was-in-your-house?*" Kai's voice has a new, murderous tone, and it's aimed at me.

Logan joins in. "What the *fuck*, Orion? I thought your house was impenetrable!"

I'm still in shock, unable to strike back as I always do. "I thought it was."

"Fuck you!" Kai yells.

"Maisy could've been killed!" Logan rages.

She tries to speak. "Milan told me if I took the three of you to Gianini's today at noon–"

"Wait, Gianini's? The people you trust? Then they're working with Milan, Kai!" I yell. *There. That's my comeback.*

"*Listen to me!*" Maisy yells, getting our attention. "Milan told me if I took the three of you to Gianini's today at noon, he'd set my sister free."

"Your sister?" I take a deep breath. "Maisy, I'm sorry to tell you this, but your sister is dead. We found a note saying she killed herself."

She frowns at my words, her black eyes slowly dying in front of my own. She blinks, too fast, then slower, like her mind is trying to restart but getting the same outcome each time.

"Wh-what?" Her voice is barely a whisper.

"We didn't know how to tell you, sweetheart," Logan says. "I'm so sorry."

"No! That's a lie!" She lunges at him with her fists. "I shouldn't have told you about Milan! You're all gonna die for these lies!"

I hold both of her wrists in my hand while she tries to wrestle free. This is bad. So bad that we're holding her down between us. But I got to know.

"Maisy, stop it. Stop. Is this what I think it is? You're taking us into a trap?"

She raises her gaze to me and when I look at her, I know all I need to know. I would've died for her, right on this very spot, but she sold us out. Her dark eyes are begging for forgiveness. For anything to keep us bathing in her waters. But they are toxic. They must be, because this keeps happening, over and over. And she's the common denominator.

I knock frantically on the barrier between Garry and us. "Stop the car! Stop it!"

With a screech, Garry stops in the middle of the road and turns to us, baffled. He lowers the barrier. There are sounds of other cars screeching to a halt behind us. "Is everything alright, boss?"

My brain goes into overdrive. In my head I'm planning every intricate detail of our attack, except I haven't been to Gianini's and I would need to know every inch of that restaurant.

"Park the car. Call everyone you can think of. Milan's set us a trap at Gianini's. We're gonna hit him back, and end this once and for all." I check my watch. "Tell them to be there in fifteen minutes."

Kai and Logan are already on their cells, talking to their families. I dial Uncle Leo's cell and wait. The glances we exchange are real, raw, like those before a gladiator's battle, when nothing is certain. Maisy's taken off her pink heels and has pulled her knees to her chest. She's terrified, but still fucking guilty. I scowl at her and shake my head, partly at my own stupidity for trusting her. She should've told us; she should've told me last night. There were plenty of opportunities. But she didn't even try. That shows how much she loves us. She came clean only because she felt guilty. That's all.

If I didn't have to think about Kai or Logan getting killed right now, I'd have shot her first. Guilt-free. *Ugh!*

12.15PM

"I don't wanna see you outside of this car, clear?" I warn Maisy.

If anyone's going to kill her, it'll be me. Her eyes are wide. We haven't addressed her at all, except when Kai asked if she knew how many people would be there and she shook her head. She knows she fucked up. Massively. None of us want to even entertain the thought of what happens next. We just know that we all want her inside the car.

This is it. Kai, Logan, and I were born ready.

On the other side of the street are seven, maybe eight cars, and everyone inside them is armed and has one aim: kill the Slavs. This is the perfect occasion for it.

I should remember to thank Maisy for bringing this fight to us sooner than we planned.

I nod at Garry, who's glaring impatiently at me in the rear-view mirror. He nods back and with a screech, ours is the first in the line of cars speeding toward the restaurant where the Slavs are waiting for us. It's a minute away, and as the noise reaches them before we do, rapid gunfire is opened on us. Someone from behind us responds, and all hell breaks loose.

Garry parks the car opposite the restaurant. A few of the cars following us crash through the front of the restaurant, and the rest alongside, creating a circle around the Slavs, who are hidden all over the space.

Adrenaline kicks in. I swing open the car door and crouch behind it as I shoot, one bullet at a time, each time getting a kill. I look back inside the car to check on Maisy. She's covering her ears and her eyes are shut.

A deafening boom blows out three cars in a row. Some of the Delgado team have sneaked in with grenades, totally disorienting everyone. The Slavs will die today. The air's thick with flying bullets and smoke. Garry takes a bullet in the shoulder; it's through and through, nothing deadly, but he's young–

"Orion..." Another spray of bullets hits him, three or four in his chest and neck. He coughs and splutters blood.

Not Garry! He's just a kid!

Turning to me was his mistake. Because of me, people die. The simple reason I'm petrified to love.

I run to him but it's too late. He's on the ground, staring vacantly at the sky. In the chaos I kneel and close his eyes, giving him his peace. Anger rolls through me as I turn in the direction the bullets are coming from.

"Cover me!" I yell. Most of us are advancing, pushing the Slavs back into the dead-end alleyway where they're sitting ducks. I pick up the semiautomatic of a dead Slav and mow down everyone in my way. *We got them! The Slavs are over!*

Amid all the commotion, Logan points his gun at someone standing on the far side of the restaurant entrance. "Is that Milan?"

"Kill everything and anything!" I shout, aiming my rifle at the figure. "Especially him!"

"*Maisy!*" Kai's voice reaches me just as I'm about to pull the trigger.

I stop, but nobody else does. I turn to see Maisy, holding a gun, firing as she advances on Milan, barely dodging the bullets raining on her.

"*Maisy!*" Logan yells when he sees her, but it's pointless. She can't hear him.

Milan doesn't have a gun, but the five goons standing around him do, and they shoot like cowboys. I aim at them, killing one, then another.

Among another shower of bullets, Kai drops to the ground next to me like a sack of potatoes. This was what I was afraid of.

"Kai!" I grab hold of him but his eyes tell me everything. There's no fight in there and he can barely keep them open. He's been shot in the shoulder again–there are multiple shots, some close to his heart. "Hey! Kai, open your eyes, you hear me? You *asshole!*"

"Maisy..." He points behind me. I look back and see mayhem. Logan's being mown down too.

"Delgados, get him!" I yell at Kai's family. They run to grab him and get him away as I go to Logan.

"I'm fine, I'm hit in the leg. My knee... nothing serious. Go, get our girl." Logan is the sane one in this world of blood and fury, although the blood coming out of his mouth is not a good sign.

I'll deal with Logan later.

I stand up and see her: fearless, proud, furious, still firing shots at Milan. *That's our fucking girl!*

"Maisy!" I yell, and she hears me this time.

She turns to me, and that's when my nightmare in slow motion starts. Her body jerks as a bullet hits her, once, twice, three, four times, all on her torso. Her pink dress slowly becomes red. Her eyes are still on me, shocked, surprised, and finally, sightless, as she falls into her own darkness and drops to the ground.

"*MAISY!*" Logan shrieks.

I try to run to her but my legs give up, my left at first, and as if in a movie, I see myself walking with a limp, and then the right leg fully gives out. I drag myself with my arms over dead bodies, under a spray of bullets and smoke, but something hot pushes on my shoulder and now my left arm gives in. Logan's voice is in my ear, he's yelling something. *I'm sorry, Logan, not now*. I was horrible to Maisy. I was mean. I want to apologize to her. To tell her I'm sorry. To tell her I love her.

I reach her limp body, riddled with so many bullets, and my heart breaks in so many pieces, leaving me feeling nothing but despair. Who hated this girl so much that they had to put so many bullets in her? I wrap my only working arm around her and give in. I cry. With no fear, no shame, no embarrassment. I don't care who sees me. I loved her. And she loved us. *My Maisy. Our Maisy.*

A black boot kicks me and only then do I become aware of the pain tearing through my body. It's utterly debilitating.

I look up to see what appears to be a shadow pointing a gun at me. I have no strength to do anything and I don't intend to, but when they pull Maisy's body from my arms, I fight. I fight with all my strength, until that boot is the last thing I see and a shooting pain in my head is the last thing I feel.

End of Book 1

ABOUT THE AUTHOR

Alexandra loves writing love stories, drinking Champagne and of course, wearing high heels.

Most days she is glued to her trusty laptop, creating magic, but on an odd occasion you'd find her on her social media accounts, connecting with her readers. Feel free to (virtually) follow her.

www.alexandraiff.com

Made in United States
Orlando, FL
22 June 2024